**BRITISH AMERICAN
PUBLISHING**

TO THE DEATH

TO THE DEATH

Robert Merritt

British American Publishing

Copyright 1988 by Robert Merritt
All rights reserved
including the right of reproduction
in whole or in part in any form
Published by British American Publishing
3 Cornell Road
Latham, NY 12110
Manufactured in the United States of America

93 92 91 90 89   5 4 3 2 1

Library of Congress Cataloging in Publication Data

Merritt, Robert, 1947–
    To the death / Robert Merritt
      p.   cm.
    ISBN 0-945167-04-0 : $17.95
    I. Title.

PS3563.E7456T6   1988
813'.54--dc19

88-21484
CIP

To the memory of my father, who was always
so proud of my every accomplishment

ONE

Michael Manning stepped from the train in Paris and for the first time in two years felt like a tourist. Even from the bowels of the train station he could tell that this was no longer his city, no longer the sanctuary that protected him from his father and from all that his father's world represented. Could Paris be so easily torn down by a single telephone call?

Not looking where he was going, Michael was jostled by two loud businessmen intent on their conversation as they pushed past him on the way to a weekend in the country. It was his own fault, but there it was again. He glared at the two Frenchmen with the growl of a tourist, and they responded in kind. Then they were gone, and he was left alone with an empty, alien ache in his stomach. All of this because of a call that made no sense at all, a call from father to son?

There were several more bumps and uncounted near misses as Michael walked against the flow, bruising his way through a plaza of high-rise steel and glass that reminded him more of New York than Europe. The steady flow of traffic convinced him that getting across town to his room at The Crillon was a lost cause, at least for the time being. He ducked into a cafe, seeking a temporary refuge.

The restaurant was a cavernous hall decorated to look like a dated version of the train station he'd just left. Sad murals haunted the walls, and the place was packed with a motley crowd. Minor politicians and junior executives sat tall in neat three-piece suits. Aging professors and their lazy students lounged in tight jeans trying to ape the great writers and artists who once walked these streets. French women of every description took advantage of the wide aisles and the latest in mini skirts with carefully crossed legs and exposed thighs.

The only available table was near the front window, and as soon as Michael sat down he knew the cafe was a mistake. Even after two years, his French was barely passable, and he wasn't in the mood for a tug-of-war with the waiter. He thought out what he wanted to say in detail before he spoke, and the waiter was surprisingly patient by Parisian standards, even if Michael's order was obviously the most difficult task of his day.

Michael tried to escape Paris by thinking about the two days he'd just spent in Pont-Aven and about the research he'd done for an article on nineteenth-century American artists in Brittany. It wasn't working. Maybe it was the noise, or perhaps the flashes of reflected sunlight as cars raced past the cafe, but his mind wandered, always to return to his father and to the call that was so out of character.

"Michael, it's Matt . . . it's your father."

They hadn't spoken in nearly six months, not since Michael's brief visit to Washington at Christmas, but the identification had seemed odd and uneasy. Michael heard the words, but he was also calculating. It had been 1 P.M. at a remote hotel in Brittany, so that would have made it 8 A.M. in Washington. It was early. His father was calling before his first appointment of the day. Something must have happened.

"What is it?" Michael held his breath. But his father couldn't do it. Michael knew the man well. He knew Matt was not a man to undertake anything without calculating the pros, cons, and all the ramifications. The call had a purpose, but Michael couldn't guess what it was, and his father was too proud to say it.

"Oh, nothing," his father came back, the casual tone so unlike the man Michael knew was on the other end of the line. "Hadn't heard from you in a while. Just wanted to see how you're doing."

It didn't work. To make this call his father had to first find out where Michael was staying. He had probably gotten his aide Allen Collins to do the tracking for him.

"Dad. Is something wrong?"

"No. No. I just had a few minutes before the meetings begin, and I wanted to call. I wondered when you might be coming home again. I haven't seen you since . . . God, has it been since Christmas?"

Michael well remembered the last time he'd seen his father, and the silence at the other end of the line told him his father was remembering too. It had been two days after Christmas, and Michael had gained an audience with the great man in the Georgetown offices that served as headquarters for the Media Associates publishing empire. He'd come to tell his father he was returning to Europe, that he still had writing to do before he settled down.

Most people thought of Matthew Emerson Manning as a giant, and it was a response to more than the six-foot-four frame or the 240 pounds the old man carried. Matt's hair was finally going white and his bulk was beginning to show signs of sagging here and there, but he still wasn't a man you'd want to meet in a dark alley . . . or even across a large desk.

However, on that day six months ago he had not seemed such an insurmountable force. He had been more like an aging, angry football coach who'd once played on the defensive line and had just watched his team lose the big game.

"It has been a long time, dad, but I've been busy. The writing is going great. Assignments are pouring in."

"How many God-damned gothic churches can you describe? This is getting fucking absurd. When are you gonna quit fartin' around and get back here where you belong?"

The real Matthew Manning had finally emerged, his Virginia drawl signaling the end of their unannounced truce, and the rest of the call became a blur of angry accusations and disappointments. The only thing Michael clearly remembered was his father saying that Kathy was gone. The child bride— she was one year younger than Michael—had disappeared, run off to God knows where with God knows who, and she'd been gone for two weeks.

Kathy was the primary reason Michael had spent the last two years in Paris. They'd never said it, but Michael knew it and his father knew it, so it hadn't been easy for Michael to express any sympathy.

"But dad, I am sorry," he had tried. "Is there anything I can do?"

"Nothing. I know what needs to be done. It's being taken care of, so don't you worry about that . . . or about me. I'll take care of it."

"But dad . . ."

"No, Michael," the big man's voice demanded silence. "I can't talk anymore right now. I've got a staff meeting to review the quarterly statements. Everyone's waiting. I've got to go."

"But dad . . ."

There had been no more. Matthew Emerson Manning, a man who calculated everything, who considered all the pros, all the cons, and all the ramifications, hung up before his son might say something that would cut too close to the core. And he left Michael haunted by the call, haunted by what had been said and by what had almost been said.

Kathy Manning hated being alone, and on a Friday evening it just wasn't right that she should be left on her own while everybody else in the world was out having fun. She'd done all the waiting around she ever wanted to do as the wife of Matthew Emerson Manning. Now she was free, and still she was alone.

She had tried to keep busy. The apartment in Old Town Alexandria was spotless. She had washed clothes, scrubbed the bathroom, even baked a chocolate cake as a surprise for her roommates. But it wasn't enough. The apartment was closing in on her, and the isolation made her dizzy.

She fixed herself a drink, moved to the sofa and stared at the front door, trying to remember where they had gone. Pete was out drinking with his artist buddies, so there was no telling when he might return. But Jackie would be home soon; surely Jackie had said she was working the restaurant and not in the bar tonight. She would get off as soon as the last straggling diners finished stuffing themselves on an overpriced meal. She could be home any minute.

Meanwhile, Kathy began counting. She counted the number of magazines on the coffee table. She counted the objects in the room, the number of furniture legs touching the floor. She tried to count the threads in the sofa cushion she hugged in her lap. She took large swallows of whiskey and counted the seconds that passed before the burning stopped and the empty pain returned.

By the time she heard the key at the door, she was frantic. She wanted to attack Jackie, to hold her close and kiss away the loneliness that had swept over her. She craved physical closeness, but at the door she drew back.

Jackie entered like a soldier returning to camp after a rough battle. Hair sagged to her shoulders, eye makeup was smeared beneath a glow of sweat, and, worst of all, she had her shoes in her hand, sure sign of a rough night.

They hugged and then Kathy took charge. She led Jackie to the sofa, lifted her feet to an ottoman and shared in the comfort of Jackie's sigh. She ran off to the bathroom to prepare a hot bath, and while the tub was filling, Jackie asked if she'd heard from Pete, or if she'd seen any more of the snoop who'd been following them for the past few days.

Kathy helped Jackie undress, walked her to the tub, and found complete contentment in washing her aching back. In holding her breasts and running soapy hands over her thighs. They stayed like that until the water began to cool, and by then Jackie was revived. They kissed—gentle, tender kisses that made Kathy want to cry. They touched. Shared caresses. Soon Kathy's blouse was wet from Jackie's fondling.

Together they moved to the bedroom. Naked, they fell on the bed and held each other close. They whispered about silly things, mostly about the obese, sweaty man who had obviously been taking pictures for Kathy's husband. They laughed about the way they'd put on a show, holding hands and enjoying friendly little kisses for the camera. They were soon giggling like school girls as their hands and tongues began to explore the smooth, damp contours of each other's body.

Another key turned in the door an hour later. Pete walked in, wobbling from too much beer with the boys, to find his two roommates still giggling in bed. The sheets were pulled out at odd angles. Pillows seemed to be everywhere, both on and off the bed, and the two women were entangled in the darkness so that it was difficult to see where one ended and the other began.

They laughed even harder when they saw Pete standing in the bedroom doorway. They shared a private joke, appreciating the way light from the living room transformed Pete into a macho silhouette of tight-fitting jeans and T-shirt.

"Well, I see you started without me," Pete said, crossing his arms and leaning casually against the doorjamb.

"There's always room for one more," Kathy offered between giggles, and the two women jumped from the bed to drag Pete into the room. They ripped off his shirt, tugged down his jeans, and started the party all over again, adding a third voice to their chorus of giggles. A third pair of hands to their fondling. A third set of lips to their kissing.

The next arrival at the apartment didn't use a key. He paused in the hallway listening for faint sounds, and when he was convinced all three occupants had moved to the bedroom he slipped a thin sheet of metal into the crack between door and frame, easing it down and back until he felt the lock slipping out of the way. With an eye dropper he carefully applied several beads of a clear liquid to one link in the chain that still held the door. He watched the acid fizz, eating into the metal, then with an even pressure he pushed on the door until the weakened link gave. The gnarled curl of metal bounced silently on the carpet.

The bedroom door was closed, but the giggles and moans were like a beacon. The stranger crept to the door, concentrating on every sound. He wondered which one of the women Pete was enjoying at the moment. He wondered what the other one was doing while she waited her turn. He listened for several minutes, enjoying the erotic scenes of his imagination, then he lifted the shotgun and checked to be sure the safety was off.

Jackie was the first to notice fresh light spilling across the bed as the door opened, and when she gasped at the new silhouette in the doorway Pete rolled off Kathy, slipping into the hollow between the two sweaty bodies.

The figure in the door moved forward slowly. No one said anything. They froze when they saw the shotgun, and then came two quick blasts that shook the building. The first explosion hit Jackie in the face as she was trying to sit up. The second ripped into Kathy's face. Her eyes had never opened. The last thing she knew was the ecstasy of making love.

There was no third shot to silence Pete's horrified scream. The stranger stood for a moment. He looked at the two women, at the bloody pulp where two faces had been. He studied Pete, not hearing the screams but staring past the noise and into the open mouth, sensing the strain of the vocal cords and the agonizing messages they received from the brain.

Then, just as calmly as he had entered, the stranger laid the shotgun across the foot of the bed, turned and walked away. He closed the bedroom door behind him as he left.

It was nearly noon, Paris time, before Allen Collins could get through to The Crillon Hotel, where Michael was recuperating from a long night of struggling with the demons of being a son. The call was short. There was no easy way to say it and no reason to drag it out. Kathy Manning had been brutally murdered, and Matthew Emerson Manning, the man who considered all the ramifications, had suffered a major heart attack.

That was all Michael knew as he flew back to Washington. He boarded the plane in a daze, trying to remember the nonexistent details of the call. He knew so little. He didn't even know if they had been together when it happened. He was sure Allen had said, but all he could remember were the words. Murder. Heart attack. It seemed impossible.

All he had to occupy his mind was that phone call of the previous day. Had his father tried to ask him for help? Had he been calling out to a son who was too deaf to hear? And, most ominous of all, he'd said he "knew what had to be done," that he was "doing it." What did it mean? What did any of it mean?

Even with the time difference, it was nearly two o'clock on Sunday afternoon when Michael's plane landed in Washington. Allen sent one of the Media Associates limousines to meet him, and from there it was a thirty-minute ride to Manning Hall, the family estate just west of Leesburg.

Michael didn't know the chauffeur and was thankful to be left to himself on the ride. As they passed through the vibrant, green fields of a sunny Virginia countryside, he remembered his father once telling him how Southerners were people of the earth, and how all of their emotions were tied to the Southern soil beneath their feet. He was shocked to discover tears running down his cheeks. He tried to chuckle at the irony but instead found himself fighting back the desire to sob as he drew nearer to whatever awaited him at Manning Hall.

The house was, above all else, his father's castle. A rambling eighteenth-century plantation house, it had originally belonged to one of George Washington's closest friends. It had been renovated top to bottom, the technological conveniences of the past two hundred years all hidden just out of sight. The house and grounds remained pure, like something out of "Gone With the Wind" bathed in the grand manner of Old Virginia. It sat like an island on a wooded tract of fifty acres, not visible from any public road. A long driveway curved in front of a majestic two-story portico standing proudly against a wall of white plaster and contrasting with the weathered brick of the house and its elegant wings spreading east and west.

The only element disturbing the scene on this Sunday after-noon were the cars parked along the gravel driveway. There was another limousine, Allen's BMW, a Mercedes, the estate station wagon, and two unfamiliar sedans, but most noticeable of all was the police car. It sat off by itself, in exile, an omen of horrors that are supposed to be seen from the safety of a comfortable den chair in front of the television or, at the least, from the distance of a newspaper story about things that happened to other people.

The front door of the house opened before the limousine came to a stop, and Allen rushed down the steps. He yanked open the rear door as if to pull it from the hinges, then stepped back hurrying Michael from the car. The two men started to shake hands, the wary distance of time keeping them apart, but then they reached to each other in a brotherly embrace.

Allen pulled back and tried to say something, but Michael shook his head. No. There wasn't time for that. Not now.

"Where is my father?" he asked. At the moment, this was all that mattered.

TWO

Michael's steps were unsteady as he entered the house. There were people in the living room, images that were only a blur off to the side as Michael walked through. He had often envisioned his return home, but it had never been like this. He imagined Matt bounding down the steps to greet the prodigal son, arms wide for the fatherly embrace Michael had always sought and never been good enough to earn. But now Michael reached the wide staircase, and there was no father. Stepping gently, he climbed with the careful tread of a mountain climber, and breathless, he paused before opening the door to his father's room.

It was an elegant room. The huge bed dated from the twelfth century and had always dominated the center of the room like a castle capable of withstanding medieval attacks, but now it seemed out of place. The room had been converted into a hospital, and the bed was a silly, overstuffed toy in the midst of so much medical equipment.

There were two nurses, one checking supplies in a white cabinet that now stood like an angelic guardian watching over the heavy wooden furniture while the other nurse sat reading a magazine. Monitors buzzed and beeped in electronic rhythms, keeping score in a deadly game that seemed of little interest to either of the two women, and in the middle of all this medical confusion lay his father.

At least Michael assumed that the man lying in the bed was his father. The figure looked nothing like the unconquerable god Michael worshipped, nothing like the spirited Matthew Emerson Manning who held Media Associates in an iron grip. The man in the bed looked dead. Only the tube supplying oxygen through his nose, the gentle rising and falling of his chest and the wires connecting him with assorted monitors gave any indication of life. The face was the same bleached white as the sheets and pillow cases that surrounded it.

Michael stepped closer, and the reality swept over him. This was his father. And his father was dying. The two nurses gracefully withdrew to a far corner as Michael walked to the bed and took his father's cold hand. He stood that way until a faintness swept over him, and a nurse, prepared for any emergency, suddenly appeared with a chair and a guiding hand.

He spent the next hour in silence. The entire house seemed to be on tiptoes, the only sound the insistent beeping of life on the monitors. Michael's breathing kept time with the sound, drawing him perhaps the closest he'd ever been to the man on the bed.

Gradually, Michael responded to a host of nagging questions. He wanted to know how this had happened. How it was possible. Who was responsible. When he finally stood, carefully placing his father's hand on the crisp white sheet, he felt firm. He wanted answers.

Allen met him at the bottom of the steps, and Michael could see the toll this was taking on his old friend. They had gone through college together, Allen only a year older. But that had been ten years ago, and now Allen had gone paunchy, his stomach not cooperating with the smooth line his vested suit was meant to hold, and his hair was quickly receding, all of this in marked contrast to Michael's thin but firm five-foot-eleven frame and his thick, ever-unkempt head of black hair.

"Things are a real mess. Michael." There was a frustration in Allen's voice that was unusual for the cool attorney.

"How bad is it?"

Michael allowed Allen to take his arm, and together the two men walked toward the den, away from the people who had encamped in the living room.

"Michael, I'm sorry. This is all madness, and there isn't time to work around it," Allen said, meeting Michael eye to eye and trying to assess just how strong the younger Manning might be. "Somebody walked in on Kathy last night and murdered her. Killed her and a woman she was living with. It was a shotgun for God's sake. An execution.

"And the police . . ." Allen paused to see if any of this was sinking in. "It's crazy, but the police think your father was responsible. They think Matt hired somebody to kill her."

Michael tried to speak, but Allen waved him off.

"Michael, I'm sorry, but it gets worse. Your father is in a coma. The doctors have been here all night, and they don't think he's going to make it."

Michael almost collapsed with this last piece of news. His legs went rubbery, and Allen had to grab him quickly to prevent a fall. Patterson, who with his wife had run Manning Hall since Michael's childhood, had been lurking just out of hearing distance and rushed forward to lend a hand. Together they helped Michael into the den, where they were greeted by a man Michael had never seen before. They tried to guide Michael to the sofa, but his head had cleared and he pulled away.

"Is this the doctor?" he asked.

"Yes Michael. Dr. Warren Epps. He's a specialist from Washington. He drove down this morning and has done everything possible. He's been waiting to speak with you."

Dr. Epps gazed at Michael, waiting until he could see the blood returning to the young man's cheeks, and then he walked to the desk to pick up a file.

"Mr. Collins insists that I give it to you straight," the doctor said, awaiting a nod from Michael before he continued.

"I'm afraid the situation is grave," the doctor said. "Sometime early yesterday morning your father went into cardiogenic shock. His heart stopped sending an adequate amount of oxygenated blood to the vital organs. To the brain. He was alone in his room, and by the time he was discovered he was comatose. There are no motor responses. We do not know the extent at this point, but there has undoubtedly been brain damage. Probably damage to other vital organs as well."

The doctor stopped, studying Michael's rigid face, and waited. He knew the question had to be asked.

"What are his chances?" Michael asked.

"Impossible to say. But not good." The doctor sighed. "It's amazing he's alive at all. The doctor who was called in last night did a remarkable job, but now all we can do is wait. There's no need to move him to a hospital. It would be too dangerous. We've brought everything here, and the nurses are specialists in these cases. We wait."

"Is there any chance?" Michael insisted.

"We can hope for a miracle," the doctor said with finality as he excused himself to take another look at his patient before heading back to Washington.

Allen walked to the bar and poured scotch into two glasses. He didn't bother with ice, but neither he nor Michael noticed. They tossed down the drinks, and looked at each other with nothing to say. Words seemed inadequate.

The silence was broken by a fragile tap at the door. Mrs. Patterson rushed into the room. She was in tears, obviously from a long day of crying, and she fell heavily into Michael's arms.

She sobbed uncontrollably, the dam of tears released, while Michael tried to comfort her. There had been many times in his childhood when she had been the comforter, but Michael shook aside such thoughts and held the woman close.

Allen caught Michael's attention and nodded in the direction of the door. There were still more duties for the returning son. When Mrs. Patterson felt the tension in Michael's hands she freed herself with firm resolution.

"Oh Michael, I'm so terribly sorry," she said. "It's so awful. Unbelievable. And Miss Kathy, too. I can't . . ."

"Ginny, please. We can't change anything that's already happened. We have to concentrate on what we can do now."

The housekeeper tried to smile. "That's what I used to tell you when you were a little boy," she said.

"I remember. And it's sound advice. Now you go find your husband and get off to bed. We can make do around here. We can get our own coffee."

"But you must have something to eat."

"No, Ginny. Not this afternoon."

She didn't argue. She came back to Michael for another hug, kissed him on the cheek and walked from the room.

Allen was pacing. He seemed angry and tense, and Michael had never seen him like this. "Michael, I know this is a lot all at one time, but the police are waiting, too. It's a Lieutenant Pemberton, from Alexandria. That's where Kathy was killed."

Michael set the empty glass on the floor beside his chair and looked around the room. There had been few changes. The antique desk, one of his father's prize possessions, and the shelves lined with leather-bound volumes were still dominant, giving the room its ageless refinement, but now three sophisticated computer consoles were lined up along one wall.

"Yes, Allen. I suppose you'd better show them in."

It was early evening in Los Angeles, and the stranger was cruising Sunset Boulevard. He sat rigid behind the wheel of the car he had rented at the airport, his leather-gloved hands controlling the slick Continental with the precision of a robot. He seemed to look neither left nor right as he drove, but he was aware of everything. He saw the girls walking the street, the pimps on parade, and the drugged-out youth wandering to their own personal dead ends amid the bright lights and the whoops of frightened laughter.

He saw everything, and he smiled. He felt good.

Michael didn't stand as the two men entered the den at Manning Hall. They were both older than Michael had expected. The bigger of the two, who had the same old-football-player intensity Michael had always identified with his father, slipped with an athletic grace to the side of the room to study Michael from a distance. It was the other man, with his thin country preacher's face, who came forward, offering a cool hand.

"I'm Lieutenant Pemberton, chief of homicide, Alexandria," the policeman said, gazing down at Michael. "The gentleman stalking the sidelines over there is FBI. Agent Garrett." The cop frowned, letting everyone know the agent had not been his idea. "The Federal boys help us out from time to time with forensic analysis."

Michael nodded to Garrett, then turned his attention to the policeman. The chief of homicide was perhaps fifty, the lines in his face more like those of a weather-beaten farmer than a veteran city cop. His hands were large and rough, the hands of a man who could get physical if he had to. And behind his cool eyes burned an anger. He was a man who didn't like to wait while an errant son made his entrance, and he wouldn't bow down to the Manning money or power. Michael wished he had stood when the policeman entered.

Allen offered drinks, but when the policeman declined he withdrew to the sofa and invited the FBI agent to be seated. Pemberton sat in a chair facing Michael.

"Mr. Manning, I realize this is not the best time for questions, but we need to know as much as possible. The more we know, the quicker we can find the truth." The cop's voice fit his look. It was quiet and hauntingly pleasant, much like a preacher who has come for a Sunday afternoon visit with the family of a sick father.

"I understand, Lieutenant. What can I do for you?"

"I believe you have been away for quite some time?"

"Two years, maybe a little more. I've been working in Europe. Freelance writing. Mostly travel stories."

"I see," Pemberton said, pondering the information as if it were the key to a hidden treasure. "And your father remarried a little over two years ago."

"He married Kathy closer to three years ago." Michael could see where the cop was going, and he didn't like it.

"Did you get along well with your stepmother?"

"I don't see what business that is of yours, but the answer is no. She was young, and it was awkward with both of us here. We didn't dislike each other, but it sometimes felt like we were competing for father's attention."

"And is it safe to say that she usually won . . . in this tug-of-war, I mean?"

"Yes. It's safe to say that, but again, this is irrelevant. It has nothing to do with anyone outside this family."

"I agree. But have you kept in touch with the family? With your father?"

Michael paused. One visit in the past year was not exactly a perfect record for a caring son. "No. The last time I was home was Christmas, and then just for a few days. I had to get back to Europe."

"What about calls? I imagine you and your father kept in touch by phone."

"No. Not often."

"I understand your father called you Friday morning."

Michael had almost forgotten the call in the confusion. "Yes. He did call."

"And what, may I ask, did he have to say?"

"Nothing much. Just hello, and he wondered when I might be coming home again."

"You hadn't spoken to your father in six months, and Friday, on the day his wife would be murdered, he suddenly decided it was time to call and say hello and ask when you might come home?"

"That's right."

"Did he mention Mrs. Manning?"

Michael went pale as he remembered the conversation. "Yes. He mentioned that she had left him. He said he didn't know where she had gone."

"I see." Pemberton paused to consider this information. He looked around the room as if seeing it for the first time. "Did her leaving bother you? Did you console your father?"

"I tried." Now it was Michael's turn to pause. He sat replaying the phone conversation, wondering if he might have said anything that would have changed all that was to happen. He spotted the FBI agent, the one named Garrett, still standing off to the sidelines, studying him, and he felt, just for a second, that the big man's eyes showed concern.

But Pemberton was waiting.

"My father," Michael said in precise terms, "was not an easy man to console."

"I see."

"Listen, Lieutenant. I know you've got a job to do, but I've traveled a long way to get here, and my father is in very bad shape. If you have anything more to tell me, or to ask me, I wish you would do it and let me get back to my father."

"I see. Well, Mr. Collins here says you're a man who likes the news straight," Pemberton said, raising his eyebrows. "Well, that's the way I like it, too."

Michael nodded his acceptance of this fact. "Okay, let's get to it. What did you really want to see me about?"

"We've got ourselves a pretty messy situation," Pemberton began, reaching inside his coat and removing a small notebook. He flipped through the pages, glanced again at Michael, then quickly slipped on a pair of reading glasses.

"On Saturday morning at approximately 12:20 Katherine Thompson Manning and Jacqueline Evonne Keaton were murdered in apartment 3C of 124 Brock Street in Alexandria. Each was shot once, in the face, with a shotgun. A third person was present, a Peter Frederick Cole, known as Pete to his friends. He caught a couple of random pellets from one of the shots but was otherwise unharmed."

Michael suddenly needed another drink, but he fought off the urge. He had to do something with his hands, and without thinking he reached in his pocket for a small leather notebook and silver pen. Everything stopped while he withdrew these and began taking notes.

Pemberton watched Michael over the top of his glasses and closed his notebook. "May I call you Mike?"

"I prefer Michael."

"Okay. Michael. This is the way it is. Late Friday night your stepmother was in bed with two people, a man and a woman, when an unknown assailant entered their apartment, walked to the foot of the bed and shot both women in the face. It was an execution. Very smooth. Very quick. The assailant laid the gun on the bed and walked away. It was very professional, and everything points to your father being responsible."

"That's absolutely absurd," Michael shouted.

"Your father is a powerful man. A man with a well-known temper, and his young wife had run away," Pemberton continued, his voice rising. "Your father found out Friday afternoon that she was living in Alexandria with two lovers. He was given the address by a Washington snoop."

Michael found the entire notion absurd. "What do you mean . . . snoop?"

Pemberton went back to his notebook.

"Two weeks ago your father hired a private detective named Louis Bottoms, a small-timer but a legitimate snoop, to find Mrs. Manning. Bottoms had a two o'clock appointment with Mr. Manning in his office at Media Associates in Georgetown. At that meeting he made his report, complete with some unflattering photographs. We've talked to Bottoms, and he tells us your father was, well let's just say he was angry. Bottoms is not a small man. He weighs in at around 240 plus, and he tells us Mr. Manning bodily threw him out on the street. There are many witnesses at Media Associates. Most of the staff seems to have seen it."

Michael could imagine the exchange. He could see his father picking up the big man and carrying him to the street, but still that was a long way from murder. "That doesn't mean he had her killed. That's not what my father would do."

"When your father had his heart attack last night he was in his room looking at photographs of his wife with these two people. The photos weren't very nice, and neither was the report with them. It was enough to make any man go a little berserk, even if he wasn't a man like your father. Even if he wasn't Matthew Manning."

"It's still crazy. My father might confront her. He would certainly want to talk to her. But he wouldn't . . ."

"Well, what about the phone call?"

Michael was caught off guard. "What phone call?"

"The murders took place at 12:25." Pemberton spoke slowly. He lowered his head to gaze over his glasses. He wanted to be sure Michael understood the time. "At 12:45, just twenty minutes after the shots were fired, a phone call was placed to this house. The call came from Alexandria. From a pay phone. It was long distance, and the number was automatically recorded in the telephone company computer."

Michael nodded that he understood.

"Your man," the Lieutenant paused and flipped quickly through the notebook. "Your man Patterson took the call. The man on the other end asked to speak to Mr. Manning, to Matthew Manning. He asked for him by name."

The room became silent. Michael tried to write the times in his notebook, but his hands were shaking too much. He wanted to look at Allen, to see what was coming next, but he was mesmerized by the policeman's voice.

"Patterson said that Mr. Manning had left instructions not to be disturbed. The man on the phone said," he looked into the notebook and read, " 'Tell him it's a friend of Pete's. A friend of Pete and Jackie. He'll want to talk to me.' "

Michael could feel himself going pale. He glanced at Allen, and he didn't like the expression that he saw. Allen looked as if he could almost believe what was being said.

"Patterson then put the man on hold," Pemberton continued. "He buzzed Mr. Manning's room, gave him the message, and your father accepted the call. An hour later it was discovered that your father had collapsed in his room."

Michael was speechless. He tried to fit the pieces together. He could see his father hiring a detective. He could see him being told about the people in Alexandria. He could feel his father's anger. But from there nothing made sense. His father would come home. He'd sort through all the facts. He'd reach a decision, and then he'd go and talk to her. The decision would never be murder.

"It's insane," Michael said, passing his personal verdict. "It's a sick joke. I don't know who killed those people over in Alexandria, but it wasn't my father. And it wasn't anybody sent by my father. It's crazy!"

"I'm just giving you the facts, as they stand," Pemberton interrupted. "The facts say that somebody was in Alexandria Friday night who knew the victims. That somebody called to tell your father something. It's too much to be a coincidence."

"Who did it? Have you found the killer? The one who pulled the trigger?"

"No," Pemberton said very coolly, "but we're working on it. This was a professional, and he's on the move. We traced him to the airport. He had a rental car that he turned in early this morning, but the name on the rental was a fake. We assume he took a flight out this morning, but we don't know to where. And he apparently used another name."

Michael still couldn't make the facts fit what he knew of his father. "It doesn't work," he said. "I know my father, and sure, he has a temper, but he could never do anything like this. If he ever got mad enough to kill someone—and I don't believe he could ever get that mad—then he would do it himself. He wouldn't hire any professional killer to do it for him.''

Pemberton gave a nod and picked up the folder he'd casually placed beside him in the chair. He opened it and studied several sheets of notes, disregarding the people in the room. Then he reached behind the loose sheets of paper and pulled out a dozen photographs. He peered over his glasses at Michael and handed him the batch.

Michael took the photos with a deliberate grasp, but his eyes stayed on the cop. When he looked down, he could feel his cheeks turning red. The top photo showed Kathy and another woman leaning against the wall of a building. There was a sidewalk, and a few blurry figures could be seen in the distance, but the two women were concentrating only on each other. They were smiling, perhaps laughing. They were holding hands like teenage lovers, and they were about to kiss.

In the second picture they were kissing. Lips to lips. Kathy had raised her hand and was caressing the other woman's cheek. The third showed the two women cuddling close to a man on a picnic blanket. The man's hand had disappeared under Kathy's blouse. Michael didn't look at the rest.

"You tell me," Pemberton said in a quiet voice. "You tell me how your father would react to those pictures. I think he'd be angry. I think he'd be out of control. I think he might be mad enough to hire somebody to pull the trigger of a shotgun."

"That's enough, Lieutenant," Allen demanded as he stepped between the two chairs. "Enough is enough. You've said what you had to say. You're wrong, but you've had your say. I think it's time you and your friend left. We've all had a long day."

"You're the one who said to tell it like it is," Pemberton said as he came quickly to his feet. "That's what I've done."

Michael wanted to stand, but he didn't have the strength. Pemberton nodded to the FBI agent, and together they moved to the door.

"Facts are facts," Pemberton said. "I wanted you to know how things stand. We're working on the assumption that your father was responsible. We believe Matthew Manning hired the killer." He turned to face Allen. "And that, Mr. Collins, is the way it is."

Pemberton walked quickly to the door, the silent FBI agent at his heels until after the policeman was out of the room. Then Agent Garrett turned back and smiled at Michael.

"We'll find our own way out," he said.

Michael closed his eyes and lowered his head. He shuddered when Allen put a hand on his shoulder, but he didn't look up. His head was pounding.

Allen took the seat where Pemberton had been, felt the warmth where the man had been sitting. He studied Michael's drained face, and tried to imagine what was going through his mind. Allen couldn't believe that the old man would have Kathy killed, and he was convinced that Michael would find it impossible.

"It is impossible," Michael said weakly, answering Allen's unasked question.

"I know," Allen said.

"But that call. Who would make a call like that?"

"It doesn't make any sense," Allen admitted. "It has to be a sick joke. Maybe somebody heard about the killings before the police released the information."

"But the killer had to know both Kathy and father," Michael said, trying hard to understand. "It couldn't have been a random thing. He knew where Kathy was. He had to know father, had the names of the people she was with. He knew everything."

"There are too many loose ends," Allen admitted.

"The only loose end is who could do something like this. It's horrible."

Both men were drained. They sat together, sharing drinks. They didn't say much, but they both felt better having the other there just in case something came up. It was two o'clock in the morning when Allen began to nod and realized that Michael had been up for nearly forty hours.

Michael sat erect in the big wingback chair, his eyes frozen open. He sat as if in a trance, gripping his glass for support. He didn't look at anything. Memories, somehow, didn't seem important now. He just stared into space and tried to imagine how anybody could do what had been done.

When Allen touched his shoulder, Michael jumped. "Let's try to get some sleep," Allen suggested.

They walked quietly up the steps, but when Allen turned to the suite of bedrooms in the east wing of the house, Michael stopped and looked at his father's door.

"There's nothing more you can do tonight," Allen said.

"You go ahead," Michael whispered. "I want to sit with him for a few more minutes."

They parted at the top of the steps. Allen went to bed, but sleep was not easy. Michael apologized to the nurse who sat at his father's side and took her chair. He was still sitting there when the house awakened late the next morning. He was sound asleep. His body sagged in the chair, chin resting on his chest. He still clutched his father's hand, seeking strength from the dying man.

When it is two A.M. on the East Coast it's only eleven P.M. in Los Angeles. As Michael was slowly climbing the steps of Manning Hall at the end of an impossible day, the stranger was just reaching the peak of his evening.

The stranger had been busy. In a matter of four hours he had worked the bars and made contact. He'd found a worthless, snivelling drug addict who could arrange almost anything, and when the stranger said he wanted cocaine—a lot of cocaine—the pathetic little man had almost wet his pants. He knew just the man to supply whatever the stranger needed. He called the man Gino.

And at 2 A.M. California time the stranger sat in a dark parking lot waiting for Gino. He was no longer in the rental car. He'd decided it was time to get something a bit more substantial, and now he sat back in the shadows looking down from the high seat of a large tank-like tow truck. He was sure it would do the job quite nicely.

Visibility in the parking lot was not good, but it was good enough to see Gino's Mercedes as it entered at the far side of the dark emptiness, cutting its headlights and coasting to a stop next to a wall that blocked the view from the street. Two oversized men stepped out of the car and eyed the perimeter.

The stranger flashed the lights of the big truck and received an answering signal from the Mercedes, which seemed so small off in the distance. And then it was time to move. To move quickly, before he lost the moment.

The stranger fired the engine of the big truck, turned his lights on full, including spotlights and spinning roof light of the tow truck, and in the moment when the bodyguards panicked he hit the gas. The stranger smiled, revved the engine and shifted gears. Tires squealed, and the truck raced toward the fragile Mercedes.

Hands reached inside jackets for weapons, but the bodyguards were too slow. They had no choice but to dive out of the way, and an instant later the huge truck smashed into the Mercedes. The impact was like an explosion as the steel plate on the front of the truck hit the Mercedes high on the grill, crushing the car against the wall. The entire front end of the car caved in, the polished silver hood and fenders collapsing like cheap cardboard.

There were two men in the car. The driver, a large black man, was instantly crushed by the steering wheel. But Gino was still very much alive. Shaken, the drug dealer tried to crawl over the front seat, but he was too big. The doors were jammed. There was no escape. His screams were like music to the stranger, a command performance for his ears only.

He took his time. He backed up, searching with the spotlight for the bodyguards, who'd run off into the darkness. Then he steered to a new angle, and charged again. The second hit rammed the car broadside and pushed the twisting heap of metal parallel with the wall. The side windows shattered, shards of glass sprayed into the car.

Tires squealed, and Gino cringed as the next hit crushed in the side of the car, pinning his leg to the seat. He screamed in agony, clawing at the leather in vain as the truck backed up and prepared for another charge.

Gino could feel blood running into his shoe as he continued to kick with his free leg. His strength was gone, the kicks little more than feeble insults to the ruined car. He was fading fast, the kicks weaker and weaker until he stopped altogether and started to sob. The truck was momentarily still, idling fifteen feet away, but the driver remained invisible. The spotlights were too bright. There were only the eyes that Gino could feel staring into his car.

Then the truck's engine revved, and Gino screamed for the last time. When the truck hit the car this time it climbed onto the roof, and Gino was crushed where he lay in the back seat.

The driver of the truck revved the engine several times, noisily shifted gears and backed away from the mangled metal of the Mercedes. He let the truck idle while he studied the crumpled waste where a car had once been. He tried to imagine what the fat man felt in the instant when he knew he was going to die. He smiled, happy with the image.

The driver then cut off the spotlights and guided the truck across the parking lot. It would take him an hour to drive the stolen vehicle to Inglewood, where he had a rental car waiting, then it would be a short drive out to Los Angeles International Airport. His plane would be leaving in three hours, and he wanted to get some breakfast before the flight.

The truck was already heading west on the Santa Monica Freeway when the police arrived at the lot. It took over an hour to cut Gino's body out of the car while a lieutenant from the vice squad stood to the side scratching his head.

There were no witnesses. They caught up with the body-guards three blocks away, but they were as dumb as they looked. They knew nothing beyond a bright light and a crash. It was certainly an odd way to kill someone, but it was undoubtedly a gangland hit, and that's the way the report would read. The lieutenant took the pragmatic approach. He appreciated it when these punks killed each other. It left less work for him.

THREE

WASHINGTON—*Matthew Emerson Manning, founder and publisher of the Media Associates magazine empire, is the chief suspect in two brutal murders that took place last weekend in Old Town Alexandria according to sources close to the investigation.*

Victims in the shooting were 31-year-old Katherine Thompson Manning, estranged wife of the 66-year-old Manning, and 27-year-old Jacqueline Evonne Keaton, one of two roommates sharing the small apartment. Peter Frederick Cole, an Alexandria artist, was also in the apartment when the murders occurred. He was not seriously harmed but has been hospitalized, unable to aid police in their investigation.

Manning, currently in a coma following a heart attack on the night of what police describe as "shotgun executions," is suspected of hiring a professional hit man to . . .

RICHMOND—*It reads like the scenario for a dime-store detective novel from the 1930s. There's the wealthy magazine publisher, a man described by all who know him as a tyrant. There's the young and beautiful wife who has abandoned him to become part of a menage à trois in an Alexandria apartment, and then there's the night a professional murderer shows up to blast away the faces of the two women with a shotgun.*

The plot appears to have been played out for real last weekend in a small apartment on one of the quiet streets in Old Town Alexandria. Two women were brutally murdered and, in a twist, the publishing giant suspected of conspiracy in the murders has slipped into a coma, unable to answer questions or defend himself.

Matthew Emerson Manning, who suffered a heart attack the night police say his wife and her lover became victims of a "shotgun execution," remains in critical . . .

ALEXANDRIA—*Police are still baffled in their efforts to track down the professional killer suspected in the brutal shotgun murders of two Old Town women last week. And the one man they think could help them in their efforts is in a coma, unable to answer questions.*

Matthew Emerson Manning, publisher and chief executive officer of the Media Associates chain of magazines, remains in critical condition at his home near Leesburg, but police detectives say he remains a suspect in . . .

The newspapers arrived at Manning Hall morning and afternoon, with each edition more vicious in its accusations against Matthew Manning. Michael read them for three days, feeling helpless and angry. Sometimes he nearly forgot that his father was in a coma. He almost expected the old man to come charging down the steps, his voice shaking the walls as he bellowed indignation at the journalistic swine and demanded that those responsible step outside.

But that was only sometimes. Michael's long hours were filled with the reality that such a demonstration was becoming less likely each passing day. His father's condition did not change. Patterson was screening telephone calls, keeping all but close family friends at bay, and Allen had returned to Washington to ease the uncertainties at Media Associates. The police remained silent.

Michael idled away the hours in his father's office. He was awed by the array of electronic marvels that linked the room to the rest of the world. The computers could check up on all of Media's publications, tie into library catalogs, and make use of an almost limitless network of information. All it took was a working knowledge of which buttons to push.

Michael knew how to do basic things, like writing a story and transmitting it to one of Media's magazines, but he was lost when it came to the more elaborate aspects of the system. He spent hours staring at the keys and switches, wondering which could be pushed to make sense of what had happened.

Allen called every few hours with some excuse to make sure that Michael was all right, and while Michael appreciated the brotherly gesture he couldn't stand being helplessly stranded in his father's house. He had to do something. He had to talk to someone, and his choices were limited.

Michael found Patterson shouting orders to two workmen and keeping a close watch on every detail as they did spring maintenance on the pool house behind Manning Hall. He didn't know how old Patterson was, but he knew the house manager had been here when he was born, and he suddenly realized he didn't even know Patterson's first name. Mrs. Patterson had always been Ginny, but he had always been Patterson. It had been that way since Michael was a small boy.

The two men moved away from the noise of hammering and sawing to find chairs in one of the ornate gazebos that marked the corners of the pool. Since his return home, Michael was surprised at how frail Patterson seemed. He remembered a robust man who'd raised him almost as a second father, filling in whenever Media Associates duties took Matt away.

"I think it's time we had a talk," Michael began. "I've been away too long. I need to know how things have been since Christmas, how things were in those months before . . ."

Patterson looked off in the distance with a serious expression. "It got bad after you left," he finally said, still looking into the distance, not at Michael. "Your father I think was in pain. I don't mean his heart, nothing like that, but he seemed to be hurting inside."

"In what way?"

"He just wasn't the same. He's always loved all that stuff with his magazines. He sure likes the power," Patterson said, breaking into a smile with the thought and then glancing at Michael before scanning the horizon in search of clouds. "But he didn't seem to be having any fun. I mean he turned more and more over to Allen, and he even had all those computers installed out here. Said he was going to run the whole thing from Manning Hall and not run off to Georgetown every day."

"And Kathy?" Michael asked.

Patterson considered his answer carefully, working his mouth silently like a cow chewing cud. "Well, I don't mean to speak evil of the dead, but Miss Kathy, she wasn't much help. She wasn't like your mother, not one bit. Your mother was a princess who made everybody feel good to be alive, but Miss Kathy was always off to herself, and then she complained how miserable she was 'cause she was all alone. They had lots of fights. Loud ones, too. They were not happy people, and the more they were together the more miserable they seemed to be."

Michael closed his eyes, struggling with images of the mother who had died of cancer when he was six and with the guilt of not seeing how much his father needed him. If he'd been here, maybe things could have been better. If he'd been here, maybe he could have taken some of the load off his father. Maybe he could have helped.

"Why didn't anybody call me? Why didn't somebody track me down before all this?"

"Oh, he wanted to call all right," Patterson said. "He always knew exactly where you were and what you were doing. Always had a telephone number on some memo Allen had sent him, listing your number in Paris or Rome or wherever you were. I even saw him pick up the phone a few times. I'm sure he wanted to call, but, well, you know how he is. He never could finish dialing the number."

Patterson was proud of his insights into the workings of Matthew Emerson Manning, but he had no idea how much pain he was causing the son. How many times had Michael considered calling home? Not enough.

"Patterson, I've got to do something. My father needs my help now, maybe more than he's ever needed it before, and I can't just sit around here and watch him die."

"Well then get out there and do something."

"What?"

Patterson shook his head and gave up on the clouds. He looked Michael in the eye and shook his head.

"You're your father's son. You're a journalist. You know how to find out things. Just get out there and do it."

With this sage advice, Patterson accompanied Michael to the garage and proudly pulled the cover off the vintage Porsche 911 that had been left in his care. The car was waxed to a lustrous red shine, and Patterson gave a detailed account of the maintenance the car had received during Michael's absence, even down to the careful monitoring when one of the handymen took it out for a monthly spin on the grounds.

Seeing the car, Michael suddenly realized there were things he could do. There were steps he could take, questions he could ask. He gave Patterson a pat on the shoulder, then climbed into the car. He quickly worked through the gears heading to the highway, then down-shifted and started all over again, letting each gear wind out as he drove east, toward Alexandria. He hadn't consciously thought about it, but as soon as he got on the road he knew where he was going. If there were answers, Alexandria was where they would be.

At least now, he was doing something.

The stranger also spent his afternoon pacing, thinking about something to do, but he didn't have a gazebo and he didn't have any fatherly advice to lead him in his decisions. The stranger was alone, pacing in his room at a Holiday Inn near Texas Stadium just outside Dallas.

Sections of the morning newspapers covered the bed. Nothing was marked, but the stranger had found several news items that interested him, most involving social events tied to the more elite Dallas circles. He considered the challenges each article offered. He was about to make a decision. He wanted to be sure it was the right one.

Finally he smiled. There wasn't a lot of happiness in the smile, but there was the satisfaction of choosing a course of action. Once the decision was made, all else would follow naturally. Each step of the plan would lead to the next step, and when it was all over the stranger knew someone would die.

Beside the bed was a small suitcase that he liked to think of as his bag of tricks. He leaned over it, picking out a small pill box. He checked to be sure all was in order. The box contained a single capsule carefully bedded in cotton.

By four o'clock, Michael was cruising the historic district of Old Town Alexandria. It took him twenty minutes to locate the address on Brock Street where the murders had taken place. He circled the block, looking at the apartment from all angles, then headed for a local bar called Jolly Jack's.

The newspaper accounts had said very little about the man who was with Kathy and Jackie on the night of the shooting. It said only that Pete Cole was in the hospital—one account mentioned he was in the psychiatric ward—and had been unavailable for questioning. But all of the papers soon picked up the bit of information that Cole had arrived home from the bar less than thirty minutes before the shooting.

Jolly Jack's was the obvious place to begin. It was a small bar, a neighborhood hangout located just far enough away from the historic shops and restaurants to avoid the crowds. It was mostly a meeting place for local artists and craftsmen who made a living through local galleries catering to the tourist trade. The paintings arranged on the walls of the bar revealed no Picassos.

When Michael arrived, prices had just been reduced for Happy Hour, and artists were beginning to arrive on well-timed breaks from the isolation of their studios. Most still wore paint-spattered jeans, and they walked into the bar with eyes wide, craving conversation to ease the tensions of a solitary day.

Michael hoped this would work to his advantage. He took a seat at the bar, and after ordering a beer asked if the bartender was Jolly Jack.

"To tell you the truth, Jolly Jack goes back about a dozen generations. I believe he was a Chesapeake Bay pirate or something." The bartender opened several bottles of beer for one of the waitresses while he talked. He had obviously told the story many times before. "But the name is Jack, and I have been known to get jolly every once in a while."

"My name is Michael. Michael Manning."

"Nice to meet you Michael. You an artist?"

"No. Kathy Manning, one of the women who was shot not far from here last weekend was . . .." Michael paused, feeling the heat of a blush. "She was married to my father. I understand the man she was living with was in here the night she was killed."

"That's right," the bartender said with a touch of pride. "He was here all right. Hadn't been gone more than a half hour when they say the shooting happened. Must of just got home."

"Were there many people in here that night?"

"Not really. We're kind of a local place, mostly artists. Just regulars. Cops have been by here and questioned everybody. There were only about a dozen people . . . and speak of the devil, here's a couple of them now."

Michael turned to see two young artists, both in jeans and T-shirts, walking toward the bar. The bartender had two bottles of beer waiting by the time they reached the counter.

"This here's Michael Manning, Kathy's stepson." He raised his eyebrows for emphasis. "I was just telling him that you two were among the unsavory characters in here the night Pete and his friends got shot up."

The two young men looked warily at Michael. The bartender did quick introductions—their names were John and Marty—then moved off to take care of orders at the other end of the bar.

"It's been really wild around here the past few days," said Marty, the younger of the two. He looked barely old enough to be out of high school, and he spoke with a drawl from the Deep South.

"Coppers really gave us the grill," added John, holding his head high and peering down a long, narrow nose as if sighting a chosen target. "We told them all about it. I mean about Pete and all his bragging. We were really givin' him a fit in here that night.

"We don't mean any offense, your stepmother and all, but Pete was really feeling his oats," John continued with a cackling laugh. "Came in here proud as a peacock, bragging about the two women living with him. He said you didn't know the true joy of sex until you'd had two women at the same time."

"Did you know Kathy?" Michael asked.

"She came in here once or twice, always with Pete and Jackie, but she wasn't into pubs. She seemed bored." John did the talking, but Marty nodded his agreement. "Mostly we just knew Pete."

"What kind of guy is he?"

"He's all right . . . a pretty good artist too, mostly landscapes and things like that. He did all right," John said. "We all like Pete, and we always knew about him and Jackie. She was a fine-looking woman. Perhaps a bit strange, but . . ."

"I wouldn't have kicked her out of bed on a cold night," Marty broke in, spilling beer down his chin as he tried to laugh and drink at the same time.

"Well, anyway," John continued, frowning at his companion's crudeness. "We didn't know where the new girl came from, but then he started telling us all about how she was the wife of some old codger, that guy Matthew Manning, the one who owns all those magazines. That night he was telling us how this guy Manning had a private eye following them."

"I know," Michael said. "Matthew Manning is my father."

The two young men looked at each other uncertainly, as if Michael's identity were a new factor. "We don't mean any offense," Marty said.

"None taken," Michael said. "Actually I'm trying to learn all I can about that night. You say the police have questioned everybody who was here?"

"Oh yeah," Marty said. "They came around to all the studios. Got each of us to make a list of everybody who was here. They talked to all of us. We didn't know anything, just that Pete was a bit drunk and kept saying he was heading home to get him some . . . you know what I mean."

"How many people were here?" Michael asked.

John and Marty both glanced around the bar, placing everybody where they had been that night. Marty's lips moved as he counted.

"I believe it was fourteen, including Jack behind the bar and the two girls—Juanita and Peg—who were working the tables." Marty scratched his ear, then waved to someone across the room. "We know everybody who comes here, and all of 'em knew Pete. None had anything to do with the shooting, though."

"Wait a minute," John said, squinting in concentration. "There was a guy here. I'm sure of it. We forgot all about him. A stranger."

"I don't remember no stranger," Marty said.

"Sure, there was. He sat down at the end of the bar. Real quiet like." John put his beer back on the bar so he could think harder. "I remember he kept watching everybody in the mirror behind the bar. Every time I looked up I'd notice he was eyeballing somebody, and listening. He was real intense."

"Did he leave here when Pete left?" Michael asked, feeling a sudden wave of nausea.

John concentrated. "I don't know. I just remember one time I looked up and he was gone. Could have been before Pete left. Could have been after."

"Hey Jack," Marty called down the bar. "You remember any stranger in here that night? I don't."

The bartender shrugged off the question while organizing six bottles and an equal number of glasses on a tray, then he ambled back to the three men.

"What stranger?" he asked.

"John says there was some guy in here that night. Do you remember? Says he was at the end of the bar."

Jack took a quick look at Michael's glass and placed another bottle of beer on the counter while he thought about the question. "I don't know. I seem to remember some guy down there. Handsome dude. Sat down at the end and drank Michelob. Was that Friday night?"

"Sure it was Friday," John said. "He sat there watching everybody in the mirror."

"Maybe you're right, but I don't think that was Friday. That must have been back earlier in the week." The bartender shrugged. "If you're interested," he added, turning to Michael, "maybe one of the girls would remember. If it was Friday night and it was this guy I'm thinking of, he looked like some kind of movie actor or something. Real slick. The girls usually remember someone like that."

The four men shared quick glances, each weighing the possibility that the stranger might be the murderer, and then the tension broke. The two artists said they'd think about it some more and went to join friends at one of the tables. Michael ordered a sailor sandwich at the bartender's suggestion and decided to wait for the new shift of waitresses due for work at the end of Happy Hour.

With sandwich in hand, Michael moved down to the end of the bar and watched the crowd. He studied the figures in the mirror that stretched the length of the bar, and he tried to imagine a killer sitting where he was. Had the stranger come here to spy on Pete and follow him home? If that was it, why didn't he kill Pete when he killed the women? Or was there some other reason he followed Pete home? It still didn't make any sense.

The meal that had just been served in the private dining room at the Highlander Club, on the outskirts of Highland Park in North Dallas, had probably cost enough to keep the entire clientele of Jolly Jack's in beer for a month. The guests of honor were Hamilton Garvey, who had just made Dallas history by winning five major New York computer contracts for Bryan Electronics, and his remarkably beautiful wife, Victoria.

The stranger sat at the public bar of the Highlander Club anxiously waiting for the private function to break up and hoping he would get his chance. He fondled the pill box in his jacket pocket, smiled at the woman bartender, and returned his attention to the wide stairway that connected the private dining rooms with the public lounge.

According to the gossip column in the morning newspaper, this dinner was being held so that Preston Bryan could formally announce Garvey's appointment as a full partner in Bryan Electronics. And everybody in Dallas knew what that meant: in five years Garvey, now only twenty-eight, would be president of the firm, with the old man serving as chairman of the board. The New York deals had set a course for the future of the company and had suddenly thrust the Garveys into the Dallas limelight.

And then they were there. The dinner had been private, just Preston Bryan, his wife Patricia, and the Garveys, but when the foursome walked into the public lounge of the club,

nearly half the people in the large room stood to give a "Big
D" ovation.

The stranger watched as Hamilton slipped an arm around
his wife's waist, his fingers tentative against the fine silk that
barely contained her all-too-visible figure. Together, they stood
at the top of the steps waving out to the crowd like the winners
in a presidential election.

Hamilton was the picture of confidence, proud and erect,
possessing not only a bright future but also a woman many
considered among the most beautiful in Dallas. And Victoria
was a goddess, long blond hair bouncing to her shoulders,
green eyes devouring the audience, and a full mouth begging
to be kissed. She was total sensuality, from the long legs
peeking through a slit in her tight skirt to the plunging neckline
that flashed bountiful breasts for all to see.

A dozen well-wishers soon circled the couple. Hamilton
shook hands and acknowledged pats on the back. Victoria
accepted hugs and kisses on the cheek, ignoring the men who
couldn't resist turning their eyes to her figure.

The stranger watched and he waited. Somehow he knew
his opportunity would come. He wasn't even worried about
it. He just had to bide his time.

The Bryans were the first to depart, obviously realizing the
employees would feel more comfortable once they were out
of the way. The remaining group, with the Garveys always at
their center, congregated at a large round table. More champagne was served. There were toasts, more handshakes, and
more kisses. It was a festive occasion filled with loud laughter.

It was another hour before the Garveys were left to themselves, and just as Hamilton was finishing off the last of the
champagne a waiter appeared with another bottle, popped the
cork, and served it with a flourish. "Mr. Bryan's administrative
assistant just called and said after things calmed down to deliver
a special bottle just for the two of you."

"Wouldn't you know it," Hamilton said, accepting an envelope from the waiter and placing it, unopened, on the table.
"The old man's timing is perfect, as always."

The stranger returned from the pay phone and again took
his seat at the bar. He watched the couple entwine arms like
newlyweds to drink from each other's glass, and he paid

particular attention as the waiter nestled the bottle in the silver champagne bucket at Hamilton Garvey's side.

Beads of sweat formed on the stranger's brow. He wiped his damp palms with the napkin beside his glass. But nobody paid any attention. Several women glanced at the handsome man, attracted by the stylish clothes and his calm presence. They sensed that he was a stranger, a few even wondered if he might be a movie actor visiting the city, but none would remember any details after the events of the evening.

The stranger concentrated only on the young couple that had attracted so much attention. He hated the way the man glowed with importance and the way the woman kept up by flashing her body for all to see. He hated the way they made a spectacle of their success, and he had decided to do something about it.

Then the moment came. Victoria Garvey stood, a bit unsteadily, to hug a woman who was leaving. She took three, four, five steps away from the table. Hamilton Garvey and the stranger stood at the same moment, and as Hamilton wobbled forward to join the good-byes, the stranger approached the table, a small capsule concealed in the palm of his hand.

Hamilton was kissing a woman on the cheek and shaking hands with her husband simultaneously, their good-bye chatter attracting everyone's attention. Of the hundred people in the room, no one noticed the stranger who bumped into the champagne stand, then caught both stand and bottle before they fell. Nobody noticed that the stranger dropped the capsule into the bottle. And nobody noticed as he calmly walked from the room.

The stranger reached the front door and turned just as the Garveys headed back to the table. His heart pounded as he watched the couple stop and kiss, the man's arm slipping comfortably around his wife in an intimate embrace. He watched the woman's face and tried to imagine what it would be like to stare into those green eyes, to feel that body pressed against his, those lips touching him.

"I believe I'm a wee bit drunk," Victoria Garvey said to her husband as she laid her head on Hamilton's shoulder. "I think maybe it's about time we headed home."

"Are you all right?" Hamilton asked. He lifted his wife's head and looked into her eyes. He laughed. "You're more than a wee bit drunk."

"I can still drink you under the table any day of the week, bud." She patted him on the rear to emphasize the point. "Let's have one more, a final toast, and then we'll go."

Hamilton nodded and reached for the champagne. He poured them each a full glass and placed the bottle gently on the table. Then he lifted the glasses and handed one to his wife.

"To the future," he said. They drank, and then they shared a final kiss.

Before they could set the glasses on the table, Victoria went into convulsions. Hamilton tried to grab her, but he couldn't breathe. He reached to his chest with one hand and watched helplessly as his wife collapsed across the table, her dress falling open as she began to twist and jerk in agony. Then his eyes began to close. His knees weakened, his chest tightened. He could barely hear the screams from nearby tables as he stumbled to the floor and died.

The stranger had wanted to stay to see the finish, but discipline told him that he must be gone. He had walked out as soon as he saw Hamilton reaching for the bottle of champagne. He stood just outside the door until he heard somebody scream, and then he walked eight blocks before hailing a taxi.

When Michael Manning ordered his third beer of the evening at Jolly Jack's, he began to realize how anonymous a stranger could be. Jack was still working behind the bar, but the two young artists Michael had talked to earlier were gone. Other than that, Michael had spoken only briefly to the two waitresses who came on duty at six o'clock—neither remembered Friday's stranger—and he was convinced he could walk out of the bar and none of the other fifteen people in the place would remember that he had ever been there.

He had also learned a great deal about the clientele of Jolly Jack's. Eavesdropping, he knew that two women at a corner table were having men problems; a man four seats down from Michael at the bar had just concluded a successful art show in Washington; and another man was having an affair with the married assistant at the Alexandria gallery that handled his work.

Michael was fascinated by this little Peyton Place and wondered what kind of stories the stranger might have heard on the previous Friday. His reverie was broken by the sound of a familiar voice.

"Drinking alone isn't good for you." The FBI agent who'd been at Manning Hall slipped onto the next stool at the bar.

"But I'm not alone," Michael replied as he tried to remember the man's name. "You're here, and so is most of Alexandria's artistic community."

"Name's Garrett. Quince Garrett. I thought you might show up here sooner or later. I asked Jack to give me a call if you did. He's also told me about your stranger."

Garrett was a puzzle. Michael could still remember the agent's smiling departure—"we'll find our own way out"—and now he studied the face of a man who didn't seem to want to take things too seriously. The creases in the rugged face were now softened. The body was less rigid, less bullish.

"I can't quite figure your game," Michael said.

"Pete Cole was sitting right over there," Garrett said, pointing to a nearby stool and ignoring Michael's comment. "He left here, went home, and a half hour later someone showed up with a shotgun to do away with his roommates."

"Has he told you anything?" Michael asked.

"Cole's out of it. Just got scratches on the outside, but he's all messed up, mental ward. He's tried to off himself twice since it happened. He has to be kept tied down."

"Has Lieutenant Pemberton come up with anything?"

"Forget Pemberton. He'll never find who killed your stepmother. He'll putter around a few days, till the newspapers relax. Then there'll be another murder, another case. This one goes unsolved."

"But he said . . ."

"Your father had nothing to do with it. We're talking a pro hit, or a psycho. And a pro wouldn't leave a witness."

"Are you saying it was a psycho?"

"I didn't say that."

Jack worked his way up the bar and placed two bottles of beer on the counter, glancing briefly at Michael to see if he was angry about the FBI agent showing up. He wasn't sure how to read Michael's expression.

"I don't understand. What's your involvement in all of this?" Michael said as soon as the bartender moved away.

"I'm strictly unofficial. I'm working on some things over at Quantico, and this case is something we're using sort of as a study tool, a test case."

"But . . ."

Garrett didn't give him a chance. "That's all I can really say right now, but if you want my opinion . . ." he paused to wait for Michael's nod, pouring beer into a glass while organizing his thoughts. "Well, the way I see it, your father's too good for this one. A wealthy, powerful man, a young wife, the private eye . . . but then the call. That call doesn't make sense. The job was too slick. A professional killer that slick wouldn't make a stupid phone call naming the victims to confirm the job done. It sounds like something a crazy man would do. Not a pro."

"It sounds like you're saying Kathy and the other woman were killed by a psycho?"

"I just don't know. It's got me baffled. It's like some phantom walked into town, picked out two women, blasted them with a shotgun, then walked away. And he stopped at a phone booth just to make a call to tell your dad he'd done it."

"Is that what you think happened?"

Garrett shrugged and took a couple of small sips from his beer. He watched the reflections in the mirror as a young couple left the bar. "I can't find anybody—not anybody official, that is—who believes it."

"What can I do?" Michael asked.

"I'm not sure. I guess maybe I'm trying to convince myself that your father's not the kind of man who would hire a killer."

"It's the last thing my father would do," Michael insisted. "I know my father better than anybody, even better than Allen. We've had our differences, and a lot of that had to do with Kathy, but my father has always been like a kid. He has built an empire by being the kid playing the most organized games in town. When he was twelve years old he started a newspaper that he sold door-to-door on the block where he grew up in Richmond. He always had meaty stories about the neighborhood, and when he was fourteen he started doing articles for newspapers and for small magazines. He was editor of his first magazine when he was twenty, and he's built from that to create Media Associates—six major regional news magazines and a wire service supplying investigative pieces to newspapers across the country."

Michael paused, uncertain what impact he was having on Garrett and wondering why the FBI man would even bother to ask. He tried to slow down, but there was a lot he wanted to get off his chest.

"I'll tell you what my father would do. Allen tells me he didn't see the private detective until Friday afternoon. He'd want to be alone after something like that. He probably didn't even open the report until he got home. He would have studied every angle, and when he was convinced he understood what was happening he would have come to Alexandria and talked to Kathy face to face. All she'd have had to do is say 'we're finished' and he would have said good riddance. My father has never been a man to want anybody around who didn't want to be there."

Garrett sighed, and Michael stopped, still trying to understand the why behind this conversation.

"I'm curious why your father decided to call you that very morning."

Now it was Michael's turn to sigh. "I just don't know. Maybe he wanted to ask for help, but as you probably realize, fathers aren't too good at asking sons for help."

Garrett took another sip from his glass, then sat silent for a few moments.

"The evidence backs up what you said about your father. We talked to your house man, Patterson, and he remembered that when he took coffee to your father's bedroom a half hour after he arrived home the envelope was on the bed. He's sure the envelope was still sealed."

"That would mean my father couldn't have done it. It would have been late Friday afternoon, probably five or six o'clock. There's no way he could hire a killer—a kind of person he wouldn't even know—and set up the murders in six hours."

"It gets better," Garrett said. "Your father instructed Patterson to cancel all of his plans for the weekend. Patterson spent most of the evening on the phone, and he's convinced your father never placed a call. We've looked at the long distance records for that night and for the past few months. They all check out."

Michael could feel a weight being lifted off his chest as he and Garrett shared a knowing look. "Then my father has been officially cleared?" he asked.

"It's not quite that simple," Garrett said. "The police still think your father did it, that he had it all set up in advance. I've talked to our Behavioral Sciences Unit down at Quantico, and they say the murders don't fit the pattern for a psycho. But it doesn't fit a hit man either. Hit men don't leave witnesses. It doesn't fit anything."

"What are you going to do?"

"I'm not sure," Garrett admitted. "There is one person who thinks I may be onto something, but she has her own ideas."

"What do you mean?"

"She's a shrink. Dr. Karen Daniels from the University of Virginia. She teaches, but this summer she's working as a consultant to the FBI, preparing profiles of violent crimes. It's part of something called VI-CAP, Violent Criminal Apprehension Program, something new with computers to help law enforcement agencies track down psychos, the ones they call serial killers. But she believes the FBI is being too narrow in its approach. She thinks killers can beat the system."

"Does she think this murderer is one?"

"She doesn't go that far, but she's interested. That's why we're using this as a test case. She's been spending a lot of time over at the apartment, trying to find things that we normally wouldn't look for. She feels that unanswered questions are just as important as the ones you can answer, and she's got a long list from this case."

"I'd like to meet her," Michael said.

"I don't believe that would be a good idea, but I'll tell you what I'll do," Garrett suggested. "You go on back to Manning Hall and stop trying to play detective. I'm meeting with Dr.

Daniels tomorrow morning over at the apartment and I'll let you know if she turns up anything."

Michael agreed. What else could he do? But as soon as Garrett excused himself, Michael paid his tab and walked over to King Street. He thought he should stick around till the morning, and King Street was where the nearest Holiday Inn was located.

Back at the Holiday Inn near the Texas Stadium, the stranger decided to cancel his flight reservations to Chicago. He should leave, the sooner the better, but just this once he would make an exception. He would stay in Dallas to watch television reports and read puzzled newspaper accounts on the double murder.

It was a wonderful two days. The police were completely baffled. They quickly discovered the cyanide in the champagne bottle. They also found that Preston Bryan's administrative assistant had never called the club to order a special bottle for the couple. They examined the unopened card that had accompanied the champagne—it read "Congratulations" and was initialed HCN, just as had been instructed over the phone. An alert forensics man had even informed homicide detectives that the initials were the chemical symbol for hydrogen cyanide.

But that was it. There were no clues. No motive. Nobody remembered a stranger who sat at the bar. Nobody could remember much of anything except that the couple had been the center of attention, celebrating and making a lot of noise.

FOUR

Michael called Manning Hall early the next morning to check on his father's condition. He got the usual "wait and see" from the nurses, then assured Mrs. Patterson that he was okay. When he got off the phone he was more determined than ever to do something, even if it was wrong.

By seven o'clock he was parked across the street from the apartment where the murders had taken place. He tried to imagine a killer with a shotgun walking up the steps and into the building with his victims already marked for death, but it was a scene that belonged to movies and television. It did not belong to real life.

Mostly, Michael filled the time thinking about what he might be getting himself into. He wondered what kind of Sherlock Holmes this Dr. Karen Daniels might turn out to be, and he was expecting the worst. She would probably turn out to be some eccentric old witch who thought everybody was paranoid and knew just what they needed to be cured.

Then there was his father. Since he had returned home he had experienced an increasing number of flashes from the past. He always remembered the good times, those brief moments when he and his father had seemed closest, like the time they'd sat in a car across the street from a house in Georgetown, playing "Twenty Questions" while his father waited for a senator who'd been avoiding his calls. There was another time when they'd gone to a steeplechase on the other side of Leesburg and it had rained so hard they'd had to sit in the car for two hours, with Michael talking on and on about the things he wanted to do, the places he wanted to go, and the stories he wanted to write when he finished college.

When Dr. Karen Daniels finally showed up at eight-thirty, she was not at all what Michael had expected. The only word he could think of to describe her was "bouncy." She was young and attractive in an athletic sort of way, like a modern dancer as she moved along the sidewalk gripping a pencil in her teeth and carrying a large shoulder bag.

He waited another fifteen minutes before he built up enough nerve to approach the building. His footsteps echoed in the empty halls as he searched for any indication of the murder apartment, and he shuddered when he stepped up to the door with a "Do Not Enter—Police Crime Scene" sign across it. A padlock had been attached at the top of the door, but the hasp was open and the lock was gone.

Michael's nerve vanished. He stood there, staring at the door and not wanting to go any further. He didn't know what might be on the other side, but he knew it couldn't be pretty. Just as he finally raised his fist to knock, a booming voice echoed down the hall and nearly scared him to death.

"What the fuck are you doing here?" It was Quince Garrett, and the FBI agent did not sound happy.

"I wanted to see for myself," Michael said, trying to tough it out.

Garrett grew bigger as he stomped down the hallway, but his anger was gradually replaced by annoyance as he got to the door.

"I thought you were going back to Manning Hall," he said. "I thought we'd agreed you'd let us play detective. You were going to wait for my call."

"But Agent Garrett, I've got to do something," Michael pleaded. "I'll go crazy sitting around that big house, and what harm can it do? I just want to see where it happened. I need to understand what took place in there."

Both men glared at the door, and Garrett noticed that the lock was open.

"Okay," he said, hating himself for doing it. "But I have to warn you in advance. Dr. Daniels is kind of new to all this. I mean she's a specialist on deviant behavior. She's talked to a lot of psychos in clinical situations, and she's interviewed a lot of guys in prison. She's on the FBI payroll, and we listen to what she has to say, too, but she does have some strange ideas."

"What do you mean?"

"It's just that this is the first time she's been involved in an actual homicide," Garrett explained, searching for the right words. "She comes up with lots of scenarios—that's one of her favorite words—and she gets real excited."

With enough said, Garrett led the way. He studied Michael for one more brief moment, knowing in his heart that this was a bad decision, and then he opened the door, making a grand gesture in allowing the younger man to enter first.

Dr. Daniels sat on the sofa, seemingly unaware that the two men had entered. Her brow was wrinkled in concentration, and she was biting down hard on the eraser end of a pencil. Her downturned eyes jerked back and forth across several sheets of paper on the table in front of her, and a hand reached to her short, dark hair, pushing it back as if she were afraid it would fall in her eyes and block her concentration.

"Dr. Daniels?" Garrett whispered.

She didn't jump. She merely took the pencil from her mouth and raised her hand. "Just a second, Quince. This new stuff is great, and I've nearly got the scenario straight."

Quince looked at Michael. His shoulders didn't move, but his eyes nevertheless offered a shrug.

"There," Dr. Daniels said. "I've got it." She stood and walked quickly to the two men. "You must be Michael Manning," she said, offering her hand. "I'm sorry about your stepmother."

Michael accepted her handshake and tried to assess the petite dynamo who now stared into his eyes. Her hair was cut the way a dancer might wear it, bobbed into neat bangs across the forehead, short and out of the way. Everything about her said tomboy, and yet there was a sexiness, too. She stood about five-foot-two, and her eyes were a clear blue that seemed to be searching for his soul.

"I'm sorry." She blushed. "I have a tendency to stare. Occupational hazard."

"That's all right," Michael said. "I understand you're helping the FBI look into the case."

"That's putting it kindly. I suppose I'm really more a nuisance, but I've been spending a lot of time just down the road at Quantico and this case is a rare opportunity to check out some of my theories. Quince has been kind enough to let me do that."

"And what are your theories?" Michael asked.

She was bubbling with enthusiasm, wanting to tell him, but she took a quick glance at Garrett and a decision flashed across her eyes. The theories would have to wait. "First, let me show you the scenario. I think I've got it all worked out . . . if that's all right with you, Quince?"

Garrett shrugged. "Be my guest."

Dr. Daniels made a face at his tone of voice, but she still grabbed up her papers and dashed eagerly to the front door.

"The way it works out, the three of them were in the apartment, back there in the bedroom. Then the killer, identity unknown, showed up at the front door."

"How'd he get in?" Garrett asked, warming to the doctor's energy.

"The lab report indicates that he used a thin piece of metal, something like the blade of a putty knife, only thinner and more flexible."

"You mean like a credit card?" Michael asked.

"Like a card, but in this case it was metal. The report says there are metal scratches on the inside of the door frame and on the lock. Then he used a strong hydrochloric acid solution containing in excess of 40 percent hydrogen chloride—potent stuff. He used it to weaken a link of the chain and force the second lock. He must have carried it in a small vial, perhaps with an eyedropper. It was precise. There was no excess spillage on the floor."

Dr. Daniels paused to glance at the two men. They had nothing to say.

"The bedroom door must have been closed, so nobody realized the murderer was here. Every light in this room was on, but we can't tell if they were already on or if the killer turned them on. In either case, he went to the bedroom door and pushed it open. There was no light on in the bedroom, so they would have seen only a silhouette. He walked to the foot of the bed and raised the shotgun. Now this is the interesting part . . ."

She stopped, motioning for the two men to follow her as she darted into the bedroom. Michael hesitated, but Garrett nodded that it was all right and they walked into the room together. The bed had been cleared. The mattress and springs were gone, but there were still a few dark blood stains spotting the wall behind the bed. The doctor stepped over the frame, into the emptiness where the bed had been, and began to use her arms to describe the action.

"This is what he did," Dr. Daniels continued. "He stood at the foot of the bed and raised the shotgun. It was a Remington . . ." she flipped through the papers, "a Remington Eleven Hundred, twelve-gauge with a twenty-eight-inch barrel. It had a full load, five 2¾-inch shells—number four buckshot. Could be bought right over the counter."

"Impossible to trace," Garrett muttered.

"The three people were on the bed. Mrs. Manning was on the left, Miss Keaton on the right, and Peter Cole was in the middle. Apparently Miss Keaton tried to sit up when she saw the killer, but he didn't just fire randomly to stop her."

She looked at her attentive audience and bit her lower lip.

"No, he stepped back a half step to get the right angle and the right distance. A shotgun blast doesn't begin to spread out until three feet, and the killer stepped back so that he would be at least five feet from the first victim's face when he fired. He wanted to destroy the face, not just kill the victim. This is the only thing that makes any sense, because he then stepped back to the foot of the bed and readjusted his angle. Mrs. Manning was still lying flat on her back, her head on the pillow. From the pattern of the blast the killer must have stepped up on tiptoes and leaned over the bed to get the proper angle and distance, a position that would destroy the face but wouldn't spread out far enough to injure the man next to her."

"You're saying that the killer didn't want to hurt Cole?" Garrett asked.

"He was very careful not to hurt him, at least not to hurt him physically,' Dr. Daniels continued. "The two pellets that hit Cole came from the first shot, the one that killed Miss Keaton. The killer couldn't control the first shot as well as he could the second. Besides, he had three more shells in the gun. He could have easily killed Cole if he'd wanted to. I think he did the whole thing to destroy Peter Cole, not physically but mentally. I think the two women were incidental. I think the murderer wanted to punish him."

"Why? For living in sin?" Michael asked softly, feeling a bit weak from the vivid descriptions.

"Perhaps," Dr. Daniels said.

"Why don't we move back into the living room," Garrett suggested, taking Michael's arm to lead him out of the room.

"I'm all right," Michael insisted, turning back to look at the room one more time before leaving.

"I apologize if I was too blunt," Dr. Daniels said as she watched Michael take a seat on the sofa. "But I believe this is a perfect scenario for what I've been trying to tell the FBI all along, that murderers don't always fit nice, neat patterns."

"That fits with the stranger at the bar?" Michael asked.

"What would he have heard?" Dr. Daniels asked.

"Only everything," Garrett said. "Cole was in there bragging about the whole setup, about how he had two women at home, about how he liked to watch them having sex with each other and could join in anytime he wanted. And he bragged about Kathy being the wife of Matthew Manning, and how he was the guy who owned Media Associates. He even bragged about a private eye taking pictures. He said it all, and he apparently said it loud enough for everybody to hear."

"Living in sin," Dr. Daniels whispered almost to herself. "That could be it."

"Now let's not get carried away," Garrett said, glancing over some of the doctor's notes. "This idea about some psycho hearing Cole in the bar and killing the two women as a punishment is one thing, and it's pretty far-fetched as it is, but jumping to one of your non-pattern psychos is too much. Let's stick with one case at a time."

"But you said it yourself last night," Michael insisted. "You said it was like a phantom walked into town and just picked these two women as his target."

Michael and Karen Daniels shared a quick glance, their minds obviously working on the same wave length, and Garrett sighed. "Now I've got two amateurs trying to solve the murder of the century," he said.

"I would take offense," Dr. Daniels said, "but even if we're not talking a serial killer, this is still a scenario that backs up my theory that these murders do exist. They should be handled as singular incidents, perhaps as parts of a whole, but never as statistics. They're . . ."

"Let's not get into that now," Garrett interrupted. "I'm sure Mr. Manning has better things to do, like getting back to Manning Hall, and then I've got to question everybody from Jolly Jack's all over again. I want to know more about this stranger."

They left the apartment together, and Garrett begrudgingly left the two would-be sleuths at the sidewalk. They watched him drive away and smiled at each other like a couple of school children who'd just pulled something on the teacher.

"I don't think he's too happy about introducing us," Dr. Daniels said, pointing to her car in front of the building.

"I think you're right."

"Well, it gives us a chance to start fresh. I'm Karen," Dr. Daniels said, offering her hand for a shake.

"Michael," he said, taking her hand, then reaching to open the car door.

"What do you say we go get a cup of coffee?" she suggested.

"I know just the place," Michael said.

Jolly Jack's looked different in the daylight. Even with placemats and napkins on the tables, the place was seedier and less romantic. The two waitresses had not been there the night before. Their uniforms were considerably longer than the short skirts of the evening shift, and judging from their figures the length was probably a blessing. They weren't happy about it, but one of the waitresses eventually stopped lining up iced tea glasses to bring Michael and Karen coffee.

"Do you really believe this could be a serial killer?" Michael asked as soon as they were seated.

"Maybe it's stretching the facts thin, but stranger things have happened," Karen said. "The important thing is that this case has a lot of questions that won't fit any pattern. And that backs what I've been telling the FBI hardheads all along."

"And what are these mysterious theories?"

"It's sort of complicated," Karen said, laughing at her own intensity. "It's this thing between the Justice Department and me about how violent crimes should be investigated."

"You mean VI-CAP?"

"You've heard of it?"

"Agent Garrett mentioned it. Said it was some sort of computer thing, a Violent Crimes Access Program, or something like that."

"It stands for Violent Criminal Apprehension Program, and it's costing big bucks," Karen said with enthusiasm. "It's really a simple idea. There are over seventeen thousand police agencies in the United States and over three thousand counties. The problem is that one law enforcement agency rarely knows what another is doing, and if somebody goes on a killing spree across the country he can kill dozens of people before anybody puts it together. VI-CAP is a computer that will offer detailed, standardized homicide reports on violent murders and attempted murders throughout the United States so that patterns can be discovered."

"What's the hangup?" Michael asked.

"The problem is the word standardized. It's too narrow in its approach," Karen explained. "The FBI Academy at Quantico is running the show, and they have brought in a half-dozen psychologists to figure the best way to train field operatives. The whole thing hinges on operatives who can go to the scene of a homicide and get the right data for the computer."

"What's wrong with that?"

"It's hard to explain, but are you familiar with the FBI Behavioral Sciences Unit?"

"No."

"They're the people who come up with profiles on serial murderers. On people like Son of Sam, on all sorts of sex killings, and on things like the Atlanta child murders. The problem is that they're using a lot of dime store psychology. They try to put everything into neat pigeonholes, and when they're right—when they hit a classic scenario—they have the profile exact all the way down to the color socks the killer is wearing. But my point is that classic cases are too rare. Those field operatives should be trained not just to file a group of standard facts into a computer but to look for the unusual, for the pieces that don't fit."

"I'm not sure I understand," Michael admitted as he stirred sugar into his coffee.

"Okay, let's take this case," Karen offered. "If we eliminate your father having hired a killer, which I believe we can safely do, that leaves us with a motiveless murder. There are five thousand such murders every year in this country, what the FBI shrinks like to call 'stranger' murders, the victim and the killer don't know each other. Everybody in the Justice Department, including the FBI shrinks, will admit these cases are unsolvable, and the best estimates are that there could be fifty people or more in this country who kill from time to time for the fun of it. They kill people they don't know, just for the thrill of doing it."

"There are really people who do things like that?" Michael asked.

"It's all too real. The Justice Department considers it an epidemic, and they've come up with formulas for deciding what type of people do these things. The victims, according to the odds, are women and children, and it's usually intra-racial—blacks kill blacks, whites kill whites. The prime motive is the desire to dominate others, to be like a judge handing out punishment. There are supposedly two basic types. They kill either by impulse and with rage, or they are cool and detached. The impulsive killer is usually young, early twenties, and he kills with whatever is at hand. He's quick because he feels threatened by the victim. The detached killer tends to be a little older, perhaps as old as thirty, and he is meticulous in everything he does. He is master of the situation, slow and sadistic. He brings his own weapon and everything he needs, such as acid to dissolve the chain holding a door. And he's cunning. He doesn't hide the body, and he doesn't worry about leaving witnesses, because he is proud. He knows he's smarter than everybody else."

"Is that our man?"

"Yes . . . And no."

"Based on the profile, and on what we know about this murder, our man is maybe thirty years old and he wants to dominate others." Michael said, trying to put the pieces together. "He left a witness, so he thinks he's smart enough to avoid capture."

"That's the way the FBI profile would begin," Karen acknowledged, nodding in approval. "But they also say when the murder includes a brutal facial attack the murderer tends to know the victim. He doesn't want to look at a face he knows."

"One thing I don't understand. Why couldn't the murderer be older than thirty?"

"Good question," Karen said. "This type of behavior tends to surface by the time a potential psychopath is thirty, usually younger. And if he doesn't get caught by age thirty he doesn't enjoy it as much as he did when he was younger. He becomes tired of looking for a new challenge. He takes more chances. He tries to get caught, or he kills himself. Quite often a psychopathic killer's final victim is himself."

"Is the FBI looking into this case?" Michael asked.

"No," Karen said. "They only do profiles on certain types of crimes, and this one doesn't fit the pattern. They did check it on the computer. They came up with other shotgun murders, but not this modus operandi. There's nothing on record quite this cool and detached. So they say it doesn't exist."

"And you think they're wrong?"

"Yes," Karen said matter of factly. "Patterns exist, but many serial murderers tend to be above average in intelligence. Some are borderline geniuses. There's nothing to stop somebody from refusing to go along with a pattern. A smart serial killer would go against the grain. He would be different. He would never repeat himself."

"How would you ever catch somebody like that?"

"That's the problem," Karen said. "You probably wouldn't."

It was obvious after two cups of coffee that Karen Daniels was anxious to join Garrett on the investigation, and Michael's mind was spinning with ideas. She certainly hadn't been what he expected, and he was sorry to see her go when they separated in front of Jolly Jack's. But Michael had a lot to think about, and the drive back to Manning Hall gave him plenty of time to work his way through all that he had learned since the previous night. By the time he reached home he had convinced himself that a phantom killer was responsible for the Alexandria murders, and he was beginning to put together a plan that just might track down the phantom.

Michael spent an hour listening to the sad beeps of the life support system that was keeping his father alive. The nurses avoided him, and even the Pattersons had begun to lower their eyes when they passed him in the hallways of the big house. He had never felt so alone in his life, but his plan was coming together. At least it had possibilities.

By two o'clock he knew what he was going to do. He believed Karen was right, that maybe there were phantom killers who avoided detection because they didn't follow patterns, and this was something solid he could examine. He could approach it as a journalist and look for answers.

Michael paced the office for two hours, pulling books from the shelf as if they might produce an answer. He opened desk drawers and cabinets looking for clues that didn't exist. He poured himself a scotch but decided not to drink it. When Ginny came to ask him about dinner, he told her all he wanted was a couple of sandwiches. Then he settled down at the computers.

At the central console he immediately realized he was in trouble. It contained three independent systems, so that his father could call material from several sources at the same time. There were large storage and power units, a printer for each system, cabinets containing programs, and additional stored data. He was familiar enough with the system to log on, but after that the computer offered options and file controls that were coded. He did manage a few commands that got him into Media's library in Georgetown, but every time he asked for something he got a "File Not Found" message.

After thirty minutes of this, Michael gave up. He knew what he wanted to do, and he was going to need help.

When Ginny brought his sandwiches, he asked her to get Patterson to stock the bar refrigerator with plenty of soft drinks. Then he called Allen Collins at Media Associates in Georgetown.

"Michael, hello," Allen said when he came to the phone. "How's Matt doing?"

"No change," Michael said, hating himself for repeating the Manning password.

"Did you learn anything in Alexandria?"

"Actually, I learned quite a bit. That's why I called."

"What's up?"

"I've been looking at the computers, and I can't make heads or tails of this stuff. I've got some research I want to do, and I need access to the system. I've used father's password—it's taped right here on the console—but this is a big project. I'm going to need a list of Media's stringers by state. And I need to know how to send out an assignment request."

"This sounds like it's going to be expensive," Allen came back, ever the company man.

"Please, Allen, no questions. Not right now. Just trust me. This is something I've got to do."

It took Allen less than a half hour to explain how to gain access to the list of freelance writers and how to contact them. But the rest was up to Michael, and he knew he was like a blind man wearing gloves to search for a needle in a haystack.

His theory was simple. He believed in a psychopathic killer, someone who had perhaps killed many people, each in a different way and for a different reason. If the killer was a phantom, impossible to find, then Michael was going to use Media's network of writers, one in the capital of each mainland state, to go hunting for the victims.

During the next twelve hours Michael turned the computer room into a command center. He began by writing an explanation of what he needed. His careful instructions asked each writer to study newspaper clippings, talk to police, and check other sources to put together a list of the most unusual murders in that state since the first of the year, a little more than five months. He wanted murders like the ones in Alexandria, murders that didn't make any sense.

Next he put together a list of primary and secondary writers for each state to cover himself if the first choice was unable to take the assignment. He decided it would be better not to mention the idea of a phantom or serial killer at this point, so he explained the assignments as research for a series of magazine pieces on unusual murders.

Michael spent a couple of hours carefully listing guidelines for including a murder on the list. It had to be an unusual killing that appeared to have obscure motives linked to some sort of punishment but with no reasonable suspects. By nine o'clock he was sending out the job to writers in the forty-eight states.

He tried to nap on the sofa, but messages kept coming back on the computers, with writers accepting the job, making excuses, or asking for further details. The time differences across the country kept things running smoothly, and while most of the East Coast was assigned by eleven o'clock, the rest of the country kept him going through the night. By two o'clock in the morning he had hired researchers for forty states, and three hours later he flopped down on the sofa with all forty-eight allocated.

"Now we wait," a sleepy Michael said to himself. The assignment had been accepted on an immediate basis. The East Coast people would soon be starting out to do the research, the West Coast three hours later. With any luck, the reports should begin pouring in some time in early evening.

"Breakfast, then bed," Michael said, still talking to himself. "No," he changed his mind. "Bed, then breakfast."

Michael checked to be sure that all three printers were loaded with paper, then climbed the steps to bed. He paused in front of his father's door, listening for a moment to the beeping of the machines breathing for Matthew Manning, then he quietly walked to his bedroom and collapsed into sleep.

FIVE

The computers at Manning Hall went active at one o'clock Friday afternoon when a phone call triggered the system and fed in details about a Duke University football player who had been chopped up like a side of beef on January 10th. Reports on three more South Carolina murders followed, and before these were fully entered a second system came on to receive equally bizarre reports from New Hampshire.

By the time Michael pulled himself out of bed at 2:30, all three computers were running at capacity. Fan-folded printouts were stacking neatly in chrome racks behind each of the high-speed printers, computer discs spinning silently, recording each report and then automatically transferring the data to one of the large storage units.

His eyes barely open after five hours' sleep, Michael stood at the doorway watching this high-tech activity and decided that breakfast would have to come first. But when he returned to the main part of the house and entered the breakfast room, he was not prepared for the suspicious stares from the Pattersons.

"Ginny. Coffee. Please." Michael begged, stopping Mrs. Patterson just as she was getting ready to open her mouth. She relented, heading for the kitchen.

"Master Michael." Patterson's official manner was out of place, but at least it dragged Michael from what remained of his sleepiness. Michael froze just above his seat at the table, and even Ginny came to a halt halfway through the kitchen door. The elderly man didn't know what to say now that he had the stage.

"What's up, Patterson?" Michael asked, realizing once again that he had never known the man's first name. "And what's this Master Michael crap?"

"Sir. Michael. There have been a great many phone calls while you were sleeping."

"And?" Michael asked.

"That FBI man. Agent Garrett. He has called at least a dozen times. Quite nasty. I told him you had been up late and were sleeping, but he just cursed and shouted. He was quite rude." Patterson blushed. "He insisted that you call as soon as you were awake."

Michael closed his eyes and pondered this overlooked side effect of his research. "Don't look so worried, Patterson . . . and you either," he said, turning to Mrs. Patterson, who still stood in the doorway. "It's nothing serious. I'm not doing anything wrong."

"And a lady called, too," Patterson continued, looking at Michael as if he were the biggest liar in the world. "She introduced herself as a Karen Daniels, Dr. Daniels, she said," though Patterson obviously didn't believe a word of it. "She also wants to know what is going on."

"Patterson, don't look so worried." Michael walked around the table and patted the butler's rigid shoulder. This time Mrs. Patterson threw her hands up and went into the kitchen before Michael could turn to her. "I'm doing some research. It may involve the police, but it's just research."

"Yes sir," Patterson said. He made a military right face and joined his wife in the kitchen.

Michael tried to imagine what, if anything, the FBI could do, but he was really more interested in the coffee at this point. He was sure he was breaking no laws, just examining the public record, tallying information. That was all.

Chimes sounded from the front door, and Michael jumped, surprised at his edginess. "Looks like I may be finding out," he mumbled to himself as he listened to Patterson's methodical footsteps approaching the front door and returning with a guest.

"I don't know what you're up to, but I want to help." Karen Daniels walked into the room, leaving Patterson at the door with his sourest expression.

"Dr. Daniels—" Michael started as he came to his feet. "This is a surprise, but please . . . please join me for coffee, and I'll try to explain. I was just having a late breakfast, if you'd care for . . ."

Karen shook her head, then apologized for barging in on him. "I don't usually do things like this, but I've been calling, and Quince has been calling. We've been getting inquiries from police departments all over the country wanting to know what you're doing. We're all very curious."

Michael finally got her to sit down for coffee. She refused to eat, so between bites Michael tried to explain, in the most basic terms, what he was trying to accomplish, and how.

"After we talked yesterday, I felt like I had to do something," Michael said. "If there is a phantom roaming the country, this may be a way to find him."

After she had heard all he had to say, Karen was very still. She stared into her coffee as if she were trying to foretell the future. "Can I see what you've got?" she asked.

All three printers were running when they entered the office, and Karen stood at the door with her mouth open, amazed at the operation. Michael tore off a stack of printouts and they moved to the desk.

"How long before all the reports will be in?" Karen asked, her mind racing with possibilities.

Michael glanced at the clock. It was after four. "All of the reports are due today, so if we figure libraries and public access to police records ending at five o'clock, add in a couple of hours to type the findings into the computer, then allow for the time difference on the West Coast, everything should be here by ten or eleven o'clock, our time."

"It's amazing," Karen said as she continued to survey the sophisticated electronics of the room.

Michael showed the psychologist around the system, explaining as best he could how Media Associates used it to connect with the computers of freelance writers across the country. He showed her how the computers were tied to three independent phone lines that automatically transferred the call to another system if the first was busy, then he pointed out how material was stored and printed almost simultaneously.

Within an hour Dr. Daniels was a firm believer. If she could have designed a network to prove her theory that phantom killers need not follow FBI Academy patterns, she couldn't have done much better than what was available at Manning Hall. She would have preferred trained analysts rather than journalists at the other end of the system, but it was a minor point. With this system and the access she had to FBI sources, she was sure she could find a phantom.

If, in fact, one existed.

Chicago was experiencing a warm spell. The Gulf Stream was sending tropical air further inland than usual, sweeping it up through the Midwest to overpower cooler Canadian winds off Lake Michigan. Daytime highs were in the eighties, a rare treat for the third week of June, and the city was in a festive mood. Everyone was feeling good.

Everyone, that is, except for the stranger who arrived at O'Hare Airport on an evening flight. The temperature was still in the low sixties, but the stranger was suffering from a vicious sinus headache and couldn't care less about the weather. All he wanted was to find the Holiday Inn on North Shore Drive, and get some sleep.

Everything was working against him. His luggage was the last to slide down the conveyor belt, and the Skycap kept dropping the large bag, grinning like a silly fool while rambling on and on about how this was a great time to visit Chicago. The weather, he assured the stranger, was bliss.

The young black clerk at the rental counter also seemed intent on doing everything except fill out the forms that would get him on his way. She too talked about the weather until the stranger felt like his head would explode.

By the time he found the car and worked his way onto the Kennedy Expressway heading into the city, there were tears in his eyes from the pain. He finally had to pull onto the shoulder of the road, barely avoiding a collision with an oil truck in the process. He popped two more sinus tablets.

Michael and Karen got down to work just before seven o'clock, reading the murder reports and trying to find details that might indicate a phantom killer. They had many heated discussions. Michael felt every murder should be included on the priority list—they all seemed so strange—but Karen was looking for the special elements, the ones that turned an odd murder into something with a presence behind it.

The last computer shut down at 12:59. By that time Michael and Karen had become so giddy from the long hours of intense work that they stopped, giggling through a moment of silence to mark the occasion.

By four o'clock Saturday morning, their list was complete. The forty-eight states surveyed had resulted in 267 "odd" murders since the beginning of the year. Each could be stretched to a point where some obscure brand of punishment might be the motive. None had suspects; if there had been obvious suspects, they had been cleared. When the screening process was completed, they had designated fifteen murders for the primary list—the ones they would study in more detail, hoping to find a link. Another forty-seven murders were included on a secondary list.

Karen was the official notekeeper. When the exhausted sleuths climbed to bedrooms in the east wing of Manning Hall, she left behind a single sheet of paper that contained the essentials concerning fifteen gruesome events:

(1) June 19—Dallas, Texas
Victims: Hamilton & Victoria Garvey . . . poison.
Couple celebrating husband's promotion. Champagne was delivered to the table as a gift, and at some point a killer poisoned the champagne with a lethal dose of cyanide.
(2) June 13—Alexandria, Virginia
Victims: Kathy Manning & Jackie Keaton . . . shotgun.
Two women in bed were joined by man who had been bragging at a local bar about his menage à trois. A killer entered and murdered both women with shotgun blasts to the face.
(3) May 17—Cape Hatteras, North Carolina

Victims: Graham Carter & Amanda James . . . drugs.

A teenage couple got off work early to go camping on the beach. Their naked bodies were found tied together, face to face, with ropes at ankles, wrists, and waist. Both had been injected with a lethal overdose of heroin. Medical reports indicated that neither of them had ever used drugs before.

(4) May 08—Denver, Colorado

Victim: Doug Flint . . . explosion.

A suspected rapist was killed when the seat of a chair exploded in his apartment. The bomb was triggered when he sat in the chair. Explosive designed for maximum damage to genital area.

(5) April 30—St. Louis, Missouri

Victim: Samantha Carter . . . clubbing.

A schoolteacher accused of spanking children was viciously murdered when a killer entered her apartment, tied her over a chair, and clubbed her to death with a baseball bat. She was also stripped and gagged. There was evidence of a spanking.

(6) April 23—Nashville, Tennessee

Victim: Sandra Homer . . . decapitation.

A stripper/prostitute was attacked in the parking lot of her apartment after performing at a private sex party. She was decapitated by an ax that was found at scene.

(7) April 18—San Francisco, California

Victim: Sally Barnett . . . asphyxia.

An advertising artist known for her loose sex life often bragged to friends about how she could hide her real life from her family. She went home to clean her apartment for a young sister who was coming to visit. Her body was found with hands and feet tied using her own sexy underwear. Death was caused by a plastic bag tied over her head.

(8) April 03—Louisville, Kentucky

Victim: Marvin Markus . . . explosion.

A land developer who beat a law suit for fraud and construction code violations was killed while inspecting a house in his new subdivision. Doors of the house were blocked from the outside after he entered and dynamite was lofted through a window.

(9) March 25—Oklahoma City, Oklahoma

Victim: Stewart Abrams III . . . crushed by car.

A bank president who foreclosed on thirty-three mortgages, then sold the property for a development, was crushed against the wall of the underground parking garage at his apartment by his own Cadillac. It was a high-security building, but the killer was waiting in the car. Considered too professional for any of the victims of foreclosure.

(10) March 05—Seattle, Washington
Victim: Benjamin Caruthers . . . fire.

The owner of a furniture company was suspected of arson in a fire that destroyed his warehouse and put 125 people out of work. Two days later he was killed in an isolated fire in his private office.

(11) February 20—Indianapolis, Indiana
Victim: Greg Patterson . . . fall.

A stockbroker died when he was pushed from the roof of a twenty-story building where he had his office. Later check of records indicated he was cheating clients.

(12) February 01—Portland, Maine
Victim: Dr. John Simpson . . . knife.

A surgeon who had his medical license revoked for performing an operation while drunk was tortured by a killer who tied him to the pool table in his home, made cuts on his body, then poured whiskey on them. There were more than 150 cuts on the body before the doctor died.

(13) January 09—Phoenix, Arizona
Victim: Diane Seeton . . . strangulation.

A twenty-one-year-old hitchhiker making her way from Florida to California by offering sexual favors to the men who gave her rides was strangled late in the evening. Commuters heading into Phoenix at sunrise the next morning discovered her body hanging upside down from a tree beside the highway.

(14) January 07—Miami, Florida
Victim: Chester Harding . . . hit and run.

A law student who had bragged about cheating on his final exams was the victim of a hit-and-run driver on campus. Tire markings showed that the killing was not only intentional, but that the driver backed up to run over the victim's head.

(15) January 02—Atlanta, Georgia
Victims: Tom Banks, Sydney Green & Carl Beswick . . . gun.

The three men had, according to newspaper reports, played some kind of hunting game with a teenage orphan who was killed on one of their hunting trips. They were each shot, at close range, in Beswick's den the night the newspaper story appeared. The gun was found at the scene.

Somewhere in all of this, Michael and Karen hoped to find a clue to the identity of a phantom they weren't even sure existed. While they were getting some much needed rest, the man they hoped to find was tossing and turning through a restless night in a Chicago motel room.

He wanted to sleep, but he could feel himself falling over the edge between his inner calm and the need for a challenge. He took a quick shower, and was still damp when he crawled back into bed. He tossed and turned for another half hour, watching the curtains in his window while the morning sky gradually brightened. It was hopeless. He'd have to get up and do something.

Dressed in a fresh suit, he wandered into the street. He tried to lose himself by enjoying the beauty of the sun as it peeked over the horizon above Lake Michigan, but he needed something more. He needed a challenge.

He turned from the water and walked to Michigan Avenue in search of food. He passed several restaurants that offered a variety of breakfast specials, but he wanted something anonymous. He found it at a McDonald's.

The place was crowded with an odd Saturday morning mix of people. Brightly dressed joggers from the North Shore Drive apartments were cooling off after their morning laps, while the rest were the urban blacks that you always found in such places, people hanging around, waiting for the warmth of a new day.

He ordered orange juice and an Egg McMuffin, then headed for what he thought would be a quiet seat in the far corner of the restaurant. He was already sitting down when he realized that a drunk was curled up on the seat across the table.

"Hey, good buddy." The drunk raised his head just above the top of the table. "Don't mind me. I's just catching me a little shuteye 'fore I go home for some breakfast." The drunk was black and probably twenty-five, but he looked to be fifty. He hadn't shaved in several days, and his breath, even at this distance, was hundred proof.

It took all of the stranger's control not to reach across the table and strangle the pathetic man where he sat. The irony was that with this new anger his sinuses no longer seemed so bad. He felt better already, just knowing he had found a new challenge.

"Here," he said, pushing his egg biscuit across the table. "I'm not really that hungry. All I wanted was the juice."

"That's mighty neighborly of you," the drunk said as he tried to focus on the food. His eyes glazed over as he discovered the sandwich, and he turned away, closing his eyes to ward off a flash of nausea. "To tell you the truth, I think maybe I should wait till I get home," he said.

"Whatever you think is best."

"Actually," the drunk said, bending over the table to get closer. "Actually I got this woman back at home . . . white woman, and she don't like for me to eat out. She likes me to come home for everything . . . if you know what I mean."

"I believe I do."

"See, I works over in one of them big 'partments on the shore, and this woman, she lives on the sixth floor and man she's built like this." He paused to pucker his lips and hold his hands a healthy distance in front of his chest. "She's big, a real foxy lady, and she gets me to come visit her on Saturday mornings . . . if you know what I mean."

"You mean you got yourself a fox to take care of you. If I had me something like that I wouldn't be hanging around in a dump like this."

"You're 'xactly right," the drunk said, glancing around and nodding his head with firm resolution. "I better get my tail home so I can get me some tail." And he tried to wink.

They shared a laugh over the drunk's joke, then the black man pulled himself out of the booth and gradually made his way to the door. Several people had to step back to give him room. The manager came out from behind the counter and showed the drunk to the door, but nobody seemed curious about the man who had taken over the corner table.

There was no hurry. As slowly as the drunk was moving there was probably time for breakfast and lunch before he'd be out of sight. Sipping his juice, the stranger pushed the egg biscuit aside. He really wasn't hungry. And his pain was gone.

Nobody paid any attention when he walked out of the McDonald's. The drunk was just turning the corner, back toward the row of high-rise apartments along North Shore Drive, and the stranger casually walked in that direction, stopping to window shop along the way.

It was the longest five blocks of his life. The drunk stood at each corner for an eternity as if trying to decide which way to go. He fell twice, sitting on the cement for several minutes each time before crawling back to his feet and wobbling gradually toward North Shore.

The sun was blazing across Lake Michigan, glaring off the glass-walled apartment buildings when the drunk finally found his destination. He turned into the driveway, buzzing like a car as he descended toward an underground parking lot. A security guard came out to meet him.

"Beep, beep." The drunk got the sounds out just before he tripped into the arms of the big guard.

"Jocko, you fool. Why ain't you somewhere sleeping this off?" the guard asked with a grin. He didn't seem at all bothered by the weight of the small man. "You know you shouldn't be 'round here in this condition, and besides, you ain't workin' till Monday."

The drunk straightened himself up and looked into the bigger man's eyes. "I's fine," he said. "Just thought I'd catch me a little sleep back in my room."

"Now you know that ain't no apartment," the guard said. "They let you put a cot in there, but that's just supposed to be for when you're on duty."

The drunk turned toward Lake Michigan, blinking against the morning sun. "Looks like another hot day," he said, changing the subject. "Bet my girlfriend will be back up on the roof workin' on her tan. What do you think?"

The guard's face twisted, then broke into a wide grin. "She'll be up there all right, but you better stop looking at that white woman. You'll get yourself in a heap of trouble."

"Now Herman, you know I ain't goin' to get in no trouble. Besides, a woman like that wants to be watched. She don't walk around in that itty-bitty bikini for nothin'. Now let me get back there and get some shuteye so I'll be all fresh when my baby goes to the roof."

"You fool," the guard said. "You ain't got the sense God gave a rusty nail. Get your ass on in here 'fore somebody sees me talking to a crazy man."

Jocko seemed momentarily sober until he tried to walk. He stumbled as soon as he took a step, and the big guard grabbed him around the waist, walking the little man past the lowered rail that blocked the entrance.

The two men disappeared into the darkness of the garage, and that was when the stranger made his move. With a quick few steps from the sidewalk he jumped the rail and headed for the cover of the cars lined up on both sides of the entrance. He was well hidden when the guard emerged from a doorway at the back of the garage and walked to his booth at the entrance.

Once the guard was out of sight, the stranger quietly made his way to the doorway. He walked into a large storage room that contained various wheeled carts, brooms, and shovels. There were two doors. The first was a small bathroom with a tub, apparently a place where the security guards and janitorial staff could clean up after a day's work. When he approached the second door he could hear snoring.

The second room wasn't much larger than the bathroom. The drunk was sprawled across an army cot that stretched the full length of one cinderblock wall. A stained sheet covered most of his apparently naked body. A shelf on the opposite wall held a hot plate, several pans, canned goods, and kitchen utensils. Below this a small refrigerator whined to the rhythms of the drunk's raspy breathing. Above the shelf were taped several magazine photographs of nude women, some black and some white.

The stranger closed the door behind him and leaned against it while he surveyed the room. His eyes were drawn almost immediately to the glimmer of a hunting knife next to the hot plate, and just as quickly he knew he couldn't do it. Killing the drunk was too easy. There had to be another way.

He bent over and picked up the knife. He studied the dirty blade and imagined the drunk poisoning sandwiches every time he used it. There had to be something else, if only he could think.

In a few seconds he had his answer. He held a hand over his own mouth to keep from laughing, and then he became serious. The stranger knew he was onto something special. He watched the drunk's breathing and examined a scar that cut through a mass of curly black hairs covering the brown chest. He looked at his watch to find that it was already nine o'clock. It was time to go.

Moving quietly back into the garage, he carried the knife with him. Two joggers struggled for breath as they came down the entrance ramp, waved to the guard, and headed in his direction. The stranger ducked back into the storage room just before they passed the door on their way to an elevator. "It's going to be another hot one," the two men said in unison, laughing as the doors of the elevator closed behind them.

The stranger went back into the garage and watched the lights above the elevator. There were twenty-eight floors listed, and the two men got off on the twelfth. Wrapping the blade in his handkerchief, he put the knife inside his coat and pushed the button for the elevator. It made no stops on the return trip to the basement.

He pushed the button for the twenty-eighth floor and straightened his clothes just in case the elevator stopped to take on passengers. He arrived at the top without incident, then walked to the exit sign at the end of the hallway. As he expected, the exit included not only steps going down but also a stairway to the roof. When he got to the top of the stairs he found the door locked. A sign warned that access to the roof was forbidden without the consent of the manager.

He shrugged, unbothered. This was even better. It meant there was no formal sundeck on the roof, but that the mysterious woman on the sixth floor—the "foxy lady"—must have her own key. She would probably be alone. All he had to do was wait.

It was nearly 11:30 when the door at the twenty-eighth floor opened. The stranger was sitting on the steps at the twenty-seventh, and he got only a brief glimpse of a woman's legs as he turned to see his victim. He counted her steps until he knew she had reached the door to the roof, and then he quietly shortened the distance between them. He heard the door being unlocked, then he caught another glimpse of her as she walked out into the bright sunlight of the roof and let the door close behind her. She was a redhead. He hadn't expected that.

He reached the door just in time to use his foot to keep it from closing all the way. He took several deep breaths to calm himself as he unwrapped the knife and laid it on the floor. Removing his tie, he folded it neatly, then used it to keep the door from closing. He removed the jacket and unbuttoned his shirt. He folded the shirt and laid it on top of the jacket, then removed his slacks and jockey shorts, making a neat pile just inside the door. This was going to be a messy job.

He listened, trying to imagine all the possibilities, then he slowly opened the door. The woman had brought a portable radio and a folding chaise longue with her and she had set them up with her back to the door. The radio was playing classical music.

He crept up to the back of the chair and looked down on a body that was perfect. She was freckled, like most redheads, but unlike most her freckles hadn't darkened in the sun. The skin had tanned to just the right shade of brown, blending with the tiny brown spots. Her breasts were large, only barely contained by the small strip of white fabric that was the top half of the bikini. The bottom half of the suit was even smaller, if that was possible, and stretched firmly across full hips. There was a slight depression in the stomach just below the navel, and he could just see the beginnings of her tightly curled pubic hair.

Taking a deep breath, he reached over with the knife, laid the blade in the crevice between the woman's breasts and sliced the top of the bikini in half. There was a gasp, but before she could react he had come around the chair and was holding the knife to her throat while he straddled her with his nude body.

She tried to scream, but he was too quick. He put his left hand over her mouth and applied all his strength for leverage. Then he took the hand away, slapped her as hard as he could and slid the knife across her throat. Blood spewed from the open wound, and the stranger trembled with excitement. He slid down the bucking body, slapping her again when she tried to sit up, and casually cut the two sides of the bikini bottom to uncover a perfect triangle of red curls.

Blood now covered most of her chest and was running down between her breasts in a tiny stream heading for the navel. Her eyes continued to stare in deathly disbelief until he reached over and lowered the eyelids with his fingers. Then he stood, watched blood rolling into her navel and raised the knife to stab the dead body in the stomach. He raised the knife again, and stabbed. Again and again. And finally he rolled away and sat with his back against the wall.

The concerto on the radio was just coming to an end. He was breathing heavily, his heart pounding as if it would explode. He conducted the last few bars of the music, using the bloody knife as a baton. He looked down at his body, spattered with the woman's blood, and felt the flush of excitement. He'd done it, and now all he had to do was get dressed and walk casually back to the motel. His sinuses had cleared. He felt great.

Michael was slow to get up on Saturday morning. He dragged himself out of bed wondering how much longer he could keep going at the pace of the past two days, but after a cold shower he felt much better. There was a brief letdown as he made the useless stop at his father's room to watch the monitors, but that quickly passed. He had decided there was no need worrying about his father—that matter was beyond his control. His duty was to get the man responsible.

There was a surprise waiting for him when he entered the breakfast room. Ginny greeted him with a cup of coffee, but behind her Michael could see that Dr. Daniels was already up, and she had a visitor. Allen Collins was sitting opposite her at the large table and they were intense in their conversation. It took a moment before they realized Michael had entered the room.

"Well, if it isn't the sleepy head," Allen stood to shake hands with Michael, acting very professional in front of company, and then he waited for Michael to take a seat. "I came out this morning, and the good doctor here has been kind enough to fill me in on what you've been up to."

"I see," said Michael, surprised at the jolt of jealousy he felt. "And what do you think of our little project?"

"Well, I can't exactly say I approve," Allen began, really playing the role of the business executive, "and I might add it's going to cost Media Associates a small fortune to have all those writers on assignment, but Karen has explained it all to me and I think maybe I can help."

This last came as a big surprise to Michael. He had barely hoped for acceptance from Allen, much less help. Karen had obviously done a super sales job.

"What have you got in mind?" Michael asked, still suspicious of Allen's help.

"Garrett showed up this morning," Karen broke in before Allen could explain.

"Oh, no. What did he want?" Michael asked.

"He demanded to see you," Karen explained, "but Patterson knew I was already up so he came to me first. It was rather tense, but he's agreed not to interfere with anything we're doing as long as we let him know immediately—he emphasized the word—if we find anything."

"And I gather," Michael said, looking from Karen to Allen and then back again, "that you two have decided what we should do next."

"We've done better than that," Allen said, taking charge. "We've talked out this whole phantom idea, and we've tried to think of a way to discover if he really exist."

"And how are we going to do that?" Michael asked, fighting off the anger he felt at being left out of these decisions.

"Karen figures that the phantom, if he does exist, is probably using commercial transportation. The FBI still doesn't have anything solid, but they did find a rental car at National Airport with a false name and address and no related plane ticket. It seems very odd."

"And Garrett thinks he has a witness," Karen added. "There's a neighbor who thinks she saw a car matching the rental's description leaving the apartment just after the murders in Alexandria."

"And if that's the case," Allen interrupted, "he could be putting in thousands of miles, flying anywhere he wants to go, then renting a car to do the dirty work. It's impossible to track him by any of the most obvious methods. Credit cards would be crazy, and airline reservations aren't much better, particularly if he's using different names."

Michael nodded, waiting for the punch line. Obviously they had come up with something.

"The next best thing is that he has to stay somewhere," Allen continued. "He couldn't sleep in the car because that would eventually attract attention and a lot of questions, so he must have money and that means motels. So we've got a man who's using rental cars and motels."

"Okay," Michael said impatiently. "I'm with you so far. He stays in motels and he rents cars. Where do we go from there?"

"We need central sources of information," Allen said, pausing to be sure Michael was following his train of thought, "and where we go is to some pretty heavy favors I've called in this morning."

"Is there a central source for motels and rental cars?" Michael asked.

"Not anything complete, but there are national chains that have everything on computer. When you check out of a room at one motel in the chain, the billing is done by computer, and that information is fed back to computers at a central location. It's something like the way writers send material to our computer here at the house. With the motels they use this data to keep track of people who pass bad checks and credit cards, people who damage rooms or steal things. When a motel registers somebody, the computer checks the files to see if that person has stayed at another motel in the chain and notes any problems. The same thing with the big car-rental agencies."

"How does this help us?"

"I managed to pick up a couple of clues from Garrett when he stopped by this morning," Karen broke in, her psychologist's mind seeing Michael's mounting irritation with Allen.

"Quince tells me he's turned over your stranger from Jolly Jack's to the police, and they're trying to tie it all together. Now there's the bar, a rental car from Hertz, and they've also come up with a motel reservation, same false name as on the car rental, at the Holiday Inn in Alexandria."

"So, I've called a couple of buddies," Allen took over. "One is a vice president with Holiday Inns, and the other is an advertising executive with Hertz. Both have access to the computers, and after a lot of begging on my part they've agreed to run the dates and cities on your primary list of murders into their systems and give us back a list of the names."

"But it's the weekend. Can they get access to the computers before Monday?"

"Actually," Allen said with a smile, "this kind of favor is best asked on weekends when not too many people are looking."

"Is it legal?" Michael asked.

Allen's grin grew wider. "As long as we don't get caught."

Before Michael could say anything, Karen stood up and came to his side. "And what all this means is we have to wait. It'll be tomorrow before we get anything, and that gives me plenty of time to run out to Quantico to pick up some fresh clothes."

Now it was Allen's turn to be surprised. Michael could tell from his expression that in all their morning conversation it hadn't been mentioned that Karen would be moving into Manning Hall until this project was complete.

"Would you like some company?" Michael asked.

"I think maybe I'd better go alone. Quince is still a bit edgy, and I don't know that they'd let you on the base. And I may stay there for tonight. Maybe I can dig around and find out if anybody's heard anything."

"But you will come back tomorrow morning?"

"That's a good idea," Allen chimed in. "Why don't we all plan to be here tomorrow, let's say at noon, and see if anything's come in on the computers."

The next twenty-four hours were a pure misery. Allen returned to Washington, and Karen departed for Quantico, while Michael waited. He ate his first full dinner in three days, and the rest of the evening he sat with his father, listening to the relentless beeping of machines and wondering what came next.

The data began coming in at ten o'clock Sunday morning. Michael stood at the computer, watching the long list of names, all the businessmen and vacationers who happened to be staying at a Holiday Inn in a certain city on a certain date. The shorter Hertz Rent-a-Car list started coming in at eleven, and it was complete within a half hour. The mass of material was more than Michael could deal with, so he waited.

Karen and Allen arrived within fifteen minutes of each other, and the trio gathered in the computer room. Allen did some quick programming so that the computers could compare names on the two lists—one had last names listed first—then he stood back and ceremoniously pushed a few buttons while Michael and Karen toasted the computer with cups of coffee.

Discs began to whirl. Fans shifted into a higher speed to keep things cooled, and three sets of eyes stared hungrily at the screen. There was nothing to say. They were seeking a single name that had stayed in a Holiday Inn or driven a Hertz car in two or more cities at the time of a brutal murder. Las Vegas was not taking odds.

Then everything came to a stop. The discs slowed. The fans dropped down to a more comfortable speed, and a single name popped onto the screen: Stephen R. Godwin.

At that very moment a man using the name Stephen R. Godwin was taking a shower at the Holiday Inn on North Shore Drive in Chicago, waiting for room service to deliver his breakfast and the morning newspaper. He had slept for two days, getting up only to eat and shower, and he was feeling more refreshed than he had in months. He'd left all his headaches back in the bed with the sweat and the bad dreams.

He tipped the waiter too much when breakfast arrived, but he was famished and it felt good to be hungry again. He wanted to share his good spirits with the world. He dived into the breakfast, certain that there would never be enough food to fill his void. The newspaper remained on the side of the tray, a tidbit for his imagination. It was an exercise in willpower not to reach for the paper, but he prided himself on willpower and was determined to wait.

Only when the meal was finished and he had poured a second cup of coffee, did the man calling himself Stephen R. Godwin unfold the newspaper. It was at the bottom of the front page, accompanied by a fuzzy photograph of an attractive woman. The photo didn't do her justice. You couldn't even tell that her hair was red. It looked almost blond. But it was the headline that said all that he needed to know:

Janitor Arrested in Murder
Of Apartment Sunbather

He wouldn't read the story, but he had a good idea what it said. He'd left the bloody knife wrapped in an equally bloody towel under the janitor's bed, and he was sure that would be enough for an arrest even if they didn't get a conviction.

He had what he wanted, and that was that. He neatly refolded the paper and placed it on the table as far from his tray as possible. Then he packed and made a quick check of the room to be sure he had left nothing behind.

On the way down in the elevator he started running the names of different cities through his mind. He went through the names alphabetically. When he came to Las Vegas he decided that would be his next destination. It fit his mood, and it might clear his sinuses. Las Vegas . . . and then maybe Detroit. Two extremes. That was what he liked. Extremes. He was devoted to extremes, and to having things work out exactly the way he planned.

SIX

Michael had a window seat on the morning flight to Dallas, and three hours in the air gave him plenty of time to consider his motives for the trip. It hadn't been easy to leave Karen back at Manning Hall, and if he was completely honest with himself he realized the trip was little more than a gesture, perhaps his way of getting back at Allen for coming up with the important data. By the time the stewardess announced the approach to Dallas International Airport he was feeling like a child play-acting as James Bond.

When they had run the name Stephen R. Godwin back through the computer the night before, it had returned two connections to brutal murders. It was on the bill for the rented car that had been turned in at Washington's National Airport the same day that Kathy Manning and Jackie Keaton had been killed. And it showed up again, a few days later, at a Holiday Inn near Texas Stadium, on the day a couple was poisoned in a Dallas club.

Michael had immediately decided he would fly to Dallas to try to learn more about the phantom they now knew existed. He thought he could perhaps find out where Godwin had gone in the past week, but on the long flight he questioned his reasoning. The truth was that it was becoming more and more difficult to stay at Manning Hall. In spite of Karen's presence and the hope of finding the man responsible for all that was happening, there was still the sad, horrible beeping of his father's life support system. It invaded the waking hours and haunted his dreams.

Karen had been the most vocal in protesting Michael's trip, but he now realized that she backed off after Allen had a chance to talk to her in private. Allen had undoubtedly felt it would be a good idea for Michael to get away for a couple of days, even if it was on a wild goose chase. Karen relented.

Everybody agreed that they had to call Quince Garrett with the results of their research, and his less-than-enthusiastic response made Michael all the more determined to do something on his own. While Michael packed, Allen had contacted Jerry Burkett, the freelance writer who had done the murder research on Texas. Burkett was asked to work through the night pulling together all the details he could find about the Garvey poisonings, and the results should be waiting at the Holiday Inn, where Michael would be staying.

Burkett had obviously been busy. When Michael arrived at the motel, there was a thick folder at the front desk. In it were not only a complete file of newspaper accounts but also the writer's typed report and transcriptions of his interviews with Holiday Inn manager, three desk clerks, and four maids, all of whom might have seen the man calling himself Stephen R. Godwin.

Michael read these quickly, and the obvious place to start was with Preston Bryan III, president of Bryan Electronics, the man who had not requested the special bottle of champagne that poisoned Hamilton and Victoria Garvey.

The receptionist at Bryan Electronics put Michael through to the president's office without hesitation, and as soon as Bryan came on the line Michael realized that he was expected. They agreed to meet in an hour, but Bryan refused to come to the Highlander Club. He insisted they meet at his office in the Dallas Market Center.

Michael had never been to Dallas before, and as his taxi took him downtown he was impressed with the sophistication and diversity of the old oil city. The offices of Bryan Electronics were located in a fifteen-story building that resembled an Egyptian pyramid built with an erector set.

Michael was met at the receptionist's desk by a man who identified himself as Mr. Bryan's aide. The quick tour on the way to the president's office took them past dozens of smiling young people working diligently for the betterment of the world through computers.

Preston Bryan greeted Michael at the door to his office, but he wasn't alone. He quickly introduced Michael to his personal attorney—no name, just "my personal attorney"— and to Lieutenant Linwood McGowan, the Dallas chief of homicide who had been quoted extensively in the clips on the Garvey murders. The attorney had the same crew cut and cold eyes familiar from assorted Wall Street hearings or stories about cult brainwashing, while McGowan was the quintessence of Hollywood cop, complete with styled hair, bright blue eyes, and a perfectly tailored suit that had never seen a rack in its life.

Michael didn't know what to make of the gathering. He was ushered to a chair that placed him directly in front of Bryan's desk and between the two other guests. While a secretary served coffee, the three men quietly studied Michael as if he were a boxer they were about to meet in the ring. When the secretary departed, all eyes turned to the chiseled face of Bryan, who sat behind his desk as if posing for an addition to Mount Rushmore.

"Lieutenant McGowan has told me why you're here," Bryan said, his voice surprising Michael with its sudden sadness. "He received a courtesy call from the FBI this morning informing him that you were on your way, and it appears that the Federal authorities believe you're playing some sort of child's game."

"I don't believe it's a . . ."

"What you believe really isn't that important," Bryan interrupted, the authority in his voice leaving no room for doubts. "I understand you're some sort of reporter, not a trained investigator, and I feel confident that the Dallas Police can find the murderer of Hamilton Garvey. We will find the bastard, and we'll do it without help from any journalists."

"Mr. Bryan, I'm not here to cause any trouble," Michael said. "If you'll just give me a minute of your time perhaps we can help each other. I have personal reasons for being here. The man who killed Hamilton Garvey may be the same man who killed my stepmother."

"I'm sorry, Mr. Manning. I'm sorry for your loss, but to be completely honest I don't trust you." Bryan's voice quivered with emotion, and his eyes clouded over. "I loved Hamilton Garvey like a son, more than a son, and the newspapers have said horrible things about him . . . about the way he did business. It's a lot of crap. I don't like newspapers, and I don't like your so-called news magazines. We don't need any of you, and in particular we don't need some smart-assed Washington journalist messing around in Hamilton's death."

The old man was near tears when he finished, and the nameless attorney quickly stepped in front of Michael as if to shield Bryan from unfriendly eyes. "Anything more you have to say can be said to Lieutenant McGowan," the attorney insisted, directing both Michael and the homicide detective to the door and closing it behind them.

Michael was shaken by the meeting. He looked for help, but McGowan just smiled, showing his bright teeth, and motioned for Michael to follow him. The policeman became completely absorbed in flirtations with the young women they passed as they left the building. He said nothing until they were in the parking lot, and then he turned to Michael and offered him a ride back to his motel.

"Actually, I'm heading to the Highlander Club. For lunch." Michael was prepared for objections.

"Okey dokey," McGowan said, "then I'll drop you at the Highlander."

Michael was wary, but when they reached the sporty BMW he followed his curiosity and got into the car.

"You've got to understand something about Dallas," McGowan said as he manhandled the car onto the highway. "An outsider trying to do good in Dallas is pretty much like a Yankee trying to sell war bonds to Robert E. Lee. People here are real friendly if you come to buy something or just to visit and tell us how wonderful we are. But no sir, you don't come to Dallas to straighten anybody out."

McGowan glanced at Michael with his Pepsodent smile, and the BMW topped eighty miles per hour on the expressway. He shook his head, pleased that Michael wasn't frightened by his driving, then concentrated as he cut between a pair of Mercedes sedans.

"And what do you think?" Michael asked.

McGowan did a quick downshift, pulling onto an exit ramp, his speed dropping to a crawl as he entered an elegant residential area. "What I think is that somebody in the computer business got upset when this hotshot started wrapping big clients around his little finger. What I think is computers are a big game . . . we're talking billions of dollars. And what I think is somebody wanted to make a point, so they offed Garvey in very showy fashion."

"Do you have any suspects?"

McGowan flashed his Hollywood smile and scratched his ear with his right hand. He jerked the steering wheel with his left hand and pulled to the curb in front of a bronze plaque that read Highlander Club.

"A few people who were in the club remember seeing a stranger—that's a stranger, not a phantom, not a psycho," McGowan said with a shit-eating grin. "We've got a description. He's tall, maybe six-one or six-two, with dark hair and blue eyes. He's well groomed, a sharp dresser, the kind of cool professional who likes to make an impression."

"Sounds like you with your hair dyed," Michael said.

"Cute. Real cute." McGowan motioned to the club with a grand gesture. "Here you are. Scene of the crime. They've got a nice menu, but I'd avoid the champagne if I were you."

"Can't we talk about this?" Michael asked.

"No."

"But the man you describe sounds like the description we got back home. We don't have the details, but a couple of guys who saw him in a bar said he looked like a movie actor. That sounds like your man."

"Listen, Manning," McGowan said, reaching across Michael to open the passenger door. "Take a little advice. If you want to write a big story, go back to Washington where people like to play games. Here we do things Dallas style . . . that's no games, and no help from the Mannings or from your *Newsbreak* magazines."

Michael stepped from the car, but before he could say anything McGowan slammed the car door and left behind a cloud of laughter as he squealed tires away from the curb.

The Highlander Club was hopeless. As soon as Michael mentioned the Garveys the manager of the club came over to inform him that the staff would discuss the case only with the police. Michael ate his lunch in silence and found himself watching the crowd, wondering what the phantom had thought as he watched the Garvey celebration.

It was a replay of Jolly Jack's. Michael was again amazed at the anonymity of a stranger and how much could be learned by simply sitting and listening. The prettier of two women at the table next to Michael's was almost in tears explaining that her husband was having an affair with his secretary; she didn't know how to prove it, or even if she wanted to. Two men at another table were discussing a business deal; their voices remained low, but Michael picked up enough to guess that somebody had been paid so they'd be sure to have the low bid on a supply contract. He heard no mention of the Garveys.

When he had finished eating, Michael called a taxi from the pay phone and instructed the driver to take him through Highland Park and past the Garvey home. He had jotted down the address from Burkett's notes, and the mansion was exactly what he had expected, a stunning white success symbol. It was perhaps a bit grander than the other houses on the block, and it seemed all the more impressive with four gardeners scurrying around the grounds, cutting and weeding and shaping just as if the family still lived there.

Michael wasn't sure when he first realized that he was being followed, but when his driver made a U-turn to head out of Highland Park he felt a sudden chill as they passed a blue sedan that had been a block behind them. He didn't see the driver's face when they passed, but he was sure he had seen that car before. It had been sitting in front of the Highlander Club after lunch, and now he was sure he had seen it pulling out of the lot at Bryan Electronics when he and McGowan sped away in the BMW.

Michael tried not to panic. He told himself he was being paranoid. He was trying to give importance to a trip that was meaningless. But when he glanced out the rear window of the taxi, the sedan was still there, still a block behind them. He looked at the taxi driver, but the young black man had a portable cassette player plugged into his ears and was oblivious to everything. Michael could see the cord running up past the driver's coarse beard, the head gently nodding to the beat.

"Hey," Michael said, surprised to hear his voice thin with fear. He looked for the driver's license, saw that his name was Hawthorne Washington and tried again. His voice still sounded unnatural.

"Name's Hawk, least that's what everybody calls me," the black man said as he removed the ear plugs. "What's up? You want to do some more sightseeing?"

"Not exactly," Michael said, trying to regain his composure. "Can you get through to the police department on your radio? Is that possible?"

"What you want, man?" the driver said, turning around in his seat while steering with one hand. "We can't do nothin' like that unless it's an emergency."

"I believe it is," Michael said. "We're being followed. It could be dangerous, or it could be a policeman. In either case we need to call the police."

"What do you mean, dangerous?" the driver asked as he reached for the radio transmitter. He didn't push the button, but stared back at Michael and glanced over his shoulder at the sedan that remained a block behind them.

"If it's not a cop," Michael said as calmly as he could, "it might be a killer."

It took several minutes for Hawk to talk the dispatcher into patching them through to the police, and every time Hawk's speed increased Michael insisted that he slow down. If this was the phantom they certainly didn't want to lose him, or to call unnecessary attention to what they were doing. Hawk concentrated on driving aimlessly through Highland Park, always aware of the sedan in the rearview mirror, while they waited for the police to transfer the call to Lieutenant McGowan.

"This is McGowan." The whining of the BMW could be heard in the background. "Who the hell is this?"

The driver handed the transmitter to Michael and showed him where to push the button. "It's Manning. Michael Manning. I'm sorry to—"

"What the hell do you want?"

"Have you got somebody following me? Somebody in a blue sedan?" Michael felt tentative with the radio in his hand.

"Hell, no," McGowan bellowed back. "What kind of game are you playing now?"

"Lieutenant, I am being followed," Michael insisted, getting angry. "There's a car following this taxi right now, and I've seen the car at least twice before. It was at Bryan Electronics, and then I saw it again at the Highlander Club when I came out."

"Bullshit," McGowan answered, but this time his voice was quieter. He was thinking. "Let me talk to the driver."

Michael handed the transmitter to Hawk, who nervously pushed the button. "Yes sir?" He was even shakier than Michael.

"Do you see this mystery car too?" McGowan asked.

"Yes sir. He's been following us at least for the past ten minutes. He's there all right."

"Where are you?"

"We're in Highland Park, sir."

"Where were you going?"

"The gentleman here wanted me to take him to his motel, the Holiday Inn out at Texas Stadium."

"All right, give me back to Manning. Listen, Manning. I think this is a deep pile of bullshit, but I'm on my way to the Holiday Inn, and I'm calling in some backup. You two head on out there. Don't drive slow, but don't try to set any records either. You got that?"

"Got it," Michael said, the driver nodding in agreement.

"When you get there, I want you to go around the right side of the parking lot, as if you were going to rooms on the back of the building. As soon as you get to the rear lot pull into the first parking space you see and duck down in the car. Whatever happens, don't get out of the car."

"Got it," Michael said. The driver nodded again.

The ride took thirty minutes, and the sedan was never more than a hundred yards behind them. McGowan checked in every five minutes to see where they were and to learn the status of the blue sedan.

"Where are you now?"

"We're almost there," Michael said. "Maybe a half a mile. And he's still with us. He may have dropped back a little bit, but he's there."

"Can you tell me anything about the car? Can you tell the make? Any distinguishing marks?"

"Nothing," Michael said. "It's just an American sedan, new, and very clean. It could be a rental."

"I think it's a Chevy," Hawk whispered.

"The driver thinks it's a Chevy," Michael repeated.

"Okay," McGowan said, all business. "Now do just what I told you. When you enter the parking lot, go to the right, around the building. There's a parking space available about four spots down, on the outside. Just pull in there and duck. There's a patrol car parked just beyond the spot, blocking the way, so don't panic. Just pull in and duck. You got that?"

"Got it," Michael said. "And thanks."

"I still think it's bullshit."

Hawk pulled into the lot and immediately had to slam the brakes to miss a car that was backing out of a narrow parking space. Then he eased around the building just as Michael spotted the blue sedan pulling into the lot behind them. The parking space was waiting just where McGowan had said it would be, and just beyond it was the promised patrol car with four uniformed policemen leaning over the hood and trunk with rifles.

Hawk pulled into the spot, jammed on the brakes, and the two of them fell across the seats. All was silent. Michael held his breath. Nothing happened. There was no sound except from the steady stream of cars on the highway.

When it did happen, it was over before Michael even knew it. He heard a car stop, then another, coming at speed, slammed on brakes. There were shouts. McGowan was on a bullhorn demanding the driver get out of his car and lie face down on the pavement, and then came running. Then more silence.

After an eternity, McGowan's smiling face appeared at the taxi window. He opened the door. "You sorry ass," the lieutenant said as he looked down on Michael's fetal crouch.

McGowan pulled Michael from the car and marched him over to a pale young man who stood next to a blue Chevy sedan. "Here's your phantom," McGowan sneered. "He's one of you. A damned journalist. At least that's what he calls himself. He's a fucking snoop for the *Midnight Express.*"

The young man stepped out from amid the smiling cops and offered a shaky hand. "The name's Jimmy . . . Jim Powers. I . . . I was hoping we could talk."

"Bullshit," McGowan said, stepping in front of the reporter to tower over Michael. "If you know what's good for you, you won't go spreading any insanity. Do you get my drift?" He bellowed like a drill sergeant.

"I hear what you're saying, but that's all," Michael shot back, anger quickly replacing his embarrassment. "I'll talk to anybody I like, about anything I like. Do you get my drift?"

The two men glared at each other, neither willing to give an inch. The uniformed policemen began to carry their rifles back to various patrol cars while Powers stood awkwardly to the side, waiting for something to happen.

"You fellas need me anymore?" came the unsteady voice of Hawk, who broke the stalemate by stepping from the taxi.

"All right, let's get out of here," McGowan roared, not realizing that the cops had already returned to their cars. Then he looked back at Michael. "I trust you can make it to your room without any further assistance."

Michael had turned away before the lieutenant spoke, and he didn't acknowledge the snide remark. He walked to the taxi, where Hawk was waiting, and tried to figure what kind of tip would cover this ordeal.

"One suggestion," McGowan yelled back across the lot. "Go play your games somewhere else. We haven't got time for this bullshit." Then he laughed and turned the corner. A few seconds later the BMW raced to the other end of the parking lot.

Hawk seemed pleased with the tip, but he was still shaking his head as he backed the taxi out of the parking space and pulled away with a friendly wave. That left Michael standing with the reporter and the mysterious blue sedan.

"Can we talk?" Powers asked once things were quiet.

"I don't know," Michael answered. "I've got to think about it. Let's go for coffee."

The reporter nodded, running around the car to the driver's side, and Michael got in. They rode in silence to the front of the Holiday Inn to park near the restaurant.

Once seated over a cup of black coffee, Powers seemed less mousy than he had in the rear lot. His eyes flashed with a reporter's instincts. He could smell a story.

"Mr. Manning, if I can just have a minute to present my case. I know I work for a rag. Everybody knows it's a rag, but it's a rag with a lot of readers. And if the vibes I've been picking up are true, I think maybe we're just what you need."

Powers was probably a few years younger than Michael. He had that baggy look reporters get after chasing too many stories over too many miles, but he also had an honest face. Michael studied that face and tried to call on all of his own reporting experience to determine if Powers could be trusted. Or if he could be used.

"And just what can the *Express* do for me?"

"I'm here to do something on the Garvey poisonings. It's big news, and it's just the type of stuff the *Express* eats up." Powers talked so fast that he was hard to follow. "But then I hear Michael Manning and Media Associates are on the case and have a hot lead. This isn't the kind of story *Newsbreak* chases down . . . too much sensationalism. Unless there's something else. And then I hear the word 'phantom' and I start to wonder. Maybe it's the kind of story the Mannings wouldn't want in *Newsbreak.* Maybe it's something that has to be handled outside of Media Associates. How's it sound so far?"

"Interesting," Michael said, deciding that this might be an opportunity to crack this thing wide open. He considered calling Allen first, to see if he agreed, but this was something he wanted to do on his own. A story in the *Express* would get everybody involved. The FBI would have to take notice. The legitimate press would demand answers.

"The question isn't if it sounds interesting," Powers said, taking out pad and pen. "The question is if it sounds interesting enough for you to tell me what you've got."

"What we've got, or at least what we think we've got is a phantom killer," Michael said without hesitation. "We . . . no, not we, it's me. I've done some research on my own—Media Associates isn't involved in any way—and I believe I've found a link between the murder of the Garveys and the murder of two women a week earlier in Virginia. One of the Virginia victims was Kathy Manning, my father's wife. My father has been in a coma ever since it happened."

"What kind of link have you got?"

"We . . . I pulled together some computer data from across the country and found that a man was here, and also in Virginia, on the dates the murders occurred."

"Does he have a name?"

"Yes. The name is Stephen R. Godwin. The only address we've got is false."

Powers jotted down the name in his notes, then placed the pen on the table and held the coffee cup to his lips without once taking his eyes off Michael's face. When he lowered the cup back into its saucer he moved carefully so that the dishes made no sound when they touched. He took a deep breath.

"If I figure right, then," the reporter continued, "you're trying to get the FBI involved and they're not cooperating."

"They don't seem to think I've got enough to bring them officially into the case."

"So you're here trying to prove that this . . ." Powers glanced at his notes, "this Godwin has crossed state lines. That he's murdered in two different states."

"That seems to be the criterion."

"This is dynamite stuff," the reporter said as he jotted down quick notes. "So why are you giving it to me?"

Michael considered his answer. "I thought that would be obvious. The FBI won't listen to me. I've tried to show them what I've got, but they're not interested. They may have made some informal queries, but the police in Alexandria, where the Virginia murders occurred, and in Dallas don't want to believe in a phantom. An *Express* story would shake things up. They'd have to look, and I could stop running around making a fool of myself."

Powers chuckled, but it fell flat. He was thinking about a big story. "Can you give me any more details?"

"There really aren't any," Michael said. "All we've got—" but he was interrupted by a waitress who came to the table to ask if he was Mr. Manning.

"I'm sorry sir, but there's a long-distance phone call. The man says it's an emergency."

Michael sensed what the call was even before he took the phone, and he was sure he was right when he heard Allen Collins' voice on the other end.

"It's your father," Allen said. "He's dead."

Matthew Emerson Manning had suffered a massive heart attack at eleven o'clock that morning. His body had arched, pulling out tubes and wires, and he was dead before the nurses could get to his bed.

By the time Michael got back to Manning Hall, Allen had completed the necessary arrangements. The funeral service would be held in Washington, but then the body would be flown to Richmond for burial in the family plot at Riverview Cemetery. Matthew Emerson Manning had always insisted that he would return to his roots.

Michael and Allen spent the first evening sitting in the den, much as they had on the night Michael returned from Paris. They sipped drinks, taking turns going to the bar, and they sat silently, gaining what little comfort they could from each other's company. Neither could think of anything to say.

Karen felt out of place at Manning Hall and stayed as far out of the sight as possible. She made a trip to Quantico and spent the rest of her time in her room, going over the murder reports again and again. She saw Allen at dinner and asked for the names of the contacts who had supplied the motel and car rental data, but aside from that she made herself scarce.

The next day Michael and Allen went to Washington. They stayed at the funeral home from eight o'clock in the morning until closing time to receive the hundreds of politicians, journalists, publishers, and others who came to pay their last respects. They spent that evening again in silence, sitting in the Media Associates' Georgetown apartment dealing with their grief. They fell asleep in their chairs.

It was Monday morning when Michael and Allen accompanied the body on the short flight to Richmond. They didn't speak about it, but Monday was also the day the *Midnight Express* hit the newsstands. The large headline read "Phantom On Killing Spree?" with a kicker, "Media Heir Blames Psycho," staring in bold black letters from news racks in grocery stores throughout the country.

Following a quiet graveside service in Richmond, attended only by a few people who remembered the Manning family from the old days, they took adjoining rooms at a hotel overlooking the state capital. When Allen came to share another evening of mournful drinking he brought the *Express* with him.

"You shouldn't have done this," he said on the second drink. "You shouldn't have gone public."

"It seemed like the right thing to do at the time." Michael spoke softly as if not to disturb the quiet hum of the air conditioning. "It may get the FBI involved, and we can stay out of it. I want the son of a bitch who did this."

They sat quietly for a few more minutes, but there were things that needed to be said, and Allen wanted to get all the old emotions out in the open.

"Michael, I know this is something I should have asked a long time ago, but what was it that happened between you and your father?"

"You really don't know, do you?"

"No. All I know is when we finished college together and you got me a job in your father's office you two seemed like the best friends in the world. I don't know if you remember, but you two did everything together."

"Yeah," Michael said. "I remember."

"So what happened?"

"You were part of it," Michael said, turning away. "Once you showed up things were different. Father saw in you all the things that I wasn't. You were so ordered, so precise in all of your priorities, and after that I never seemed to measure up in his eyes. I hated you for it. You were my best friend, but you were also my worst enemy."

"And Kathy?" Allen asked.

"I thought you knew that. I thought you at least sensed it even if you weren't sure."

"What?"

"Kathy and I were lovers. We met one summer when father and I took a trip to Monte Carlo. We partied. We had a good time, and then dear old dad invited her to Manning Hall when she came back to the States. Next thing I knew they were an item in the gossip columns and an engagement was announced. I guess he didn't think I was good enough for her either."

Perhaps Allen had known, but he'd never been sure. Now everything seemed to make sense, especially the tension that had kept father and son apart for the last two years.

Allen picked up the *Midnight Express,* with its glaring headline, and dropped the paper in the wastebasket. "What now?"

"We go on with our lives as best we can," Michael said. "You'll run Media Associates, and I'll do whatever I do."

"But what if there is a phantom?" Allen asked.

"I don't know what you mean."

"I mean if there is a phantom, he's sure to see that story. Don't you think that maybe he's going to be a little bit upset?"

"I hadn't thought about that."

"I think you should stay close to home for a while. There are going to be a lot of details to take care of, but I can handle most of it. You stay close to Manning Hall until the police, the FBI, or somebody finds out what is happening."

Michael didn't bother answering. He knew Allen was right, but in his heart he wished the phantom would pay him a visit. He'd never thought about killing anybody in his life, but if he could get his hands around the throat of the man responsible for all that had happened in the past few weeks he had no doubt that he could kill. And he would give anything to have the chance.

SEVEN

Karen had not been able to leave it alone. There had to be another angle. There had to be something they had missed.

When Matthew Manning died, Karen felt out of place at Manning Hall. She had never met the man, had never even seen him. The closest she'd ever been to the ruler of the Manning empire was to pass his door and occasionally meet one of the nurses in the hall. She drove to Quantico that morning, having made the decision to move back into her dormitory at the FBI Academy until after the funeral, or until Michael invited her back to Manning Hall.

But still she kept thinking about the phantom, knowing there was something more. There had to be an answer. It was impossible for anyone to travel around the country without leaving some sort of trail. There had to be something that could be followed.

The drive to Quantico helped clear her head, but when she arrived at the FBI Academy she didn't feel like unpacking. She was restless. She went to the Academy library, but she knew the answer wasn't there. She tried to find the other psychologists who had been brought in to study the VI-CAP program, thinking she might talk it out, but they had all finished their work and taken off to enjoy the rest of summer vacation.

It took less than an hour for her to make the decision. She would return to Manning Hall, and sequester herself with the computers until she found the missing link. It was there. Somewhere. And she was going to find it.

No one took any notice of her return. Probably no one even knew she had left. The driveway in front of Manning Hall was empty. Michael hadn't yet returned from Dallas, and Allen was in Washington making arrangements for the funeral. The Pattersons were nowhere in sight, but Allen had brought in a college student, the daughter of one of Media Associates' secretaries, to serve as a temporary housekeeper.

Karen stayed in her room with the list of murders until Michael and Allen departed for the funeral home in Washington the next day, and then she moved to the computers. She had learned a great deal about the Manning system. Working closely with Michael, she had soon discovered that once you knew the basics of computer communications, one system was pretty much like the next. She had previously spent hundreds of hours with the computers at the University of Virginia and had quickly adjusted to the elaborate coded system at the FBI Academy. The computer room at Manning Hall fell somewhere between the two extremes.

Karen went to the refrigerator for a soft drink and cleared a place at the desk by pushing aside the printouts from their murder research. Then she pulled out a legal pad, wrote across the top "Who are we looking for?" and leaned back to consider the possibilities.

He stays at motels, and he rents cars. She sat up and wrote these things under her question. He had to be traveling alone, but maybe his driving was strictly on a local basis. The car rental in Godwin's name had come from National Airport, and that opened up the possibility that he was using commercial jet transportation to get from city to city, state to state. Perhaps, in addition to flying, he also used trains, even buses, then rented a car when he got where he was going. She wrote these down with question marks.

She rolled the cool drink can across her forehead and thought about money. Traveling like that, with planes, car rentals, and motels, it would be expensive. How does he pay for all of it? What is his source of income? She added the word "Money" to her growing list.

Something was still missing. She pulled out the sheets of computer printout with the name Stephen R. Godwin circled. In addition to the name there was an address listed in Boston. They'd already checked that with their Boston researcher—a guy named Raymond Hart—and it didn't exist. But there was a Parkman Street near Massachusetts General Hospital, and the address was only one number higher than that for the last house on the block. Perhaps the killer knew Boston. She added Boston to her growing list and put a question mark beside it.

More. She needed more. The rest of the computer printout on Godwin was meaningless. It was a series of coded symbols, each representing some detail that the motel and rental car chains wanted to know about their mysterious client.

"How does he pay?" Karen finally mumbled to herself. "How does he pay for all these motels, cars, and trips?"

She stared at the printout sheets willing them to give her the answer, and then maybe, just maybe, she saw something. The first symbol after Godwin's name on the Holiday Inn listing was a "C." Could it be for cash? Then she found the Hertz listing, and the first symbol was "$".

It was beginning to make sense. He was traveling alone. He obviously had money—some unknown source of wealth— and most important of all, he paid for everything in cash. That was why he had used a piece of metal, and not a credit card, to open the front door when he killed Kathy Manning and Jackie Keaton in Alexandria. He didn't have a credit card. He always paid cash.

Suddenly Stephen R. Godwin, or whoever the phantom really was, had connected himself to a group. A minority. With tax records and the worries of carrying money, almost nobody paid cash for things like motel rooms and rental cars. Certainly not for plane tickets. But perhaps the phantom did.

She reached for the pad and wrote at the bottom of her list, in large letters, the word "Cash," adding four exclamation marks behind it.

Now she had to figure a way to use this information. The phantom had become part of a small group. What she needed was more data. There couldn't be many people using cash. They were freaks. It was practically unAmerican.

Karen found a telephone book in the bottom drawer of the desk, then went back to her list, started a second sheet and began to put down the information she would need. At dinner the previous night she had made an appearance long enough to ask Allen for the names of the two contacts, but otherwise she had left the two men with their private sadness.

She called the Holiday Inn number first. The "C" did stand for cash payment, and Allen's friend acknowledged that cash had become a rare means of payment in recent years. The contact at Hertz confirmed the information. The "$" stood for cash, and it was very rare. Neither seemed very comfortable when Karen asked if they could run up a list of customers who had paid in cash.

"It could be done, but I don't really know if I should," the man at Hertz said. "I ran that first list because Allen is a good friend, but I could get into trouble."

"What if it were an official FBI request?" Karen asked.

"That would be different. We'd be glad to cooperate."

It was obvious that Karen was going to need help, FBI help, and she believed she knew just the man who could supply it. She hesitated for only a moment, then placed a call to Quantico and asked for Robert Besswick, head of the Justice Department's VI-CAP analysis team.

"Hello, Bob. This is Karen Daniels," she said tentatively, not sure if Besswick would remember the pass he'd made at her on her first day at Quantico.

"Karen, what a nice surprise." He remembered.

"Bob, I wonder if I might get a little help on a research problem. I've been thinking about VI-CAP, and about different kinds of information that might help in tracking violent crime. I started to think about how people might travel around the country. How they might use credit cards or checks, but also how they might use cash, thinking it wouldn't leave a trail."

"It's an interesting theory," Besswick said. "But what exactly are you trying to do?"

"Well, you know I've been working out at Manning Hall. They've got this incredible computer system, and they've turned it over to me for my research. I don't have to wait in line like I would at Quantico."

Besswick's laugh was stiff. He waited for the punch line.

"What I'd like to do is get some cooperation pulling together random names, people who use cash on things like hotel rooms, rental cars, plane tickets . . . things like that. I want to see if there are any patterns. I figure there are some central locations for most of the national chains, and for the major airlines. And if there isn't a central computer, we could ask for a list of names in a few key cities . . . say maybe twenty cities across the country."

"That's a pretty tall order."

"All it would take is a few phone calls. I've worked up a list of what I'd need. It's the airlines, maybe a dozen motel chains, and a half dozen of the larger car rental companies . . . all national chains. With just a few calls from you, requesting the information on Justice Department business for research, the names would be in your computer before the night is out. And then we could set up a link from Quantico to Manning Hall. You could pop all the information to me, and it would be over before you know it. And Bob, I really think I'll come up with some interesting data that might be useful for VI-CAP."

She stopped, breathless, and waited.

Besswick laughed. "You make it sound so simple. I mean, sure, it would just take a few phone calls . . . about thirty based on the list you just mentioned, but then it would take months for me to explain to the Justice Department why I need the information. And I'd have to get permission to send anything out to a private system. The paperwork would take years."

"Now Bob, you and I both know there are ways around paperwork," Karen said, trying to tease the agent into service. "If you don't fill out the first sheet, the one that says why you're doing what you're doing, then you don't fill out any of them. You just do it without raising any questions, and that way you don't have to give any answers."

"I don't know, Karen. I could really get my ass in a sling over something like this."

"But it's research," Karen pleaded. "You're in charge of research, and this is good nuts-and-bolts research."

"I'm going to have to get back to you on this. It's asking a lot. And I'll have to see who's working the computers this afternoon. Where can I reach you?"

"Thanks, Bob. I knew I could count on you." Karen gave him the direct number to the office at Manning Hall, and Bob assured her he'd call back.

At Quantico, Bob Besswick hung up the phone and turned to Quince Garrett, the FBI agent "unofficially" assigned to the Manning phantom. Garrett had been listening in from the start, and now that the conversation was over he continued to stare at the phone as if he expected to hear Karen's voice tell him what he really wanted to know.

"What in the hell is she up to?" Garrett squinted, taking aim at the silent phone and mumbling more to himself than to the Justice Department researcher.

"It's hard to tell." Besswick reached for his own stack of computer printouts and looked up the name Stephen R. Godwin. "Here it is," he said. "Godwin paid cash for the motel rooms and for the car. She could be onto something."

Garrett glanced at the sheets and made his decision. "Wait forty-five minutes, then call her back. Give her whatever she wants, but keep tabs on it. Tie the Manning computer into Q Section. I want to know every move she makes."

The number was twenty-seven. Stanley Walker had hit it three times in little more than a half hour, and while Las Vegas was not in danger of going bankrupt because of his winnings, the pile of chips in front of him did look impressive. He'd started the night down three hundred dollars, and now he was ahead more than six thousand. He was beginning to attract attention, and he loved it.

Mostly, he noticed the brassy blonde on the other side of the table, and he knew what she was after. He might be only a junior accountant with a large firm in Oklahoma City, but he hadn't been born yesterday. He'd heard stories about the "party girls" who would cozy up to a winner, go to bed with him, then steal everything while the sucker slept. He'd had dreams about it, but he wasn't stupid enough to fall into the trap.

Then he looked up into eyes more beautiful than any he had ever seen before. He looked down at lips that glistened with neon-red lipstick, down to bare shoulders, to skin as smooth as porcelain, to breasts that threatened to burst free from the sequined gown that caressed them. And then he looked back at the lips. God, what lips.

With this as competition, it was no wonder Stanley didn't notice the stranger who was staring at him from the opposite end of the table. The stranger also knew the score. He had seen the woman moving in. He could see what was happening, and he knew he was going to have to do something about it.

The computers at Manning Hall were going crazy. Michael and Allen were still gone, but Karen hadn't left the office in more than thirty hours. The names she wanted were pouring into the system. Bob Besswick had come through with everything she wanted, and the computers were at full load.

It took another twelve hours for all of the data to arrive, and the results were too much to handle. Karen prepared a program to note multiple-city listings of people using cash, but when the list topped four hundred names she canceled the program and tried to think of a better way.

Besswick called in the late afternoon, and he seemed as tired as Karen. "How's it going?" he asked without enthusiasm.

"Not good," Karen said over a yawn. "I can't believe how many cash freaks there are in this country. I thought everybody had been converted to the mighty plastic."

"It's not as bad as you think," Besswick said while shuffling through some papers. "I found some figures on credit card usage. It seems that 56 percent of all Americans now have credit cards. But when you break that down to travel expenses, it comes out that approximately 92 percent of all air tickets, motel rooms, and car rentals are put on plastic. Another 5 percent pay with traveler's checks, and that leaves only 3 percent paying in cash. It doesn't sound like much, but when you figure on hundreds of thousands of motel rooms and flights, it adds up."

"I'll say. I'm drowning in printouts."

"What are you going to do now?" Besswick asked.

"I'm not sure. I'm trying to come up with a program that will compare the list of names against actual murder cases, but it may take a while."

"The way you sound, you ought to get some sleep. I know that's what I'm going to do."

"Bob, I don't know how to thank you."

"I can think of a few ways, but you're too far away and I'm too sleepy. Just let me know what you find."

Angel grabbed Stanley's hand, dragging him into the hallway as soon as the elevator doors opened on the twentieth floor of the casino hotel. By all appearances she could hardly wait to get to the room. As they ran into a second hallway, Angel was still pulling, whispering an urgent, "Hurry, hurry."

And then everything went blank. Stanley never saw it coming, but as they walked past a utility closet someone stepped out of the darkness. There was a sudden pain across the back of his head. Then nothing. As he sank to the floor, strong hands grabbed him under the arms and dragged him back into the closet while Angel reached inside his coat for the packet of hundred-dollar bills. The whole thing took less than ten seconds.

"Bill, drop him. Somebody's coming." Angel's voice was a whisper that carried the full force of command. She was all business. Gone was the sultry vision of small men's dreams.

Laughter and the loud, drunk voices of a party poured out of the elevator. It was heading in their direction, but they didn't panic. This was an old game, and they were pros. Bill quickly stepped from the closet and took Angel in his arms. He leaned her against a wall, ran a trembling hand across her hip and lifted the side of her skirt to mid-thigh while they embraced in a deep kiss.

They broke apart, embarrassed, when they heard the hoots and hollers of the party crowd. They looked sheepishly at the six faces. The three men leered at Angel while the three women reacted much the same way to Bill's muscular physique. Angel became flustered, holding a hand to her face. Her hips swayed as she walked down the hall, and Bill quickly caught up, slipping an arm around her waist while the party crowd turned to their own intentions and disappeared into a room.

They'd pulled it off again. But this time there would be no celebration. They turned the corner and found themselves staring into the long barrel of a .45-caliber revolver.

The man holding the gun had watched the whole thing. He'd watched Angel make contact at the roulette table, had followed them to the bar, and had even accompanied them into the elevator. He'd gotten off at the nineteenth floor after seeing Angel push the button for the twentieth.

The man with the gun had only arrived from Chicago the night before. He was almost sorry to find new victims so quickly, but Bill and Angel deserved to die, and he couldn't turn his back on that.

"Did you kill him?" He spoke calmly, making a quick assessment of Angel's companion. The accomplice was young and strong, his chest stretching the fabric of a satin shirt. Tight curls of dark hair crawled up into the open vee of the neckline.

"No," Bill said, sneering. "But he'll have a headache when he wakes up."

The stranger reached over and slapped Bill across the cheek with the barrel of the gun, leaving a nasty cut that turned anger into fear. There had been something in the young man's eyes that had insisted the stranger take charge. The look was now gone. It was safe.

"Now, let's do this by the numbers. Number one is that both of you turn around. Number two is that we're going to walk to the end of this hall, then left to the service elevator. And number three is that if we pass anybody I'll have the gun out of sight but you'll be real quiet. I'll kill you on the spot if I have to. Now that's simple enough, isn't it?"

Bill and Angel looked at each other, nodded, and turned around. "What are you going to do to us?" Angel asked.

"If you do everything . . . by the numbers, then nothing. I'll relieve you of that little roll of bills you went to so much trouble to get, and then we'll part company, nice and easy. It's that simple."

Angel looked back over her shoulder at the handsome stranger and tried to smile. She wanted to believe him.

When they started down the hallway, an older couple dressed in clothes meant for a Hawaiian luau stepped from a room just in front of them. Everybody tensed, but Bill and Angel moved to the side, offering feeble smiles, and kept walking. They reached the service elevator without incident.

"You've got to have a key to operate that thing," Bill said, nodding at the door.

The stranger smiled. "Actually you need two keys. One to open the door and one to operate the panel." While he spoke he removed a key ring from his pocket and let the two keys dangle.

"Now, backs up against the door. Hands out in front."

It was a command that left no room for discussion. Bill backed up against one side of the door, Angel against the other. They raised their arms and stared at the stranger.

"Let's not forget the money."

Angel reached into her purse, acknowledging the barrel of the pistol not more than a foot from her head, and handed over the loose hundred-dollar bills.

"Now the hands." The stranger fanned himself with the money, then shoved the stack of bills and the elevator keys into one jacket pocket. He reached into another to produce two pairs of handcuffs. "Here, little Angel. You do the honors on the kid."

Angel took a pair of the handcuffs, securing Bill's wrists. The gun touched the side of her head and she pushed them on tight, then stepped back while the stranger slipped the other pair around her wrists and pushed her back against the door.

"I believe that covers just about everything." He took the keys from his pocket and stepped in front of Angel. He placed the key on her cheek and lowered it tenderly across her neck, then lower, following the neckline of her dress. He glanced over to see Bill's hate-filled glare, then he pulled the key away and reached over Angel's shoulder to unlock the elevator.

The doors opened with a whoosh that almost pulled the two handcuffed victims off their feet. Bill threw his weight forward and stumbled to his knees, realizing immediately that there was no elevator behind him, only an empty shaft that descended twenty floors. But he wasn't quick enough. The man with the gun kicked him in the chest and Bill reeled back into the void, his hands helpless as he tried to grab the edge. His scream echoed back up the shaft, cut short by a sudden silence.

It took a moment for Angel to realize what was happening, but she never had a chance. When she tried to run, the stranger grabbed her by the neck with one strong hand. She kicked but couldn't get her bearings and kept hitting nothing but air while the stranger walked her back to the edge of the empty elevator shaft. Her eyes bulged with fear. Her face turned pale, and she gasped for air.

Then the grip relaxed. It held her, but it suddenly seemed almost tender. She looked into the stranger's face and shivered at the smile that held her in its power.

"Shhhhh . . . don't scream." The stranger whispered, then he bent forward and kissed her on the lips. It was a soft, loving kiss, and in that moment he changed his mind. He let her go, and she fell to her knees in front of the open elevator doors, her head hanging as she sobbed.

The stranger looked down at her and ran one hand through her hair, pulling her against his crotch while he reached in his pocket with the free hand for the money. He ran his tongue over his lips, tasting her mouth and feeling the tremble of her skin. Then he pulled out the stack of hundred-dollar bills, took five bills from the pile and sent the rest fluttering down the open grave of the shaft.

He was reluctant to leave. He savored the moment, proud of his perfect timing and the way everything had worked to the last detail. He then lifted Angel's face, squeezing until she opened her mouth. He stuffed the five hundred-dollar bills between her pearl-white teeth, then turned and walked away.

Karen couldn't sleep. With all the new material she decided the primary list of fifteen murders they had selected for analysis wouldn't be enough. She spent seven hours feeding into the computer the dates and locations of all 247 murders that had been supplied by the researchers. Then she struggled to create a program that would digest all the material coming into the system and focus any overlaps into a single terminal.

All this, and what she was really looking for was quite simple. She wanted the name of any lone traveler who had paid cash for anything—plane, motel, or car—on the same date as two or more of the vicious murders. Nothing could be simpler.

She dozed off at the console while the three computers did the work, but she didn't sleep for long. Only five minutes passed before the computer bleeped and a name appeared on the screen. Karen raised her head to see the name Stephen R. Godwin, and she felt panic. Had all the work been for nothing? Would Godwin be the only name on the list?

But then the computer bleeped again, and another name joined Godwin on the screen. Bleep. A third name appeared. When the computers finally wound down and the central terminal listed "Program Complete," there were twelve names on the list.

Karen's eyes were half closed. She was running on the last ounce of adrenaline as she reached over to one of the peripheral computer terminals and pushed a few buttons to get a more complete read-out on the twelve mysterious cash fiends. And then she came wide awake. Seven of the twelve names listed Massachusetts addresses. Five were in Boston, the other two in Cambridge and Salem, just a few miles from the city.

Ripping off a printout of this information, Karen took a swallow of bitter, cold coffee, made a face, and waded through the printouts to fall across the sofa in the room.

On the piece of paper she clutched to her chest were the seven names she was sure formed a link to the phantom:

Stephen R. Godwin	2713 Parkman Street	Boston
Lester D. Haisley	1412 Beaver Place	Boston
Daniel J. Johnson	2666 Philips Street	Boston
Kenneth A. Murphy	314 Derby Street	Salem
Curtis G. Pearsall	1569 Byron Street	Boston
Stephen S. Stoddard	2750 Cedar Lane	Boston
Benjamin L. Wynn	3412 Kirkland Street	Cambridge

And with that, she slipped into sleep. She dreamed of a man, a handsome man about thirty years old. A man who lurked in shadows and killed people. It wasn't really a nightmare. She didn't see any blood. No severed heads. She saw only the handsome face, heard only the Bostonian accent. She dreamed of catching a phantom.

EIGHT

Karen was roused from sleep by a buzzing sound that was coming from somewhere beneath the stacks of paper on the desk at Manning Hall. It took her a few seconds to get her bearings, but when she saw the list of seven names on the printout she still clutched in her hand it all came back to her. She glanced at the clock, realized it must be Wednesday morning, then she dug down to find the intercom.

"Dr. Daniels, there's a gentleman from the Federal Bureau of Investigation here, and he insists on speaking to you." The temporary housekeeper was obviously frightened.

"Did he give a name?"

"Yes Ma'am . . . yes doctor. He said to tell you it's Quince Garrett. He says you know him."

Karen tried to think of all the reasons Quince might show up at Manning Hall, and there was only one that made any sense. He was keeping tabs on the Manning phantom, and he surely knew all about the computer data she'd received from Besswick.

She'd figured it all out except for the article in the *Midnight Express.* As soon as she entered the living room, Garrett walked up to her and stuck the headline "Phantom on Killing Spree?" in front of her face.

"Have you seen this?"

"No. I don't know anything about it."

"Where is Manning? I'd like to know what in the hell is going on."

"He's still in Richmond, burying his father. I can't believe Michael did this." Karen quickly scanned the article. "This is bad. He shouldn't have done it." She spoke more to herself than to the FBI agent.

"What are you going to do?" she asked.

The agent dropped down on the sofa, grunting with the stiffness of a running back who has just been plowed under by the defensive line. He ran a hand across his head, but he already knew the score. His team was trailing, and he didn't like the game plan.

"What can we do? If we jump into the case now, the media will be all over us. The FBI will look bad, and this disgusting rag will become a hero. If we don't get into the case and it turns out that there is a phantom killer, then we look even worse. You know how it works. With government bureaucrats looking over our shoulders at every move we make we can't afford to get caught in traps like this."

"So it's going to stay unofficial?"

"That's the way it stands at the moment. I'm strictly an observer. I've talked with Pemberton over in Alexandria, and with some squirt named McGowan out in Dallas. I've even talked to a few others . . . to some of the people on your list." He dropped his eyes away from Karen. "When we tied into your system yesterday we started pulling back copies of everything you've done. We've got your list of murders."

"And . . . ?"

"And nothing," Garrett said, exasperated. "I've talked to two dozen homicide detectives, and they all have baffling cases. It doesn't take a genius to read your profile. They are all murders that could be based on some sort of punishment where the obvious suspects don't fit. These cases read serial killing, if you want to look at them that way, but they're not like any serial killings I've ever seen before."

"But what do the detectives on the cases say?"

"What they say is sure, they'd love to have a phantom. It takes one more murder off their unsolved list. But not a one of them believes it. Phantoms are too easy. Too pat. They're all convinced that they're dealing with somebody local, and they don't want the FBI butting into their business."

"Seems like everybody's worried about looking bad."

Garrett didn't answer. He stood, paced the length of the living room and came back to Karen.

"We've got the list of twelve names that you pulled out of all that computer crap," he said with fresh anxiety. "What do they mean? What have you got?"

Karen tried to avoid the agent's eyes while she thought about the priorities. Since he'd said twelve names, that meant he had gotten them off the main computer console, not from one of the peripheral units she'd used to call up the addresses. He didn't have the list of seven names indicating Boston as a home base, and for some reason she didn't want him to have them.

"I haven't got anything you haven't seen off the computer," she said. "I'm working on a few things, but then you know how crazy my ideas are. Probably nothing but a wild goose chase."

Garrett read what she was saying between the words. The FBI had refused to listen when she first came to them. They had illegally tied into the Manning computer system to keep tabs on her, and even now they were only unofficially involved. Why should she cooperate?

"I'll see that our computer link is cut as soon as I get back to Washington." He waited until Karen looked at him. "You will get in touch if you find out anything?"

Karen led Garrett out of the living room and opened the front door for him. She watched him cross the porch and descend the steps to his car.

"Tell me, Quince. Do you believe there is a phantom?"

"There are many phantoms," he said, turning to face her. "And you may be onto one of them. I just hope you'll know when to let it go. It's a dangerous game. Phantoms bite back."

There was a reservation waiting for him at the Detroit Metropolitan Airport in the name of Lester D. Haisley. He had selected Tampa as his next destination, so there would be a connecting flight out of Atlanta.

He stood in the airport shop scanning the local newspaper headlines and feeling quite proud of his past few days. His story was all over the front page—the death of Sam McGruder was big news, particularly since he had met with such a fitting end.

McGruder had been an machinist, one of the many automotive workers laid off in a recent cutback. But McGruder had been different. With no job to keep him busy, he had taken to abusing his family. Three days ago McGruder's wife had stumbled into the Detroit Medical Center carrying Stacy, her three-year-old daughter. Burns covered 36 percent of Stacy's body. McGruder had thrown a pan of boiling water on the child.

Last night McGruder got his due. Out on bail, the child abuser had drunk himself silly and passed out in bed. No one would ever know all the details of what happened in that house, but the stranger scanning the headlines knew. He could remember every pleasing moment of tying the drunk to the bedframe, the torture he had inflicted with several pans of boiling water, and finally the fire that had engulfed the bedroom and ended the life of a man who didn't deserve to live.

All the newspapers had to say was that the body was burned beyond recognition, when in fact it had been little more than a pile of charred bone. The police were even suspecting suicide, so it was doubtful they would look close enough to find out they were wrong. It would take them another week just to confirm the identification.

The man calling himself Lester D. Haisley stood in front of the news rack in the airport gift shop feeling content, thinking about a possible vacation. Maybe something quick in Tampa, then perhaps he'd take a couple of weeks off. Perhaps he'd take a casual train ride up the East Coast, making several stops just to relax and see the sights along the way. Perhaps he'd even fly to Europe and really get away from things for a while.

But then he spotted another headline. "Phantom on Killing Spree?" He broke into a cold sweat. He froze where he was standing and glanced at the other people in the shop. He looked back at the headline, hoping he'd read it wrong, but this time his eyes were drawn to the kicker. "Media Heir

Blames Psycho." The name Manning popped into his mind. He remembered Alexandria, remembered the phone call to some old man named Manning.

He picked up the *Midnight Express,* a Detroit *Morning Star* and a *Time* magazine. He paid the cashier and headed to the restrooms. He didn't look at the article until he was safely in one of the stalls. Then he sat down and quietly cried, letting large tears flow across his cheeks.

When he walked out of the restroom a half hour later he was a new man. The tears were gone, and he'd washed his face. It was all he could do not to laugh. He was happy again. He had a plan. He went to the phones, called information in New York and asked for the number of the *Midnight Express.*

"Hello, may I speak to James Powers, please?"

"I'm sorry, sir, but Mr. Powers is out of the city on assignment. Can someone else help you?"

"I must speak to Mr. Powers. It's urgent. I may have some information on the phantom killer."

"One moment please."

He drummed his fingers on the side of the phone.

"Hello, this is Sandra Taylor, may I help you?"

"I must speak to James Powers. About the phantom."

"I'm Mr. Powers's editor. May I help you?"

"No. It must be Powers."

"Where are you calling from?"

"I'm in Dallas . . . Dallas, Texas," he said.

"Mr. Powers is also in Dallas, covering the—"

"I know who killed the Garveys."

There was a moment's pause. "Let me give you a number in Dallas where Mr. Powers can be reached."

She gave him the number.

He thanked her and gently hung up the phone. From where he was standing the man calling himself Lester D. Haisley could see the board listing departing flights. There was a jet leaving for Dallas in forty-five minutes.

Betty Grant was not proud of her job, but she was good at it. Maid duty for a Holiday Inn was methodical work. You had to have a routine—making beds, vacuuming, cleaning bathrooms, replacing towels and the little bars of soap, making

sure there were no hidden secrets in any of the drawers.
There was really nothing to it, but Betty prided herself on
neatness. She'd been working at the Holiday Inn near Texas
Stadium for three years, supporting two children that her
husband had abandoned when he took off for California. Her
life, like her job, had fallen into a neat, if unexciting, routine.

However, Betty Grant was not herself on the morning of
July third. Because of seniority she'd managed to get a four-
day weekend over the Fourth, and she was rushing to finish
her rooms. She'd torn seven of those silly strips of paper that
go across the toilet. She had dropped three glasses that had
shattered in their paper wrappers, and she couldn't get the
sheets to fold into neat hospital corners the way she wanted.
Instead of saving time she'd fallen half an hour behind schedule
as she approached the next to the last room on her floor.

Under normal circumstances she would have been prepared
for anything when she opened the door. Maids know better
than anyone the strange things that go on in motel rooms,
but she'd met the nice young man who was staying in room
208. He was a reporter for the *Midnight Express*, and over the
past week her cleaning schedule had often disturbed his work.
He'd be writing on a fancy little computer or be on the phone
trying to track down new information on the Garvey poisoning,
but he'd always been so nice. He'd told her a few jokes. He'd
asked her a few questions about some guy who'd stayed there
a week earlier. And other times he'd gone for a cup of coffee
just to get out of her way. When he didn't answer her knock
she thought that maybe this once she wouldn't be disturbing
him.

Nobody would ever disturb Jim Powers again. He was seated
just a few feet inside the door. His bare feet were tied to the
legs of the chair, his hands pulled behind him and tied. His
head was bent to his chest and blood covered his body. His
tongue had been cut out, and he'd been left to bleed to death.

It was a sight that would haunt Betty Grant's dreams for
the rest of her life.

Michael returned to Manning Hall late on the evening of
July third. The house was dark, but the Pattersons rushed
down to greet him at the door, insisting they were ready to

go back to work. Michael tried to talk them into taking a few days off, but he realized that after thirty years they didn't like having a temporary housekeeper in their home. And perhaps it would be better to get things back to normal—or as close to normal as things would ever be without Matthew Manning.

Michael hadn't seriously considered what he would do now that his father was gone. It was obvious that Allen would run Media Associates, at least for a while, and as Michael had said back in Richmond, he would do whatever it was he did.

Then Karen peeped around the corner with a tired face and bloodshot eyes. Suddenly there were things to do.

"Hi," she said, her voice slow with the need for sleep. "I know you just got back. You've got to be tired. But I've got something I want you to hear."

Michael silently followed Karen into the office. Her steps were slow and shaky, but she would accept no help. She held her head high and led the way.

The office was a mess. Computer printouts were two inches deep on the floor, and empty soft drink cans covered nearly every other flat surface in the room. Karen fell into the chair behind the desk and made a gracious but tired gesture for Michael to be seated across from her.

"I've been trying to track down our phantom," she said. "I'll explain how I did it later. I ended up with seven names that seemed to be connected to Boston, so I got Raymond—that's Raymond Hart, the freelance writer we used in Boston—to check on them. And they're connected. I was so tired I put the call on tape." She pointed to the recorder. "Listen to it while I get some sleep."

Michael stared at the recorder, and when he turned back to the desk Karen had laid her head down and was asleep. He went behind the desk, picked her up, and walked the limp body to the sofa. When he had her tucked in, he returned to the desk and pushed the play button on the recorder. The voice was that of Raymond Hart, and he went straight into his report.

"Okay. None of the seven names is listed in either the Boston telephone book or the city directory, but I found birth certificates on five of them. Then I looked for death certificates and drew a zero until I got to the name Lester D. Haisley. He died less than a month ago, on June 18th. For his place of residence it listed the Underwood Clinic. It's a private mental hospital just outside of Boston."

The recording paused, and there was the shuffling of papers. Hart's voice was pitched high with excitement when he started talking again.

"I tried to get to the clinic, but they wouldn't even let me in the door. So I did some more checking back in town and found another name. Kenneth A. Murphy, he's on your list, too, he was admitted to the Underwood Clinic when he was six years old after he took a knife and almost killed his sister. The only reason I could find it was because it made the papers."

There was another pause. More papers were shuffled.

"There was nothing else, so I assume he's been there ever since. He should be . . . that's what, twenty-two years plus six . . . that makes him twenty-eight."

The voice of Karen Daniels came on the recorder.

"Raymond, you've done a wonderful job. I'll see to it there's a bonus in your paycheck."

"Mrs. Daniels, it may not be any of my business, but you sound like you need sleep. I'll keep looking. I imagine all the names might be from Underwood Clinic, but I don't know how much more I'll be able to find with them being so secretive. What else do you want me to do?"

"I'm not exactly sure," Karen said. "Let me talk it over with the other editors here. Maybe I'll want to come up and try to question the clinic people myself."

"Mrs. Daniels, I don't know how important this story is, but I think you better take a nap before you do anything."

"Thank you, Raymond. I will."

Then came the click of both phones hanging up.

Michael looked at Karen sleeping soundly on the sofa. Her body was twisted to fit the narrow space, but her breathing was smooth and deep.

"Good God," Michael mumbled to himself. "She's found him."

Michael wanted to wake her, to learn more, but he resisted. He tiptoed to the desk telephone and called the airport. With the July Fourth weekend beginning everything was booked solid, but a single ticket had just become available in first-class on a morning flight to Boston.

Just as he hung up, the phone rang again. Karen sat up, but she was still sleep. Her eyes opened for a moment, but she was so tired that she couldn't quite manage it. She sat there in a daze, her body unable to tell her what to do next.

Michael answered the phone, and it took him a moment to recognize Quince Garrett on the other end. He'd never heard the big man sounding so sad.

"Michael, is that you?"

"Agent Garrett, yes." Michael panicked for a moment, wondering how much Garrett knew about Karen's work. "It's late. What's up?"

"I wanted to let you know before the papers get ahold of it." Garrett spoke slowly, the sadness in his voice preparing Michael for the worst. "I just got a call from Dallas . . . I believe you met Lieutenant McGowan when you were there."

"Yes."

"Jim Powers, the guy you gave the story to, the one from the *Midnight Express*. He's dead. His body was discovered earlier today in a Holiday Inn. He had been cut up bad and left to die."

Michael felt faint. He looked at Karen, but she was still out of it. Her eyes were closed, and her head had tilted to one side, resting as best it could on her own shoulder.

"Michael, are you there?"

"Yes, Quince, I'm here."

"Do you know what this means?"

Michael tried to think, but all he could remember was the rumpled young reporter who'd so badly wanted the big story.

"Michael, this means there is a phantom. It means you've stirred him up, and he's angry. It means he might do anything. He might even come after you."

Michael trembled, but he couldn't think. He couldn't make any sense out of what was happening.

"Quince, can we talk about this in the morning?"

"Okay. You stay close to home tonight, and tomorrow we've got a lot to talk about. This could get messy."

Michael hung up and suddenly felt very tired. He walked over to Karen, trying to think how best to get her up to her bedroom.

"What is it?" she asked when he touched her shoulder. "We've got to find him."

"It's nothing," he said. "Nothing at all."

She was still sleep, and the climb upstairs would be impossible. Michael sat on the sofa and gently laid her down, letting her use his shoulder for a pillow.

"We've got to find him," she mumbled again in her sleep. "He's ours."

"Yes, I know. We will." Michael trembled with the thought. They might not have to find him at all. The phantom, whoever he was, might find them instead.

NINE

Michael picked up a rental car at Logan International Airport and joined the holiday traffic heading north through Boston on Interstate 93. The fact that only one ticket had been available gave him an excuse for leaving Karen behind, and he was glad she couldn't come. With the phantom now a reality, possibly hiding behind any tree, it was important that he not take any chances. He had also needed someone to run interference with Quince Garrett while he tried to see if Boston held any answers.

Was this just another grand gesture, he asked himself as he jockeyed for position on the interstate. He didn't like to think that it was, but still he wondered how he was going to get anything that Raymond Hart hadn't been able to get. His morning call had, however, at least gained him a begrudging invitation to the Underwood Clinic.

Hart had also called Manning Hall before Michael left for the airport, and while he hadn't discovered anything new about the list of names, he had managed to put together a brief introduction to the clinic. The place had been opened in 1956 by Dr. Emerson Underwood, a brilliant child psychologist with credentials as long as your arm; a man not only with the professional respect but also with the moneyed friends to make the private hospital a reality.

There wasn't much personal information about Dr. Underwood, however. He had suddenly retired as director of the clinic twelve years ago, and soon after that his wife and child had been killed in an automobile accident. After that the doctor had disappeared.

The clinic itself was just what Michael had pictured. Located in lush countryside just north of Silver Lake, the central building looked more like a country club than a hospital. Red brick walls stretched in several directions, with carefully placed columns and white-framed French doors spaced at precise intervals. Other buildings, also of brick but much simpler in design, were hidden deeper in the wooded tract, with a tall black iron fence surrounding the entire estate.

A guard at the front entrance didn't seem happy, but his name on the check-in sheet permitted Michael to enter. The first of many white jackets came down from the central building, arriving at the edge of the driveway just as Michael pulled up.

"Mr. Manning, if you will please follow me."

Michael didn't like the cool sound of the man's voice, much less the officious, robot-like way he did an about-face without introducing himself.

Another white jacket took over just inside the door, and this one didn't even bother to speak. He just made a gesture with his arm and led the way down a long hallway that had the gloss of an army barracks floor.

"Mr. Manning, please do come in," said a smiling face when he was shown into an office at the far end of the hall. This one also wore a white jacket, but he at least seemed human. He was obviously the man in charge.

"I'm Dr. Bartholomew. I believe you spoke with one of my assistants this morning, but we felt it would be better if you talked with me. I'm director of the clinic, but I'm afraid your trip has been for nothing. I can tell you nothing about our patients."

Michael sighed, already exasperated, but he knew he had to give it a try. "I don't believe you realize the importance of the information you might have here at the clinic," Michael said, hearing the desperation in his own voice. "If the data we have gathered is correct, then this clinic is clearly linked with a phant—, with a man who could be responsible for murders all over the country."

Dr. Bartholomew smiled like a kindly grandfather accepting some silly story from a grandchild. His fingers tapped gently on the desk, his only acknowledgement of impatience.

"Mr. Manning, I hope you do understand," the doctor said, shifting into his most professional voice. "The Underwood Clinic is a private institution, and a very expensive institution. One reason people are willing to pay more to have their needy family members stay here is that they know we will keep it private. What goes on here, and with whom it goes on, is the business of no one beyond the walls of this clinic."

"But . . ."

"No, Mr. Manning. Our records are closed. Beyond a court order for a list of names of patients, not even the police can gain access to our files."

Michael reached into his pocket for the list of names, passing it across the desk.

"Can you at least tell me if these seven people are patients here?"

Dr. Bartholomew tried to act like he wasn't even looking at the sheet of paper, but his eyes darted to his desk, each time catching a name, his fingers continuing to drum primitive rhythms as he studied Michael.

Then he pushed the sheet back to Michael.

"I'm sorry, my hands are tied. Perhaps it would be best if you saw the police in Boston." Now it was the doctor who seemed exasperated. Perhaps he didn't like the names he saw on the sheet of paper. "As I said, even the police would be limited to a list of patients, but perhaps they can ease your mind that Underwood Clinic has nothing to do with any murderers."

"I will do just that."

"In fact, Mr. Manning, we have already made contact with the police for you. A Lieutenant Patterson is waiting in my outer office. He will be glad to escort you to the city. His superior is a man named Richardson, Captain Richardson, and the captain has agreed to speak with you on this matter."

"But . . ."

"I'm sorry, Mr. Manning. Any further contact with Underwood Clinic will have to come through Captain Richardson."

Walking through Logan International Airport, he felt out of place, a stranger in his own land. So much had changed, nothing seemed to same, and he had stayed away so many years for the most foolish of reasons, simply to avoid a city that held bad memories.

There was a small mixup over his reservation for a rental car, but the clerk insisted it was a simple matter due to the busy holiday weekend. Things were quickly straightened out, and the stranger climbed behind the wheel of a new Thunderbird, ready for his tour of the old places.

He drove north on Interstate 93, gliding in and out of the traffic. He took the exit at Somerville, casually making his way into Cambridge and moving gradually north to Harvard University. This had not changed, at least not so much on the surface, but it was still depressing.

Nothing was quite as it had been in his youth. The home where he'd spent the few semi-happy years of his childhood was smaller than he remembered. It looked the same, even if the new residents, whoever they might be, had not taken care of the yard the way his father had always insisted.

He found the other house, too, the one that represented so much misery. Even after all these years it was difficult to accept the fact that it was just a house, not unlike so many others in North Cambridge. The house itself seemed evil. It cast a spell over the stranger, reminding him of where it had all begun, and then he didn't want to be there anymore. He wanted to get as far away as possible, but he still had one more stop on this trek down memory lane.

Working his way back to Interstate 93, the stranger again headed north, this time in search of the Underwood Clinic.

"I don't believe it." Captain Richard "Dick" Richardson paced behind his desk at Boston Police Headquarters, chomping on an unlit cigar. Richardson was ex-Marine. Above his desk were photos of Vietnam buddies, and his voice was that of someone who would get his men out of any jam. It was raspy, filled with authority. It held back nothing of what he felt.

"You think you've tracked a phantom right here to Boston, right to the front steps of the Underwood Clinic. And this Dr. Daniels of the F-Fucking-BI believes it, too. Well, I'll tell you something young man, I think both of you are full of crap."

Michael was getting used to rough edges. He had been with Richardson and a uniformed stenographer for nearly an hour, telling them what he had discovered and trying to convince them to call the FBI, and Richardson's expletives had dominated the session. Michael glanced at his watch, convinced that it had stopped running hours ago if only the second hand hadn't been so casually clicking off the seconds in slow motion.

"Won't you at least look at the list of names," Michael pleaded for the hundrendth time. "I tell you, when I showed these names to Dr. Bartholomew he recognized them. No, he didn't say it, but it was there."

"You just sort of read his mind, is that it?

"No, I didn't read his mind. I saw it in his eyes. He glanced at the list, and he didn't even have to read the names. He knew them."

Richardson paced the office, up and down, shaking his head the whole time.

"I sure hope you realize the can of worms you've opened with all this crap. I'll still be doing the paperwork five years after I retire, and that won't even begin to take care of the crap the FBI will want in triplicate. Now, tell me again, why is it I'm staring into your lovely face instead of one of them fucking hotshot G-Men."

"I've told you and told you . . . Dr. Daniels and I just wanted to check things out first. Maybe we're in this thing over our heads, but we found the names, and we wanted to see where they led."

"And this Dr. Daniels stayed back home to play with the FBI boys. Is that it?"

Michael could feel his face flush, but he controlled his temper. "We're not getting anywhere, Captain Richardson. I've given you a list of seven names, and I've asked you to call Agent Garrett. I'm sure the names are connected with the Underwood Clinic, and they're also connected to a man . . . to somebody who is roaming this country using those names and killing people."

Richardson picked up a copy of the *Midnight Express*—the one with the psycho headline—and frowned at Michael.

"And your psycho . . . this phantom . . . he killed the writer for this piece of shit too?"

"It has to be. Call Agent Garrett. He'll tell you."

"And you think I should just go out there to Underwood Clinic and find out who he is?" Richardson asked.

"From the reception I just got, I don't believe it's going to be that easy. But yes. I believe you should go out there and find out what it is that connects these seven names."

Richardson huffed and puffed some more. He paced the length of the office, then came back, and flopped down into his chair behind the desk. His stenographer, never taking his eyes from the pad on his lap, jumped at the sound.

"Hell, I'm gonna have to talk to the FBI, to this Garrett. There ain't no way out of it, but there's not a reason in hell for me to do it till your Dr. Daniels fills him in. I need to know what they've got, what you've got, and what the blind old lady down on the corner has got, and maybe then I'll really see how screwed up all this mess is."

"Dr. Daniels is meeting with Agent Garrett right now." He involuntarily glanced at his watch one more time.

"Shit." Nothing pleased Richardson. He turned to his stenographer. "I want a transcript of tonight, and anything else you can find on this Underwood Clinic—personnel, patients— I don't know what you'll find, but find it. Once the FBI starts nosing around they're gonna want answers, and by God, I'm going to have them. I want all of that on my desk at 0600."

Richardson waited while the stenographer closed his notebook and marched from the office.

"And you," he demanded of Michael. "What are your plans?"

"There's nothing more for me to do," Michael said. "I've got a room near the airport for tonight. I'll be heading back to Virginia in the morning."

"Good." Richardson was again pacing. He snatched the *Midnight Express* off his desk and glared at the headline. "You really shouldn't have talked to this trash—" he slapped the paper. "If your phantom is actually responsible for killing this writer, then there's no telling what he might do next. He may run for cover, he may come home, or . . . ."

"Or he may come looking for the guy who has gummed up the works," Michael finished.

"You just get yourself back to Virginia, and I'll worry about any Boston phantoms. If I have to make waves, I sure as hell don't want you looking over my shoulder. I want you out of here."

Richardson tried to smile as he ushered Michael to the door. Then the captain returned to his desk and stared at the *Midnight Express.*

"All right you son of a bitch," he mumbled at the paper. "Come to daddy."

Michael slept soundly. Perhaps it had been the drinks he'd had after his visit with Richardson. Maybe it was knowing that the case was now in the hands of professionals. Or perhaps it was just pure exhaustion that brought on a deep sleep as soon as he got to his motel room near the airport. Not even the constant roar of jets landing and taking off with the morning rush stirred him from the bed.

It was almost noon before he began to think about getting up, but even then he couldn't make himself move. He was glad he had decided to reserve an afternoon flight back to Washington rather than rushing to join the morning crowd. He was anxious to see Karen and find out what steps were being taken on her end, but he'd just as soon avoid Quince Garrett as long as possible.

That was when the telephone rang.

"Hello," Michael said. He tried not to give away the fact he was still in bed.

"Mikey, you've been a busy boy." It was a taunting challenge. "I've had a few people get close before, but you've been good. Really good."

"Who is this?"

"Aw, Mikey, wake up. Who in the hell do you think it is?" The anger in the voice made Michael shudder.

"It can't be."

"Oh yes it can."

"You're—"

"I'm your worst nightmare. I'm the devil . . . I'm the Blob from Outer Space . . . I'm Frankenstein . . . I'm the Phantom of the Opera . . . and I'm all those crawly things that get under your skin and drive you mad. Tell me, Mikey, which one do you see me as in your dreams?"

Michael's throat tightened. His heart pounded as he threw back the covers and sat up straight on the edge of the bed. "What do you want?"

"Like I said, you're good. You've gotten closer to me than anybody, and I just wanted to meet the man who's smart enough to do that. I'm wondering how you did it."

"You're sick. You're crazy—"

"I expected better from you," the voice broke in, cutting Michael short with its bitterness. "I'm good at what I do, and you're good, too. I thought maybe we could talk over our, what should I call it? Our crafts. Our opposing crafts, if you will."

Michael's head was spinning. He couldn't get his mind to sort through the cobwebs. There were a thousand things he wanted to say all at once, but his mouth wouldn't work at all.

"Come on, Mikey. Cat got your tongue? Tell me. . . . Just tell me how you did it."

"You're a real sicko," Michael said.

The laughter from the other end of the line had a piercing clarity to it. "You've already said that. Don't tell me I was wrong about you. Now just take a minute. Calm yourself down and talk to me. I really want to know."

"The cops are onto you," Michael blurted. "I've talked to the Boston police, and I've got the FBI into this thing. It's all over."

"The opera isn't over till the fat lady sings . . . oh, Mikey, please, forget I said that. I'm sinking to your level. Let's make it . . . oh, how about, the killing isn't over till the bad buy croaks? Or maybe, the croaking isn't over till the bad guy stinks?" He sang these like verses in a bar song.

"Richardson said you might come back to Boston."

"Who said anything about Boston? And who's Richardson?"

"What do you want?"

The voice shifted, mimicking a child telling a story.

"I want Mikey to come out and play. I'm all alone out here in this big, bad world, and I think Mikey probably knows some new games. We could have fun together . . . at least we could have fun until I decide it's time to kill you."

"Oh, my God—"

"No, Mikey. It isn't God. It was just me. But then, you don't know me, do you? You just know there's someone. So what do you guys call me? I'll bet its the phantom, like in the newspaper headline. Am I right?"

"You can't get away with this."

"Oh, but I can. I've been getting away with it for years. Actually a lot of years if you count dear old Granny. But then, I don't much like to count Granny. I mean she was family and all that. I almost hurt myself more than I did her. I've learned a lot since then."

"You mean you've been killing all along."

"Oh yes. I thought you knew that. Let me see, if we add last week to the list that makes 483 dead. How would you like to be my 500th customer?"

"You're really sick."

"Not that again. Come on Mikey, get with it. I'm offering you a real honor—number five hundred. Maybe I could make up a big banner like a supermarket honoring its one millionth customer. No, that's no good. Then I'd have interviews and all that mess. Besides, I'm not even sure I want to kill you."

Michael knew he had to think of something to do. There had to be some way the call could help the police track this madman, wherever he was.

"Where are you?"

"Okay, Mikey. Now you understand. Let's say I'm not as far away as California, and I'm not as close as being in bed with you. Does that help?"

"What do you want?"

"I told you. I want to know how you did it. How you tracked me all the way to Underwood Clinic. I saw you there. Well, I saw the cop who came out with you and escorted you into the city. But I don't know how you possibly got that far."

"You left a trail."

There was silence on the other end of the phone, and Michael held his breath.

"This is distressing news." The voice turned icy in its sudden calmness. "I would say it was impossible, but you're here. I don't make mistakes, but you are here. This is not good."

"Take my word for it," Michael said. "You left a trail. How else could we find you?"

"Oh, well, maybe it's time for a vacation." There was a long pause. "What do you think? Do you think maybe I ought to retire? Take a lengthy leave of absence? Tell me, Mikey. What do you think?"

"I think your days are numbered, asshole. You've got to realize that as soon as you get off the phone I'm calling the police. They'll have the FBI tracking you within the hour."

There was a long pause.

"I know you're trying to scare me, Mikey, but that sounds exciting. The police have become such a bore. They just don't have the time to devote to me. They look at one of my victims and they decide it's not worth the effort, or maybe they just arrest the wrong person. Maybe the FBI will offer some new challenges."

"You're—"

"I know, I'm a sicko. By the way, I was sorry to hear about your father. I read the story, and I just want you to know that even though you blame me for his death I'm not going to claim that one. All I really wanted was to let him know I'd taken care of that bitch of a wife he had. She was a cutie too. A real shame she was both a bitch and a lesbo. I don't suppose she ever knew if she was coming or going."

Michael had to take the phone away from his ear to escape the brutal laughter. He wanted to hang up, but something refused to let him do it. "You bastard," he hissed.

"We don't seem to be getting very far, Mikey. I've gone from a sicko to an asshole to a bastard. I don't know, but that last one sounds like an improvement. Maybe I should call at a more civilized time. I mean noon, what kind of time is that for me to call and introduce myself. What do you say? Do you want me to call back later, after you're fully awake?"

"Yes. That might be nice."

The phantom gave a hearty laugh. "You still think you're dealing with some simpleton, don't you? Do you really think I'm going to give you a chance to get the cops in, tap the phone, and do all those crazy things they like to do? You can't possibly think I'm stupid."

"Okay," Michael said as calmly as possible. "What is it you want to do?"

There was a pause. "I don't know. Do you want to die today? No, I don't think so. Mikey, I've changed my mind. I was going to kill you this morning, but no, I'm not going to do it. You know that nice rental car sitting outside your room? Don't . . . I repeat DO NOT get in that car."

The phone clicked, leaving a hollow silence on the line.

It took the Boston police an hour to clear the motel parking lot of all cars except Michael's rental. A dozen patrol units plus a special bomb squad were on hand to help cordon off the western half of the lot, moving everything that wasn't nailed down.

Michael stood with the crowd that gathered behind barriers far from the car. They all watched while one of the bomb squad specialists suited up with flak jacket and other protective gear, and a buzz passed through their ranks as this single policeman began to edge toward the suspect vehicle.

All eyes were on the policeman, and absolutely no one paid any attention to the man who came out of a room on the second floor of the Holiday Inn. The man glanced at the crowd as he left his room carrying two small suitcases. He shrugged, uninterested, and quickly made his way to the lobby, where he almost had to drag the desk clerk from a window to clear his bill. He paid in cash.

A few minutes later the phantom placed the suitcases in the trunk of his car. He was parked at the opposite end of the lot, far from the area that had been cordoned off by police.

Sitting behind the wheel of the car, he could barely see Michael's rental car. The crowd occasionally blocked his view, but in the glimpses he could see a young policeman, with the thick padding across his chest, cautiously approach the car.

He smiled, then started his own car and pulled up a slight rise that led to the highway service road. When he looked back over his shoulder the young policeman was trying to peer in through the window on the driver's side of Michael's car more than a two hundred yards away.

That was when the phantom removed from his pocket a small case that looked like a portable radio. He raised a thin antenna at one end and wondered if the device would work. He had never trusted remote controls, always worrying that something would go wrong and mess up the timing he had so carefully arranged. He counted backwards from five and pushed the button.

The blast blew the top off of the distant car and the shock waves knocked down several spectators standing more than fifty yards away. The young policeman almost disintegrated. What was left of his body landed sixty feet from the car in a bloody heap of charred muscle and bone.

The crowd began to scream and policemen ran in circles trying to control the panic. The phantom slipped his own car into gear and carefully pulled onto the highway. There was no rush. His flight wouldn't be leaving for another eighty-five minutes.

TEN

The room was the size of a basketball court, with desks arranged in clusters through the middle. Teletype machines and electronic terminals stretched the full length of one long wall, busily collecting data from a variety of sources. A row of glass cubicles, each with shutters for privacy, dominated the opposite side, while the wall nearest the main hallway opened into a smaller room set up with a podium and folding chairs to handle press conferences. At the other end, closest to the rear of the building, there were two more small rooms; one had a large conference table in the center, the other a smaller table and three simple wooden chairs—a place for interrogations. This was the Action Room, operations center for special cases.

Michael sat against the wall next to the interrogation room and watched an uninterrupted stream of activity. Half a dozen detectives and twice as many uniformed policemen worked telephones, preparing files and studying data collected by officers in the field. The Manning phantom had become an overnight celebrity, the subject of media speculation and the elusive target of a manhunt undertaken by hundreds of Boston policemen. During the emotional twelve hours following the

131

car bombing, Michael had seen policemen in tears as they were briefed on the malicious killing of one of their own, and now he watched as those tears turned into an angry determination to catch the "thing" responsible.

Attitudes had also changed regarding Michael. After the bombing he had been bodily dragged into a patrol car by Captain Richardson and brought to this room. There had been more questions, long hours trying to reconstruct every word of the telephone conversation between Michael and the phantom.

Michael told his story over and over, with new faces in the audience for each recitation. Then came more hours sitting on a hard chair, feeling helpless because he didn't know more, because he couldn't help the policemen in their search. He was just beginning to doze off when one of the uniformed policemen approached and asked him to step into Richardson's office.

The homicide detective looked as tired as Michael felt. When he spoke it was still the voice of authority, the voice Michael had heard the first time they talked, but Richardson had been worn down by the past twelve hours. He looked shorter, his pin-striped suit was rumpled, the jacket and vest piled on a corner chair. His tie was loosened and the top of the shirt opened. The sleeves were rolled up.

"Mr. Manning, please, have a seat. I believe you know Agent Garrett, Quinton Garrett, with the Federal Bureau of Investigation."

Michael turned warily to face Garrett but was surprised to find not the anger that he expected but rather a caring, worried look. Perhaps there was a lot more to this man than just a government identification and a tough exterior. It was something Michael would have to think about.

"Well, looks like you've done it now," Garrett said without menace. "You've found your phantom, or he's found you, and that means we'll be spending a lot of time together."

"That's what we wanted to talk to you about," Richardson broke in. "As you might imagine, we've had a long talk about what to do with you. I'm sorry, I don't mean that the way it sounds, but you have to admit that it's something of a problem. This fucking psycho has tried to kill you once, and odds are he'll try again. And he's gone."

"He decided not to kill me," Michael whispered.

"It appears that . . . what do we call him, the phantom, I guess . . . he's left Boston," Garrett added. "Using the names you've supplied of patients at the Underwood Clinic, we believe he was staying in the same motel where yesterday's bombing occurred. His room, in fact, was practically next door to your own. This raises some interesting questions about the method he chose for killing you."

The two professionals shared a quick glance before Garrett continued. "My personal opinion is that he was playing with you, like a cat with a mouse."

"What do you mean?"

"What we mean," Richardson's voice shook the walls, then calmed to a simple roar. "What we mean is that this psycho is gone. We don't know where. He used one of the names you gave us for the motel room, and he returned a rental car to the airport less than a half hour after your car exploded. And what Agent Garrett was saying about a game, well, we've learned that the car bomb was set off by remote control. The bastard probably knew you were nowhere near the car when it blew. He was making a point."

Garrett broke in again. "He was showing you, first hand, what he's capable of doing."

"So, what do we do now?" Michael asked.

Richardson sat back in his chair. It had obviously been decided that Garrett would give the explanation. "We want to get you back to Virginia as soon as possible. I'll be handling the case out of Washington and, with your permission, we'll establish a command center at Manning Hall. I'll be bringing in some of my best people, and while we work things on the national level, Captain Richardson will work with one of my men here in Boston. We're basically convinced your phantom will try to reach you again, and that he'll probably do it by calling Manning Hall."

"We know he has, or at least had, the telephone number," Richardson added.

"Travel arrangements have been made. Our flight leaves Logan in two hours. A car will meet us at the airport in

Washington and take us straight to Manning Hall." Garrett seemed almost fatherly in his concern. "And this is important, Michael. From now on I'll be with you, right beside you all the way through this thing. We don't know what to expect, but we'll all be working to catch this psycho as soon as possible."

"Right," was all Michael could think to say. "I understand."

Garrett stood up, towering over Michael's chair. "You've got to understand, Michael. This guy has apparently been killing at random for years, and in the last day he's given up the randomness of his travels to focus on you. Something is going on in his mind. We don't know how he came to Boston or how he knew you were here, but when we ask ourselves why there is only one answer. He's showing off. We've talked to Dr. Daniels and to the other agency shrinks, and they all agree. You've reached this psycho, and he wants you to know that you're in danger. He must prove himself superior. That's what it's all about. The quicker you accept the reality of that situation the better for all of us."

Michael stood, but his legs were weak. "I understand. Really, I do."

Two days later, at three o'clock in the morning, the telephone rang at Manning Hall.

Michael was so primed by the drills explaining what to do and not to do when this happened that even in his sleep he reacted automatically. The natural instinct to reach for the phone next to his bed had been programmed out of his behavior, and instead he grabbed a robe, and ran for the hallway.

He met Quince Garrett at the top of the stairs just as the phone pealed for the third time. Agent Bill Travers, who'd been brought in as Garrett's assistant on the case, was working night phone duty, and he waited anxiously, staring up from the bottom of the steps. That meant he'd already signalled the telephone company to begin tracking the call.

By the fourth ring, the whole house was in movement. Karen emerged from her bedroom deeper in the east wing of the house, and two more FBI agents came running to grab special hookups, one to stay in contact with the telephone operators tracing the call and the other to monitor the call while it was being recorded. Travers had already flipped on the two tape recorders and the speaker that would allow everybody to hear both sides of the conversation.

Michael answered the call on the sixth ring.

From the other end of the line came laughter.

"Mikey, what is this? Is it the servants' night off?"

Michael shivered at the sound of the taunting voice, and everybody in the room shivered with him.

"Mikey, it's me. Aren't you talking to me?"

"Okay. What do you want?"

"Please, Mikey, call me . . . what's a good name? How about Houdini? I like that. And don't worry. I haven't placed any more bombs anywhere. Not yet, anyway."

Michael looked at the faces around him trying to find Karen. They had discussed so many things for Michael to say, things that would keep the psycho on the phone, things that might cause him to make a mistake. Michael drew a complete blank.

"Mikey, this is getting absurd. I call, and you never have anything to say. I end up doing all the talking."

Michael shook himself. "Okay . . . okay, Houdini . . . let's talk."

"That's more like it. What shall we talk about?"

"Let's talk about murder."

"Oh, my, a juicy subject indeed. Shall we talk about guns, knives . . . or car bombs?"

"Car bombs."

"Good choice." There was a pause. He was acting like he had all the time in the world.

"Why did you do it? Why blow up an innocent man?"

"Oh, Mikey, that's the greatest question of all time. Why? But the answer is so simple. It's all part of the game."

"Is that all this is to you? A game?"

"That's it. That's all there ever is." There was another pause, and Michael could almost hear the wheels turning. "The game is everything. That's why I've called, so we can get straight on the rules of the game."

"You're really sick."

"Not that again." The voice was angry. "We've been through all of that. I'm sick, I'm a dirty bastard, and I'm . . . what was the other one? Oh yes, I'm an asshole."

Michael caught sight of Karen out the corner of his eye. She was making a gesture, holding her hands flat, telling Michael to be cool.

"Okay, what now? You're making the rules as we go along. What's the next part of the game?"

"Hey, Mikey, you learn fast. If I didn't know better I'd think maybe you've been getting some coaching. Huh, Mikey? You got yourself some help?"

"I don't know what you're talking about."

"What I'm talking about is The Law. The guys with the white hats. You know what I mean, but just for the sake of argument, let me see. If we're going to play, I need to know the players. Who's there with you?"

"What are you talking about?"

"Just give me a second. Let me think. Oh yes, surely that cute young lady doctor is there. What's her name? Karen? That's right. Good morning, Dr. Daniels."

Michael looked up at Karen's face. She had gone pale, and she looked as if she were about to faint until Garrett put an arm around her shoulder.

"And is Allen there? Good, solid, uptight Allen Collins, the man behind the man behind Media Associates. Is he there, or is he in Washington keeping the Fourth Estate afloat and the bucks pouring in?"

Michael didn't answer.

"Oh yes, and our men in blue. I won't bother them. I'm sure they're busy trying to figure where in the hell big bad Houdini is calling from. But, let me see. If the newspapers are correct—and I make no guarantee for their accuracy—then Agent Quinton Garrett of the nation's glorious capital can't be far away. Add in a few flunkies, and that would make maybe six in all. How did I do?"

"Let's say you're close. Now let's get back to the game." Michael said.

"This is the game, Mikey. Remember, I make the rules, and the rules say that this is the game."

"When do I get a chance to play?"

"But Mikey, you don't know the rules. You can't play the game unless you know the rules."

"That doesn't sound very fair."

"Who ever said games were fair?"

"Even unfair games give the underdog a fighting chance. Even if I don't have a chance of winning, at least I've got to feel like I'm going to get to play or there's no need in staying on the line. I might as well hang up."

"Spoken like a real trouper. But now we both know you won't hang up, not without prior approval. Besides, hanging up on me would be a big mistake. I might have to assess you penalty points . . . you know, like bodies."

Michael looked at the two agents for help, and they looked at their equipment, acting busy.

"This is the way it is, Mikey. I like you a lot. You're smart, and all that, but I'm in charge. Now we both know that the FBI has put me at the top of the ten most wanted list. Cops everywhere are hoping for a shot at the phantom. But I'm still in charge, Mikey, and what I say goes. Do I make myself clear?"

"Yes."

"Good. Now the game." Then came the laugh, such an honest, clear, exuberant laugh that it was difficult to remember it was coming from a murderous psychopath. "Like all games, this one is made up of penalties and bonuses. I decided not to kill you back in Boston, and you did good. You didn't get yourself all blowed up, and that means you get a bonus. See how simple it is? You do good, and I give you a bonus. Do bad and you get a penalty."

"You're crazy."

"Now be quiet Mikey, I'm just getting to the good part. The bonus has to be nice, but it should also help us get to know each other better."

Michael was distracted by a sudden flurry of activity in the room. The agent who was keeping track of the trace on the call was speaking frantically into his headset, and both Garrett and Travers were leaning over his shoulder, reading what he was writing on a pad.

"Now, doesn't that sound nice, Mikey?"

"Yes. I see your point."

"Do you want the bonus or not? If I'm disturbing you we can forget the whole thing."

Michael took a deep breath, and the two agents turned back to listen. "No. Please. What is the bonus?"

"Well, you see, Mikey, like I told you before, I've been at this for quite some time. I'm very good at what I do. I believe I've already given you the count. I don't keep track on a daily basis, but the last time I checked there were seventeen people in jail for murders that I committed."

Michael looked at the two agents, but neither Travers nor Garrett would look his way.

"Did you say something, Mikey?"

"No."

"Oh, I thought I heard something nasty, but it must have been my imagination."

"Must have been."

"Where was I? Oh yes . . . seventeen people in jail. On occasion, I like to see how far I can go, and sometimes putting the blame on somebody else can be . . . well, fun. That's really why I called your daddy after my little fling in Alexandria. See, I was hoping the cops would think he was responsible. I never thought he'd go to jail or anything. He was too rich and powerful for that. And I certainly didn't think he'd go and croak on me, but I just thought it'd be fun to let the police question him. Do you see what I mean?"

"Yes," Michael whispered. "I see."

"Good. Well, there are others who weren't so lucky. I mean they were arrested, charged, tried, and convicted."

"What has this got to do with me?"

"Well, what I was thinking, Mikey, is that for your bonus I'm going to give you one of these people wrongly accused of a crime I committed. Would you like that?"

Michael looked at the two agents. "Yes."

"Actually, the guy I've decided to set free hasn't been tried yet. The trial isn't for two weeks, but he doesn't stand a chance. I doubt the trial would last more than two days, and he'd be gone. Up the river for a long, long time. He lives in Chicago. He's a janitor at an apartment building on North Shore Drive. Do you know where that is?"

"Yes."

"Well, they say he cut up this beautiful redhead on the roof of his building. She was up there sunbathing, and they say he took a knife and cut her all to pieces. He cut off this little white bikini so he could look at her beautiful body, and then he stabbed her, over and over again. But Mikey, he didn't do it. I did it."

Michael remained silent.

"I know how you found me, Mikey. Somehow you got hold of the names I've been using. I got sloppy, but never mind that. If you check you'll find that I was staying at the Holiday Inn just a few blocks from the apartment on the day it happened. I was using the name Godwin. Stephen Godwin."

Michael still didn't speak.

"Aren't you even going to thank me? Never mind. But I do want you to do something for me. I can't stand the thought of your being cooped up in Manning Hall just waiting for me to call. I want you, personally, to go to Chicago. See the janitor. Tell him I'm sorry. And before you say no, and before our FBI friends come up with all sorts of reasons for you not to go, let me remind you about the rules. Penalties and bonuses. If you don't show up in Chicago tomorrow morning, I'll know it. I'll cut up six women that will make what that redhead got look like a little scratch. Do I make myself clear?"

Michael's voice was so weak he could hardly be heard. "Yes. I understand."

"Good. Who knows, maybe I'll see you in the Windy City. Would you like that?"

Michael's anger gave him strength. "Oh yes, I'd like that very much."

"I bet you would. And oh, before I go, tell your friends I'm calling from Wisconsin. From a nice little place called Appleton. Just for your education, Mikey, this is where Houdini was born, but tell your fellas there's no need to come all this way. By the time they get here I'll be five hundred miles away, but I thought they'd like to know. See you later, Mikey."

The phone went dead.

O'Hare was fogged in for most of the morning. The flight from Washington circled above Lake Michigan for a half hour until the sun began to peek through the clouds and the jet was given clearance to land. When the pilot came on the intercom an audible sigh of relief passed through the cabin, a sigh enjoyed by all except Michael Manning.

Michael had a window seat near the front of the aircraft, and landing meant that he would soon be in jeopardy. There was a very good chance that Houdini was waiting somewhere down there to play another game with his life. At least that was what Garrett told him over and over during the endless sessions following the morning call at Manning Hall. Everybody agreed they had no choice, that Michael would have to go to Chicago, and while Garrett spoke gravely about how much protection Michael would be given, their real thoughts were obvious. They hoped the psycho would make a try for Michael so they'd have a shot at catching him.

Three seats behind Michael on the other side of the aisle sat two men who, from all outward appearance, were very much like all the other businessmen on the flight. Garrett had not made the trip, fearing the phantom might know what he looked like, but these two were cut from the same pattern. Wearing vested suits, each with an attache case across his lap, they played the part well. Michael didn't know their names. He had been told they would be there, but he wasn't supposed to notice.

Michael had been told to stay in his seat until most of the passengers were gone. It was one of the reasons he'd been assigned a window seat, so that it wouldn't be obvious that he was lagging behind. The crowded aisle would make it impossible for him to leave for a few minutes, anyway.

The two agents also took their time. They compared notes as if working out a day's agenda, then slowly closed their cases and began gathering the newspaper they had shared on the flight. There were only a few stragglers when Michael stepped into the aisle, glancing at the agents as he joined the end of the line leaving the plane.

The stewardess, an exotic Oriental girl with bright red lipstick, wished him a pleasant stay in Chicago.

The terminal was frantic. Flights had been backed up all morning because of the fog, and businessmen were dashing through the airport, all late for appointments. Others seemed lost, looking for people who had expected to meet them an hour earlier.

It had been decided that Michael would be met by two uniformed Chicago policemen. Since Houdini knew the FBI was on the case and knew that the Chicago police would be aware of the previous morning's call to Manning Hall, an officer escort was mandatory.

The two policemen stood as Michael entered the terminal, and for a brief moment Michael felt almost safe as he walked through the crowd. Seeing the two blue uniforms, and knowing there were two armed FBI agents just a few feet to his rear he almost wished the bastard would make an appearance. But the sense of security was fleeting. As he walked deeper into the terminal crowd, jostling for position with the faceless masses, Michael realized Houdini could come from any direction.

"Mr. Manning?" One of the officers offered quick introductions with names that Michael couldn't catch. "Don't worry, sir. There are two agents nearby, plus the men you brought with you. You're fully covered."

Michael might have gained comfort from these words if the two young policemen hadn't looked so nervous. It was warm in the terminal, but not warm enough to cause the sweat that glistened on the forehead of both men.

"You have a car waiting?" Michael asked.

"Yes. Right this way."

They pushed onward through the crowd. As they walked, Michael could imagine this cluster of people—agents and uniformed policemen—moving against the flow. He couldn't see the box they formed around him. He was only aware of the two policemen who flanked him and the stares from people trying to guess what he might have done to require an escort from the airport.

The two policemen were alert. There was no idle chatter. Michael's eyes darted from face to face in the crowd, the two policemen doing the same, watching for any quick movement, any hand mysteriously slipping inside a jacket. Anything out of the ordinary.

The patrol car that would take Michael to his visit with the janitor sat in a no-parking zone just beyond the glass doors leading into O'Hare's monstrous parking lot. There would be just a few steps between building and car, no way for a sniper to pick him off.

Then they heard the loud speaker paging Michael Manning, a woman's dry voice being amplified throughout the terminal.

"Mr. Michael Manning. An emergency phone call for Mr. Michael Manning. You may take the call at one of the white telephones at any ticket counter or information desk."

Michael and the policemen froze in their steps while the message was repeated. All three looked at the patrol car just a few yards away, so close and yet so far, but then Bill Travers, the agent who had been lurking just over Garrett's shoulder the past few days, stepped out of the crowd.

"Follow me. We're patching the call through to one of the offices. We had a feeling this might happen." Travers left no room for discussion as he cleared a path in that direction. Michael and the two patrolmen had no choice but to follow.

Travers jumped over a luggage scale next to one of the ticket counters, flashing his identification to the various clerks who looked up in surprise, and then they barged through the door to a small office. Travers didn't bother to knock.

The office contained three small desks jammed against walls to take full advantage of the space, and it was crowded. Two agents were already rushing managers from one of the midwest airlines out of the office and clearing a place for Michael at a desk. Wires had already been attached to the phone, one leading to headphones, the other to a tape recorder.

"Sit." Travers was a man of few words.

Michael sat, staring at the telephone. But nothing happened. It didn't ring. Michael looked up at Travers, who was adjusting the headphones over his ears. Travers was unlike Garrett in every way except size, both standing over six-foot-two. But Travers was dressed impeccably, with a cool that made you think he was a doctor, someone unshakable. Garrett dressed in standard suits and ties, always fresh and crisp, but Travers went that little extra. There wasn't a wrinkle anywhere, the creases in his slacks razor sharp, his hands manicured and certainly never sweaty.

Now those hands were signaling Michael to pick up the phone. "The call has been patched through. Take it."

Michael picked up the receiver.

"This is Michael Manning."

There was a click. A long pause.

"Good morning, Mikey. Have a nice flight?"

"What now?"

"I'll say this for you, Mikey, old buddy. You've got guts. And you're learning the rules real fast. I'm proud of you. Are you looking forward to meeting Sambo?"

"What?"

"Sambo. My janitor friend with the hunting knife."

Michael didn't answer.

"Well, he's a nice fella. I'm sure you'll have a pleasant visit. But that's not why I called. I just wanted to welcome you to Chicago. I would come over and say hello in person, but you know, with all your friends I wouldn't want to make a nuisance of myself. You know what I mean, don't you Mikey?"

"Yes. I know what you mean."

"You sound tired. I'm not wearing you out, am I? I don't mean to do that. In fact, just for showing up you get another bonus. How do you like that?"

Michael gritted his teeth. Another agent joined the group at the telephone.

"The way I see it, Mikey, you and I have a lot in common. I mean it. I've been reading all about the Manning family, and your daddy did all right. It's great when a man can be born poor and build his own future . . . build a magazine empire."

"I really don't want to talk with you about this." There was a tightness in Michael's chest. He could hardly breathe.

"Mikey, Mikey, Mikey. You sound tense. Don't be. Please. It's been a long time since I've had anybody to talk to, and I really believe you and I share a lot more than you realize. See, my daddy was a big man, too."

Michael glanced at Travers, but he got no sign from the agent. Travers remained cool, listening on his headphones, leaving Michael to deal with the phone call the best he could.

"I don't understand. In what way are they the same?"

"Well, maybe not the same exactly. My daddy didn't publish magazines, but he did . . . well, I better not get into all that. Not now, Mikey, but some day I hope we can talk about it."

"I'd like that," Michael answered, trying to sound positive, knowing that any connection between him and the psycho might bring them closer to the day when the man was caught.

"Would you really do that, Mikey? I mean, if I could arrange for the two of us to talk, just you and me—talk about our families, about the problems of being the son of a big man—would you do that?"

Michael shivered at the possibility. "Sure, if—if I thought I would be safe."

And then came the laughter. The phantom laugh, with it wondrous purity, its shocking love of life. "Mikey, you are something else. I almost believe you're serious."

"I am."

"No, Mikey. You and I sitting down for a nice quiet talk is something that can never be. You brought the FBI into it. They will never let you out of their sight. Not until I'm caught—or killed. Think about that, Mikey. Think about spending the rest of your life in the custody of your government friends."

"Why do you do it?"

"Why, Mikey? Why did you come to Chicago? Better yet, why did you start hunting for me in the first place? What made you think that I even existed? Were you that sure your father hadn't hired a killer? Did you believe in him that much?"

"I certainly knew my father hadn't killed Kathy," Michael said, surprised to find himself honestly trying to explain. "And things just happened after that. I didn't just figure it out; just suddenly you were there. But I still don't know your name. I still don't know."

Michael was stopped by the firm hand of Bill Travers grabbing his shoulder. The agent was shaking his head. He wasn't to say what they didn't know.

"What's the matter, Mikey. Have they stopped you from talking?"

"I seem to have gotten a bit carried away."

"Well, think about this Mikey. When you came home and found your stepmother brutally murdered and your father dying because some psycho played around with his head, and maybe his heart, you reacted the only way you could. You went hunting for the person responsible."

"Yes."

"Well, I had some trauma in my childhood, too. Mine was not a loving family. I told you about Granny—well, I probably shouldn't have done that, but it's done. She caused me all sorts of pain, a pain you will never know."

"I don't understand. Please tell me." Michael felt like he was close. If he could just keep the phantom talking.

"Let's put it this way, Mikey. Think about the pain you felt when you came home to all this mess."

"Yes."

"Well your pain was so great that you came after me. You probably want to kill me. Right?"

Michael didn't answer.

"Well, regardless of that; when I was young I suffered so much pain that I couldn't strike out at just one person. I mean, sure, I killed old Granny. She was my first. But that wasn't enough. My pain was still there. I hate everybody. I hate everybody because everybody's life is better than mine. And they don't deserve it."

"And me?"

"I haven't decided about you yet, Mikey. You've had the good life for a long time, but I sense that you've also had pain. I feel like maybe you've been alone too. That's the worst of all, being alone."

"Yes. You're right."

There was a long pause on the phone. Michael couldn't think of anything to say, and the phantom had gone further than he had planned.

Then, again there came the laugh. It filled the small airline office, and it challenged everything that had been said.

"Mikey, you're good. I was going to kill you today, a quick sniper's bullet. I'm right here, in Chicago. I've decided to let you live a bit longer, but I'm worried about you. I think right after you visit Sambo you'd better get back to good ol' Virginny. Go back to Manning Hall and get some rest. That, by the way, is an order."

Michael didn't answer.

"Mikey, this is from the heart. If I could have known you a few years ago—well, maybe a lot of years ago, maybe none of this would have happened. I believe we could have been friends, and if I'd had a friend like you maybe I wouldn't have been so lonely. Maybe there wouldn't have been so much pain. Think about that."

And the phone went dead.

Interrogation rooms tend to look alike. The one in Chicago was not much different from the one in Boston. There was the simple wooden table, scratched and stained with the memories of many previous encounters. The chairs were uncomfortable, with hard, straight backs. The light was harsh and unpleasant.

Michael sat in the room and waited for the janitor. He didn't really know why he should meet the man who'd been charged with one of the phantom's murders, but it had been decided for him that he would follow his orders exactly as stated.

The black man who was ushered into the room was not at all what Michael expected. He was young, although you couldn't help thinking he looked older than his years. Michael had anticipated a bully, someone who at least looked capable of mutilating a sunbather, but this man was thin, almost delicate, and he was frightened.

"Are you Mr. Manning?" The voice trembled. "You're the fella told 'em I didn't do it."

"Yes, in a round about way, I'm the one who told them. And please, the name is Michael."

"My name's James Gunther, but friends call me Jocko. I sure do 'ppreciate what you done."

"I really didn't do that much. I don't know how much they've told you, but the man who apparently killed the woman called me and told me he did it. The police were there when he called, so they know. And he said some things he shouldn't have known. He knew she was wearing a white bikini."

"I used to watch her all the time," Jocko said, ducking his head in embarrassment. "I mean, she was sure somethin' to see. She had a whole bunch of them little bikini things. It was like she had a different color for every day of the week."

Michael smiled, and Jocko seemed to relax.

"I imagine they've been asking you a lot of questions."

"They don't ever run out of 'em," Jocko said, showing stained teeth behind a half smile. "I do believe I've told 'em everything happened to me since the day I was born. Everything I remembers, anyway. Don't 'member much when I's drinkin'."

"Were you drinking that day?"

"Oh, yeah. It was my day off. Only reason I was at the building was I needed to sleep it off. But they done ask me all 'bout that. I figures it must of been this guy I talked to. Fella I met over at breakfast. But I can't 'member him. We talked a few minutes, then I left. I needed to get me some sleep, and I never seen him after that. Next thing I knew I had policemen hanging all over m."

Michael tried to be comforting.

"I suppose they told you I was wrapped up in her robe when they found me. It had all this blood on it, and the knife, it was under my cot. I don't know how that stuff got there."

"And you don't remember anything about the man?"

"Naw. And Lordy, I sure wish I could. All I know is he's white and 'bout your age. I wasn't 'zactly seein' straight."

"Well, Jocko, I don't think you've got anything to worry about. They know you didn't do it, and they'll get the man who did."

Jocko squinted at Michael. "They say they doin' the paperwork get me out of here. Then they say they goin' take care of me . . . for my own protection. Is that right?"

"It's probably a good idea, at least until we know more about the man who did it."

A guard knocked at the door, then stepped quickly into the room. Jocko responded automatically by standing, but he kept his eyes on Michael.

"If I's in danger, what 'bout you?" Jocko asked. "I mean, he's already done me, but if he knows to call you and tell you stuff, what make you think you safe on the outside?"

"I can't really answer that," Michael said. "But I can tell you, I don't feel very safe."

Jocko nodded, then bowed his head to the guard, ready to return to his cell.

"I tell you one thing, Michael. Anybody'd do what this fella done, he bad. I mean he ain't just a mean dude. He has to be born bad to do somethin' like that. You be real careful now, you hear?"

Michael nodded, and the two men shook hands.

ELEVEN

Who is Michael Manning?

The stranger sat in the restaurant at the Indianapolis International Airport carefully scanning the headlines of *The New York Times* looking for a cause. But he was tired, and he couldn't get Michael Manning out of his mind. It had been a long drive from Chicago, and his shoulders ached with the tension of a new challenge.

Michael Manning, Michael Manning, Michael Manning—he wasn't sure why Mikey was special, but he knew he had to do something special to mark this new . . . what should he call it? Was friendship too foolish? It didn't really matter because it was fun, too. He hadn't had so much fun in a long time, and now he needed a biggie. He needed something really special.

Outwardly, sitting over a cup of black coffee, he blended into the crowd. He was just another well-dressed executive, perhaps a bit more handsome than most, reading the newspaper and waiting for his flight. But inwardly, his stomach was in knots and the paper blurred in front of him as he tried to understand what was happening with Michael.

There were many questions. How had he allowed Michael to become such an obsession? Why couldn't he just let it go,

149

or kill him? Why did he insist on this game when the odds
were quickly turning against him? If he kept playing around,
it was certain he would make a mistake, or somebody would
get lucky, and it would be over. One mistake and it would
all be over; would that be such a bad thing?

It didn't matter. Nothing mattered except that he find
something juicy, something that would show Michael Manning
the extent of his powers. There was nothing else, and as he
focused in on this mission he tried to convince himself that
he felt good. Another day. Another challenge. Life was still
worth living.

He flirted briefly with the waitress who came to refill his
coffee cup, then he turned seriously back to the newspaper.
But there was nothing. Politicians were politicking. Businessmen were making big deals and losing fortunes. Baseball teams
were playing other baseball teams. Some were winners, others
were losers, but there was nothing that popped out and said
"Do me."

He pushed the coffee and the newspaper aside, staring for
a moment at his hands. They were clean, strong hands, capable
of doing anything. But they needed something to do. He
picked up his change from the table and bounced it in his
hand as he left the restaurant and headed for the telephones.
He still didn't know what he was going to do next, but it was
time to stir things up again at Manning Hall.

He was still bouncing the change when he got to the phones.
He glared at the one thing that formed a link between him
and Michael Manning, and then he changed his mind. There
would be no call. Not now. It was time for something better.

Pocketing the change, he walked to the ticket counter. An
attractive young girl smiled up at him, showing the cleanest
and straightest white teeth he had ever seen.

"May I help you?" she asked, sounding like a television ad.

"Yes," he said, returning the smile. "Your next flight to
Washington. One way."

Michael arrived home late in the evening, traveling with
two FBI agents. Bill Travers had remained behind in Chicago
to coordinate what little hope there was of finding a trail to
the phantom.

Quince Garrett had come over to give Michael a pat on the shoulder when he arrived home. Garrett had already heard the tape of the telephone conversation between Michael and the phantom in Chicago, and he felt Michael had handled it well.

Michael was tired, and there wasn't really much for anybody to say. He and Karen took a brief walk around the grounds, trying to enjoy the clear, star-filled sky, imagining how nice it could be to take this walk if there weren't a phantom. The agent assigned to follow them kept his distance, but they felt his presence.

It was dark when Michael and Karen made their way back to the house. They ate dinner in the den in silence, wondering what came next and knowing, deep down inside, that if the phantom wanted Michael dead, odds were he just might pull it off.

Michael thought about reaching out to Karen every time he looked at her face and their eyes met. He could see that she was worried for him, and it had been a long time since he'd seen that look in anybody's eye.

Karen was confused. She had made this phantom happen, but now she looked at Michael and questioned what was really important. She had wanted a phantom, a man who symbolized all that was wrong with the world. And what she had was Michael, a man who seemed to represent all that was good.

When Michael joined Karen for breakfast the next morning, he was surprised to find that Allen had arrived, having made the long drive from Washington to learn the status of the investigation. Allen wanted to talk. He wanted to ask questions, but he met with a sad silence. Only when one of Garrett's agents stepped into the breakfast room to request a meeting did the threesome take any notice of each other.

When they gathered in the den after breakfast, Garrett was on the telephone. Finally he stood and walked to the center of the room, where he studied the faces before him. Michael and Karen sat beside each other on the sofa, leaving Allen a nearby chair. The aide moved to the far corner, dragging another chair over for Garrett and placing it so that he would be in direct line with his audience of three.

Garrett was uneasy. "The situation is getting pretty intense," he began. "I think we all know that. Agent Travers will be staying in Chicago, at least for a few days, to see if he can find any leads. We know the call to Michael at O'Hare was placed from the city. The goddamn call was placed from right inside the airport, and we haven't got a clue where he went after that."

There was a tap at the door, and Mrs. Patterson entered with a tray, bearing a pot of coffee, cups, and saucers. Garrett took advantage of the well-timed interruption to put his emotions in check while Michael poured a cup for everybody.

Garrett started again, this time taking a different tack.

"The situation is that Michael is out of it. Regardless of what this psycho demands next, Michael, you won't be doing what he says. We won't let him jerk our chain anymore. He'll call, we're certain of that, but there will be no more direct involvement." He stopped to see what effect he was having. On the surface, at least, the three seemed very willing to leave things to the professionals.

"We have no leads on where he is," he continued, grimacing at just how little they did have. "We've been running a lot of stuff through the computer. The same data you used—airline, motel, and car reservations. But we're getting back nothing. He apparently has a new list of names to use."

"He's not using the clinic names?" Karen asked.

"No. Since the car bombing in Boston, none of the names has been used anywhere. He had a rental car in Boston that morning, turned it in at the airport, and since then he has disappeared. We cannot find any of the names on anything. We don't know how he's moving around, but he's probably got a backup list—names that could come from anywhere. There's no way to check them all, even if we knew what they were."

"What about Chicago this time?" Michael asked.

Garrett sighed.

"Nothing. Travers knows which pay phone he used. We even have the usual description—he's tall, handsome and well-dressed—the same stuff we've gotten before, but it all adds up to zero. We even found a witness who saw him leave the airport, but once he walked out the door—nothing. He could be anywhere."

"What about car rentals? If his past is any indication, he probably rented a car from O'Hare?" Michael asked it as a question.

"Do you have any idea how many cars are rented at O'Hare in a given day?" Garrett snapped. Then struggling to regain control of his emotions he added, "Again. We're checking everything. So far, nothing has turned up."

"What about his profile?" Karen asked. "Is there anything new in that area?"

"You should know that better than any of us, Dr. Daniels." Garrett's voice was again showing strain. "We've profiled the son-of-a-bitch up one side and down the other. He doesn't profile. He fits everything. And he fits nothing. He's an absolute fucking freak."

They sat for a few minutes in silence. Karen finally stood to refill her cup of coffee. She brought the pot back to the sofa to freshen everybody's cup. They had hardly been touched, but at least it gave her something to do.

"What do we do now?" Michael asked.

This was the question Garrett hated most. He didn't know what came next. "Unfortunately, Michael, you're still our best lead. We're certain he'll be calling again. We don't know when, or from where. We've alerted every FBI office in the country to be on standby. Police departments in every state are ready. They know what we're up against, and they're ready to respond at a minute's notice. All we need now is to know where he is."

"And you expect to find that next time he calls?"

"If he calls, we've got a location. There's no way around it if he's calling long distance. The number called and the number from which the call is placed are fed into a computer automatically as part of the billing cycle. We can have a location, and even a damned phone number within a few minutes. And that's regardless of how long he talks."

"It's just a matter of getting there before he leaves?"

Garrett winced. "Yes."

Michael stared at the agent, then looked at Allen, who had been sitting silent, uneasy in his stiff chair. The meaning was clear. The chances weren't good.

"What are we going to do about the media?" Allen asked.

"That's another tough one," Garrett admitted. "We're trying to keep this thing as quiet as possible, but the media boys are crawling all over our backs, and they all saw the *Midnight Express*. They know we're looking for a phantom. They just don't know the extent of what we're dealing with."

Garrett took a break to sip his coffee, and everybody in the room took it as a sign to do the same. Cups rattled in saucers, and then everything became quiet.

"We're trying to handle everything out of Washington so we keep everybody away from here," Garrett continued. "And Patterson is helping us with the phones here. He transfers personal calls to a second line, and basically insists that everybody else get off immediately. We have an agent there to back him up if anybody gets stubborn. A matter of official business. The local sheriff's department has people at the gate to keep reporters away from Manning Hall, and since nobody but Allen at Media Associates knows anything about what is happening, the calls to them are coming up with blanks. We'll handle the rest out of press conferences in Washington."

Michael was beginning to feel a tightness in his chest.

"Does that mean we're trapped here?"

"Not trapped, exactly, but yes. Until we catch the son-of-a-bitch, you've got to stay under wraps. We would appreciate it if Mr. Collins would return to Washington as soon as possible and not return to the house until . . . until this thing is over. Dr. Daniels will stay here to help us sort through the psychological profile if and when he gives us any new clues."

Allen started to say something, but they all realized what Garrett was saying. He didn't want to give the phantom any more targets than was absolutely necessary. Allen was being dismissed from the list.

There was not much more to say. War had been declared. The phantom was taking them all on, and somehow the advantage in numbers didn't make any of them feel very comfortable.

"One more thing," Michael said. "What do we do if he calls and tells me to go somewhere? What then?"

Garrett stood up, taking his cup of coffee with him. He placed the cup gently on the tray, thinking.

"We've been talking over that very situation for the past twelve hours. We all agree that we simply cannot walk into any more uncontrolled situations. It's too dangerous. If he wants you to do something, you say no. You tell him he isn't playing fair, so you won't play."

Driving into Washington, the phantom felt good. It was a beautiful day, and the traffic heading up Interstate 95 to the Fourteenth Street exit seemed to flow with a rare kindness. Cars were even slowing down to let him change lanes when he signaled.

He decided to circle the Mall, turning at the Washington Monument and moving down past the Smithsonian Institution castle and the strange roundness of the Hirshhorn Museum. Proof of just how nice a day it was came when a parking space opened up in front of him just as the Hirshhorn came into view.

Michael Manning would have to wait. A parking space was too good to pass up. He pulled into the space and took a brisk walk through the Hirshhorn Sculpture Garden. He hadn't been to Washington in a long time, not for anything as casual as viewing art, and the sculpture garden was something new.

He tried to forget Michael for a few moments, but he was never entirely successful. He missed Michael almost as if he were a long lost brother. He ached to hear Michael's voice on the phone. He wondered how easy it would be to upset Michael's balance. He wondered what he could do that would really shake things up.

And still, he didn't have an answer. He glared at a nude figure by Rodin and pondered the process of the imagination. Why couldn't he think? Why couldn't he come up with anything that was good enough for Mikey?

Following the morning meeting at Manning Hall, Allen Collins abruptly said he would keep in touch by phone and departed for Washington. Quince Garrett returned to the office command post, taking his aide with him and leaving Michael and Karen alone in the den.

"What do you think is going to happen?" Michael finally asked.

"I don't know." Karen's voice was small. "That's what scares me. I have no idea what he might be capable of doing."

"Are you .. ."

"Yes. I'm afraid . . . afraid for all of us. I believe he may be smarter, or at least more determined, than any of us can realize."

"I'm sorry we started all of this," Michael said. "I wish we had just left it alone. We didn't need to know."

Karen looked at Michael carefully. Sometimes he looked so young, but this morning, hair messed and in need of a shave, he looked surprisingly mature.

"You don't mean that," she said. "You had to know, and I had to know. And it isn't over yet. When all is said and done, it's still going to be us against him. I can't give you any psychological reasoning for it, but I feel it. This whole thing is between him and you, him and us. He's not going to let it end any other way."

Michael turned to look at the doctor. There were tears in her eyes, and she was visibly trembling.

"Do I have any chance at all?" he asked.

"I don't know."

Michael reached out to wipe a tear away from her cheek, and she took his hand.

"Michael, please hold me."

And Michael moved closer. He put his arms around her, and he held her close.

TWELVE

The waiting was toughest on Michael. He was the odd player that neither team wanted, an embarrassment who stood on the sidelines and kept meaningless statistics during a tie game.

Karen went to Quantico to work with a team of psychologists from the FBI Academy's Behavioral Sciences Unit. They went over all the known facts, the taped telephone conversations, and a growing list of murders now linked to the phantom's known aliases. They profiled and re-profiled the insanity of the man, but they got nowhere. He was capable of doing anything, anywhere, to anyone. It was as simple as that.

Quince Garrett had become moody. He was a field man, and the days of waiting at Manning Hall were driving him crazy. He stayed only because he was so sure the phantom would have called by now, and this hope remained the best bet.

Bill Travers was still in Chicago, trying to discover how a man disappears from the face of the earth. If he could understand how the psycho had gotten out of Chicago maybe it would be helpful if he ever got another shot.

Manning Hall was in the care of eight agents who moved quietly through the house on rotating shifts, and Michael

wandered the estate making up stories for each of them. At
least it offered a few minutes of escape from the thoughts
about the phantom. Where was he? Why had he insisted that
he and Michael were alike, and that they shared so much?
What did this psychopathic killer want, and how could he use
it, how could he get at the thing that had caused so much
pain? He even tried to imagine a young boy growing up, a
boy not unlike himself, except that this child had a mean
streak. Michael gave himself headaches imagining the things
that must have happened to a child to make him turn out
like the phantom.

Michael volunteered to carry sandwiches and iced tea to
the front gate, where the county sheriff's unit was stationed,
but even for this he had to have an escort. He tried taking
walks, but found it difficult to relax while a stranger in coat
and tie watched the horizon for any sudden movement.

Mostly, Michael swam laps in the pool, pounding the water
while he replayed the telephone calls over and over, wondering
if there was anything he could have done, anything he might
have said that would have made a difference. There were no
answers. Only questions. And the certainty that something
horrible was going to happen.

A stack of newspapers was delivered to the house each
morning and afternoon. The stories about the phantom killer
made Michael question the family profession of journalism. It
was all guesswork and shaky sources. After the *Washington Post*
had run an article stating that Michael and the phantom talked
on the phone once a day, newspapers across the country picked
up the story as gospel.

The phantom had no name, but everybody had a theory.
Several newspapers dragged up local stories about shadowy
figures and strange murders in the community, convinced
they'd found a link to the mysterious killer who was stalking
the country. Several even went so far as to run photographs
of people who had been cleared of murder charges in the
past, convinced that these people, simply because they had
disappeared after their trials, had become the phantom.

When he wasn't reading the newspapers or swimming frantic
laps, Michael was drawn to the room where his father had
died. It was almost empty now. All of the medical gear

was gone. The bed had been cleared and remade with a colorful comforter. There was something soothing in the quiet of the room, and in that peace Michael hoped for some of his father's strength.

The phantom was standing in line for the buffet breakfast at the Watergate Hotel when the solution suddenly came to him.

He was listening carefully to the proposals and counter proposals exchanged by two attorneys in front of him as they spooned scrambled eggs onto their plates. They were discussing high-level corporate merger possibilities that were far beyond his comprehension, but then one of the two moved down the line, picked up a biscuit, and turned to the other.

"Listen, it's simple," the attorney said. "There are no rules in something like this. Why don't you just wait and see what he does? You can always take action later if he doesn't do exactly what you want. And if it really gets bad, you can get tough. You can always send in a troubleshooter."

That was it. It was that simple. He had become so obsessed with trying to find a suitable "event" for Michael that he'd lost track of the most important thing. There were no rules. At least there were none until he made them. And at that very moment he knew what he was going to do.

He paid for his breakfast and moved to a table far away from the crowd. He felt as if he hadn't eaten for days. The warm blend of smells—eggs, sausage, toast—was like nectar from the gods, and he plunged into his meal with an intensity that drew stares from all who glanced his way. For once in his life, he didn't mind being noticed.

He ate with abandon. Once his appetite was sated, he drew out a leisurely third cup of coffee while he completed his plan. It was a gamble. There were so many things that would have to fall perfectly into place, so many things that could go wrong, but that wasn't important. It was the game. It was all that mattered.

He smiled, pleased with himself. As of the moment, he was on vacation. There were things to do, but there was nothing that couldn't wait. He deserved a treat. He'd spend the day at the National Gallery, perhaps take an afternoon stroll through

Georgetown, and for the evening there was the Kennedy
Center. The American Ballet Theater was presenting "Don
Quixote," one of his favorites.

When Karen Daniels returned from Quantico, it had been
five days since they'd last heard from the phantom. She was
delivered by an unmarked FBI car, now the only visitors to
Manning Hall, and she was exhausted, drained by the endless
sessions with the FBI Academy shrinks. Nothing had been
accomplished. Their phantom, they had concluded, was capable of anything. And they'd echoed what Garrett and Travers already knew—that he was unstoppable unless someone
happened to come across him in the act.

As exhausted as she was, Karen could see immediately that
things were bad at Manning Hall. She stopped in the kitchen
for a glass of Mrs. Patterson's lemonade and to get a report
on how everybody was holding up under the pressure.

She didn't like what she heard. Michael was moping around
the house, not speaking to anyone. He hadn't shaved, and he
was only eating when Ginny insisted. Karen first tried to
comfort Mrs. Patterson, then she hunted down the agent in
charge—Garrett was off on some unknown errand—to discuss
procedures. The agent was not happy with her request.

"My orders are to keep Mr. Manning in sight at all times,"
he explained. "We let him go to the pool, with proper escort,
and we've offered to escort him on walks as well. That's the
best I can do."

"But don't you see," Karen insisted. "What he needs is to
get away from your people. And it's a safe bet our phantom
is nowhere near here. The one thing we do know is that our
crazy has a lot more games to play before he makes any move
to kill Michael. You can take my word for it. He won't be
trying anything at Manning Hall. He's too smart for that."

"I'll have to get clearance."

"You do that. And in the meantime I'm going to get Mrs.
Patterson to pack us a nice lunch."

She found Michael standing at the large window in his
father's room, looking out at the green hills of the estate.

"Father used to love this view," Michael said when he
realized someone had entered the room. He didn't turn to

see who it was. "This time of year the sun goes down just over those hills." He pointed off into the distance. "He would often leave whatever he was doing, even get up from dinner, to come up here and watch the sunset. He liked little things like that. Most people didn't know him, but he was really a tender man."

"Michael, it's me."

"Karen—hi." Michael turned from the window. "How was Quantico? Did you learn anything?"

"Things were hectic, and no, there's no news. But more than a hundred agents are working on the case, and I'm sure they'll have something soon. We just have to relax and leave it in their hands."

She tried to sound happy, but it wasn't easy while looking into Michael's sad face. His eyes were bloodshot, and he seemed to have aged ten years. She walked over and put an arm around him.

"Guess what? We're going on a picnic."

Michael looked disconcerted. "Have you cleared it . . ."

"I've told them we're going out on the grounds."

"Are they giving us an escort?"

"No escort, Michael. We're safe here. We'll just walk out and find a nice spot up in the hills. What do you say?"

Michael gave the invitation unwarranted consideration. Then he grimaced in what she realized was an effort to smile.

"Okay," he said. "If you're sure it'll be all right."

Michael was tense as they strolled. They found a secluded place to picnic, and when they had eaten he remained quiet, lying back on the blanket soaking up the sun like a prisoner given a day off for good behavior. Karen was about to give up trying to make conversation when he finally spoke, but his choice of subject caught her by surprise.

"I've been thinking about you, wondering what might have happened if we'd met—I don't know, if we'd met in a situation that wasn't quite so crazy."

Karen picked her words carefully. She didn't know what games Michael's mind had been playing in his solitude, nor did she know what games she'd been playing in her own loneliness. She'd thought a lot about Michael, and she hid behind the careful words of her background.

"We've become very close in a very short time," she finally said. "I don't think I could have gotten through all this without you being here. A friend. Someone outside of the profession to talk to."

Michael looked up at her from where he lay on the picnic blanket. "I've been wandering around for a lot of years, trying to get away from who I am. Somehow I feel you've been doing the same."

"I see what you mean."

"No," he finally said. "I don't mean that the way it sounds. When we first met . . ." he paused. "I guess I seem pretty childish to you . . . I mean you've settled down and accomplished things while me, I've been running all over Europe with no responsibilities. Nothing I have to do."

"It sounds lonely."

"That's what I've been thinking. I mean I know a lot of people, but I've avoided anything close. I've kept my distance from everybody . . . my father wasn't the only one. I guess I've seen too many marriages . . . too many relationships that get in the way and mess up people's lives. At least that's what I tell myself . . . that I have some special goal in life and even if I don't know what it is, anybody—anybody special would just get in the way, keep me from getting the job done."

Karen sighed, wondering how he had seen so clearly into the way she thought.

"Maybe, maybe when this is all over we should talk about it."

Michael faded away with his own thoughts. "Yeah. Maybe we should. But this being lonely. I mean I think about the phantom, too. I can't get him out of my mind. He has to be very lonely, and I keep trying to understand why he would do these things, and I can't make an answer fit. I can't find any logic in killing people—strangers—just as some kind of game."

Karen sighed. She still had to be careful, but Michael was ready to talk about the phantom, and that was a big step.

"Our phantom is very complex. He's dealing with the traumas of his childhood the only way he knows. There could be physical causes, but even if there aren't, these killings are apparently what he feels he needs. He was perhaps beaten, probably made to feel worthless. And murder—or more specifically the control and careful planning of the whole murder scenario, plus the success he feels after making it happen— these things came to him as a salvation from the only life he'd ever known."

Michael looked at her, trying to understand.

"He does it well," she continued. "He found something he can do perhaps better than anyone else. Once he'd killed his grandmother, and obviously gotten away with it, he dedicated himself to this. Murder became his vocation. His art. He's an addict, and murder is his fix."

Michael nodded, the words confirming the theories he'd considered over the past few days, but there had to be more.

"But why has he focused on me?" Michael asked. "It doesn't make any sense. I mean, if he's been killing for so long, why hasn't he done this before? He's taking a lot of chances, and he really hasn't tried to harm me—just scare me."

"That's what we've been talking about for the past few days," Karen explained, moving closer to Michael. "For him, murder is a creative act. He loves it. He loves the control, the imagination. But we do believe he's also very lonely. He's been roaming the country for years, apparently never staying in any one place for more than a few days. And then, when he discovered that you had found him, all of that changed. You became a challenge, but it has gone farther than that. You have become his equal, and in some bizarre way that makes you his friend. I believe he sees in you the man he might have become if he hadn't been deformed."

Karen tried to find in Michael's sad eyes an understanding of what she was trying to say. "It's pitiful, Michael, but you're the closest thing he has to family."

Michael held her tightly. He didn't want to let go. "I wonder if he realizes how lonely I've been. I wonder if he knows that all of us—the ones trying to catch him—are probably just as misunderstood and just as uncertain as he is."

Karen held Michael tighter and tighter as he spoke. She wanted to cry, thinking about getting the job done when it didn't seem all that important. When holding Michael was all that seemed important.

It was not clear who moved first. They turned together, and they kissed. They had a need, and with the crowd at Manning Hall, the picnic blanket was probably as much privacy as they'd ever find. They undressed each other gently, but they made love with desperation. And for a few moments they both escaped the phantom and found something they'd lost a long time before.

The strip show was pathetic. The woman dancing on the bar was built, but her large, drooping tits showed deep blue veins as she swung them from side to side, and her hairy legs were covered with small blemishes and scars, the combined result of bad hygiene and too many off-stage tricks against alley walls. It was just about what he had expected from the smallest of the seedy bars along Fourteenth Street, a half block from the small park that an assortment of D.C. junkies called home.

He ordered a beer, and gradually his eyes adjusted to the gloom. He was surprised to find himself getting an erection as he watched the woman's naked body gyrate through her methodical routine. It had been a long time since he'd been with a woman, and perhaps that was another thing he'd have to take care of before this vacation ended. But not now, and not here.

He had come to the bar on a mission, and over the next bottle of beer he assessed everybody in the place. Men looking to get laid learn to pick available women. Others can spot a hooker from four blocks away. Homosexuals can always find their own kind, and those who wander the fringes of kinkiness acquire certain mannerisms that attract others of the same persuasion.

The stranger, however, was looking for something special. The man he wanted was sitting alone in a booth against the far wall. He was a junkie, unshaven, his clothes shapeless rags hanging over a body that hadn't seen a decent meal in months. And he was sniffing, badly in need of a fix. But what caught the stranger's attention, what he could see from across the bar, was a cold, black emptiness in the man's eyes. They were the eyes of a madman. To those eyes everyone was a victim.

To those eyes people were worth only what they could do
for him.

Ordering two more bottles of beer, the handsome stranger
walked across the room. He stood at the end of the table and
watched the junkie run a filthy hand across the stiff whiskers
of his chin and down over his throat as if trying to force
himself to swallow. The junkie was perhaps two hours from
the panic stage.

"Here," the stranger said. "This will quench that dry throat."
He pushed a bottle across the table. "Okay if I sit down?"

The junkie looked up at him with black, bottomless eyes
while he wrapped a hand around the bottle and tilted it to
his mouth. Some of the beer ran down across his chin, but
he did nothing to stop it.

"I ain't no queer, mister. You lookin' for a queer, you
better keep away from me."

The stranger gave a casual laugh and slipped into the booth
on the opposite side of the table. "No problem," he said.
"I'm not a queer. I'm just looking for somebody who could
use a few bucks. Maybe a lot of bucks."

The two men stared at each other across the table. The
junkie tilted his head back and finished off the bottle of beer,
then slid roughly across the seat and tried to stand.

The stranger reached out a strong hand and pulled the
junkie back into the booth. "Wait a minute, buddy. Give me
a chance."

"I ain't no buddy of yours, mister."

He held tight to the junkie's arm with one hand while
reaching inside his jacket with the other. When he brought
the hand out of his pocket it held a small cellophane packet.
He slid the junkie's salvation across the table.

"How about now? Are we buddies yet?"

The junkie stared at the packet. He began to rock, excitedly,
back and forth in the booth.

"What I got to do for that?"

"Let's call it a present. Why don't you slip in the back and
take care of yourself. You take care of business, and then
we'll talk. I'll wait here."

The junkie reached hesitantly for the packet and held it
tightly in his hand. His cold, dark eyes never left the stranger's

face, but his knees began to tremble. He could almost feel the fix in his veins just by holding it in his hand.

The phantom released his grip, but just as the junkie was about to stand he jerked him back into the seat.

"Now that we're friends, I'm sure you'll come back to talk with me after you fix yourself."

The junkie's eyes turned blacker, but the stranger smiled.

"If you aren't back out here in twenty minutes I'll come looking for you." His grip on the junkie's arm tightened. "And you wouldn't like that. I'm a mean son of a bitch, and you wouldn't like that at all."

The junkie tried to stare the stranger down, but the grip on his arm became painful and his eyes betrayed a sudden fear. He glanced around to see if they were attracting attention, but this was a place where people came to mind their own business.

"I'll be back," he said, nervously, as the grip on his arm relaxed. "Folks call me Artie. I won't ask your name, but I'll come back. Just give me a few minutes with the stuff."

The phantom let go. He watched the man stumble through the door to the bathrooms, then he turned his attention to the new stripper. She wasn't so bad. Her body was tight, the tits small but erect. He watched her sway and counted the minutes.

Fifteen minutes later, Artie walked back to the table, standing tall, with fresh flecks of fire in the black void of his wide-eyed stare. He sat opposite the man who'd made him feel good, and he held his back straight.

"People sometimes call me Houdini. Here," the stranger said, pushing another packet of white powder across the table. "Why don't you hold this for later."

The junkie stared at him in disbelief and the packet disappeared below the table.

"There's plenty more where that came from," Houdini said with a happy grin. "There's plenty more. And also maybe five thousand dollars. How does that sound?"

Artie kept his eyes on the table while his fingers destroyed the label on his bottle of beer. When he looked up his fist gripped the bottle, and his eyes had the power. The eyes were empty of any feeling except hate for anything that would dare stand between him and five thousand dollars.

"Who do you want killed?" he asked.

THIRTEEN

Day nine. And still there was no word from the phantom. The weather became unmercifully hot, the mid-July Virginia humidity setting daily records, but at Manning Hall everyone lived under a growing cloud. He was out there, somewhere. No one thought for a moment he had disappeared from their lives, and the waiting was driving them all toward a private madness.

Karen stayed next to the pool, going through her notes for the thousandth time or simply reading and sunbathing, while Michael swam furious laps. There had been no more picnics. Both sensed that they didn't want to get any closer until something happened.

On the ninth day Garrett awakened with a premonition. He had started each day certain this would be the one, but this time it was different. He was sure the phantom was about to make a move. He quietly called together his team of agents and had them survey the perimeter of the estate looking for signs of anyone spying on the house. The report was negative, but he remained uneasy.

Garrett had begun to avoid the office and its silent telephones. He stopped by the room a few times, just to see that the phones were still there, but it was too depressing to stay for long. As the afternoon wore on, he felt sorry for the men working that shift. One was reclining on the sofa with a copy of *Playboy*, the other folding little airplanes out of typing paper and sailing them at a trashcan across the room. He'd obviously been at it for some time.

Garrett preferred to hang out in the kitchen. Since Ginny was continually fixing some meal, it was the one room where something was always happening. Moreover, the window above the sink offered a private view of Michael at the pool. Garrett could stand there, unseen, and try to figure what was going on in Michael's head. He didn't like the signs. Aside from the obvious frustration, Michael looked as if he were in training for a showdown, and Garrett didn't like to think what that might mean.

As he watched, Karen walked to the edge of the pool. It took her a few minutes to get Michael's attention, and while Garrett couldn't hear the words, he knew the scenario. She was trying to get Michael to come out of the pool. But he refused, shaking his head and plowing back through the water.

Karen walked away in frustration. Garrett watched until he saw the agent he'd assigned to her. The agent held back about twenty yards, just close enough to keep her in sight.

Michael swam to the edge of the pool and stopped, panting and wheezing while he watched them walk away. It was impossible to read the expression on his face. It was bland, unemotional, yet there was something hidden just below the surface.

Michael swam another lap, but his heart was no longer in it. He climbed from the pool, feeling a healthy ache in his shoulders. He flexed his arms, enjoying the tight feeling across his chest as he walked to the bath house behind the pool.

The bath house consisted of a central lounge with bath and dressing room facilities on either side. Michael entered the bathroom traditionally designated for men and walked to one of the three sinks. There were three toilet stalls along the opposite wall, and at one end of the room arches led to the showers and the communal sauna that joined with the women's dressing room on the other side.

Michael stepped to the center sink, threw water in his face and reached for a towel. He felt a chill breeze in the room, then . . .

"Mikey, please. Please don't turn around."

Michael froze at the sink, his hands under the water. He tried to glance in the mirror, to find the figure somewhere behind him, but there was nothing to see.

"Mikey, I've been waiting a long time. I've been camped out in these less than glorious surroundings for two days. I've watched you swimming, watched you pounding away at the water. And I've watched that sweet, sweet Dr. Daniels, too. Have you two got something going on I don't know about?"

Michael turned quickly, without thinking about the consequences. He had to see this phantom. He wanted to tear him apart with his bare hands. But he wasn't at all prepared for the calm face that stared back at him.

"Hi, Mikey." The man held a large revolver, but he seemed to be holding it without harmful intention.

"How did you get in here?"

The phantom laughed. It was that same clear, penetrating laugh from the telephone, and Michael stared, etching the face in his memory. The psycho did not look at all like Michael had expected. Yes, he was handsome, just as all the witnesses had indicated, but he also seemed so normal that it was disconcerting. He stood, at six feet, perhaps an inch taller than Michael. His eyes were blue, his hair a brown that was nearly black. And his manner, like the laugh, was one of self-content. The phantom seemed happy with himself, and that was one thing Michael certainly hadn't expected.

"Well, Mikey, what do you think? Do I live up to your expectations.?"

"No. Not at all. I mean—you're not what I had envisioned."

"Well, you're exactly the way I pictured you. And Manning Hall . . . wow! It's just what I thought it would be—Tara. Gone With the Wind. The whole bit. You folks sho' do live mighty fine, Mr. Mannin'."

Aside from the gun, the conversation seemed so casual that Michael had to shake himself to realize what was actually happening.

"Is this it?" he asked. "Is this when—when you kill me?"

The phantom looked down at the gun as if he'd forgotten it was there. And he laughed.

"No, Mikey—well, at least maybe no. I've been thinking about our telephone conversations and decided I had to meet you man to man. I'd thought you were going to be such a worthy opponent, but every time I've called you've sounded like such a wimp. Which are you, Mikey. Are you a wimp? Or are you a worthy opponent?"

Michael didn't try to answer.

"I figured the question might be too tough. You probably don't know if you'd have a chance against me or not. So I've decided on a little test."

Michael heard a noise in the storage room, but his hope that it might be one of the agents checking on him was shattered when a small, nasty-looking man stepped into the room. This man looked crazy, his eyes like those of a snake that sees its victim coming nearer and nearer. And in his right hand he carried a long-handled ax.

"Mikey, please, let me introduce you to my buddy. This is Artie."

The two men stared at each other across the room. Artie's expression never changed.

The phantom laughed. "Artie here is going to help me decide if you're a worthy opponent. You want a shot at me, then you've got to survive him."

The laugh grew louder, and then without another word the phantom was gone. He ducked into the storage room, shutting the door behind him and leaving Michael face to face with a madman and an ax.

Things happened so quickly that Michael barely saw Artie coming at him. A flash of movement, and the long, twin-bladed ax rose, poised to strike. The man was less than three feet away when Michael saw the ax swinging right at him. In that instant Michael knew he was dead. Pure instinct made him dive to the right. The swoosh of the blade whizzed past his ear, but it was the wooden handle that crashed into his left arm, the metal blade passing on to shatter the porcelain sink.

The arm was useless. After a mercifully brief, searing pain it went numb. The blow threw Michael off balance. He tried to grab the handle of the ax with his right hand, but the effort pushed his balance over the edge. He fell to the floor with a heavy thud.

The ax raised, and Michael scrambled out of the way. The blade cut a huge gash in the floor. The ax went up. Michael dodged again and crawled to his feet. This time the blade missed his left leg by inches.

The man with the ax stopped, not believing he'd missed again. His breathing was heavy. He stared at Michael with cold, black eyes, and then he started across the room again, this time swinging the ax from side to side. The blade whistled in the air, each swing getting closer to the target.

Michael backed against the wall, too busy keeping away from the blade to look for a way out. Then, with Michael boxed in a corner by the sinks, the ax was raised for the final blow.

Michael dived. He tried to grab the madman around the legs, but missed and rolled across the floor toward the toilet stalls. The ax whizzed over his head, tearing into one of the thin wooden partitions and sticking there.

Michael pushed himself up from the floor, aiming his right shoulder for the madman's chest. The hit was solid. He heard air blasted from lungs, then the crack of a rib and a scream, but the killer held tight to the ax.

Michael whipped about and sprang for the door to the yard. He glanced over his shoulder just in time to see the ax pulled free from the stall. He couldn't make it. Just as he got to the door he heard the ax slicing through air. He stepped aside as the blade ripped through the center of the door.

Michael spun back into the middle of the bathroom, tripping to the floor and twisting to face the next charge. He kicked, aiming for the groin, but he missed. His foot landed on the thigh with just enough force to throw the next ax swing off center. The blade landed inches from Michael's head.

He crawled away and climbed breathlessly to his feet as he got to the stalls. Holding a partition with his good arm, he kicked his right leg with all his might. The man with the ax turned to avoid the blow, and Michael's foot landed on the back of the leg. The leg collapsed, and the man fell.

Michael kicked again, but the man still held tightly to the ax. With both arms, Michael would have had a chance, but the left arm was still numb.

The man rolled away, jumping to his feet and growling in pain. He stared at Michael, shifting the handle of the ax from hand to hand, and then he charged.

Michael turned and fell, his head missing a toilet bowl by inches as the ax came down behind him. The porcelain shattered, sending water cascading across the room.

Michael scrambled out of the way and again came up on his feet. Water was flooding the room quickly. Michael charged again, using his good shoulder. Again he heard the moan of air blasted from lungs. This time the madman gave ground, and Michael pushed, ramming the man's back into the wall.

Michael was finished. He crashed into what was left of the bathroom door, tripping and falling into open space, taking most of the door with him. Someone screamed, and Michael twisted onto his back to look up into a crazed face. The ax was raised high in the air, and the cold, black eyes stared down into Michael's face.

Then came shots. Four of them, and they all seemed to be fired at once. The madman's chest exploded. He was jerked back off his feet and, taking the ax with him, crashed backwards through the shattered frame of the bathroom door.

Agents appeared from everywhere. Quince Garrett was there, Bill Travers, and the two agents who had been on telephone duty. They had formed an arc facing the door of the bath house, their guns drawn in firm, two-handed grips. It was Karen who had screamed as she came running up the path, her escort right behind her.

While Garrett and Karen helped Michael to his feet, ignoring his angry shout that the phantom was there, the other agents went to the dead body of the junkie. Travers came up with five one-hundred-dollar bills.

"That's not him," Michael screamed, pointing back into the pool house. "He's in there. He was here."

The agents found nothing there. The storage room window faced away from the house, out of sight. By the time they called in helicopters, the phantom had disappeared into the lush wooded terrain that surrounded Manning Hall.

Just as they all entered the French doors at the back of the house, two policemen from the gate came charging through the front door, dragging with them a taxi driver, a nervous balding man of about forty.

"He just showed up with this," one of the policemen said, holding out an envelope. Even from a distance the printing stood out clearly. In block letters was the single word—"Mikey."

Inside was a single sheet of Watergate Hotel stationery, supported by a piece of corrugated cardboard cut to the same size.

Written in the same block letters as the envelope, the letter read:

> Dear Mikey:
> If you're reading this, I must assume that you've sur-
> vived my little friend. I'm glad to hear that, but I'm still
> not sure. It's just a guess, but I'll bet you got some help
> from our friends of the FBI. I still can't decide if you're
> truly worthy of me. I'd hate for us to get into a little
> one-on-one action and find out you're not the man I
> thought you'd be. Are you ready for the fight of your
> life—or the fight of your death, whichever way you want
> to look at it? Do you want to take me on, Mikey? Do
> you want to come out and play? Oh, I do hope so. I do
> so very much hope you want to play. I need a new game.
>   Love,
>   Houdini

Michael dropped the letter on the table, and turned toward the taxi driver. He wanted to hit something, and he struggled to fight off the violent urge.

"Where is he?" Michael roared, stepping up into the frightened driver's face. "Tell me, damn it, where is he?"

Garrett and Travers reacted quickly, pulling Michael back. They walked him toward the den, and Karen met them at the door, taking Michael's arm and leading him into the privacy of the room. She glanced at Garrett, then closed the door.

Michael sat rigidly in one of the large chairs, his eyes cold, his breathing deep. Karen handed him a drink, which he held in both hands without knowing it was there. He stared just above the rim of the glass, seeing things that weren't in the room.

It was not easy for Karen to shift suddenly into being a psychologist again. She didn't know what to say as she sat down opposite Michael and looked into his unseeing eyes.

"Michael—please, look at me."

There was no immediate response, but the eyes made a subtle shift. Some of the blackness left. He recognized her voice.

"Michael, can't you see what he's trying to do? He's trying to get at you every way he can, and it's working. You can't let this happen. You've got to hold onto who you are. Don't let him manipulate you."

Michael's eyes grew softer as he listened to her talk, but he still wouldn't look at her. Every muscle in his face was tensed. His right cheek quivered with anger.

"Michael—talk to me?"

She waited. She could see he wanted to talk, but she wasn't prepared for the growl in Michael's voice when it came.

"I'm going to kill that son-of-a-bitch," he said, still not taking notice of her. "That's what he wants. There's going to be a showdown. Me and him. I'm going to kill him."

Karen walked to Michael and put her arms around him, being careful to avoid the deep blue bruise that showed through a rip in the sleeve of his shirt. She was surprised when he laid his head on her shoulder, and then she heard him crying, sobbing softly as he buried his head.

Michael was still shaky when they gathered in the dining room for a late dinner. He had spent two hours with an FBI artist helping to work up a drawing of the phantom, but the image on the paper never quite matched that which haunted his mind. He had showered and changed clothes, but when he came down from his room he insisted that he wasn't hungry. He wanted only coffee. He sat at the head of the table, embarrassed by his afternoon rampage, with Karen on one side, Garrett on the other.

The dining room doors were closed to hold down the noise, but they all still jumped every time the phone rang. It had been ringing at least once every few minutes with reporters on a relentless quest for details. Garrett had left the house for an hour to conduct a press conference at the county sheriff's office, telling no more than was absolutely necessary, and then he had rushed back to Manning Hall, leaving a trail of unanswered questions.

When Patterson showed up at the door to the dining room, they all knew what it meant. Michael was the first to move. He crashed his chair back against the wall and ran from the room. The agent on duty in the living room tried to hold the phone until everybody could get into position, but Michael quickly grabbed it out of his hand and roared into the mouthpiece.

"Where are you?"

There was silence.

"All right, asshole, don't get shy on me now. Where the hell are you?"

Then came the familiar laughter.

"Is this Mikey? Is this Mikey Manning, civilized human being, upstanding member of uppity-up Virginia society? Is this THE Mikey Manning?"

"All right, let's do it. Me and you. You name the place and the time. I'll be there."

There was a long pause. All eyes at Manning Hall were on Michael, but attention moved gradually to Garrett, who shifted it back to Michael. The two men stared at each other, the tension so thick it was difficult to breathe.

Laughter came from the phone. It filtered through the speakers, flooding the room with its insanity.

"Mikey . . . welcome aboard. I knew I could count on you."

"You make the rules. Just name the place and the time. I'll be there."

Michael and Garrett continued to stare each other down, and it was Garrett who turned away, busying himself with the agent who was tracking the call.

"But Mikey, it's not going to be easy. I mean your friends will never let you come out and play, not all by yourself."

"I don't care about that," Michael snapped. "You want a game, and I'm ready to play. This has nothing to do with them."

There was a long pause. No one breathed.

"By the way, Mikey, how did you and Artie get along?"

"He's dead."

"Oh, Mikey. I'm sorry to hear that."

"If you want the job done right, you'll just have to do it yourself."

There was another long pause. Karen turned away from the group and walked back toward the dining room. She didn't want to hear any more. Garrett was mesmerized by the change in Michael's attitude. He wondered if he was going to be able to handle two madmen at the same time.

"Are you sure this is Mikey Manning? I must apologize if I've got a wrong number."

"Quit stalling, asshole. You and me. It's simple. You still write the rules. Just name the place and the time. You've got something planned—now let's do it."

There was another long pause.

"I must admit, Mikey, that I have given it some thought. But I tell you, it won't be easy."

Everyone in the room froze, waiting for the phantom's new game.

"Mikey, are you sure this is what you want?"

"Oh yes," Michael growled. "I want it."

"Well, Mikey." There was a theatrical sigh. "Tell you what I'm going to do. I'm going to think about it real hard. I've got some ideas, but I'm going to have to play this hand close to the chest. I'm going to do something big. Watch the newspapers. You won't have any trouble finding it. And when it happens, you can just come and get me. I'll think of something interesting by the time you get there."

It took a few seconds for Michael to realize what the phantom was saying, but he was running on pure anger now. He didn't give a damn.

"Forget all that crap," Michael insisted. "Let's skip to the final game. We don't need anybody else. You and me."

"How could I possibly make that happen? Your friends would never allow it. They'll probably never let you out of Manning Hall again."

"I'll be there. Trust me."

This was the longest pause of all. Garrett finally looked up, meeting the cold, dark emptiness in Michael's eyes.

"No, Michael. I'm sorry. I can't do that. Not right now. You see I've already picked my victims. I've got it all worked out. I can deliver, and then it's up to you."

"But there's no need. I'm ready to play."

The laughter filled the room.

"Mikey, trust *me*. Our day will come, but for now this is really important to me. You just come get me when it's done."

"But—"

"Oh, and Quince. Agent Garrett? Are you there? I just wanted to let you know I'm calling from Atlanta. I flew down here on the 4:50 out of National. Nothing fancy. I'm in a phone booth at the airport. You won't catch me."

"Please—"

"No, Mikey. Now don't pout. This one is for you. Tomorrow is the day. I'm going to deliver something really special, and it's just for you."

The phone went dead.

FOURTEEN

"Forty-eight . . . forty-nine . . . fifty."

Wearing only jockey shorts, he completed his pushups, dropped his feet down off the edge of the bed, and gracefully coiled into a sitting position in front of the television. He was on the third floor of a small hotel on Chartres Street, in the French Quarter of New Orleans, and there was a summer breeze blowing through the opened French doors. It was Sunday morning, and the streets were quiet. The smell of lilacs was in the air.

The newscaster had a mild Southern accent, but the phantom paid very little attention to the commentary. He was watching for the third time the news footage of two men— one young and trim, the other middle-aged and pudgy— forcing their way through a crowd in front of the courthouse. Screamed obscenities were barely covered by the mass roar of the mob. Policemen, with determined looks on their faces, formed a corridor to the street, but one crying woman broke from the crowd and swung wildly at the older of the two men. A policeman hesitantly grabbed the woman around the waist and dragged her out of the way while the two men ran to waiting cars at the curb. The whole thing was over in less than thirty seconds. The events had taken place two days earlier, on Friday morning, following a trial that had attracted all three networks and a half dozen cable news stations.

On trial was Joseph "Joe Cool" Balducci, who had been running most of New Orleans's drug traffic, prostitution, and gambling for the past decade. A man who prided himself on the fact that he had never spent a night in jail.

Then the body of a sixteen-year-old girl, a runaway from Alabama, was found in a warehouse at the docks. She was naked, hanging upside down, her feet nailed to a support beam. Her hands were gone, ripped off at the wrists, and she had been slowly tortured to death. Every bone in her body was broken.

One of the lesser punks in Balducci's "family" was arrested, and after twenty-four hours of intense questioning he agreed to testify. He'd seen it all. The girl was a hooker who had tried to skip town with ten thousand dollars in gambling receipts. Balducci, he claimed, had administered the torture in person.

The trial, however, had turned into a farce. The witness chickened out on the stand and refused to confirm his earlier statements, insisting that he had been forced to sign the confession. The cattle prod found in Balducci's car, with his fingerprints and the girl's blood on it, was ruled inadmissible evidence due to an illegal search. The jury was out for eleven hours before returning with no verdict. The two men being escorted from the courthouse were the two jurors who had refused to find Balducci guilty. Rumor said they had been bought. Both men publicly denied any bribes, insisting that they couldn't find Balducci guilty on the basis of the legal evidence. Both refused police protection.

The phantom pulled a towel from the bed and wiped his face and chest. He took several deep breaths, then returned to the bed and picked up pad and pencil. Written on the pad were the name, address, the make of car, and family status of each juror. Both men lived in the New Orleans suburbs. Greg Mosby, the elder, was married, but his three grown children had families of their own. Robert Pratt, the younger man, was also married. He and his wife had sent their seven-year-old daughter to stay with an aunt in Florida until things calmed down. All of the information had come from news reports.

He chewed on the eraser end of the pencil while reading the information, poised to add anything he'd discovered from the most recent newscast. There was nothing to add. He had all that he needed.

Dropping the pad and pencil back on the bed, he removed his shorts and walked into the bathroom for a shower.

Bill Travers arrived at Atlanta International Airport at one o'clock Sunday morning, just four hours after the latest call to Michael Manning. Agents from the FBI office in Atlanta had already been at the airport for three hours, but they hadn't come up with anything interesting. Agents checking Atlanta motels had similar results.

They showed their drawing of the phantom to everyone, especially at car rental agencies, calling in all the clerks who had been on duty over the last twenty-four hours. They also questioned every taxi driver who regularly serviced the airport.

It was six o'clock Sunday morning when Travers called Manning Hall to talk with Quince Garrett.

"We've got three possibilities," Travers said without pre-liminaries. "Three different clerks, three different car agencies, and all three are convinced that our man rented a car from them last night."

Garrett had been up all night. He had a headache.

"That sounds promising" he said without enthusiasm.

"What else have we got?"

"Nothing."

Travers had a headache too.

"Okay, Quince, what now? There's got to be something we can do. Anything at your end?"

"Nothing. Zilch. Zero. The profile boys are taking a vacation on this one. Dr. Daniels says he's going to do it—not saying, I might add, what the IT is. And I sit here waiting for a madman to call and tell me what he's done. Do you want me to come down to Atlanta?"

"You'd better stay there," Travers said. "There's nothing to do here. We've got an APB out on all three cars. If he's in one of them, maybe we'll get lucky. If he's not, then we'll try again. After IT happens."

Garrett paused. In twenty-three years with the FBI he'd never known such frustration. Everything he wanted to say sounded wrong.

"I think we both need some sleep." It was the best he could come up with.

"I'll let you know as soon as I hear anything."

"Bill, what do you think? I mean do you really think he would call from the Atlanta airport and rent a car from the same place?"

"It's all we've got, Quince."

The house could have been in the suburbs of any city in the United States, and the phantom didn't think that was right. Cities have a distinctive character—certainly New Orleans was unique—but its suburbs were Anywhere, U.S.A. He was fed up with middle-class America. He had watched the home of Mr. and Mrs. Greg Mosby for two hours, and the bedroom lights on the upper level had been off for half that time. It was eleven o'clock on a Sunday evening, and the streets were quiet. He left his car parked more than a hundred yards from the Mosby house, and moved cautiously, aware of everything. He had seen children returning home earlier in the evening so he knew no neighborhood dogs would come out barking at a stranger. He was in complete control.

The solid, wooden front door was held by a dead-bolt. He could have gotten around the lock, but he didn't want to make any noise. Not yet, anyway. So he moved slowly to the back of the house. He found the main junction box for the telephone near the roof line at the rear corner. Balancing delicately on a metal lawn chair, he snipped the wires just above the spot where they disappeared into the house.

The rear door was also locked, but there were glass panels in the upper half of the door. Using a small glass cutter, he followed the line of the molding around the pane closest to the doorknob. He cut a small triangle in the upper right corner, tapped out the tiny piece of glass and used the opening to get a finger hold and pull the pane free.

The kitchen was clean almost to the point of obsession. Nothing was out of place. Even the shopping list and a few other notes were neatly organized on a magnetized board, held in place by little apples and oranges. The only sound was a duet played in electronic hums, the refrigerator supplying the bass while a wall clock drifted high as the tenor.

He gradually found his way around the lower level of the house. The dining room was as spotless as the kitchen, and the parqueted floor in the living room sparkled in the moonlight. He stepped quietly and unlocked the front door. Then he climbed the open staircase that reached up into the shadows at one end of the room. He found the expected double switch at the top of the steps and guessed that one would light the living room. Next he worked his way down a small hall to locate the door to the master bedroom.

Convinced he now knew the lay of the land, he returned to the living room. He removed a long-barreled .45-caliber revolver from inside his jacket, flipped off the safety, and began searching for the props that he needed. He selected a small, fluffy pillow from several on the sofa, then found a delicate ceramic figurine of a ballet dancer on one of the corner tables.

With these he again climbed the steps, checked the bedroom, then retraced his steps to the top of the staircase. From there he lofted the ceramic figure down the steps. He was already moving back down the hallway when the figurine shattered on the hard parqueted floor.

A light went on in the bedroom almost immediately. There was the muffled sound of voices, the hesitant rustle of covers, and a man grunting as he put on slippers and robe.

Light poured from the bedroom as Greg Mosby stepped into the hall, but the phantom was far enough away to remain in the shadows. Mosby shuffled to the top of the steps and peered into the darkness. He was reaching for the light switch when the phantom moved quickly and shoved the older man from behind.

There was nothing to grab. Mosby tumbled down the short flight of steps, his head bouncing off the wall twice as he tried to gain control. He landed face down at the bottom, his nose broken against the hard floor. He was trying to crawl to his feet when he felt pressure at the back of his neck.

The phantom placed the pillow gently at the nape, then pushed the barrel of the revolver into the center of the pillow at the base of the skull. The whole house shook with the blast of the single shot, but the pillow disguised the sound. The few neighbors who awakened later described the noise as a distant explosion or a rumble of thunder. Not even Mosby's wife was immediately aware of what had happened.

No lights came on as the phantom walked to his car and drove off to perform his next execution.

Bill Travers called Quince Garrett late Sunday evening.

"I believe we know the car he's driving. It's a red Ford Thunderbird. License number GCY-405."

"Are you sure?" Garrett asked.

"We found the other two cars this afternoon. Both check out as legitimate businessmen. We can't find the third one. I've questioned the clerk in detail. She's convinced it's the man in our drawing, and the rental is checked out for return to another location."

"Where's he taking it?"

"We don't know. He told the clerk he just wanted to see part of the South. He said he was on vacation and didn't know where he'd end up when he had to return to Boston and get back to work."

"He said Boston?"

"She's sure that's what he said. But it doesn't help us. He could be anywhere. He said today was the day, but he could have covered a lot of miles. He could be back in Virginia, in Florida, or even west—Louisiana or Texas."

Garrett felt a sudden rush of excitement and reached for the *Washington Post* beside his phone.

"New Orleans. I'll bet that's it. There's some hood who just got off for killing a teenage runaway. It's big news."

"Do you think he's going after the guy?"

Garrett quickly scanned the story about Joseph "Joe Cool" Balducci, then saw the names of the two jurors.

"The hood is Joe Balducci. He could go after him, or the jurors, the guys who hung the jury. Names are Mosby and

Pratt. The way this psycho's mind works he could go for them."

"What do you want to do?"

"You're closer, and we've got nothing to lose. Catch the next flight to New Orleans. I'll get in touch with our office there. We'll put out an APB on the car and get agents out to watch these people."

"Right. I'm on my way."

The Pratts were not at home. It was nearly midnight, and the phantom had been completely through the apartment. The dishwasher was empty, so he assumed they were out for dinner. The suitcases in the hall closet were a good sign. They hadn't packed for a trip. He decided to wait.

Robert and Sandra Pratt lived in a large suburban complex west of the city. The apartment was not as neat as the Mosby home, but the furnishings were more modern, with lots of chrome and glass. Parking for residents was directly in front of each building, with two spaces reserved for each apartment. An old Volkswagen, obviously a second car, occupied one of the Pratt spots. Visitor parking was off to the side.

He backed the red Thunderbird as close to the walkway as possible and played out the coming events in his mind. First he placed the big .45-caliber revolver in the glove compartment. From the trunk he removed a breech-loading, double-barreled shotgun. He loaded two shells of number four buckshot and decided to keep two extra shells in his pocket. He also slipped a small .32-caliber pistol in his waistband, then entered the apartment from the rear.

Leaving the sliding glass doors open, he moved into the living room and tried the light switch next to the front door. Several lamps came on. He flipped the switch off and moved through the maze of furniture, finding each lamp by touch and unscrewing the bulb. When he finished, the only working light was one on the ceiling just inside the entrance.

He slid the best of the living room chairs as far from the front door as possible, then checked the light switch once more to be sure the chair would remain in the dark. When all was ready he sat down to wait. He had not yet decided what he was going to do about Pratt's wife. She had done nothing wrong, and there was no reason to kill her. She would live, he decided. He would leave her screaming over the body. The blood from the shotgun blast should put her into shock. It would be enough to keep her well out of the way.

It was nearly two o'clock when headlights flooded the front of the apartment and a car pulled into the Pratt parking space. He could hear a man and woman laughing. They sounded drunk. The car door slammed, and a pair of high heels tripped at the first step. The laughter drew near.

The front door swung open slowly, but no one entered. Robert Pratt stepped back and was bowing in a gentlemanly gesture to his wife.

"Ta-da," he said, his head lowered almost to his knees. "Home at last, my lady."

Sandra Pratt giggled and started through the door, but then her husband reached around her waist and lifted her into his arms. He stepped into the darkness of the apartment and paused just inside the door, swaying from side to side while Sandra tried to find the light switch. They turned quickly toward the darkness when they didn't see the amount of light they expected.

"Keep quiet, and close the door." The phantom's voice seemed to echo from a dark cave.

"What is this?" Pratt demanded, lowering his wife until she stood on her own feet. As he spoke his eyes began adjusting to the darkness and he saw the barrel of the shotgun.

"Shut the door," the phantom demanded.

Pratt looked at his wife, then reluctantly reached behind him to close the door. They stood, side by side, staring at a figure they couldn't quite see.

"What do you want?" Sandra Pratt asked. Her voice trembled as she reached for her husband's hand.

The phantom sat silent and looked at the couple. They were Mr. and Mrs. America, perhaps not beautiful but certainly attractive in an All-American sort of way. Sandra started to cry and the illusion was broken. It was time to get it over with.

"Mrs. Pratt, Sandra. I wish you no harm. I'm here to see your husband. If you would please step aside."

Sandra looked at her husband, then slowly took a step closer to his side. Robert reached out and pulled her to him.

"Please, don't make this difficult."

Robert stared into the darkness. His eyes had adjusted, but he still couldn't quite see the man in the shadows. It was with something much keener than sight that he sensed the evil in his presence. He shuddered, took a deep breath, and pushed his wife away. She tried to resist, but then he slapped her and pushed harder, tears in his eyes.

The phantom was sitting only eight feet away. He stood, glanced behind him to make sure the sliding door was still open, with nothing in his path. Then he braced the shotgun against his shoulder and pulled the trigger.

Suddenly, everything went wrong. Just as he pulled the trigger there was a rush of movement. Sandra Pratt stepped in front of her husband. The shot caught her in the stomach, and the force of the blast threw her back off her feet. In that instant Robert Pratt charged into the room.

Before he could react, Pratt had hold of the barrel of the shotgun. Adrenaline and fear made Pratt strong. They wrestled for control, and it was all the phantom could do to hold on as he crashed backwards over the chair.

He tried to pull free, but the young executive was too strong. They rolled to the floor, still fighting for control, when for just an instant there was an opening. The phantom pushed with all his strength, and Robert's hands lost their grip.

The force of the shotgun blast blew Pratt five feet across the room. His back slammed against the hall wall, leaving a bloody smear as he slid to the floor next to his wife.

The phantom stood, gasping for air, then he ran on instinct for the open door. Lights were coming on in several of the nearby apartments as he tossed the shotgun through the open window of the car and jumped into the driver's seat. He could see apartment doors opening as he started the car. There was no need to be subtle. He jammed the car into gear and squealed tires out of the parking lot.

His head was pounding. Everybody had seen the red car. He'd have to get rid of it fast. Then he'd have to come up with another plan. He still had one more stop.

It was near three o'clock on Monday morning when Patrolman Scott Butterfield, making rounds near the New Orleans Baptist Theological Seminary, spotted a red Thunderbird with Georgia license plates. He drove around the block, and on the second pass saw the number. It was GCY-405.

Ten minutes later, Bill Travers stepped out of a patrol car and approached the red Thunderbird. He flinched when he looked past the open window. Lying across the back seat was a shotgun. The smell of burnt gunpowder was still strong. The glove compartment was open. And empty.

Joseph "Joe Cool" Balducci had been in jams before, but this was different. Awakened at five o'clock Monday morning with news of the executions, he broke out in the cold sweat of a man who knows he's in trouble for something he didn't do. An hour later Balducci, flanked by bodyguards in the back seat of a black Cadillac, left his river plantation east of Baton Rouge and beat the morning rush into New Orleans.

When Balducci panicked, everybody panicked. Even Charles P. Anderson, senior partner in the law firm of Anderson, Cable and Dominick. Both parties had decided it would be best for them to meet to discuss the situation before the office crowd arrived. And, if possible, before the police showed up.

The offices of Anderson, Cable and Dominick occupied the seventeenth and eighteenth floors of a restored building a few blocks north of the Superdome. The building had two sets of elevators, the first operating only to the sixteenth floor, where those wishing access to the prestigious law firm could buzz a secretary for clearance to use the second elevator that serviced only the sixteenth, seventeenth and eighteenth floors.

Balducci's driver pulled to a quick stop in a no parking zone in front of the building. There were a surprising number of people of the sidewalk, and the three passengers quickly surveyed the crowd before stepping from the car. The two bodyguards took their positions on either side of Balducci, their eyes darting from face to face in the crowd, then the three men walked into the building as if they were bolted together, all part of the same machine.

Two people waited in front of the elevator, a man and a woman. The doors opened, and the man stepped aside to allow the woman to enter first. The man was just about to follow when Balducci's machine approached. Balducci raised his hands, a benevolent sign that told the anxious bodyguards not to get physical with the innocent bystanders. He graciously insisted that the nervous man enter first.

The woman got off at the sixth floor, lowering her head as she moved past Joe Cool. The nervous man departed at the seventh floor, begging everyone's pardon as he left.

When the elevator stopped again at the eighth floor, one of the bodyguards reached inside his jacket. The doors opened to reveal a small man wearing wire-rimmed glasses. The man took one step into the elevator before looking up at the three passengers. Recognition flashed across his face, and he quickly apologized, stepping backwards into the hallway. The doors closed.

The elevator arrived at the sixteenth floor without further interruptions. The doors opened, and Balducci almost collided with the large attache case carried by a man who rushed past him to grab the elevator doors. The bodyguards growled, but Balducci raised his hand, calming them the way he would a pair of dogs. The man standing at the elevator looked horrified and bowed his head, begging forgiveness.

Balducci smiled, appreciating the fear that he caused. He apologized in a quiet voice, explaining that it was he who hadn't been watching where he was going. His two goons growled one last time, and turned their backs to walk away.

Then the phantom stepped into the elevator, opened the attache case with one hand and removed the large .45-caliber revolver with the other. He turned and fired four shots into Balducci's back from point blank range, dropped the gun, and watched the two bodyguards spinning in horror as the elevator doors closed.

FIFTEEN

Quince Garrett took a small private plane to New Orleans Monday morning. There wasn't much to do on the quick flight—no room to pace—and radio contact with New Orleans supplied one frustration after another. All the proper steps were being taken. A sketch of the phantom was being circulated to airports, train stations, bus terminals, car rental agencies, even to taxi services.

Bill Travers met Garrett at the Lakefront Airport with a sedan from the local FBI stable.

"We believe he's still in the city," Travers said, but when he saw Garrett's face perk up, he quickly amended his statement. "Perhaps believe is a little bit strong. There doesn't seem to be any way he could have gotten out unless he had a second car, and if he does have a second car, we can't find out where it came from."

"What's the situation with the media?"

Travers frowned. "We're checking everything. Local police are making the rounds of hotels. We've released the sketch to TV and newspapers—" He paused to slide an early afternoon edition of the newspaper across the seat, the stiff sketch of a handsome stranger covering a quarter of the front page.

"TV is also giving us good play. The creeps have begun calling in, but there hasn't been anything of substance."

"And the media?" Garrett insisted.

"I don't know that I like this plan of yours, and I don't believe the brass—"

"Have the media been alerted?" Garrett interrupted.

"It has been suggested that the head of the phantom investigation would be arriving this morning," Travers said. "It has also been suggested that he might be going first to the Mosby home to investigate the scene."

"Good," Garrett said. He didn't know what chance he had, but he felt that letting the phantom know he was in town might trigger some sort of reaction. Maybe he could divert the attention from Michael.

"Listen, Bill. Maybe this is crazy, but this is the closest we've gotten to him. We picked New Orleans. We were just a few minutes late. And if he's still in the city, or even if he isn't, he'll at least be aware that I'm here. He's waiting for us to show up. I sense it in my bones. And he will get in touch, maybe through the police station, television or even the FBI office."

"And then?"

"And then—maybe—we catch the son-of-a-bitch."

Michael and Karen had been left behind like family pets abandoned at summer vacation. They had watched Garrett leave just as it was getting light, and they had learned what little they could from the two agents who'd been left behind to babysit.

The morning newspapers had nothing on the events in New Orleans, and television coverage was spotty. It wasn't until the first of the afternoon editions arrived at Manning Hall that they learned the true scope of what had happened. They read the articles quietly, and then Karen suggested a walk around the pool. Even with the phantom in New Orleans, the agents on duty refused to let them go any farther on their own.

"This is not good," Karen said as soon as they were away from the house.

"I know," Michael said. "It's horrible. Four people dead, and for no reason."

"No," Karen said. "I don't think you understand what this means. He's got a plan—something big and obviously complicated. New Orleans is only the first step."

Michael didn't even want to think about it. "But Quince is down there. He'll find out what's happening."

Karen shook her head. She wasn't so sure. "I hope so, but . . . I don't know. New Orleans has been too simple . . . too obvious. I don't know what he's got in mind, but whatever it is it won't be down there."

"Shouldn't you tell Quince about this?"

"Tell him what?" Karen asked. "Tell him I don't trust Houdini? Tell him I'm worried? Tell him I'm scared to death?"

Michael took her in his arms and was surprised by the passion with which she returned his kiss. It lasted only a brief moment, a time when they could close their eyes and forget, but then Karen pulled back.

"It's still going to be him and you. I know that now more than ever," she said. "And I'm scared."

The phantom was so pumped up that he could hardly contain himself. He sat over a plate of hamburger and fries in a diner trying to act casual when all the time he felt like a Greek god who had come down from Mount Olympus to walk among mortal men. He was power. Television spoke of him with awe. Newspapers honored him. People lowered their voices when they spoke of the things he had done.

From his window seat, he could see the metal box of afternoon newspapers that sat at the curb, chained to a nearby telephone pole. Even from the distance he could see the picture of himself staring back across the sidewalk, and he was pleased with the likeness. It made his face a little fatter than it was, but otherwise it was close. Very close.

He almost laughed out loud. Several people in the diner turned to stare, but he didn't care. He continued to chuckle while he looked out into the broiling midday sun. Across the street was a small used-car lot, and he had spent most of the morning considering whether or not the dragnet had reached as far as the bald-headed man checking batteries in the lot.

He knew which car he wanted—the 1972 Comet, white with a black racing stripe. The left fender had a dent in it, but that was no problem.

His meal finished, he decided that it was now or never. He would know immediately if the man recognized him, and armed with this confidence he paid his check, left a tip, and darted across the highway, dodging cars like a matador.

He walked straight to the Comet, fondled the dented fender, then glanced in to read the odometer. It said sixty thousand miles, an obvious lie.

"Howdy." It was the bald-headed man. "Anybody out walking on a day like this certainly needs a car, and that one's a beauty."

The phantom looked serious, frowning at the fender, then he opened the passenger door and ran a hand over the bucket seat.

"Don't let that fender bother you. A hundred bucks and you can get that thing fixed so it'll look like new." The salesman laughed. "In fact, that little scratch is going to get you a real deal. I can let you have it for eleven hundred."

The phantom sneered as if the man was a fool. He slipped into the car and hoisted himself over onto the driver's side. The key was in the ignition. The engine roared to life, and the salesman looked through the open door, beaming like a proud father.

"I'll give you eight hundred. Cash."

A cold shadow fell over the salesman's smile. "A thousand, and that's the bottom line. Can't go no lower."

The phantom reached into his pocket and pulled out the folded bills he'd prepared in the restroom at the diner. He carefully counted the fifty-dollar bills onto the passenger seat. There were eighteen of them.

The salesman looked at the money arranged neatly to form a green fan. The two men shared a knowing smile. Then the salesman reached up and scratched his head.

"If you'll step this way I'll fill out the paperwork and have one of my boys pop a temporary tag on this beauty for you."

Forty-five minutes later, the phantom had a car registered in the name Emerson Underwood and was headed back into New Orleans. He could hear the tapping of a valve in the engine, and the windshield wipers only worked at half speed. He tried the radio and found that all five buttons were set for country music stations. He tried the dial. It was 1:30, and he had his choice of newscasts. He stopped turning when he heard the name Quinton Garrett. He listened to the latest news, then he looked for a telephone.

The arrival at the Mosby home went according to plan. Travers drove past the driveway, braking hard to attract the attention of photographers lounging on the lawn, then Garrett stepped from the car, acting most annoyed by the crowd. Travers came around from the driver's side of the car, and together the two men used their shoulders to plow a wide path through the waiting reporters.

They turned briefly when they reached the front door. "I'm sorry," Garrett shouted, "but there will be no statement at this time. We're dealing with a real sicko, and a press conference will be held later this afternoon at police headquarters. We will try to answer your questions at that time." He didn't wait for the roar of questions. He and Travers stepped past the policeman at the front door into the cool emptiness of the house.

Travers had already seen the taped silhouette at the bottom of the stairs. He gave Quince a chance to survey the surroundings. "He didn't worry about fingerprints this time. We've got good prints on the door handle, on the broken pieces of the figurine, and on both of the guns—the pistol used here and on Balducci and on the shotgun. No match yet, but at least it's something."

Garrett studied the room silently for fifteen minutes, and then they left.

"The other one didn't go so smoothly," Travers said as they rode to the Pratt apartment. "It's a real mess. Shotgun. And the woman apparently jumped in front of her husband. It's the only thing that makes any sense."

Another patrolman met them at the door of the Pratt apartment. There were no reporters here; they had been told where to be, had gotten what they were meant to get, and now they were off to their various television stations and news desks trying to milk it for all it was worth.

The apartment, so calm on the outside, was a bloody mess. Dried stains, more black than red, were everywhere. It started in the hallway, not only covering the floor but with splatters also on the walls and ceiling. It continued into the living room, spotting everything and forming two large puddles that had turned the blue carpet to purple. A chair was overturned, a table smashed. The tell-tale tape showed the twisted forms of two figures.

Garrett turned away from the blood-soaked room and found himself looking at a framed collage of photographs on the wall. There was a shot of the Pratts playing with their daughter in front of a Christmas tree. There were Easter baskets and picnic tables, the three of them smiling over a large slice of watermelon, and another of the couple kissing under a piece of mistletoe.

Travers was explaining the murder scenario when the telephone rang. The agents looked at one another, and the patrolman peered in from the front door.

"My watch commander said I shouldn't answer the phone," the young patrolman said. "But it's been ringing every ten minutes for the past hour."

Garrett grabbed the receiver.

"Who is this?" Garrett demanded.

"Who do you think it is?" a voice answered back. "And to whom do I have the pleasure of speaking?"

"This is Agent Quinton Garrett, Federal Bureau of Investigation. Please identify yourself."

"Quince, baby. At last. I've heard so much about you. And I, for one, think you fellas do a real bang-up job. It's great to hear the voice of The Man. Really great."

"Who is this?" Garrett demanded again.

"It's me, of course. Who-dini. Who were you expecting?"

Garrett froze. He'd known it was the psycho, but there was something in the voice—a pride, a sincere superiority—that had thrown him off, made him unsure.

"Hey Quince, baby. Don't go to sleep on me. Now where's my buddy, Mikey? Let me talk to him. Please?"

"He's not here," Garrett said, puzzled. The phantom obviously knew that Michael wasn't with him.

Then came the laugh, the same clear, mesmerizing laugh they had all come to know.

"I am truly, truly sorry to hear that." There was a pause. "Well, Quince, baby. I guess that means it's you and me."

"Okay, Houdini. That's more like it. It's me you've wanted to challenge all along, isn't it? And you've done what you said you were going to do. You said you were going to kill, and you've killed. You've made us look like a bunch of fools twiddling our thumbs while you spill blood all over the country. Now it's my turn."

There was a long pause. Garrett could feel the wheels turning, decisions being made.

"I never knew you felt so strongly—so personal about everything, Quince, baby." The wheels were still turning. The phantom was weighing the situation. "I know you think I'm an evil, disgusting person, but that woman . . ." he waited, giving Garrett plenty of time to view the taped silhouette where Sandra Pratt's body had fallen. "The woman was a mistake. I mean it was horrible. Poor Sandra, she just jumped out, and I'd already pulled the trigger. Believe me, Quince, I didn't want to kill her. The only thing she ever did wrong was to marry a jerk."

"You bastard."

The phantom sounded almost in tears, and Garrett couldn't make up his mind if he wanted to believe it or not.

"I deserve that. It's true. I get started, and I don't know when to stop. But Quince, you've got to believe me. The woman was a mistake. She killed herself."

"You wanted her to just stand there and watch you kill her husband?"

"What would you have done?" The mood suddenly changed. Now it was cold and bitter. "Come on, Quince, what would you have done? You're standing there with a shotgun staring. . . . You got any family, Quince?"

"I have a son."

"A son? Great. That's just wonderful. Let's say we're standing there and I've got this big old ugly shotgun aimed right at your son's face. I tell you I'm going to kill him, and you know I mean it. What do you do? Do you jump out in front of him and get yourself killed, too? Knowing damn well that I'm still going to kill your beloved as soon as I roll your body out of the way?"

Garrett didn't imagine his son—he hadn't seen him in five years—but in his place he saw Michael. He saw Michael Manning about to have his head blown off, and yes, he saw himself step in front to take the blast.

"I'd try to stop you," Garrett said, weakly. "You can be sure of that. I would do whatever it took to stop you."

There was a long pause. Garrett looked at Travers, and together they stood there, wondering what was going on at the other end of the line. They waited for the next move of the game.

"Quince, I'm sorry. I can't talk right now. I mean that woman and all these cops looking for me. It's just too much."

"What do you want?"

"I want to talk. Honestly. We need to talk. Please say you'll talk to me. Please."

"When?"

"Oh, Quince, thank you, thank you, thank you. Please stay there . . . at the apartment. It may take a while, but I'll call as soon as I can. I'll try to call tonight. If not, first thing in the morning. Things are a bit sticky for me right now. I have to pick my spots carefully, if you know what I mean."

"Yes," Garrett said, almost tasting victory. "I understand."

"Then you will wait for me? Please say you'll wait. I really do need to talk to you."

"I'll wait."

"Bless you, Quince. You're a good man. I'll call, I swear, as soon as I can, probably first thing in the morning."

Garrett heard the phone go dead. "He says to wait here. He'll call back when he feels safe . . . by morning."

"And you believe him?" Travers asked.

Garrett didn't answer right away, but he wanted to believe. "I'm beginning to see how his mind works. Now he wants to play a game with *me*. I can feel it in my bones. He'll call."

SIXTEEN

With the battle line moved to New Orleans, security at Manning Hall was suddenly relaxed. The police at the front gate were relieved, and there was even talk of disbanding the command post. Karen was the only one with a new agenda. Reports were being fed to Quantico on the New Orleans murders, and she was helping in the search for any detail that might trip up Houdini.

She was up early, anxious to examine the material at Quantico, and Michael accompanied her to the driveway. They shared a glass of orange juice while they waited for the FBI sedan. It felt cozy, standing arm in arm, almost like a married couple. And everybody at the house was being careful not to let on that they knew about the new sleeping arrangements that had started two nights ago.

"It shouldn't take long to go through the lab reports," Karen said as she finished off the juice and handed Michael the empty glass. "I should be back in time for dinner."

They kissed goodbye, then Karen climbed into the car, and it pulled away. Michael watched her go with a happy sigh.

"I know this is a silly question after all the time we've spent together," Michael said, turning to the agent left behind to guard him, "but have you got a name?"

"It's White," the young agent said with a smile. "Bernard White, but my friends call be Bubba."

"Well, Bubba," Michael said, "I've got a feeling this is going to be a good day, maybe even the day Quince catches this guy and we can get on with our lives. Why don't we go get ourselves a cup of coffee and you can tell me all about the FBI business."

Karen had become bored with the ride to Quantico. She figured this was probably her twentieth trip since moving into Manning Hall, and even the Virginia countryside had become uninteresting. The agent who was driving was a quiet one, but she thought she'd at least try to start a conversation.

"You're Agent Church, aren't you?"

"Yes, Ma'am."

"How long you figure this morning?"

"We should be at Quantico in an hour." Very official.

Karen sighed. She was just leaning back in the seat when the phone on the dashboard sounded. Agent Church picked it up, then handed it over the seat to Karen.

"Somebody's been trying to reach you at Quantico," he said. "Operations says it sounds urgent."

"This is Dr. Daniels. You have a call for me."

The operator seemed overly pleased to hear her voice. "Well, I'm sure glad we found you. This lady has been calling every five minutes. She's real upset."

Karen tensed. She took a deep breath, and she waited. Two more clicks, and a line opened on painful sobbing.

"This is Dr. Daniels. Who is this?"

The sobbing continued. The person on the other end of the phone was losing control and hyperventilating.

"This is Dr. Daniels," she repeated. "Now calm down and tell me who you are."

There was deep breathing. When the sobbing was finally under control, the voice was that of a young girl, perhaps a teenager. It was also the voice of somebody frightened to death.

"Dr. Daniels, please. You've got to help me. I've seen your name in the papers. I know the man you're looking for. I

know the psycho . . . the phantom, and he's going to kill me
. . ." She broke into more sobs.

Karen froze. Then she reached over and slapped Agent
Church on the shoulder, gesturing for him to turn on the car
speaker and pull to the side of the road. He looked at her,
puzzled, but obeyed.

"Where are you?" Karen asked the sobbing girl. "Please.
Tell me where you are. I can help."

"I've got to talk with you," the girl said between deep
breaths. "He called me this morning to tell me he's coming
back. He'll be here this evening, and I'm scared."

"I can help. Now, where are you? You've got to tell me
where you are. We can help."

"No." The voice on the other end was in a panic. "He
knows. He knows everything. You must come alone."

"Stay calm," Karen pleaded. "I can't do that. I can't come
alone, but I'll bring only one person with me. He'll be an
FBI agent, and he can protect you. But I can't help you unless
you tell me where you are. Please. Trust me. I can help."

The girl continued to whimper, but she seemed to have the
crying almost under control.

"Please," Karen pleaded. "Please. We'll come alone . . .
just me and one FBI agent. I promise. We can talk and decide
the best thing to do."

"Yes . . ." the girl gulped between sobs. "Please."

"Where? Tell me where."

"Yes," the girl said. "I'm at an abandoned farm. It used
to belong to my uncle. On Route 234 about ten miles west
of the Interstate. But you've got to hurry. He knows everything. If you're not here in fifteen minutes I'll have to leave.
I've got to get away from him."

"I'll be there," Karen promised.

The voice on the phone was now that of a little girl.

"You can't miss the place. There's a little motel and service
station, then there's just this dirt road off to the right. There's
an old wooden sign beside the road. The place used to be
called Goose Neck Farm."

"I'll be there in fifteen minutes," Karen said.

"Please. Please hurry."

Karen and Agent Church stared at each other, both realizing this could be the break they had been hoping for. Then Church grabbed the phone and called Manning Hall.

Bubba White took the call.

"We've got something, Bubba," Church shouted into the radio while he spun tires turning the sedan around on the narrow highway. "We got a patch from Quantico. A girl said she knows the phantom and she wants to meet. We need backup."

"Where?" White asked.

"A farm on Route 234, right there near the house. It's supposed to be off the road beside a service station and a motel. Place called Goose Neck . . ."

"I know the place," Michael interrupted. "It's just a few miles from here."

"We've got a time problem," Church interrupted. "The girl said she'd wait only fifteen minutes."

"We're on our way," White shouted.

Quince Garrett and Bill Travers, backed by a telephone team from the New Orleans office, waited in the Pratt apartment for over twelve hours. Just minutes after Karen received the frantic call from the girl, the Pratt phone finally rang.

Garrett answered on the second ring.

"Quince, baby, is that you?"

"What did you want to talk about?"

There was a pause. A chuckle. "I'll say one thing for you, Quince. You do get right to the heart of the matter."

"So, tell me. What do you want?"

"Well, Quince, baby. I've been giving this thing a lot of thought. You and Mikey have been talking mighty big lately . . . all this you-and-me crap. So I've been trying to come up with a little game. You know, man against man. That kind of stuff."

"And what have you decided?"

"Oh, Quince. I've come up with a good one. I hope you're going to appreciate the planning that went into this."

Garrett felt himself slipping. He thought he had reached a point where he could be calm and handle anything the psycho dreamed up, but his resolve weakened. What he felt now was a complete hatred, and an utter, inescapable fear.

"What'll it be?" He decided to tough it out. "Guns at twenty paces? Knives? How about hand to hand combat? We'll lock ourselves in a room and the winner goes free."

The phantom broke into one of his heartiest laughs.

"Now come on, Quince, be serious. It's been nearly impossible for me to get a face-to-face with Mikey. Trying to get one-on-one with you would be even more ridiculous. You travel with an army."

"I could make an exception for you."

"Hey, Quince, you're not in any cage. This thing can be over right now. All you've got to do is call it quits, and you're free. As a matter of fact, if you hang up right now, right this second, I'll promise never to contact you again. That'll be it. Over. No more calls, and that goes for Mikey too. He can get back to his fun with the Manning millions, and you can get back to shuffling papers. What do you say? Time is running out. Hang up. Now or never."

There was a long silence at both ends of the line.

"Can't do it, can you Quince? I didn't think so. As the Olympians would say, let the games begin."

"Enough bullshit. Just give me the rules."

"Quince, Quince, Quince. What am I going to do with you. I mean I let you call me names. I let you tap the phones and bring in all your FBI buddies to play with all their buttons and things, and still I get no respect. It's a real shame, Quince. In another lifetime . . ."

"Let's worry about this lifetime," Garrett interrupted.

"Good, Quince. That's good. This lifetime. That's very good, and it also has particular meaning this morning."

"Come on, bastard. Quit stalling."

"Okay, Quince, baby, here it is. Hope you've got your recorder going 'cause I'm only going to say this once."

"Ready."

"Okay. To begin with, every game must have a prize. Do you want to know what the prize is, Quince?"

"Yes."

"It's a grand prize. To the winner goes the lovely, the effervescent, the cruelly sensual and heart-stopping Karen Daniels, Doctor of Psychology and Associate Professor at the University of Virginia."

Garrett almost dropped the receiver. He turned to signal Travers, but the agent was already reaching for one of the phones.

"Quince, you still there? What do you think of the prize?"

"You don't want to do this. Let's keep it between you and me. She's no challenge for you, but trust me, I'm your match. Just give me a shot."

"But Quince, if I were going to do any you-and-me stuff it would be with Mikey. You're just a cop, but Mikey . . . well, he's special. In another lifetime, Mikey and I could probably have been good friends . . . just a couple of wealthy kids out for a good time. What do you think? You know him better than I do. Do you think he and I could have been buddies?"

"You asshole."

"But you . . . just listen to you, Quince. You're low life. You have no class. You're just a flatfoot with a federal badge. That's all. No, Quince. Anything personal in all this is going to be with Mikey. You remember that."

Travers was screaming into the other phone, but it was gibberish to Garrett. He didn't know what was being said, but he knew the word from Manning Hall wasn't good.

"Now listen to me, Quince. I figure the sides aren't very even. You've got half the Federal government on your side, plus all the men in blue, and I just have one little me. So I've given myself a little head start."

"What have you done?"

"Be patient, Quince. I've placed myself a bit closer to the playing field, so to speak. And I've also taken the liberty of sending your lovely friend on what you might call a wild goose chase. She's not at Manning Hall, and she's not at Quantico, either."

"Where is she?"

"Oh, Quince. I haven't got her. I don't want that much advantage. But I believe I can get her before you can find her. And finding her is only the beginning, Quince."

"Can't we talk about this. Please," Garrett begged.

"Quince. You're wasting time. Sweet Karen is out there somewhere, and she's all alone. On your mark, get set . . . Go!"

Agent Church and Karen found the dirt road exactly where the girl on the phone had said it would be. A weatherbeaten sign identified the place as Goose Neck Farm, but the land hadn't been worked for many years.

The house was not visible from the highway. The road disappeared over a small hill then followed a gradual curve around the edge of a wooded area before opening into a long straight section. Agent Church drove two hundred yards before they saw the small farmhouse and barn sitting in a clearing.

The house had once been painted white, but now the color was peeled away, the boards warped and twisting from the walls, exposing equally worn supports. Birds had nested in many of the openings.

A station wagon was parked near the front of the house, but nobody was in sight. Karen shivered as Church cut the engine. They got out of the car together, but no one came out to meet them.

"Hello. Anybody here?" Karen hollered, motioning for Church to wait.

The only response came from swarms of insects drawn to a new presence in the humid August heat. Gnats came to play in front of Karen's face. A dozen large grasshoppers soared through the air in all directions, waking up an assortment of other unseen things that crawled and hopped in the tall grass.

Still no one came. Karen walked to the front of the station wagon. The engine was still warm, making gentle popping sounds as it cooled in the shade of a rotting apple tree.

"Hello," she called again. "It's Karen Daniels. Is anybody here?"

There was a sound, and they both spun, Church reaching for his gun. A rabbit disappeared across the road into the thicket. A dog barked off in the distance.

Still there was no answer. Karen was becoming frightened. Part of her wanted to let Church go to the house first, but she knew it had to be her. The girl was probably hiding, too frightened to speak. Karen glanced back at Church, holding up a hand to tell him to stay put, then she tentatively stepped onto the rotting porch. Tattered curtains, black with dust, stared at her from the windows. Every panel of the screen door was ripped, and the frame hung tentatively from the upper hinge. The tilted roof seemed ready to close over her like the mouth of some giant beast.

"Hello!" she called again. "Hello! It's me. It's Dr. Daniels. Please say something. I want to help."

A silence haunted the house. A warm breeze swept across the porch, raising dust and a few scraps of yellowed newspaper. She tried to consider the psychology of her fear as she took another step and reached with a trembling hand for the doorknob.

She turned the handle and pushed. The door was stuck. It didn't budge. She glanced back at Church, shaking her head no, and she pushed again without success.

"Hello," she demanded. "Anybody there?"

She put a shoulder against the door and pushed again. The door came free, opening onto the musty smell of mildew and age. The only sound was the buzzing of flies as they reacted to the sudden breath of fresh air.

"Hello," she called again, embarrassed by her own hollow voice. She glanced back, making sure Church was still there, then she stepped into the house, feeling a sudden chill. Things weren't right. The flies were buzzing too loudly. She could feel a presence, and her belief in the teenage girl wavered. She looked back again, feeling some comfort that Church was still in sight.

She turned the corner, then tried to block out what she saw before her. She heard herself screaming. She collapsed to her knees, but the screaming wouldn't stop.

Karen had found what she was looking for. Hanging on the door to the kitchen was a teenage girl. Her hair was blond and stringy; her eyes, frozen open in death, had once been a powder blue. She was wearing only her panties, the rest of her clothes piled next to the door. What held her in place was a long strand of barbed wire. It was wrapped entirely around her body, cutting into the flesh of legs, arms, feet, hands, and across the soft expanses of white skin. One end was wrapped tightly around her throat, then looped over a nail placed high on the door. Blood was still oozing from the cuts in the neck, covering the body with a thick red that had drawn dozens of excited flies.

Karen was still bent forward, her arms wrapped across her stomach and her head almost to the floor. Then she heard a cold, breathless voice, and she knew her most horrible nightmare had come true.

"Dr. Daniels, I presume," he said, stepping behind her and placing a firm hand on her shoulder. "Allow me to introduce myself."

She scrambled from the hand, hearing that frightful laugh as she crawled away on hands and knees. She circled a table, then climbed to her feet and dashed for the front door. She got a glimpse of Church, lying beside the car, a large bloody spot soaking his white shirt from the collar down. And then a large shadow blocked out the sight.

The phantom stepped in front of her, gently closing the door behind him, and when Karen turned to get away he grabbed a handful of her hair and almost jerked her off her feet. With the easiest effort, he threw her against the wall, then placed a hand around her throat.

Her toes barely touched the floor, and she was choking, hanging helplessly in his grasp. She looked straight into a face contorted by a mocking smile, then she closed her eyes.

He stared into her face as he lowered her, willing her to open her eyes and acknowledge his big smile.

"The sweet Dr. Daniels, or may I call you Karen?" he asked. "I feel we've known each other for so long. I think I'll make it Karen. And you must call me Houdini. I like that."

Karen choked for breath and tried to think. She cautiously tested the strength in her legs, then kicked with her knee, catching the madman in the groin. She stared helplessly as he blinked and tightened his grip on her throat.

"Now that's dirty pool, sweet Karen," he said, shaking his head and gently rubbing his crotch with his free hand. "I had no idea you were the kind that would hit below the belt. Shame. Shame. I'll have to pay you back for that later, but if I've figured this right, I imagine Mikey and maybe a friend or two are getting pretty close by now."

Karen tried to kick again, but this time he turned and took the blow on the thigh. His grip tightened, and with his free right hand he slapped her across the face.

"Now we can do this the easy way, or we can do it the hard way. I don't plan to harm you. You're only the bait to draw Mikey out here. This is the end of the game, sweetie. Today, he dies."

Karen gazed into his face and felt herself fading again. She closed her eyes, and when the grip relaxed she tried to kick again, but he was too quick for her.

He lifted her off the floor, holding her against the wall with only his left hand pressed against her throat. He slapped her twice with his right hand, then threw her across the room like a toy doll. A cloud of dust blew up like a storm in the middle of the room, then her head slapped the floor with a thud and she blacked out.

He carried her down the rotted porch steps, past Agent Church, whose throat showed a gash of red blood, then dropped her face down across the hood of the station wagon. He left her there while he walked to the passenger side of the car, pulled open the door, and reached into the glove compartment. He slipped a new .45 into his belt, then he pulled out a syringe and removed the cap protecting the needle.

Karen slowly raised her head, but everything was a blur. She felt herself being lifted. A hand popped the front button on her jeans and lowered the zipper. Tears came to her eyes as she felt her jeans being tugged down over her hips, but then the needle pricked her on the thigh and she faded quickly into a painless sleep.

The phantom tossed the needle aside, patted Karen on the backside, then yanked the jeans up over her hips. He effortlessly lifted her into both arms, carried her to the front porch, and dropped her. Then he got a rope and tied her, leaving her toes barely touching the ground, her arms stretched above her head to a hook extending off the roof. She looked dead, her head hanging down to her chest, but it didn't seem quite right. With a quick move he tore her blouse open. Now he was satisfied.

He climbed into his station wagon, placing the gun beside him on the front seat. He had just started the engine when he saw a trail of dust rising above the dirt road.

"Now, Mikey," he muttered to himself, "all I ask is that you be there." He threw the station wagon into gear, spun it in a circle and raced for the narrow dirt road.

He spotted the car as soon as he pulled into the long straight section. With the accelerator pushed to the floor, he had to use both hands to keep the station wagon from spinning into the ditch on either side of the road.

Bubba White saw the station wagon coming. If the phantom was driving, it was a deadly game of chicken, and Bubba had about three seconds to maneuver. He shouted for Michael to hold on, pulled the car as far to the left as possible, then turned hard to the right, sliding the car sideways until it completely blocked the road from one ditch to the other.

Houdini saw what was happening. Just before he rammed the car he hit the brake and threw the station wagon into a bootleg turn. The back wheels jumped over the ditch as the car made a 180-degree spin and came to a stop facing back toward the farm house.

He hit the gas, accelerated for about twenty yards, and slammed the brake. Then he threw the station wagon into reverse and jammed his foot on the gas, looking over his shoulder to keep the car on the road.

Bubba White reached inside his jacket for a service revolver that he had never used except on the firing range, and he pushed himself and Michael out the passenger door. They had just cleared the car when the station wagon plowed backwards into the driver's side, crushing in both doors and lifting the side of the car off the ground.

Houdini kept his foot on the gas, the tires spinning in the dirt, but he couldn't get enough traction to push the sedan off the road. Cursing, he shifted gears and pulled away. Through the mirror he saw two men running. He was sure one of them was Michael.

Bubba and Michael ran for their lives. When they heard the station wagon pulling away, Bubba spun, came into a kneeling position and used both hands to steady the revolver.

The first shot shattered the rear glass in the station wagon, and the second shot hit the side panel above the rear tire.

The wagon swerved to a stop, and the madman grabbed his .45 off the seat and ducked. He glanced through the shattered window, shifted into reverse, and stomped on the gas again.

He was going at least forty miles an hour when he hit the front corner of the FBI sedan. The fender crumpled, and he stayed on the gas until he had pushed the car into the ditch. The road was cleared, but with his station wagon facing the wrong way he was a sitting target. Two more shots shattered glass in the side of the car as he pulled away. He swerved sideways and stepped from the car, lifting the pistol as he came.

Bubba White never had a chance. Kneeling at the side of the road, he realized too late that the madman had come out of the car ready to fight. He saw the figure lean across the hood of the station wagon, heard an explosion, and felt the bullet rip into his chest.

Michael watched in horror from the ditch as White fell backward. Then, without thinking, he charged into the road, his eyes riveted on the spot where the agent's service revolver had landed in the dirt. There were two explosions, and Michael rolled on the ground, reaching for the gun.

He came to his feet firing, the gun jerking in his hand with each shot. And then it clicked on an empty cylinder just as a bullet ripped into his chest and sent him sprawling on the road. Michael cried out in agony and began clawing at the dirt trying to get away.

The phantom had won. His heart pounding, he casually walked toward the two downed men. He watched Michael crawling to the side of the road and chuckled at man's will to survive, then he blew across the barrel of his pistol like a Wild West sheriff while he reached into a jacket pocket for more bullets.

He walked first to young blond agent, slowly raised his pistol, and fired a single shot into the center of the agent's forehead.

When he looked up, Michael was gone. Somehow the wounded man had made it to the edge of the woods and disappeared. Houdini wasn't worried. If he'd timed it right, he still had a few minutes before more cars arrived on the scene.

"Mikey, Mikey. Come out, come out, wherever you are." He jumped the ditch, noticing a few drops of blood in the dirt, and he peered into the brush. It was thicker than he'd expected. This was not good.

"Mikey, are you in there?"

He looked for any movement, for any sign of life, but there was nothing. Twisting vines and a thick green engulfed everything. The phantom began to sweat. How could this happen? How could everything work so well and then suddenly go bad? He glanced at his watch. He hadn't planned on climbing through thick brush. It was supposed to be all over by now.

Sweat formed on his brow, and he was angry. He fired into the brush, reloaded and fired again, listening carefully to see if he got lucky. His anger grew with the silence, and then, far off, he heard sirens.

He wanted to cry. It wasn't supposed to be like this. It was supposed to end. He threw the pistol as hard as he could at the green brush and ran back to his car. That was when he saw Karen still dangling in the sun and realized there was a better way.

He laughed, just a momentary laugh that wiped away the tears and put him back in charge. He ran over to Karen's limp body, untied the rope and slung her over his shoulder. He had to pull several times to get the crumpled rear door of the station wagon open, and then he tossed her across the seat.

The closest police car was less than a mile away, but that was more than enough. He had studied the farm carefully, and there was a small back road that would take him through the woods and out to the main road.

Mikey would have to wait for another day.

SEVENTEEN

Michael was floating. He could look down and see his toes sticking up, see hands clasped in his lap, knuckles turning white from the pressure. But he was in a void. If he wiggled his toes he could see it happen, but he couldn't feel it. He could make no contact with anything around him, not with objects or the people who hovered over him. He didn't know if it was morning or evening, only that there was an impossibly white light shining down on him.

He remembered his own tears in the woods and how difficult it had been to breathe. He'd passed out, and when he came to in an ambulance . . . or was it a helicopter . . . or was it the hospital . . . somebody was looking down at him. Was it Quince Garrett?

As Michael came awake, he knew that he was in a hospital room. He could smell it before he could even open his eyes to see the whiteness and the antiseptic cleanliness. There was a window, and it was sunny outside. A policeman sat in the corner reading a magazine. He looked up as Michael turned his head, but then Michael faded back into sleep.

When he awakened for the second time, the room was dark. A figure sat in the corner chair, barely visible in the light from an open door to the hallway. The figure was snoring, and the steadiness of the sound put Michael back to sleep.

The third time, it was morning. There was a special smell and an urgency. Michael opened his eyes, knowing that this time he would stay awake. Sitting in the corner was Quince Garrett, and in front of the agent was a hospital tray stacked high with eggs and sausage. Michael was hungry.

"Good morning," he said, woozy as he tried to slide up in the bed. "How does a fella get some breakfast around here?"

Garrett almost knocked over his tray of food as he stood, smiling, and rushed to Michael's side.

"Are you okay?"

"You tell me." Michael's throat was dry. "Where's Karen?"

"She's alive. That's all we know. She's alive, but he's got her. We don't know where."

"Karen?"

Garrett's happiness disappeared, and in that moment Michael could see how tired the big man was. His eyes were bloodshot, and his face sagged like a paper bag that had been used to carry too many lunches.

"We haven't found her," Garrett said. "We haven't heard anything. Every policeman in Virginia, West Virginia, Maryland, and the District of Columbia was alerted not twenty minutes after they left the farm, and nothing."

Garrett paused to study Michael's face. "Do you remember the farm? I don't know how much you remember."

"I remember enough," Michael said, letting his head drop back on the pillow. He felt faint.

"I'd better get the doctor," Garrett suggested.

Michael nodded, gripping the sides of the bed and forcing himself to stay awake. The room tilted, but he concentrated and forced it to level. The numbness faded, too, and in its place, like molten rock, was anger.

The doctor gave Michael a quick once over, explaining how the bullet had missed the heart and the lungs but had still left a messy hole. He seemed more worried about shock and listed the drugs Michael had been given to bring him out of it. When Michael asked again for breakfast, the doctor proudly announced him to be on his way to a quick recovery.

Michael's portions were neither as large nor as appetizing as those on Garrett's plate, and a nurse stood by his side, insisting that he eat slowly and chew everything thoroughly before swallowing. He had not eaten for two days, so his stomach would have to adjust to food that didn't come through a needle.

"I wanted to be here when you came to," Garrett said as Michael finished, "but I'd hoped I'd have more to report. Are you up to it?"

Michael nodded and tried to cover the stiffness as he pulled himself up in the bed.

"The bastard put together an elaborate trap to get Karen . . . or to get you. We can't be sure who he was after. He picked up a young hitchhiker and forced her to make the calls. She called Quantico and they put the call through to Karen in one of our cars. I've heard the tape. She was very convincing, and she got herself killed for the trouble."

Michael winced. He tried to remember the day at the farm.

"He strung the girl up with barbed wire, then he waited for Karen in the house. We don't know exactly what happened after that. He killed Agent Church and drugged Karen, and when he came out of the house you and Agent White were apparently approaching on the road into the place. The rest we can only guess."

Michael could remember most of it, but it was hazy.

"Agent White managed to block the road," Garrett continued, "but there was a lot of crashing between cars. White was shot down in the road, and I imagine that's when you tried to be a hero. The son-of-a-bitch walked over and fired a .45-caliber bullet into White's brain at point blank range, but you . . ."

"I crawled into the bushes."

"He must not have had time to come after you . . . that is, if he wanted you. So he took Karen."

Both men sat silent, each imagining the scene.

"We found his car, a station wagon he'd stolen that morning. It was shot up pretty bad. He ditched it in Fredericksburg, about fifteen miles from the farm, then rented another car. It was another alias, but the clerk identified him from the drawing. He abandoned the rental in Richmond some time yesterday afternoon, and we haven't been able to determine where he went from there."

"And Karen?" Michael asked.

"As far as we know she's still with him. When we found the car in Richmond there were lots of wrappers from a McDonald's. There are two sets of fingerprints, and one set belongs to Karen Daniels."

"Where do you think they're going?"

"At this point I don't know where the sorry son-of-a-bitch might be. We've spread the alert to all bordering states, the Carolinas, Kentucky, Tennessee. And there's nothing. He seems to be able to disappear at will, and we have absolutely no idea where he's heading . . ."

"Or what he has in mind." Michael added.

"We're covering everything we know to cover, checking everything we know to check," Garrett said hopelessly. "We've got people on the phones at Manning Hall, and there's been nothing. Not a peep. At least three hundred people are working on this case, and we're finding nothing. We can't even find out how he left Richmond."

"When can I get out of here?" Michael asked.

"The doctor says you need to stay still and let that hole in your chest heal. I've got to get back to Washington, but there'll be somebody with you twenty-four hours a day. I'll keep you informed every step of the way, but the doctor says you have to rest."

Michael closed his eyes, but it wasn't exhaustion that made him do it. He wanted to hide the anger that he knew Garrett could see there.

"Take care of yourself, Michael. I'll call if we get anything. I'll be here sometime tomorrow."

Uncontrollable tears rolled from behind Michael's closed eyelids.

"Are you going to be all right, Michael?"

"Just catch the bastard. Please catch him."

Garrett started for the door. He wanted to hit something. Anything.

"Quince," Michael called from the bed.

The agent stopped at the door and turned around.

"I just wanted to say thanks for everything. I appreciate your being here."

"We'll get him, Michael. I promise we'll get him."

Scotty Bowman had been with the police department of the District of Columbia for five years, and if there was any duty he hated more than all the others it had to be babysitting. He hated waiting for something to happen.

Bowman also hated coffee, but he was just sitting over his fourth cup from the machine at one o'clock in the morning when the cutest of the night nurses came from behind nurse's station and started in his direction. And she wasn't smiling.

Bowman came to his feet.

"There's a telephone call," she said breathlessly as she reached him. "He says his name is Houdini."

It took a second for the name to register.

"Holy Christ," Bowman said. "What in hell does he want?"

"He says he wants to talk to Mr. Manning."

"Where can I take the call?"

She pointed back to the nurse's station, and together they ran down the hall.

Bowman paused at the phone, trying to place everything in perspective. He couldn't think what to say. He couldn't even remember his name.

"This is Patrolman Bowman, D.C. Police. Who is this?"

There was a cold silence at the other end of the line, then a chuckle.

"This is the one, the only Who-dini. I hear my buddy is in the hospital. A bit under the weather, I understand. And when I call to wish him well, the dumb broad tells me I can't speak to him. What kind of place have you got there? Is it a hospital or a prison?"

"It is one o'clock in the morning," Bowman said, taking his ear away from the phone for a moment to escape the laughter that followed.

"Is this really a policeman? My, my, it's a sorry world we live in. Now tell me, Patrolman Bowman, I imagine you're there to protect Mikey from the bad people in the world— people like me. And based on our conversation to this point,

I assume you have a superior that you can call in the case of an emergency. Don't strain yourself now, but am I correct?"

Bowman tried to hold back, but it was no use.

"Listen to me honky, I don't know if you're the psycho or not, but I wish you would show your face around here. I'd break your smart ass real quick like."

The phantom laughed so hard that he dropped the phone.

"Guess what, Patrolman Bowman, sir," he said when he picked it up. "You'd lose."

"Come on down here, motherfucker. Let's see 'bout that."

The laugh only grew louder, and then it stopped suddenly.

"Okay, enough of this stupidity. Now listen carefully. Maybe you'd better take notes. It is now five minutes past one. In exactly nine hours and fifty-five minutes—that's at eleven o'clock A.M., I'm going to call the hospital again. At that time I expect to speak either to Michael Manning or to somebody in authority who can tell me what's going on. You'd better make it Quince Garrett or somebody else with the FBI. Have you got it?"

"I've got it," Bowman said.

"Good. Now remember, I'm calling at exactly eleven o'clock. And I do believe everybody knows what'll happen if I don't get what I want. The lovely Miss Daniels . . . oops, I mean Dr. Daniels. She's with me, and at the moment she's alive. Let's see if we can't keep it that way."

Bowman had a lot more he wanted to say, but the phone went dead before he had the chance.

Quince Garrett was sleeping on a cot in his office at FBI headquarters when the call came in. He was at the hospital twenty minutes later. The doctor assured him that although Michael had been sedated for the night, there was no medical reason he shouldn't be allowed to take the call at eleven o'clock.

Garrett waited until after Michael had eaten breakfast before he approached the room.

"What's happened?" Michael knew Garrett's expression meant trouble.

"Michael, it's him. He's called."

Michael sat up in bed, carefully swinging his legs over the edge and then holding tight to avoid falling into the floor. He was weaker than he thought.

"Where is he?" Michael demanded. "What does he want?"

"He called here at the hospital. He wants to talk to you. Do you feel up to taking another call?"

"Of course," Michael demanded. He dropped off the bed, standing on wobbly legs, and reached to Garrett for support. "I'm still pretty weak."

"We've got time. He's not calling until eleven," Garrett said, easing Michael back onto the bed. "Are you sure . . ."

Michael stopped him. "What choice do we have?"

"None."

"Where do we do it?"

"We're using an office at the end of the hall. Can you make it?"

"I'll make it," Michael said bitterly.

They stayed in the room together until it was almost eleven. Then they slowly made their way down the hall. By the time they reached the office Michael felt stronger. The setup looked familiar—a collection of three telephones, headsets, a speaker, and a tape recorder. Agents surrounded the table, and there was also one black policeman in uniform.

The clock on the wall said five minutes to eleven. One of the agents served coffee, then they sat, staring at the lights on the telephone. With two minutes to go, Garrett lit a cigarette. He hadn't smoked in three years, but earlier in the day he'd picked up a pack.

The clock clicked to 11:00, and everybody in the room focused on the telephone. It was so quiet that they all jumped when the clock clicked to 11:01 . . . and then 11:02 and 11:03. At 11:05 they began to look at each other, puzzled, and at 11:10 an agent burst into the room waving an envelope.

"A cab driver just delivered this to the front desk," the agent said. "It's addressed to Mikey Manning."

Garrett grabbed the envelope, peering through the open door at the cab driver.

"Hold him for questioning," he snapped, shutting the door and rushing to the table. He ripped open the envelope and dumped the contents on the table. A Polaroid photo showed

Karen tied to a chair in a motel room. She was nude. With the photo was a cassette tape.

Garrett grabbed the tape recorder, pulling it free from the telephone, and popped in the tape.

"Mikey, I don't know how to say this, but you should be dead." The voice was laughing so much at his own sick joke that he couldn't continue. "But really, Mikey, if you had died out there like a man, then the game would be over and sweet, ever so sweet Karen would be safely tucked in bed somewhere."

Michael was holding the photograph of Karen. Not looking at it, just holding it. When he did finally see it, he placed it face down on the table and pushed it as far away as he could reach.

"Now, Mikey," the tape continued, "imagine, if you will, a lovely young lady—I do believe you have a photo of her. Now, imagine a motel room. Imagine an evil death machine, something that slowly, ever so slowly, causes pain and suffering. And then it kills. Have you got that image in your mind?"

Michael lowered his head, and Garrett was clenching his teeth so tight that the muscles knotted in his jaw.

"I've studied this very carefully," the voice continued, shifting to mimic a German accent. "I am just about to start the machine. If the cab driver delivered the tape as instructed, then it should be 11:15, give or take a couple of minutes. You should have five hours, till four P.M., to find her. I'm leaving now, and I'll tell the maid my wife has one of her migraine headaches so please not clean the room."

Michael was weeping. He tried to stop, but he couldn't help it.

"A simple game, don't you think, Mikey. And, oh yes, you get two clues. We registered as man and wife, using one of the names you already know. And the motel is located in Atlantic City, New Jersey. Lots o' luck, Mikey. You're going to need it."

Before the tape ended, Garrett was on the phone barking orders. Michael just sat at the table. He was numb. He saw nothing and he felt nothing. At that moment, if he could have felt anything, he would have cracked. He was going to Atlantic City, and there wasn't anyone who could stop him.

EIGHTEEN

The digital travel clock beside the bed read 11:28 as the phantom paced the motel room on the outskirts of Atlantic City. The breakfast tray on the bed contained a hearty meal—a western style omelet, sausage, toast, and juice—but he was too keyed up to sit down and eat.

It took an eternity, but when the clock flipped to 11:30 he approached his breakfast smiling. He picked up a piece of toast, smeared grape jelly on it, then walked to the bathroom while he ate. When he finished he wiped his fingers on a towel and smiled down into the tub, into the frightened eyes of Karen Daniels.

Karen was already tied, her arms pulled tight behind her back, her legs bound at the knees and again at the ankles. A washcloth was stuffed into her mouth, with plastic tape wrapped around her head to hold it in place.

"And how are you this morning, sweet Karen?" He looked down at her naked body, reached out and ran a hand around her chin, down across her neck, and between her breasts. The skin was taut, the muscles tight. The nipples stood erect in fear.

"Aw, sweet, sweet Karen, how I do wish we could spend more time together. Lots more time." He shook his head,

221

then bent down and picked up a thick piece of rope from the floor. A towel rack was built into the wall above the foot of the tub, and he tried to shake it with his hands. It was solid.

He smiled, then wrapped the rope around the bar with scientific deliberation. When he finished, the two ends of the rope extended to the rim of the tub. Pulling on the ropes, he was satisfied they wouldn't give. He stood back for a moment, admiring his work, then he turned his attention to Karen.

"You really are a sight for the hard and the horny," he said, shaking his head. "My, my, and brains, too."

This time he reached down with both hands, caressing her cheeks and letting his hands fall to her breasts. He let his fingers glide to the nipples and gave them a gentle squeeze, then casually followed the contours of her body, down across her stomach, widening to trace the hips, then farther down, along the thighs and across the rope at the knees. When he reached the ankles he took a solid grip with both hands and lifted.

Karen's head smacked against the porcelain of the tub. She blinked, and when she opened her eyes the rope was already cutting into her ankles. Her legs were extended upward at a 45-degree angle, and she was helpless. She tried to twist, but it was impossible. It only made the ropes tighter. It was at that moment she realized what was about to happen.

Houdini smiled. He reached over again and tugged on the ropes, wrapping the loose ends around the towel bar and tying each into a quick knot. He placed a large rubber stopper over the drain just above Karen's head and used plastic tape to secure it.

Breathing heavily, he stepped back and surveyed all that he had done. He was pleased. He bent forward and kissed Karen on the forehead while reaching to the cold water tap. He twisted the knob until there was a slow, steady trickle.

"Well, sweet Karen. How smart do you think they are? They know where you are—at least they know the city. And they know you've got only four, maybe four-and-a-half hours to live. Will they find you in time?"

Karen's eyes were pleading. She tried to scream, but the washcloth made any sound beyond a frantic hum impossible.

He took a glass from the sink and held it under the slow stream of water in the tub. He started timing. It took seventy-three seconds for the water to fill the glass, and when it was done he raised the glass to eye level, studied the contents, then dramatically glanced at his watch. He smiled and tossed the water into Karen's face.

"It is now 11:40," he said. "You can figure on being dead by four o'clock, give or take a few minutes."

He left the room but returned a moment later with the clock. Using the plastic tape, he attached it to the wall just above the towel bar, tilting the face down so that Karen could see the time.

"I wouldn't be too hopeful," he said. "Your friends really aren't all that smart."

And then he was gone.

The LearJet was cleared for takeoff at 11:38. On board were Michael, Quince Garrett, and two young agents. As soon as they were airborne, the two agents returned to their phones with a vengeance. Michael knew that one was a link to Atlantic City, but he wasn't sure about the other.

Garrett made a quick trip to the cockpit, and when he returned he didn't look happy.

"We should be there in forty minutes, maybe less," he said, glancing at his watch. He tried to smile. "Don't worry. We'll find her."

"Do you really believe that?" Michael asked.

"Yes, Michael. I do."

One of the agents handed Garrett a note. He read in silence, then turned to look out the window before he spoke.

"He chartered a plane out of Northern Virginia yesterday and got to Atlantic City in the afternoon. They found the plane in one of the leased hangars at the airport. The pilot is dead. He was strangled."

Michael turned to his own window, but his eyes were closed.

The taxi driver was in a talkative mood, but the passenger didn't mind. He felt fresh. He had on a new suit, with a

224 To the Death

pocket full of cash, and a few hours to squander at one of the casinos.

"You ain't no tourist. You look like a serious gambler," the driver said between puffs on a cigar. "Where you from?"

"Actually, I'm from the coast," the phantom said. "But I spend a lot of time on the Continent . . . in Europe."

"Working the big casinos, huh?"

"That . . . and other things," he said, enjoying the game. "Casinos are only one form of gambling."

"What's your game?" the driver asked.

"At the casino . . . probably Black Jack."

"Good game." The driver nodded his approval.

"But then I like to gamble at anything."

"I know what you mean. Me, I bet the ponies, and my wife gives me a fit. I mean, I win some and I lose some. But what she can't understand is . . . you know. I need the game."

"We all need the game," the phantom said. "It's the game that keeps us going."

They were pulling up to the entrance of the Tropicana. Two police cars blocked the door. The taxi driver had to double park to let him get out.

"Here," he said, handing the driver a fifty-dollar bill. "Bet this for me on the next long shot."

He walked between the two patrol cars and entered the casino. The time was 12:20. It was crowded, but he found an opening at one of the Black Jack tables, took the seat, and bought five hundred dollars in chips. He bet a hundred dollars on the first hand and drew a Black Jack.

The LearJet didn't land until 12:35. Garrett was the first to leave the aircraft, with Michael and the other agents close behind. No one bothered to introduce Michael to the local agents who met the plane.

"Nothing," said Scarborough, head of the FBI Trenton office. "We're covering every casino, every motel and every dive in the city. It's going to take some time, but if the deadline is four o'clock, and this guy is shooting straight with you on the names, then we should make it."

Garrett glanced at Michael to be sure he'd heard, then the cluster of people began to move toward the cars.

"Tell me, Garrett," an Atlantic City police lieutenant challenged, "what makes you think this guy's on the level? How do you know he isn't in Texas or California or even Idaho, for all we know?"

"He wouldn't do that," Michael said before Garrett could answer. "This is a game . . . and he plays by the rules."

"Who is this guy?" the cop asked Garrett.

"He's right," Garrett said. "We've been following this bastard for weeks. This is a game to him, and he won't lie unless he's got a better game to play." Garrett thought about the lie that had held him in New Orleans while the phantom kidnapped Karen. "He's not lying about this."

"You mean he'll kill the girl, but he won't lie about doing it . . . or where?"

"No. He won't lie," Garrett said.

The patrol cars at the front and rear of the line flipped on their sirens as they left the airport. They passed quickly through the traffic heading into Atlantic City. The time was 12:55.

The water reached Karen's ears just as the digital numbers flipped to 1:00. Her eyes were closed. She had been breathing too fast, and now she was holding her breath, trying to fight off the panic of hyperventilation. Blood was rushing to her head, and her arms were numb. She tried to wiggle her fingers, but she could feel nothing.

She closed her eyes tight and held her breath. An eternity passed. She opened her eyes. She did it again. Then again.

The water coming from the tap suddenly slowed to a drip, and Karen opened her eyes wide. She leaned her head back to see. The water had almost stopped. Far off in another room she could hear somebody singing in a shower. The water pressure had dropped. She twisted, and her ankles burned with a sharp pain as the ropes cut deeper into her bruised skin. She tried to scream, but it was hopeless.

The far-off singing stopped, and the water regained its pace. The drips turned into a steady dribble, and Karen again closed her eyes.

When she opened them again her ears were below water, and she screamed. Everything in her screamed, but no sound came from her lips. She gagged on the washcloth. The tape held, and the clock clicked to 2:00.

Quince Garrett had decided that they should split up. One group patrolled the Boardwalk area, another headed toward Ventnor City. Garrett and Michael stayed with Scarborough and moved toward Absecon Inlet.

The radio buzzed frequently with reports from police patrols and agents. All went to the command center at the Atlantic City P.D., and each indicated that another motel had been checked off the list.

At 2:45 the radio popped with urgency.

"This is car 217. I think we've got it. We're at the Cobbler's Inn on Melrose. There's a Godwin, a Stephen Godwin registered. Car 324 has arrived. We're going to investigate."

"This is Command Central," came a frantic reply. "Use all caution. Repeat. Use all caution. Attention all units in Sector Seven . . . all units Sector Seven to the Cobbler's."

Michael craned forward in his seat to listen, and Garrett grabbed the dashboard as Scarborough sent the sedan into a tire-squealing turn. They were on Atlantic Avenue approximately half a mile from the motel.

"What's the Cobbler's Inn?" Garrett asked as they maneuvered through traffic.

"It's a dive," Scarborough said. "A real meat house."

Four patrolmen moved cautiously up the stairway of the Cobbler's Inn. Stephen Godwin was registered in room 304. It was at the end of the hall at the rear of the third floor. A window next to the door opened onto a fire escape.

The senior patrolman unfastened the snap on his holster and edged up to the door of the room, moving his ear close. He could hear water running. He motioned for one patrolman to take the fire escape. The other two stood on either side of the door, but the leader motioned them away and knocked loudly.

"This is the police. Open up."

There was no answer. Together, the three stepped in front of the door and kicked. The door splintered back into the room, and all three dived through the opening.

Someone in the bathroom shrieked, and they ran in with guns drawn. What they found was a fat New York insurance salesman named Stephen Godwin. He was sharing his tub with an equally fat hooker known on the streets of Atlantic City as Buttercup.

The time was 3:25.

He was ahead seven hundred dollars. The time was 3:30. From where he sat he could see a group of people gathering at the door. They had the look of tourists—housewives who had played hooky from their chores, office workers who had called in sick so they could take the bus to Atlantic City.

He decided to make one more bet. He slipped five hundred dollars to the betting square, and the dealer passed around the cards. He was dealt a Jack and an Ace. He'd started the game with a Black Jack, and he'd finished the same way. It was time to leave.

Scooping up his chips, he cashed in and followed the last of the tourists into the driveway. Their bus was marked Pittsburgh.

He hung back watching until all the passengers were inside, then he stepped up to talk to the driver. He reached out a hand, introducing himself, and when they shook the driver accepted the fifty-dollar bill he had been palming.

"Looks like you've got a few extra seats," he said. "I'm heading to Pittsburgh. It certainly would save me a lot of trouble if I could catch a ride."

The driver slipped the fifty into his pocket and looked back over his shoulder. Nobody had noticed the exchange. Without answering, he reached forward and pulled the handle, closing the door.

"Welcome aboard," the driver said, looking at the stranger but speaking into a microphone that amplified his voice through the bus. "Have we got any winners? Any losers?" The latter brought a painful moan. "Well, everybody take a seat, and we'll have you home in time for supper."

It was 3:55 when Michael glimpsed the sign for a small motel as they went by one of the smaller sidestreets. Something about it struck a familiar chord. Then he had it. The phantom had signed off his taped message by wishing Michael "lots o' luck," and that was the name he'd just seen—the Lots o' Luck Motel.

"That's it," he shouted. "The Lots o' Luck—that's where they'll be."

Scarborough slammed the car into a broad U-turn in the middle of the block.

The water was rising over Karen's cheeks, and the one thing she wanted more than anything was to go to sleep. She had to arch her neck to keep her nose above water, but she was fading. There was no more energy. The pain that had consumed her whole body was now gone. She could feel nothing. Her arms and legs had passed beyond cramps, beyond all feeling, and into a sleep all their own.

All she could feel, all that she was aware of, was the play of water around her nostrils. She couldn't lift her head anymore. The water was there. If she didn't stay perfectly straight the water rushed down her nose and she choked.

Four o'clock. It would be over soon.

She closed her eyes, deciding this would be the last time. She willed herself to keep them closed. The water continued to rise. Blessed sleep was coming. Some urgent message from the brain forced her to take one last breath, and then water closed off everything.

She held that last breath for an eternity. Her lungs burned, knowing this was the last oxygen they would ever have. She couldn't hold out any longer. The last breath had given her all the life it had. She exhaled.

Quince Garrett was out of the car before it came to a stop, Michael at his side. A patrol car pulled in beside them, and two patrolmen emerged with guns drawn.

They found a sad-eyed clerk reading *Hustler* at the front desk. The young man looked like he wanted to run when he saw the cops charge into the lobby.

"Let me see your register," Garrett demanded. And the name was there . . . Stephen E. Stoddard. He pointed at the register, and the clerk read the name, not knowing what else to do.

"The room number, damn it. What room is he in?"

The clerk finally understood. "504" he said. "Down the hall on the right."

Less than fifteen seconds later, Garrett and Michael hit the door simultaneously with their shoulders.

The thin wood splintered, knocking both men off their feet as they fell into the room. Water was running.

Michael was the first up on his feet. He dived through the bathroom door and reached into the cold water to pull Karen up. Her face was blue, her legs and arms a deadly white. Michael held on with all his strength, keeping her head above water.

Garrett reached over him and cut the ropes at Karen's ankles. The sudden release dropped both Michael and Karen to the floor in a heap, but Michael took the shock across his shoulder.

Garrett pulled them apart and sliced more ropes while turning Karen flat on her back. He pushed Michael out of the way and climbed over her, lifting her head, pulling off the tape and yanking out the waterlogged washcloth. He tilted her head, forced her mouth open with his fingers, and started mouth-to-mouth resuscitation.

Michael fell back against the wall. It was over. Garrett continued to puff into her mouth, but Michael knew she was dead. They were too late. The phantom had won.

Then she began coughing. The first one was low and brief, but the second was louder. She twisted to her side and began spitting up the clear water.

Michael crawled forward to hold her head, and Garrett reached up to accept a towel from one of the patrolmen standing in the doorway.

NINETEEN

Six days passed before Michael realized that he hadn't heard from the phantom. It took that long for the doctors at Memorial Hospital in Philadelphia to repatch the hole in his chest—the stitches had burst open when he hit the door at the Lots o' Luck Motel—and to grant him permission to fly Karen back for medical attention in Washington.

Everyone insisted that both patients were doing fine, but Michael wasn't so sure about Karen. She had barely spoken. Every time she tried she broke into tears, sobbing until she was given a shot that eased her into sleep. She had not slept without the aid of drugs since what everybody gently referred to as "the incident." When she was awake, she sat for hours on her bed, rubbing her arms and legs where the bindings had cut off circulation.

Michael hadn't seen Quince Garrett since the day they had pulled Karen out of the tub in Atlantic City and flown her to Philadelphia for treatment. Bill Travers had also disappeared. New agents with fresh faces kept Michael company every minute of every day.

Back in Washington, Michael returned to reading newspapers and discovered that the phantom was page one news across the country. Michael remained in the hospital as much to be there for Karen as for his own health. They had adjoining rooms, both surrounded by agents twenty-four hours a day. There was also an army of journalists to contend with.

The ninth day was a day of breakthroughs. When Michael entered Karen's room that morning she was gently crying, but when she saw him she called his name and raised her arms for a hug. They held each other for a long time, and when they finally parted she was trying to smile. She lay back on the bed, exhausted, but she held onto Michael's hand.

"Have they caught him?" she asked, gripping Michael's hand tighter.

"No."

"When can I get out of here?"

"Soon," Michael said. "Very soon." Then he went to call the Pattersons, to tell them he and Karen would be coming home as soon as it could be arranged.

Quince Garrett was getting too old for this crap. He was angry, but it wasn't a sudden flash of anger that comes and then goes. No, this was the kind of anger that gets inside you and won't let go. The phantom was like a disease, and Quince had a lethal dose.

It was a subdued Captain Richardson who greeted Garrett in the same Boston office where they'd met three weeks earlier. Richardson was still camping out in the Action Room even though most of the special investigation team had been taken off the car bombing. But Richardson, like Garrett, couldn't let go. He had the phantom disease too.

"What have you got?" Richardson asked.

Garrett winced. The question still hurt.

"Not much. From Atlantic City, we found a tour bus driver who gave him a ride to Pittsburgh. He just stepped on the bus as it was getting ready to leave one of the casinos, handed the driver a fifty and asked for a ride. The driver would have been a fool to resist an offer like that, and now he'll probably lose his job over it."

Richardson looked as if he wanted to mark down one more victim on the phantom's score card.

"And what brings you back to Boston? Is he here?"

"We know where he got off the bus in Pittsburgh, and we found the motel where he spent the first night. He used a new name—Dr. Kenneth Daniels. The next morning he disappeared. We checked everything, no last-minute airline reservation, no car rental. On an off chance I tried the bus terminal, and it seems a guy fitting our description bought a ticket to Buffalo, and in Buffalo he rented a car and . . ."

"Let me guess," Richardson interrupted. "He rented a car and mentioned he was heading to Boston."

"Not quite. He said he was going to tour New England."

"So, where do we go from here?" Richardson asked.

Garrett sighed.

"Let me guess." Richardson knew the answer to his own question. "You don't know. We just keep looking."

"Right."

Richardson looked again at the pile of junk that had accumulated on his desk. All questions. No answers.

"Why would he come back to Boston? What's he up to?"

"If we knew that," Garrett said, "we'd be a step ahead of him for the first time. We don't know. So what have you got on your end?"

"That fucking clinic has fought me every step of the way." Richardson's temper was finally getting the best of him. "We got a list of current patients, and all those first names are on the list except for the one who died. And I can't even get a fucking court order to see any records. They won't tell me anything about any of these guys. They won't tell me anything about former patients, former staff. They won't tell me shit."

"So you have nothing." Rephrased, it was still a question.

"I've got no answers. I've got six men working this thing, and I sit here poring over files. I don't know what I'm looking for. I'm looking for his granny, the one he said he offed. I've looked at every unsolved case for the past twenty years, and she simply ain't there."

Now Garrett knew why he'd dreaded this meeting so much. He hated the idea of hearing Richardson echo what they didn't know.

"I'm going to get some sleep," Garrett said, looking at his watch. It was only four o'clock in the afternoon, but he'd been up for thirty hours straight, and he was beat. "If any miracles happen, I'm at the Holiday Inn just down the street."

He sat over a cup of black coffee, a small smile playing across his face, reflecting on the plans and counterplans that raced through his mind. The cafe was noisy, but he barely noticed. The waitress smiled as she freshened his coffee, and he smiled back without ever really seeing her. Sitting at his window seat, a gentle afternoon shower pelting rain off the glass, he had the concentration of a chess player working out a strategy ten moves ahead. If I do this, he'll do this, and then I'll have to do that . . . and when it all ends, I win.

It all worked. That was the important thing. If he did what he had to do, and Karen reacted the way she should react, and if Michael was willing to take the ultimate gamble—with his life—then every piece would fall into place. The game would be exciting, and in the end . . . checkmate. He would win.

The phantom liked it. It felt good. It felt right. He looked up to notice that the rain had stopped, and just as he peered out the window he saw a figure walk out of the building across the street. He knew that man. He'd seen his photograph in the newspaper and on television.

The man was Quince Garrett and the building was the headquarters of the Boston Police Department.

The phantom smiled. All was right with the world, and he was ready to play. It was time to make the first move . . . pawn to king four.

Karen was recovering much quicker than anyone had expected. As soon as she arrived back at Manning Hall, she seemed to come alive. She even managed to sit down and tell Michael the whole story of her kidnapping, somehow cleansing her own mind by sharing it.

Michael was trying to exercise as much as he could. Karen still needed a lot of sleep, and when he was alone he became silent and brooding. One of the nurses was always there to remind him to exercise his shoulders on a weight machine that had been installed at Manning Hall for that purpose, and he worked out religiously. Once he started, the nurse had a difficult time making him stop. He would leave the new exercise room with a sharp pain burning in his shoulders, and it felt good. It felt real.

It was on the fourth day back at Manning Hall that Karen suggested they sit under a tree and watch the sunset. The two agents were far enough away to guarantee them a few minutes of privacy. Karen curled into Michael's arm, but then she became serious.

"How strong are you feeling?" she asked.

"I'm good. I think the weight machine is the best thing that ever happened to me. I feel great. Why?"

Karen paused, choosing her words carefully.

"Do you still dream about your father?"

"Yes." Michael answered weakly, not wanting to talk about it. "I wish you had gotten to know him. He was a fascinating man, so strong and so determined in everything he did. Most people only saw us fight, but there were lots of good times, too. I loved that man more than I ever realized. I dream that he's still alive, and I save him."

"You save him from the phantom?" she asked.

"Yes."

"Do you kill the phantom?"

"Yes." He said the word quietly, as if it might bite.

Karen sighed. Then she trembled.

"That's what I thought. I have the same dream . . . where I kill him . . . I cause him some horrible death."

"Are you okay?"

"Yes . . . I'm just scared. Remember when I said this was going to come down between him and you? I still believe it, now more than ever. Something is going to happen. I know it. And when it does . . . when it does, he's going to remove everything that stands between you and him."

"I'm ready."

"Are you sure?" She turned to look up into his eyes. "He's a monster. He's inhuman. Are you sure you're ready for that?"

"I'm ready."

"It's not going to be easy." She spoke slowly, almost in a whisper. "As long as the FBI watches us, he'll stay away. He'll have to keep his distance until he can figure a way to get around them."

"I'm ready."

"I'm scared."

They watched the sunset. It was beautiful, a red glow spreading over soft clouds as the sun floated below the trees to the west. They watched. They saw the red. And they held each other.

TWENTY

Derek Russell.

That was the name. The phantom. Captain Richardson had known that if he strained his eyes over enough old police files he'd find it, and there it was. Derek Russell.

It was all there, an old file stored safely among the yellowing sheets of ancient Boston Police reports. Derek Russell was a madman, all right. He'd been a patient of Dr. Emerson Underwood, the retired founder of the Underwood Clinic who now lived, self exiled, in the picturesque town of Salem, twenty miles north of Boston.

Derek Russell was the only son of the late John Russell, an archaeologist who had amazed the world with his knack for locating the lost sites of ancient civilizations. John had inherited a fortune from Pennsylvania coal mines that had been in his family for generations, and he'd sold them at their peak, before alternative fuels and labor problems plagued the industry. He'd used the money to travel the world, financing more than a dozen digs, then he'd come to Boston to accept a full professorship at Harvard. He married a brilliant graduate student—not a very original story—and six months later the child Derek had been born.

The Russells, however, continued to travel, leaving the child in the care of his maternal grandmother. And when the Russells were killed in a plane crash in Egypt, the four-year-old child was placed in the custody of a grandmother who hated him. To her, the small boy looked too much like his father, the man who had stolen her daughter and carried the innocent young girl off to death in a distant land. She would have her revenge.

After that, the story was mostly theory, recorded long ago by a doctor who spent years with the tormented child. The statement was in Dr. Underwood's own words:

"From the little that Derek told me when he was under my care, it seems that the grandmother locked him in a closet for days at a time, barely feeding him. She destroyed anything the boy tried to do. If he tried to build a model airplane, she would tell him he was doing it all wrong and throw it away. If he wanted to play baseball with the other boys, she'd tell him he would just embarrass himself, then she'd lock him in the closet until he calmed down. She convinced him that he wasn't capable of doing anything."

Richardson took a sip of coffee and tried to imagine what it would have been like growing up under such circumstances, and then he returned to the doctor's testimony.

"When Derek was thirteen, something horrible happened. Nobody had seen the boy or his grandmother for three days, and when neighbors went to investigate they found the grandmother tied to her bed and butchered to death. Someone had taken a knife to her and mutilated the body. She had obviously been tortured for hours before she died. Much of the mutilation seemed to have sexual overtones, and this became a major point in the events that followed.

"Derek was found in a closet, in the same closet where he had been sent for so much punishment. He was almost dead. His hands were tied to a hook in the ceiling, his feet barely touching the floor. His face and body showed severe cuts from the same knife that had been used on his grandmother. There was lots of blood, but the cuts weren't very deep. What almost killed him was dehydration. He also appeared to be suffering from shock. He didn't speak for six weeks, and in the course of that time he was brought to Underwood Clinic for extended care."

The report went on, page after page, detailing the scientific analysis of Derek Russell's case and the treatment that was administered while he continued in a catatonic state.

"I was with him when he said his first words," the doctor's report continued. "I was called to his bed because he had slipped into a fever and was shaking violently. When I got there he became very calm, opened his eyes and said, 'I did it.' He said it with great pride."

More pages followed. A few doctors, including Dr. Underwood, believed that the boy had killed his grandmother and tortured himself to escape blame, but nobody wanted to believe it. Doctors questioned Derek for months, but all they got from him was that a man had forced his way into the house. Derek said he had been tied in the closet, hearing and seeing nothing of what happened to his grandmother. He'd described sexual things the man had done to him while he hung helpless and weak from the closet hook. He had the cuts, and he described the sexual acts so innocently, seeming to be so pure, that the team of doctors decided he couldn't have done it. He was the obvious victim.

Richardson found it painful to read the next few pages of police reports. These documented a similar case of mutilation a year later and rationalized a quick decision that the same man had done both.

"Derek remained in my care, one of a select group of severely traumatized patients," Dr. Underwood's comments continued, and Richardson was sure that select group included seven names on a list Michael Manning had brought to his attention. "He stayed always to himself, and when he tried to get involved in things—games, sports, school—he became very nervous. He lacked the confidence to try anything, and if he did try he became so agitated that it inevitably went wrong."

How could such a child become such a demented but brilliant murder machine? Richardson asked himself the question and continued to read for the answer.

"There was a complete change in Derek's personality when he was fifteen. He started to talk in our sessions together, but always he maintained control. He never said anything from the heart. It was all from the surface, mostly innocuous things, mostly about his grandmother and the eccentric things she did. Only occasionally about the closet punishments.

"He also talked about the scars, particularly the scars on his face. They remained very visible, but he was completely against the idea of plastic surgery. He would stand at the mirror and run a finger over those scars. I always sensed that he was proud of them.

"He eventually became involved in school and reading, and turned out to be a brilliant student. He had a passion for books dealing with true accounts of murder, but when he realized we were keeping track of the things he read he turned to knowledge with a passion—science, history, even the Bible. He excelled as a student in spite of the time he had missed from school, and he became athletic, avoiding all team sports but working out with weights, building his body as if with great purpose."

It was clear from the reports that Derek Russell had become an obsession to Dr. Underwood. The doctor had studied the police records and had done his own investigation. He'd found that the knots holding Derek to the hook in the closet had come right out of a Boy Scout's manual that was in Derek's bedroom. Even the cuts, on closer examination, could all have been made with a knife held in his own hand. The doctor was convinced Derek had killed his grandmother and was capable of much more evil, but nobody would listen.

The file went on and on, explaining scientific evidence for what might be going on in Derek's mind, but talk of the limbic brain and vertical spikes on EEGs was beyond Richardson's understanding. He skimmed ahead, looking for the meat of the story.

"Derek remained always in control, and I sensed that he had a plan. Just before his eighteenth birthday, that plan surfaced. He contacted his trustee. The family fortune—more than four million dollars—was in the care of a bank until Derek turned eighteen, if he could be proven competent. He brought in an independent psychiatrist and a high-powered lawyer, and on his birthday they went to court and demanded his release from the clinic."

The bastard had won. Richardson read in disbelief about how calmly the scarred teenager sat in the courtroom while experts testified about what a remarkable recovery he had made from such a traumatic childhood. Dr. Underwood had been outnumbered. Not only did they set Derek free, but they also congratulated him on all that he had accomplished in his years under Dr. Underwood's care.

"I retired shortly after that," Dr. Underwood's statement continued. "Something broke in me. I couldn't handle looking into all those young faces that wanted to be well. My wife was also a psychologist. We talked it over, and we both decided to get out, to leave Boston and move to one of the smaller towns along the coast. I tried to keep track of Derek as best I could, and then I learned, almost by accident, that he was undergoing extensive plastic surgery with Dr. Henry Redford, a prominent man in the field."

Four months later, Dr. Redford died. His wife had gone away for the weekend, and he had, according to police reports, gone to his car in the garage, started the engine, and died of carbon monoxide poisoning. It was ruled a suicide.

"It was three months after that I received my call," Dr. Underwood's statement continued. "It was four o'clock in the morning. My wife and I had just completed all of the paper-work to turn the clinic over to new directors, and we were going to spend the weekend driving up the coast looking for a new home. My daughter, Cindy, was six years old at the time.

"It was a man's voice on the phone. He said I had to pay for my sins. He said there was a bomb in my daughter's room and that it would go off before I could get to her. I dropped the phone, ran to Cindy's room, and pulled her from her bed. My wife was awake, and I rushed both of them out of the house. I forced them into the car and told them to go to a neighbor's house and call the police. Then I turned back to the house. I don't know what I was thinking, maybe that I could find the bomb and throw it into the backyard. I just don't know, but just before I got to the porch there was an explosion.

"Something hit me in the legs, and I blacked out. When I awakened at the hospital I was sure everything was all right.

242   To the Death

But then they told me it wasn't the house that had exploded.
It was the car. My wife and daughter were killed instantly,
and one of the doors had been blown off the car with such
force that when it hit me it took off both legs at the knee."

Richardson closed his eyes for a moment of silence, thinking
first about the pain of this poor man who'd known the evil
when nobody would listen. And then the pain turned to anger
at realizing this should have never been allowed to happen.

There was only one more paragraph to Dr. Underwood's
statement:

"I always thought Derek would come back. But gradually
I became convinced that he knew exactly what he was doing.
He knew I'd get the family out of the house, but somehow
he also knew I wouldn't go with them. He probably watched
from somewhere until I moved away from the car, and when
he guessed I might be far enough away to live through it he
triggered the bomb. I waited for years, wanting him to come
back and finish the job, but he had finished. He got just what
he wanted. He never intended to kill me. He just left me
dead."

Richardson had a difficult time reading the remainder of
the official documents of the investigation. The plastic surgeon's records had disappeared. The money had been transferred through a dozen banks and eventually disappeared.
And Derek had disappeared with it.

Richardson forced himself to complete the file, and then
he quietly closed the cover. He took one moment to sit there,
alone with what he had discovered, and then he reached for
the phone to call Quince Garrett.

While the Holiday Inn was putting him through to Garrett's
room, Richardson received a call on another line. He put the
Holiday Inn on hold and took the call.

"Captain, this is Sergeant Barkley. I just picked up something
on the Telex I thought you'd want to know. It's about that
Underwood Clinic. The guy who started the place was murdered tonight out in Salem. Name was Dr. Emerson Underwood. No details, but it sounds like a mess."

The next morning, a package was delivered to Manning
Hall. Bill Travers and two of his agents carried the large box

into the yard and had it examined by bomb experts before it was opened.

The box contained a large trophy. At the top was a small chrome-plated statuette of a he-man raising his arms in victory. The plaque at the base had only one line—

"For Michael Manning . . . A Worthy Opponent."

Also in the box was a thick file folder embossed with the emblem of the Underwood Clinic. Inside was everything Dr. Emerson Underwood had ever known about Derek Russell.

TWENTY-ONE

Karen spent four hours alone with the psychiatric file on Derek Russell before giving it up to the Behavioral Sciences Unit at Quantico. She sequestered herself in the den, away from the watchful eyes and pleading questions of Michael and Quince Garrett. She read every line on every scrap of paper, and then she went back and read it all over again. It wasn't until the third reading that she began to take notes, trying to pull together all that Dr. Underwood's file had to say with all that had happened since that time, fourteen years ago, when Russell blew up Dr. Underwood's car and became a phantom.

"We have to look at this thing on several levels," Karen began when she finally faced her elite class of two. "We begin with the childhood psychology.

"You've read the police file, so you know most of it. I don't have to tell you that Derek was a battered child, but there's another element here—the father. Derek's father died when he was four, but even at that age he adored the man. Under hypnosis he described the scent of his father's aftershave, the stiffness of a shirt collar as he had climbed on his father's lap for a hug. These were powerful images."

Michael tensed, thinking about his own memories. His own father. He, too, could remember the scent of his father's aftershave, the thickness of his shoulders as he had carried the young Michael on his back.

"I don't know how or when Derek conceived of his father as a genius, but it must have been quite young," Karen continued. "Perhaps he read articles or perhaps his grandmother used the father as a symbol of what Derek could never become. This ability to do something better than anyone else became Derek's obsession. His father had been the best—the absolute best at archaeological discovery, and Derek was determined to be the best at something. At anything. It didn't matter what. It only mattered that he be the best at it.

"I agree with Dr. Underwood that Derek murdered his grandmother. Probably with each slash of the knife, with each moan of her pain, he felt stronger. When he came out of that first murder, he felt he had found the one thing he could do better than anyone. He could kill."

"Does he feel that what he does is wrong?" Michael asked.

"No." Karen was emphatic. "Right and wrong never enter into the question. There is only doing it well or not doing it well. There is getting away with it, and there is—what for Derek is impossible to conceive—there is getting caught. That would be the ultimate failure. He could never face that.

"Now, there's another side to this. There's a medical implication. Dr. Underwood found evidence of possible damage to the limbic brain." She waited for the puzzled looks from her students. "The limbic brain is a small but vital complex at the top of the brain stem that controls all feeling—pleasure, pain, fear, aversion, rage. There is some evidence that damage to this sensitive area of the brain is linked with violent behavior. When Dr. Underwood put Derek Russell on the electroencephalograph the reading would sometimes be interrupted by a sudden vertical spike in the EEG, a spontaneous and uncontrollable release of energy in the limbic brain."

She scanned her notes. "In his examinations the stylus would sometimes stagger across the page as a result of these high-voltage discharges. And this, combined with his childhood, gives Derek a classic physical and mental makeup for violent behavior."

"He found what he was meant to be?" It was Michael who made the statement, turning it into a question.

"In an eerie sort of way, yes. He decided to become the best damned killer he could be."

"How do we stop him?" This came from Garrett.

Karen paced behind the desk, glancing down at the notes, and then returned to the two men in the room.

"There is no easy answer," she said, pausing between each word. "Even in giving us this information, he made the decision. He knew we were getting close, that the Boston police were sure to come up with a file—a name—so he gave it to us. He's made it part of his game. It's another victory—that he can give it to us, and that he doesn't care. He has given us all of this information as a way of saying it doesn't matter— that he's still smarter than all of us."

"You still haven't answered my question," Garrett insisted.

"There's only one thing that will get Derek Russell." She looked Garrett in the eye, until he blinked. "You've got to make Derek Russell blink. You've got to force him to make a mistake—one undeniable mistake that he can't fix. When he kidnapped me, that was a mistake. He wanted to kill Michael that day, but he rationalized it. He had me, and in his mind he decided I was a better game anyway. He was still in control."

"And what about the fact that he didn't kill you?" This came from Garrett.

"He didn't make a decision to kill me. He decided to test Michael. He wanted to see if Michael was a worthy opponent. Because Michael, with the help of the FBI and the police, was able to save me meant that he could be considered an equal."

"And now he wants a showdown with me." Michael had known it was coming to this.

"And now . . ." Karen paused. "Now, having accepted you as an equal, he must kill you. He must prove that he's better . . . that he's even better than you."

Karen didn't have a minute alone with Michael until they climbed the steps for bed at one o'clock in the morning.

"I've been going insane," she burst out, digging into the pocket of her slacks while Michael smiled, misunderstanding her urgency. She looked up, smiling back at his thought, then backed away and handed him a piece of paper.

"This," she announced, "was stuck in the middle of the Derek Russell file."

Michael took the piece of paper, glanced at it and then back at Karen. It was just a simple scrap, apparently a few quick notes jotted down by Dr. Underwood in the middle of doing something else. But then he saw what it said.

> To MM (care of KD)
>
> Request a private meeting at your earliest convenience to discuss the Derek Russell case. Imperative that we get to the heart of the matter. It's time for a showdown over just how we are going to conclude his treatment. Dr. Arthur Bottoms, the drug specialist from Washington, has been kind enough to take a suite at the Ritz-Carlton in his city so that we can get together without the usual interruptions. You and I have important matters to conclude. The room is reserved for the week. I ever so anxiously await your arrival.
>
> Yours,
DR

Michael read it a second time, considered all the ramifications, especially that Karen had kept this from the FBI.

"We've got to do it, Michael." She anticipated his question. "It's the only way."

"You want me to go after him?"

"It's the only way," she repeated. "Derek is too smart to let Quince get close to him. If he senses anything not exactly right he'll be gone and we'll lose him. And if you don't go after him and accept his challenge, then we lose the one thing we've got going for us. If you don't do it, you will no longer be his equal . . ."

"And if I'm not his equal . . ."

"Then you're not worth bothering with. He would go back to random killing with a vengeance, convinced that there is nobody who even has the guts to challenge him."

Michael couldn't think straight.

"In its own sick way, this is Derek's highest compliment."

Michael looked at her as if she had gone crazy.

"If we don't do this, Michael, then we've lost it all. I know. Derek will never call again, but he'll go on a killing spree that will make everything else look like play time."

"I've got to do it."

"No, Michael. We've got to do it. It's got to be both of us."

"Yes."

"Now, we need to figure a way to get out of this place."

"I think I know a way."

The telephone rang an hour later, and there were no preliminaries.

"Get Mikey to the phone," Russell demanded as soon as he realized an agent was on the line.

The buzzer sounded. Doors opened everywhere, and Michael led the pack down the steps, pulling on a robe as he ran. They were all in their places in less than thirty seconds. Michael looked to Garrett for the signal, then he picked up the phone.

He couldn't think of a word to say.

"Mikey. Are you there?"

"Yes. I'm here."

"Mikey, I've been bad again. I kept thinking about you, and about how you saved sweet Karen, so I went out and I got me a girl tonight. We had ourselves a real good time, but now she's dead. I just killed her, and it's all your fault."

Karen had already warned Michael that Russell would probably call with some gruesome details. Now every point counted, and Derek would do whatever it took to keep the lead. He had to keep the upper hand.

"No way, Derek." Michael stumbled as he said the name. "If you killed somebody tonight, it's because you're sick. It's because you haven't got any control. And it's because you feel safe killing people who aren't ready for you. They're all substitutes because you know I'm ready and you're too chicken shit to come face me man to man."

It was as direct as Michael could be. He avoided Garrett's face, hoping Karen was explaining their strategy—to put Derek on the defensive.

Russell was silent for a moment. "Maybe you're right, Mikey. I feel bad about this one. I mean it should be you that's dead. It shouldn't be her."

"Then let's do it, Derek. Come here . . . or tell me any place you want. Let's get down to me and you and settle this thing. We don't need all these bystanders. Just you and me."

Russell sighed. The game would be ending soon, and he was sad. It wouldn't be the same once he'd killed Mikey. "Maybe you're right. That's probably why I called. I mean, Mikey, I'm bored. It's no good anymore. I don't feel anything. I know I can go out and kill all the people I want. Nobody can stop me. There's no challenge."

"I'm your challenge, Derek. Let's do it."

Michael was deliberately taunting him, and Russell couldn't figure out why. If Michael had received the message, that was it. They both knew what had to be done.

"So let's do it, Derek. You name the place. You make the rules. Just don't do me in the back. Make it face to face like a man. Me and you. One on one."

Russell laughed. "Mikey, I look forward to the day."

"So do I, Derek. So do I."

"Good night, Mikey."

"Good night, Derek."

TWENTY-TWO

Michael and Karen were standing at a bedroom window in their wing of Manning Hall just before six A.M. when Quince Garrett, suitcase in hand, left the estate. Garrett had said he would be leaving for Ohio, following the call from Derek Russell and the discovery of another body just off the campus of Ohio State University, and the only question had been whether or not he would leave in time.

As soon as the car was out of sight, Michael went to the private phone line that had been installed for personal business. He knew the agents on duty downstairs would see the light come on, but he and Karen had tested it the night before. She had gone downstairs while he made a call, and the agents were not keeping tabs on the line.

A call to Allen Collins was the first move in a chess game that, if all worked according to plan, would soon bring Michael face to face with Derek Russell. It was a short call. Michael knew exactly what he wanted.

He and Karen then spent the next two hours going over their escape plan again and again, and the alternative strategies if any step along the way failed. The important thing was the rendezvous at the Ritz-Carlton Hotel in Washington.

When they came down from their rooms at nine o'clock, Michael was dressed in a crisp lightweight suit, a clear contrast to the usual jeans and T-shirt. He nodded to the four agents on duty, then continued into the kitchen to have Ginny prepare breakfast. He returned to the living room sipping a glass of orange juice just as Karen came down the steps.

"Where is Quince?" Michael asked.

"He left a couple of hours ago for Ohio," Travers said, failing to disguise the wary edge in his voice. "He can be reached if you need to talk to him."

"That won't be necessary, but you might want to let him know what is happening." Michael studied the attentive faces and took a deep breath. "I called Media Associates a couple of hours ago, and they've set up a press conference for eleven o'clock this morning. I'm going into Washington to talk to the press, and I've already consulted my attorney. I don't believe there's anything you can do to stop me."

Travers took a step forward, ready to state chapter and verse, rule and regulation.

"I know, Bill. I know you can pull some material witness crap, and get a court order, and fill out eight thousand forms, but I can tell you right now," he paused, making sure Travers was looking him in the eye. "I'll fight you every step of the way, and when I win I'll have a lot more to tell the press."

Finished with his statement, Michael didn't wait for the arguments. He emptied the glass of orange juice, took Karen's hand, and together they walked into the breakfast room. Ginny was just setting out eggs and sausage.

Travers waited until they were gone, then signaled his team. One reached for a telephone to track down Garrett. A second dialed headquarters in Washington. The stenographer in the group began logging in what had been said and what steps were being taken.

When Michael returned to the hallway, Travers stepped forward. "Mr. Manning, Agent Garrett would like to speak to you." He motioned to a phone held by one of the other men in the room.

"No, thank you. I don't care to speak with him until after the news conference."

"We must insist."

"Check your manual," Michael said. "You don't do any insisting while you're in Manning Hall."

Travers's face went red, more with surprise at Michael's attitude than anything else.

"Okay," Michael continued. "Who, if anybody, has been assigned to accompany me to Washington?"

"What about you?" Travers asked, looking at Karen. "Are you in on this little escapade?"

Karen smiled at the stenographer, poised to record her response.

"No," she said. "Michael and I have talked it over. I believe what he's doing is a good idea, but there's no need for me to go to Washington. I'll stay here and behave myself."

Travers nodded to an agent, who then picked up car keys from the table and left the room.

"Agent Randolph and I will accompany you, Mr. Manning," Travers said, putting as much bite into his formality as possible. "Agents Chambers and Fredericks will remain here with Dr. Daniels."

"Good," Michael said.

The board room at Media Associates was packed. It looked like a presidential news conference, with perhaps seventy reporters seated in rows before the podium, television crews just behind the seats with their bright lights and cameras.

An anxious Allen Collins, now acting publisher of Media Associates, met Michael in the hallway and pulled him into a side room away from the crowd.

"Good God, Michael, what's going on?" Allen nodded to the door. "It's a zoo out there, and a couple of hours after you asked me to set this up I had FBI people all over the place. These are not happy men."

Michael put his arm around Allen, remembering how they'd spent so many summers together in that other lifetime. Few people knew how Allen had supported Michael's decision to go to Europe and be on his own for a couple of years, and Michael needed that same kind of support now more than ever.

"Everything's okay, Allen. I promise. It's just that this phantom thing is getting out of hand, and I'm afraid it's up to me to make the next move. It's the only way. You've got to trust me on that."

Allen thought for just a moment before he answered. "Sure, Michael. You do what you've got to do."

"Thanks, Allen. I appreciate your taking care of this for me. Things will be clear in a few minutes, and then I'll need to see you after the news conference."

The two men walked together into the conference room. Camera shutters clicked, and the bright TV lights blinded everybody as Michael stepped behind the podium.

"First things first," Michael said. "I'm not going to be able to answer any questions. I've come to you this morning without the blessing of the Federal Bureau of Investigation. I'm acting on my own. I've seen the information the Bureau has released, and I've read the speculation that has resulted. What I hope to do this morning is set a few things straight."

Michael's eyes gradually adjusted to the bright lights. He looked over the silent crowd of reporters, some holding tape recorders, others busily scratching notes. Red lights flashed at him from the row of television cameras, and he could spot at least a dozen FBI agents in the crowd.

"We believe—no, make that I believe—that a man named Derek Russell is responsible for the murder of hundreds of people. He has been roaming the country for fifteen years, killing people for sport. It is all a game to him, and he's good at it. He's managed to avoid police investigation—in fact, he was unknown to all law enforcement agencies, including the FBI, until two months ago. He remains at large. He claims responsibility for the murder of Kathy Manning, and indirectly for the death of my father. More recently, he has murdered several other people, including two FBI agents and a prominent Boston psychiatrist. He has kidnapped and tortured Dr. Karen Daniels, a close friend of mine, and he has shot me."

A buzz passed through the room, and sweat began to form across Michael's forehead.

"This man has for some reason chosen to make me part of his game. He has called me at intervals over the past two months, taunting me and the FBI. He has challenged us and always managed to escape. He has hinted about some kind of showdown between him and me, but he has refused to live up to this one challenge. He has hurt everyone around me, but he is unwilling to face me."

Michael's throat was dry, but he forced himself to swallow. He had to keep going.

"When he kidnapped Dr. Daniels, he vowed that he would set up a showdown—between him and me. I have proven myself a worthy opponent. Dr. Daniels is now recuperating from the horrors of what he did to her. She is alive. It has been nearly two weeks since then, and still Derek Russell avoids me. There has been no showdown."

Michael's throat had reached the raw stage. Sweat dripped from his brow, and his eyes were burning, but he stared out into the cameras.

"I challenge Derek Russell to come forward. I challenge him to meet me anytime, anywhere. That is the message I want you to deliver. Tell Russell I'm ready. I'm tired of waiting."

Michael turned away from the podium as soon as he had said the last word. There were shouts from the audience, reporters screaming questions, but Michael didn't stop. He walked out of the room, leaving the FBI agents to block the path behind him.

Allen Collins came into the office from a side door and handed Michael a glass of scotch. He said nothing until Michael had gulped down the drink.

"Do you really think they'll run that?"

"They'll run it," Michael said. "Maybe not all of them, but enough will."

"Jesus, Michael. I hope you know what you're doing."

"I hope so, too. And I need your help."

Quince Garrett walked in, looking like the side of a mountain about to cave in.

"We need to talk—alone," Garrett demanded.

"Allen, would you mind? I promised Agent Garrett I'd talk with him as soon as the conference was over."

Allen left the room.

"Okay, Quince, calm down," Michael said before Garrett had a chance to start. "I thought about this a lot. I knew you wouldn't approve and that if I gave you enough time you'd find a way to stop me. I also know there's no way you can stop all of them from releasing the story. That means I've done it, and there's nothing you can do about it."

Garrett stood in the middle of the room. When Michael stopped talking, he opened his mouth, but none of the things he wanted to say were going to make any difference.

Michael walked to the far wall and pushed a hidden button at the side of a picture frame. A panel popped open to reveal a small bar. He filled two glasses with scotch and returned, handing one of the drinks to Garrett.

"Let's drink to catching the son of a bitch," Michael said, raising his glass and meeting Garrett eye to eye.

Garrett raised his glass. They drank.

"Now that that's settled," Michael said, "I need a few minutes alone with Allen. Company business. Decisions about how our magazines should handle the story. As soon as I finish we can go back to Manning Hall, where Dr. Daniels and I will try to explain what it is we're trying to accomplish."

Garrett was still guarding his tongue. He looked at the young man who had become almost like a son to him, but he wouldn't say anything. He was afraid that if he started, he wouldn't be able to stop. He was angrier than he'd been since this thing began. His exit was clean and quick.

"Okay, what now?" Allen said, coming into the room.

"You're not going to like this," Michael said. "I need to escape. I've got to get away from the FBI. I need a Media Associates credit card, something with any name except Manning on it, and I need to go through the offices and out the side door."

"Are you sure, Michael?"

"Yes. And there isn't much time."

Allen reached into his wallet and handed Michael his own credit card.

"I'll stay and run interference for you," he said. "I've gotten good at that over the years."

The two men tried to smile, and then Michael was gone.

Karen Daniels wandered around Manning Hall. She went to the den with the excuse that she needed to go through her notes, but that didn't work. Then she went to her room and checked the large shoulder bag that served as her purse.

It contained all the bare necessities in terms of makeup and underwear.

Now. Now, it was time to move.

Downstairs, she found Mrs. Patterson in the kitchen. Michael had casually suggested that Ginny make some of her famous chocolate chip cookies, and the first batch was just coming out of the oven. Karen grabbed one, then walked into the office.

The agent she and Michael had nicknamed Chow noticed the cookie almost before she got into the room. His sensitive nose had zeroed in on fresh-baked treats, and he could resist no longer. He quickly excused himself and headed in the direction of the kitchen.

The other agent, nicknamed Fifi, continued to lounge in the living room command center like a fat cat. He was theoretically reading a newspaper, but actually seemed half asleep. Karen nodded a hello and wandered back into the hallway.

Everyone was in place. From the living room and kitchen no one could see the garage. If she was really careful, the engine of Michael's Porsche probably wouldn't be heard either.

She grabbed her shoulder bag off the steps, eased out the front door, and dashed for the garage. Michael had given her the electronic code to unlock the garage door, and in less than a minute she was at the main road, turning toward Washington.

There was no barometer designed to measure Garrett's anger when he discovered that he had been had.

"I want to know where he is, and I want to know, now!" Garrett screamed at least a dozen times to at least a dozen operatives on the phone.

Garrett remained in Washington, heading up the search for Michael, while Bill Travers returned to Manning Hall to pick up Karen's trail. It took two hours before they knew anything.

An APB on the red Porsche turned up the car in the parking lot at National Airport. From there Karen could be almost anywhere, certainly with Michael by her side and Derek Russell closing in for the kill.

Then there was Allen Collins.

Garrett grilled the Media Associates senior man for an hour, getting back a lot of legal mumbo-jumbo for his efforts. It was only in the second hour that Allen began to falter in his support for what Michael had done.

"You realize he's going to get himself killed? You do realize that?" Garrett insisted for about the one hundredth time.

"All I know," Allen came back, "is that he said he needed to get away. He never mentioned Derek Russell, never said anything about any plan. He only said he had to get away from you, away from the FBI."

Garrett stormed around the office. "And there's more," he demanded.

"The only thing is he asked me for a credit card." Allen felt like the biggest traitor since Benedict Arnold. "I gave him my credit card. Anything he buys with it will be in my name."

The special telephone rang at Manning Hall at two o'clock that afternoon. Bill Travers let it ring while he patched through to Media Associates. Garrett was going to have to handle this one.

The phone continued to ring . . . five, six, seven rings. Then Garrett answered.

"Hello." The patch had created an echo, and the word bounced back through the receiver over and over again.

"Quince, baby. Is that you?"

Now the phone was clear. The voice was unmistakable.

"Let me talk to Mikey."

This was it. Garrett had tried to think how he was going to play the scene, and none of his ideas worked.

"He's not available at the moment," Garrett said, trying to make it sound as natural as possible.

"Would you repeat that, please?" Derek asked.

"Michael is not available to come to the phone. He does not wish to speak to you. He . . . ."

But there was no need to say more. Derek Russell had hung up.

TWENTY-THREE

The view from the fifth floor of the Ritz-Carlton took in the heart of Washington's Embassy Row, its architecture standing tall with a European grace while the colorful flags of many nations flapped in an afternoon breeze. Trees, spaced evenly along both sides of Massachusetts Avenue, added a touch of serenity to the steady flow of traffic. A party of high school students gathered at the corner of 21st Street while a teacher tried to herd them into the Phillips art gallery.

Michael stood at the window of the suite that had been rented for him by Derek Russell. Behind him was a locked and bolted door at which he expected Derek Russell to appear at any moment. There was a bar stocked with assorted liquors—actually there were two, one in each bedroom—but as much as Michael needed a drink he was determined to avoid the temptation. He wanted to be alert.

There were also five televisions—a large-screen version in the living room, portables built into armoires in each of the two bedrooms, and additional small units in each bathroom. There were nine telephones, king-size beds, and a marble fireplace.

Derek had spared no expense. He had registered the suite for Dr. and Mrs. Arthur Bottoms, anticipating Karen's insistence that she join Michael, and Derek was obviously out to impress.

Michael had been in the room for a little over an hour, hiding like a criminal on the run and wondering why this absurd escape had seemed like the only reasonable thing to do. He had no weapon, and he was standing in the middle of a room that a psychopathic killer had rented for the exclusive purpose of killing him.

Karen's knock almost sent Michael through the window, but her voice calmed him and he raced to the door. They embraced.

"Are you okay?" she asked. "You look like you've just seen a ghost."

"I've been seeing ghosts all afternoon," he said, trying to smile.

Karen gave the suite a quick once over.

"Is this completely foolish, what we're doing?" she asked.

"I don't know. Just before you arrived I was ready to call Quince and stop the whole thing, but I couldn't do it."

"This is the only way?" she asked.

"I believe it is. If the FBI were in on this, Derek would just stay away."

Karen pulled back, looking at Michael carefully before she went to the large shoulder bag she'd dropped on the sofa. She took out a revolver—a .38-caliber police special.

"I've had this all along," she said, holding the weapon like a fragile art object. "I've got a permit—for my protection— but I've kept it in my room. I keep it cleaned, and it's loaded. I think we're going to need it."

She handed the gun to Michael, who had flashes of a dirt road next to an abandoned farm. He remembered the feel of the dead agent's gun in his hands.

"What do we do now?" Michael asked.

Karen moved to the sofa and patted the seat beside her.

"We wait," she said.

Michael placed the gun on the coffee table. The barrel pointed directly at the door to the room.

"I noticed that Derek registered the room for Dr. and Mrs. Bottoms," Karen said, almost at a whisper. "He knew I'd come."

"He seems to know everything we do," Michael answered, his whisper smaller than hers.

"We're going to have to change that," she said, and this time the words were barely audible.

Quince Garrett figured the odds were fifty-fifty, maybe sixty-forty, with the advantage going to Derek Russell. And if Derek did find Michael and Karen first, the odds were probably 99-to-1 that they would die.

Garrett was back in his office at FBI Headquarters on Pennsylvania Avenue. It was 2:30. Michael and Karen had been on their own for three hours, and finally the calls were beginning to come in, the first from an agent sifting through hundreds of reservations at National Airport.

"I think we've got a lead on Dr. Daniels." The agent spoke fast, excited. "A woman fitting her description bought a one-way ticket to Richmond at 11:45 this morning. She paid cash. The plane departed on time at 12:20, so she's already there. It's too late to hit the airport."

Richmond? Why Richmond? Because it was close but also far enough away to avoid immediate detection? Or was it just a detour, a brief stop in transit to somewhere else?

Then there was another call.

"We've got a lead on Michael," Travers reported without preliminaries. "He bought a suitcase and what appears to be a single change of clothes from one of the Georgetown boutiques, then he taxied a few blocks and rented a car. All of this is on the Allen Collins credit card."

"We've traced Karen to Richmond. What do you think?" Garrett asked.

"I don't know. Something in my bones tells me they haven't left Washington. Why would they bother?"

"To get away from us?" Garrett tried.

"But if they're after Derek Russell, why would they go away? He connects them to Washington. If he's going to get in touch, it almost has to be here."

"Somehow, I feel like they've already made contact," Garrett said. "Something we missed at Manning Hall. That's what my bones are telling me."

"What now?" Travers asked.

There was a moment of silence while Garrett crushed out his cigarette with a vengeance.

"Put out a Washington APB on the car. Let's find the damn thing."

Seconds after they hung up, the phone rang again. It was Travers.

"We just got a bonus," Travers reported. "Local police just ticketed a silver Corvette parked on the Mall across from the Smithsonian. The car is registered in Columbus, Ohio. It's Derek Russell's car. He's here."

The telephone rang in the suite of Dr. and Mrs. Arthur Bottoms at four o'clock. Michael moved to the antique desk in the living room and answered on the second ring.

"Mikey?"

Michael's heart almost stopped as he nodded to Karen.

"Mikey, I know I've said it before, but I've got to say it again. You've got balls. I had no idea you'd actually accept my invitation. I hoped that you would, but this—well, to tell you the truth, I'm just flabbergasted."

"So, what happens now?"

Derek laughed. "Mikey, please. Give me a second. Your showing up is a lot to take in. I've got to think."

"You, think," Michael came back, suddenly feeling nasty. "How can you possibly call what you do thinking?"

"Mikey, Mikey, you cut me to the quick." Again the laugh.

"So, what now?"

There was a pause.

"Relax, Mikey. Let's talk. This is the first time we can really talk, with no FBI and no Quinton Garrett around. They aren't around, are they, Mikey?"

"No, Derek. I'm all alone."

"Well, tell Karen to hang up the extension. I heard it click when she picked up. This is between you and me."

Karen hung up the phone and sat on the sofa listening to Michael's end of the conversation.

"Okay, Derek. What do we talk about?"

"Let's talk about—how about fathers?"

Michael trembled.

"Tell me about your father, Mikey. Was he big and strong? Did he carry you on his shoulders when you played in the park? Did he hold you around the waist the first time you tried to ride a bicycle? Did he play catch with you in the yard and show you the proper way to pass a football? Did he give you your first typewriter and say 'be a writer, my son'? Did he take you fishing in mountain streams and hunting in the Canadian wilderness?"

Derek finally stopped. Matthew Emerson Manning had done all those things.

"Talk to me, Mikey." There was anger in the demand.

"Yes, Derek. Yes. My father did those things and a lot more."

"I thought so." Now the voice was sad. "My father never had time. He was too . . . too important. And then he died."

"Yes, I know, Derek. I read the files."

"Tell me, Mikey. How do you think you would have turned out if you'd lived the life in those files? Do you think you'd be the same person you are today?"

"No, Derek. I wouldn't be the same."

"Do you think you could have become me?" This was said quietly, calmly . . . importantly.

"No, Derek. I could never have been you."

"Are you so sure?"

"Yes, Derek, I'm positive. I could never have done the things you've done."

There was a long pause.

"Do you think I could have been you, Mikey?" There was hope in the question.

"I don't know. Maybe, if you'd had my father, my kind of life. Maybe you wouldn't have felt like you had to hate the world. Maybe—"

"I don't hate the world." Now there was anger. "I certainly do not hate the world, Mikey. The world is wonderful, filled with unlimited possibilities. It's the people who ruin it. I hate the people, Mikey, not the world."

"I'm sorry."

"So am I, Mikey. There are times, honestly, when I wonder what I might have become. Maybe an archaeologist, like my father. Or maybe an artist. I have always been fascinated with

the creative spirit, with the willpower that it takes to make a
piece of art come alive."

"I wish you could have had that, Derek. Honestly, I do."

There was another pause.

"I believe you do, Mikey, and that's the nicest thing anybody
has ever said to me. It's a shame I've got to kill you."

Michael almost dropped the phone.

"Why, Derek? Why do we have to do this?"

"Don't you see, Mikey? Haven't I taught you anything? This
is what I am. You're a journalist with a publishing empire
filled with possibilities. My father was an archaeologist with a
whole world to uncover. And me, Mikey. I'm a killer. My
world of possibilities is in what I am capable of doing. I can
do anything, and there's not a soul in the world who can
match me. Not a soul, Mikey, and certainly not you."

"But it's wrong, Derek. You have ruined so many
lives—"

"They have all ruined mine," Derek shouted into the phone.

"No, Derek. They have not ruined your life. These people
are innocent. They are trying to live their own lives as best
they can. That's what we all do. That's what my father did,
what your father did. And you step in and—"

"I step in and take over," Derek interrupted. "I control
life and death, Mikey. Think about that. I control who lives
and who dies. The ultimate power. It's more than anything
you'll ever write, and it's more than any old bones my father
ever dug up."

Michael closed his eyes.

"When are we going to meet, Derek?"

"Soon, Mikey. Very soon."

"Am I going to have any chance at all?"

Derek laughed, but this one wasn't quite so jolly. "Yes,
Mikey. I promise you'll have a chance. It probably won't be
a fair chance, but it will be a chance."

"When?"

There was another pause.

"Mikey, you take it easy tonight. Consider this evening my
treat. Have dinner in the Jockey Club. I've already told them
to put it on my bill."

"What are you going to do, Derek?"

"Don't you worry about me, Mikey. I'll spend the afternoon seeing the sights. Then there's this dumb party I'm supposed to go to tonight."

"But Derek—"

"No, Mikey. You enjoy this evening. Consider Karen your last request. Tomorrow you will die."

Bill Travers and a team of federal agents stormed the East Building at the National Gallery of Art just as Derek Russell was hanging up the pay telephone on the lower concourse. When the agents found the telephone booth, tucked away in a marble alcove near the restrooms, there was a card taped to the door.

Printed in block letters, the card read "Closed by order of the FBI." It was signed with the name Quince Garrett.

Travers ripped the card from the door and balled it in his fist. Both buildings of the National Gallery were sealed off within three minutes, every exit manned for a gallery-by-gallery search.

Derek Russell was gone.

How? That was the question. They had only located Michael's rental car, parked in the valet lot used by the Ritz-Carlton, thirty minutes before the call. The manager had identified the couple registered as Dr. and Mrs. Bottoms, and Garrett had arrived in the basement of the hotel just as the tap had been completed on phones in the suite. They had made it with five minutes to spare, and Garrett was sure they had him when Derek's call rang through.

"God damn it?" Garrett shouted when he got the news. "How does he know?"

Travers tried to be calm.

"What now? Are you going to tell Michael you've found him?"

"Hell, no," Garrett snapped. "If Michael wants to play the fucking hero, we'll just have to let him do it."

"It won't be easy to cover him, not with the traffic in and out of the Ritz-Carlton."

"I know. I know."

"And Derek knows we're onto him," Travers continued. "He's sure to do something nasty."

"I know."

TWENTY-FOUR

A formal gathering was taking place in the private second-floor dining room of a restaurant on Pennsylvania Avenue, just two blocks above the White House. The long buffet was piled high with appetizers, as colorful as they were tasty, while white-jacketed bartenders maintained the lively mood by serving from bottomless bottles of champagne at each end of the room.

Derek Russell moved casually through the room. When he spotted Phyllis Kenworthy, he was delighted by her radiant beauty. He'd seen her only twice before, both times from a distance as he weighed the possibilities and planned his strategies.

Russell gradually made his way in her direction. He waited until she was alone at one end of the buffet table and watched until she carefully chose a tiny sandwich. He moved in.

"What are these?" he asked, edging down the opposite side of the table without looking at her.

"I believe it's chicken liver," she said, popping one in her mouth for a test.

Russell glanced up.

"Suddenly, I'm not very hungry," he said, allowing his appreciation of her beauty to sparkle in his eyes.

She laughed, and took a sip of wine, but her eyes flirted ever so slightly over the top of the glass.

"I would really like to meet you sometime when I'm completely sober," Russell said, setting his glass on the table as if he were sorry he'd ever started drinking.

"You don't look drunk to me."

"I'm not," Russell said. "But I have a feeling I'd want to be completely alert—with not a trace of outside intoxicant—when I'm with you."

"Why's that?"

Russell laughed, a low conspiring chuckle that showed off his smile. "To use one of my mother's expressions—I feel I would need to have all of my wits about me."

She smiled. "I don't believe we've met," she said.

"Kenneth, Kenneth Daniels," he said, walking around the table to take her hand.

"Phyllis Kenworthy. I'm with Amberson & Wade, the New York publisher. I'm trying to make contact with—well, let's just say with a very mysterious author."

"And I'm in the same boat—mystery that is." Russell laughed his most conspiring laugh. "I'm here trying to do some business for someone who must, at present, remain anonymous."

"Sounds very cloak and dagger."

"It is. Very definitely cloak and dagger—perhaps a bit more dagger than cloak."

"Do you live here in Washington?"

"For the present," he said.

Someone motioned to Phyllis from the other side of the room, and she waved back.

"Must run," she said. "Very nice to meet you."

"But wait. You haven't said how I can meet you . . . when I'm sober."

She thought only for a moment.

"You can call me at the Ritz-Carlton. I'll be here to the end of the week, working mostly in the morning. Most afternoons and evenings are free."

"I will call."

"I'll look forward to it," she said, toasting him with the glass of wine. And then she was gone.

Russell wandered through the party, knowing that the rest of his plan relied on too many uncontrollable details. He knew that Phyllis Kenworthy had no car and was using taxis to get around the city. He simply had to hope no one offered her a ride back to the Ritz.

When Phyllis emerged from the restaurant just before eleven o'clock, she immediately began looking for a taxi. Russell stepped up beside her, then bent forward looking up and down Pennsylvania Avenue.

"May I offer you a ride?" he asked.

She started to decline the offer, but before she spoke Russell raised his hand and a black limousine pulled up in front of them. The driver, the quintessence of formality in his uniform and cap, jumped from the car and came to the sidewalk to open the door.

"Well?" Russell said.

"I thought you wanted to be sober before we met?"

"I do. But the fresh air has made me bold."

Phyllis flashed her bright eyes and slid into the car, making room for Russell beside her.

"To the Ritz-Carlton," Russell instructed the driver.

"That's at 21st and Massachusetts," Phyllis added.

During the short drive Russell asked her about her job in New York, then about the books she had handled. She listened intently as he talked about his travels around the world on behalf of his mysterious client. When he asked her to dinner the next night, she accepted.

When they pulled into the driveway of the Ritz-Carlton, Phyllis was feeling rather good about herself. She suspected that this mysterious Kenneth Daniels would make for an interesting week. She almost invited him for a drink in the Ritz bar, but decided at the last minute that it would be too bold.

"I insist on seeing you to your door," Russell said, stepping from the car before she had a chance to object.

"It really isn't necessary."

"But I insist. Besides . . . I might get lucky. You might invite me in."

"Don't count on it," she said, laughing.

"Just in case . . ." Russell bent back into the car and patted the driver on the shoulder. "If I'm not back in an hour, turn into a pumpkin and roll away."

The driver smiled, but then Phyllis stuck her head into the car.

"Don't worry. He'll be back."

Phyllis smiled confidently as she took Russell's arm and they walked to the door. Many eyes watched their entrance, but they were all too far away to identify the man with the beautiful woman.

The Ritz lobby was arranged with two front desks, the concierge on the left, registration on the right. Derek turned toward the gentle older man who was obviously the concierge, a subtle move that hid his face from the obvious young FBI man trying to get a glimpse of the tuxedoed man who had just entered with the beautiful hotel guest.

"Good evening, Miss Kenworthy," the concierge said.

"Good evening," she responded.

Russell's nod went unnoticed. One advantage of being with a beautiful woman, as Derek knew, is that you're rarely seen.

As the elevator doors closed, the agent at the registration desk was on the radio.

"This is the lobby. Kenworthy. Room 535. She's registered as a single, but she just came in with a man. She's all dolled up, and he's in a tux. I didn't see his face, but he's going up with her."

"Don't sweat it," came a radio reply from an agent watching the front door. "Big limo out front, and I don't think that's our phantom's style. What do you think, nest?"

"I don't like it," Garrett said. "The fifth is our man's floor, and I don't trust the tux. Get one of our waiters up there to keep an eye on this dude."

"Roger," said the agent at the front desk.

In the elevator, Derek Russell was playing things cautiously. He slipped an arm casually around Phyllis's waist, and while there was no real resistance she did move away. He moved close again, and she playfully kissed him on the cheek.

"There, are you satisfied?"

"Pleased, yes," he said. "Satisfied—well, let's think about that one for a while."

The elevator came to a stop, and they stepped into a long hallway on the fifth floor. A maid at one end of the hall was rolling a small tray that contained roses and chocolate mints to be placed on every pillow when she turned down the beds for the night. A waiter who had apparently dropped a tray at the opposite end of the hall was busily cleaning up the mess.

Russell only glanced at the maid, but his attention riveted on the back of the waiter.

"My room is right down here," Phyllis said, motioning to a door midway down the hall.

Russell became playful again, acting drunk and using Phyllis for support, causing them to stumble and sway as they made their way to the door.

"Looks like we've got a real jerk here," the waiter reported, mumbling softly into a microphone pinned to the lapel of his waiter's jacket. "A real loser."

As they approached the door to Room 535, Russell moved close to Phyllis and began to whisper to her, pulling his jacket over his face to avoid the waiter.

"They're watching us," she said, nodding to both the waiter and the maid. She laughed as she put her key in the lock. Just as she turned the knob, Russell reached for her shoulder and turned her around.

"With all this watching going on, I think we ought to give them something to watch." He nodded toward the waiter. "How about just a little kiss good night. Something for him to take back to the kitchen. A little kiss, and we'll no longer be strangers."

Russell very deliberately lifted each of her arms, placing them around his neck, where she obediently laced her fingers. Then he placed his left arm around her waist and bent forward with a tender kiss on the lips. As he moved up against her body he reached into his jacket pocket with his right hand, removing an eight-inch switchblade. The blade sprung open just as their lips met, then he pushed the full eight inches of steel between her ribs and turned the point upward, to the heart.

There was no struggle. Their lips stayed together. Russell used his strength to hold her still against the door, then he slowly pushed her backward. The door opened, and to the kneeling agent it appeared that she had dragged him into the suite. The door closed.

"Well I'll be damned," the agent reported. "The son-of-a-bitch scored. She put her arms around his neck for a little good-night kiss and zoom . . . the lucky bastard is into the room."

"You can never tell about women," came back Quince Garrett's voice, relieved that it had been a false alarm.

Twenty minutes later Russell backed out of Room 535 carrying his jacket. There was blood down one sleeve, but he carried the jacket folded over his arm so that it wouldn't show. There was no one in the hallway, but just before he closed the door he waved back through the crack, then he stood straight and stuck out his tongue at the imaginary figure who might be standing there.

When his elevator arrived in the lobby, he made a quick dash for the door, mumbling angrily to himself and catching the agent at the registration desk by surprise. He was outside before the agent had a chance to see his face.

"Wait a minute," the agent at the front desk said into the transmitter. "Romeo is either the fastest gun in the west, or he was just called on a third strike. He's out."

Laughter came from all stations.

Michael had checked the doors a half dozen times, to be sure each was locked and bolted. A bottle of champagne that Derek had ordered for them sat unopened on a nearby table, light from one of the bedside lamps reflecting off the metallic embossing on the label. The same light reflected off the hard gray barrel of the police revolver.

"Do you think you are going to be able to use that thing when the time comes?" Karen asked, seeing that Michael was staring at the gun.

"That's what scares me most," he said. "I don't know."

"What do you think he's going to do?" Whenever one of them mentioned Derek Russell, it turned into a whisper.

"I don't know." The question made Michael angry. "I have a feeling he's out there . . . somewhere . . . killing somebody. He's doing something really bad, and then he's coming after me."

"What can we do?"

"There will be a moment. I don't know when, and I don't know how long it will last . . . but there's got to be a moment when we can change things. We've got to believe in that moment."

It was nearly midnight, and Quince Garrett was going stir crazy. Michael and Karen had remained in their suite all day, even ordering their evening meal from room service, and there had been no more calls.

At last count, Derek Russell had used his assorted names to reserve more than thirty motel rooms in and around Washington. He was staying in none of them. There was no record of a car rental or purchase. No taxis reported picking up anyone who matched the drawing they had circulated. There was nothing but the aching knowledge that he was there . . . somewhere . . . just out of reach.

"I've got to get out of this place," Garrett said to the agent beside him at the telephone tap. "If anything comes in—and I mean anything—you can reach me in my car."

TWENTY-FIVE

The telephone rang at 12:15. The sound sent shivers through the suite on the fifth floor, and brought the agent in the basement to attention.

Michael answered on the second ring. He picked up the phone with his right hand, his left moving with a will of its own to rest gently on the revolver.

"Derek. This is Michael. Where are you?"

And Russell laughed. "Easy, Mikey. You don't have to scream. I'm close. I'm very, very close."

"Have you—" Michael couldn't ask the question.

"Yes, Mikey. I have. And it was a good one. She was a real beauty, a warm and wonderful girl."

"Bastard." Michael said the word quietly. Sadly.

"I know, Mikey. It is hard to sit there and hear about all the fun I'm having—fun at your expense, I might add. But Mikey, it is fun. Can't you see that. God, it's exciting."

"Please Derek, no details."

"But Mikey, you're missing the point. I mean, tonight I put everything on the line. It was thrilling. I spent the evening in a large group of people. These were people who know what's going on. Any one of them could have recognized me.

Any one of them could have seen the sketch your FBI buddies
have plastered all over town, but they didn't. Then I walked
right into the hotel, Mikey. Right in front of Quince Garrett
himself, right in front of everybody. And I walked right back
out again. And nothing. Not a peep out of anybody."

"I wish I could have been there."

"Now, Mikey, listen to me." The tone changed. This was
it. Derek was making his move.

"I'm here, Derek."

"Mikey, this is very important. Which room are you in?
Which bedroom?"

Michael had to think.

"The one on the right, to the right of the living room."

"Good, Mikey. In the drawer of the table to the left of the
bed, the one with the phone on it—look in the drawer."

Michael carefully opened the drawer. The only thing there
was a folded sheet of hotel stationery.

"Have you found it, Mikey?"

"Yes, Derek."

There was a pause. Derek was giving him time to read the
note:

> Mikey
> The FBI has followed you. If you're serious about this
> showdown, you've got to escape. Do not listen to the
> rest of this call. Get out. Get out now. Do not use the
> main elevator. Leave your room and turn right. There's
> another set of elevators at the end of the hall. It will
> bring you down to the side entrance. This is it, Mikey!
> It's now or never! Move!
> Derek

"Are you there, Mikey?"

"Yes, Derek. I understand." He had read the note quickly,
passing it to Karen, and she was already slipping on her jacket.

"Then do it," Derek demanded.

Michael dropped the phone on the bed, pushed the revolver
into his belt, grabbed the sportcoat Karen was holding for
him, and they ran for the door.

"All right, Quince, are you there?" Derek laughed, continuing on the phone. "This is for you, Quince, baby. Take a
look in Room 535. I've left a little present for you."

The hallway was empty. Michael and Karen stepped from their room, looking both ways, and ran to the right. The elevator was exactly where Derek had said it would be, and Michael frantically pushed the button.

Just before the doors opened, he had a thought. Could this be it? Is Derek in the elevator? Michael pulled the gun from his belt, grasping it with both hands as he aimed at the door, but the elevator doors opened, and it was empty. Karen stepped into the opening, pulling Michael with her, and the doors quickly closed behind them.

"Michael," she said, breathlessly. "This is it. If we're going to get our moment, it's got to be soon."

Michael nodded his agreement.

The elevator doors opened on a quiet hallway flanked by rooms reserved for conferences. The rooms were all empty, and the main lobby was far away, its bright lights visible through ornate doors at the far end of the hallway.

The double doors directly in front of them were intended for use only in an emergency. A sign warned that if you opened the doors an alarm would sound, but Michael didn't even slow down enough to see it. He hit the safety bar on the door, his left arm around Karen's waist, and they stepped into the darkness as a loud bell sounded behind them.

"Which way?" Karen asked, but Michael had already made the obvious choice. They had to go left, away from the front entrance and move quickly to one of the darker side streets. If the FBI had the hotel staked out, they couldn't be far behind.

"We've got to get to my car," Michael said. "I believe the valet parking uses a lot at the next corner. We should be able to pick up the keys there."

Then, out of nowhere, Bill Travers stepped in front of them.

Without thinking, Michael grabbed the revolver from his belt.

"Michael, please." Travers held both hands out from his side in a show of peace. "Let's go back to the hotel and talk."

"No, Bill. We can't do that."

"Well, Michael." Travers spoke calmly, keeping his hands far from his sides. "We have a stand-off. I don't plan on stepping aside."

Karen glared at Travers and stepped around him, as if to continue. When Travers turned toward her, Michael moved, bringing the barrel of the gun down on Travers's head. The agent collapsed.

"Oh my God," Michael breathed, looking at his hand and the blood-stained barrel of the revolver.

"We've got to move, Michael." Karen grabbed his arm and almost dragged Michael along.

They reached the corner, but there was nowhere to go. Directly across the street was the parking lot, with Michael's rental visible in the second row. But in front of the shack where the keys were kept sat a police car, the two uniformed officers inside listening to instructions over the car radio.

"We can go for my car," Karen said. "I parked on the street. I didn't use the valet service, and I'll bet Quince doesn't even know I have it."

Just before they stepped off the curb, a taxi pulled up in front of them and stopped.

"Would you by chance be the gentleman named Mikey?" the driver asked.

Michael looked beyond the taxi at the police car in the parking lot, his head spinning with what was happening. Karen took charge, pulling Michael into the back seat of the taxi.

"Did Derek send you?" Michael asked.

"Don't know his name," the driver smiled back over the seat. "But this dude just gave me five crisp new twenty-dollar bills and said to pick you up and carry you to the Hay-Adams."

"The Hay-Adams—another hotel?"

"That's it. Now what's the clue?"

"Clue?"

"Yeah," the driver came back. "He said y'all was playing a game, and the Hay-Adams was your clue. He said room number 535 . . . that would tip it off."

"This doesn't make any sense."

The driver frowned, not happy at being left out of the game.

"Who gave you the money—the hundred dollars?" Karen broke in, all business.

"I told you." The driver was becoming annoyed. "Don't know his name—just this dude."

Michael reached over the seat, shoving the revolver into the driver's face.

"Holy shit."

"Where is he?" Michael demanded.

"I don't know. He was around the corner. A big celebrity-type dude in a tuxedo—had himself a big black limousine. He paid me and headed on down 21st Street."

"Take us over to that car," Karen demanded, pointing to a beige Chevrolet parked thirty yards away on Massachusetts Avenue.

The driver looked at the gun, then at Michael.

"Move! Now!"

The driver raced the half block, almost sliding the taxi to a stop when he hit the brakes to make an awkward U-turn next to the beige sedan. They had to go right past the spot where Michael had knocked down Travers, and they caught a glimpse of the agent crawling to his feet as they passed.

"You've already been paid," Michael said to the driver.

They transferred to the rental car, keeping as low as possible just in case Travers looked up. Karen's hands were surprisingly calm as she unlocked the car door, climbed into the driver's seat, and waited for Michael to sneak around to the passenger side.

"Now get out of here," Michael called across to the taxi driver, who didn't need urging. The taxi spun tires down the street, running a red light at 21st Street as he raced down Massachusetts Avenue.

Karen was right behind him. She steered the Chevy into the street, then swung a hard right as she passed the corner entrance to the Ritz-Carlton. There was no traffic on 21st Street, so she gunned the engine.

The whole escape had taken less than three minutes. With a little bit of luck from the traffic lights, Derek Russell was only a few blocks away.

Quince Garrett had gotten the call from the Ritz-Carlton command post less than a minute after Derek Russell's call rang in at 12:15. When he arrived at the hotel twelve minutes later, it was all over. FBI agents were running in and out of the elevator, the phones rang continually as hotel personnel tried to calm the other guests, and in the midst of it all sat Bill Travers, cursing everybody in sight while someone from the hotel staff tried to put a bandage on the nasty cut in his scalp.

"I haven't been upstairs yet, but I understand Derek has left another mess for us to clean up." Travers was trying to shake off the rage. "And Michael is gone. The son of a bitch bashed me over the head. He and the good doctor got out of here in a car, apparently another rental. We don't know where it came from."

"Michael is gone?" Garrett couldn't believe it.

"We knew Derek was onto us—well, it appears he was onto us before we even knew he was onto us." Travers shook his head.

Garrett waited for an explanation that made sense.

"Russell left a note in the room telling Michael to get out because the FBI was here. He must have figured you might use Michael as bait—I don't know, but somehow the bastard had it figured out, and he told Michael to run."

"And Michael ran?" Garrett still couldn't believe it.

"He did so with a vengeance." Travers said, nodding just enough for Garrett to see the bloody bandage on his head.

"Have you got a description on the car?"

"It's real screwy, Quince. You're not going to like it," Travers began. "Russell is in a limousine. Michael and Karen are—"

"A limousine!"

"A limousine and a tux, and he sent the fella over there"— Travers pointed at a taxi driver who sat quietly in one of the big lobby chairs—"to pick Michael up when he ran."

Garrett tried to follow it.

"The taxi picked them up, Michael pulled a gun, they switched cars, and, from all we can figure, Michael and Karen have taken off looking for Derek."

"Oh my God."

"We've got APBs on both cars, black limo and beige Chevy." Travers paused. "Now, shall we go see the mess upstairs?"

Michael spotted the limousine as it made a right turn onto M Street. Karen, intent on her driving, saw it a moment later and moved to the right in pursuit. Only a block and a half separated the two cars.

The limousine had to stop when M Street merged with Pennsylvania Avenue, and the beige Chevy moved closer. They were heading into Georgetown.

There wasn't much traffic after both cars made the turn. Karen tried to keep a hundred yards between them, but it was difficult on the nearly empty street, particularly when the uppermost thought was not to lose Derek now that he was so close. Michael sat beside her, the revolver in his lap.

Then the limo moved to the left lane and turned onto Key Bridge. Derek was heading into Arlington, not taking any chances that someone might be looking for a shiny black Cadillac.

The beige Chevy also made the left turn onto the bridge.

The body of Phyllis Kenworthy was stretched out on the crisp white sheets of the bed in room 535. She was nude, the sheets pulled to her waist. The bed was soaked in blood, and several lamps were on, the shades tilted to highlight the body.

A half dozen agents stepped aside when Quince Garrett and Bill Travers entered the room. Nothing was said. Each man remembered the sexy young woman who had entered the hotel lobby less than an hour before. And every man in the room remembered the barely seen man who had been with her. The tux. The limo. The wounded pride as he had limped back to his car in the driveway.

Pinned to the headboard, just above the girl's open eyes, was a note on a piece of hotel stationery. It looked as if had been written with finger paints, but the color was a red that could only be blood. Its message was simple:

Quince. This one's for you.

TWENTY-SIX

Derek Russell sat in the center of the plush back seat, rubbing his hands together in his lap to avoid stiffness. He'd been in the limo too long, and by now he knew there had to be an APB out on the car. Just a few minutes more. That was all he needed. He had instructed the driver to an address just off Glebe Road near Marymount College.

Just a few minutes now, and the driver would discover there was no house at the address, only a dark parking lot with many of the lights broken by neighborhood kids. Also in the lot would be a fresh rental car, one that Derek had acquired in Bethesda earlier in the day. It was time for a change.

There was no expression on the driver's face as he found the proper street, but there was a moment of indecision when he neared the corner parking lot. He had followed the instructions precisely, but he had arrived at an empty lot, with one car parked near a far wall.

"There seems to be a problem," Derek began, anticipating the driver's question. "Are you sure this is 425?"

"Yes sir."

"Maybe you'd better pull up in the lot for a second and let me find my notes. Maybe I read the address wrong."

The driver circled the limousine around in the lot so that the headlights faced the street sign at the corner. Derek reached into his jacket pocket, fumbling for a small leather-covered notepad.

Derek laughed. "My eyes must be going fuzzy on me. Too much of the bubbly, I expect. I can't make this thing out. Would you take a look?"

The driver reached over the seat for the notepad. When he turned back to the front, he flipped on a small dashboard light to read by, bending his head down to study Derek's scribble.

Derek reached over the seat, arching his strong left arm around the driver's neck. He had his grip before the driver knew what was happening. There was a moment of resistance, the driver suddenly kicking his feet and trying to pull away, but it came too late. Derek pulled back with all his weight, and twisted. The neck snapped with a shocking, brittle crack.

Derek reached over the seat to flip off the dash light. He glanced out into the darkness, seeing nothing out of order, then he stepped from the limousine and walked straight to the rental car.

Michael and Karen saw the whole thing. Karen had been hanging back when the limousine made its turn off Glebe Road, but she circled around, coming to the parking lot from a different direction. They spotted the limousine from a block away, and they parked just as the dash light flickered on.

"We've got to do something," Michael whispered, breaking the silence.

"What? Are you going to walk over there and stop him?"

"We've got to—" he began.

"We've got to be patient, Michael." Karen responded without taking her eyes away from the limousine. "We're only going to get one chance, and if we blow it we'll both be dead. This is the only way, Michael. It's up to us, or he gets away again."

Michael didn't get a chance to answer. Derek moved to the new car, a midnight-blue Chrysler La Baron. They were on the move again, retracing their steps back toward Georgetown.

The Ritz-Carlton remained Quince Garrett's base of operations, with calls pouring in at the front desk and driving the hotel staff crazy.

"We've found the limousine service," Bill Travers reported, stepping from the hotel manager's office. "It's some small outfit out of Chevy Chase."

"And where is the car?" Garrett bellowed.

"We don't know. They just tried the car phone and they didn't get any answer."

Derek Russell drove through the dark, quiet streets of downtown Washington. He found a parking space just off Ninth Street, removed a suit bag from the trunk of the car, and walked three blocks to The Bank, a disco that had been fashioned out of a deserted bank building in the center of downtown. It was the perfect place for Derek—the bank lobby had been converted to a dance floor with spinning lights that were for atmosphere, not for seeing anybody too clearly, and behind that was a dark, cavernous maze of small rooms and hallways.

There was a cover charge to get in, but Derek handed the large black man at the door an extra twenty and asked if there was somewhere he could get out of his glad rags and slip into something more comfortable. The bouncer didn't blink twice, but nodded to an arched doorway at the far end of the bar.

The music was loud, lights flashed, and the crowd was dominated by men in a ratio of about four to one. Derek made his way through the room, drawing only a few curious stares because of the tux. The arch led to the restrooms. Derek changed quickly, stuffing the tuxedo into the suit bag and leaving it in the restroom stall. When he stepped out he was dressed in charcoal-gray slacks, dark shirt and tie, with a black-on-white silk designer sportcoat. He fit right in with the disco crowd.

Michael and Karen circled the block three times trying to decide what to do. They had passed Derek just as he was removing the suit bag from the trunk of his car, and they passed again just as he was entering the disco.

"Now what?" Michael asked.

Karen pulled to the curb in front of the disco. "You've got to go in. There could be other ways out. He's obviously changing clothes. You've got to find him and keep an eye on him."

"What will you do?"

Karen thought for a moment. "I've got to stay with the car, in case he decides to move again. I'll park as close to his car as I can, but I'll try to get a block this side of it. That'll give you time to find me if he goes for his car."

"Right." Michael said it, but everything in him screamed that this was all wrong.

"This is the only way, Michael. Trust me."

Michael paid the cover charge and stood to the side until his eyes adjusted to the gloom. The crowd was a strange mix of sixties' hip, seventies' punk and eighties' chic, the combination producing a sort of time capsule of clichés.

Gradually, he moved in among the crowd trying to imagine what he would do if he bumped into Derek Russell. Then he saw the face. Derek was on the dance floor, dancing with a young woman, a bright blonde in tight white pants and a dazzling gold blouse.

Michael watched the entire dance, mesmerized by the man who had caused so many horrors. He reached inside his jacket to convince himself that the gun was still there, then he turned his back to order a drink. The disco was far too crowded to do anything. He had to wait. Be patient.

When he turned back, Derek was gone. The blonde stood on the sidelines, flirting with several men at the same time.

Michael was already moving. He scanned the crowd, sliding in and out of the maze created by the huddled groups. He remembered the jacket, a random mix of black and white, and then he saw it just as it disappeared through a doorway on the other side of the room, moving off into the rear of the building.

There was panic as Michael charged across the floor, bumping dance couples left and right, his hand gripping the gun inside his jacket. He stumbled off the dance floor, then plunged through the open doorway. A narrow hall snaked its way to small rooms at the right, with an equally narrow stairway leading to more rooms on a basement level.

Michael opted for the steps.

Derek found the quietest phone in the disco. He sat at the small downstairs bar, ordered a beer, and dialed the Hay-Adams Hotel.

"Dr. Arthur Bottoms, please," Derek requested. "Room 616. He's expecting my call."

The clerk hesitated for a second.

"I'm sorry, sir. We do have a room reserved for Dr. Bottoms, but I'm afraid he never checked in. Would you like to leave a—"

But Derek Russell had already hung up the phone.

He sat at the bar, staring into his beer, his eyes squinting as he considered the possibilities. He had waited to see the taxi pick up Michael and Karen. The instructions had been simple, and Michael certainly would have done whatever Derek had ordered. What did it mean?

He picked up the phone and dialed a familiar number. The phone rang three times at Manning Hall before there was an answer.

"Manning residence, may I help you?" The clear, precise voice was unmistakable. It was another in the endless supply of FBI agents.

"Where is Michael?"

"Who may I say is calling?"

"It's me, asshole. Derek Russell."

"Please hold, I will transfer you to Mr. Manning's new number."

There were several quick clicks and buzzes. Then a familiar voice came on the line.

"Derek. This is Garrett. What the—"

"Quince, is that you?"

"What kind of game are you playing now?"

Derek paused, weighing the honest anguish in the voice.

"What do you mean, Quince?"

"You know what I mean. Where is Michael, and what's this game you two are playing?"

Derek decided on the honest approach.

"I haven't spoken to Michael in almost three hours. Where is he?"

Garrett considered the possibilities. Had Michael and Karen found the limousine? Had they lost it? Had they missed a rendezvous with Derek?

"I haven't spoken to him either."

Derek hung up the phone, drained his glass of beer, and moved quickly from the bar. He took the steps two at a time, bumping into a man who was on the way down. He didn't look at the face, but he had just passed Michael Manning.

Karen Daniels saw Derek move past her parking space as he walked to his car in the next block. She ducked down, but it wasn't necessary. Derek was in a hurry. He wasn't looking at anything.

She closed her eyes for a moment, trying to calm her nerves, and then she started the engine, looking back over her shoulder to see if Michael was coming.

She counted under her breath, and when she got to nine she saw Michael move cautiously down the steps at the disco. At twelve, he was at the car, sliding into the seat beside her.

Michael was as pale as a ghost.

"He just passed me on the steps," Michael said, fighting to control his breathing. "I think he might have made a call. I believe he knows we're not where we're supposed to be."

"What will he do now?" Karen asked.

"I wish I knew."

Ahead of them, the midnight-blue Chrysler squealed tires as it pulled out of a parking space and headed uptown.

The limousine was spotted at 3:35. The APB included strict orders not to approach the vehicle, so the patrolman working the Marymount College area kept his distance and waited for help.

Quince Garrett arrived fifteen minutes later to find the limousine sitting alone in the parking lot, an ominous reminder that Derek Russell was always two steps ahead of them. The body of the driver was still in the front seat, the head at an awkward tilt, the eyes staring into the darkness, seeing nothing.

Garrett only glanced at the body, then returned to his car to use the radio. Bill Travers was on the other end at FBI Headquarters.

"They're still here—still in Washington." Garrett was sure of it.

"We've got every available man out there looking."

"I know, damn it," Garrett yelled back, "but make more men available. Get the D.C. police to bring in everybody. Call in extra men from Quantico. I don't care how you do it, but I want these fools found."

TWENTY-SEVEN

They'd lost him again. Karen had been less than a half block behind the blue Chrysler when Derek drove down 21st Street and made a right onto Virginia Avenue, heading toward the Watergate Hotel and the Kennedy Center. When she made the turn she was caught by a traffic light, and by the time she was able to pursue it the car was gone.

Derek was gone.

"We call Quince. That's all we can do." Michael spoke more in desperation than anything else.

"And what good will that do?" Karen asked, bitterly, never taking her eyes off the street.

"He has the manpower. He has—"

"Quince Garrett has been trying to find us now for six hours. He's probably got every cop in D.C. and every FBI agent he could pull in from a radius of a hundred miles looking for one simple beige Chevrolet. And he can't find us."

Karen glanced at Michael for emphasis.

Michael sighed. "We've got to do something. We can't just keep following him."

Karen wasn't even listening.

292   *To the Death*

"The way I see it, he was only a minute ahead of us. He had to turn into one of two parking lots. Either he's at the Watergate or at the Howard Johnson's across the street. Or he went up New Hampshire to the Kennedy Center, and that seems highly unlikely at five o'clock in the morning."

Michael sighed. "I'll take the Howard Johnson's. You take the Watergate."

"Right."

Derek paced his room, trying to make his mind focus. Why had Michael disappeared? The logic didn't work. Michael had to get away from the FBI, so he ran, just as Derek had instructed. But he had to be someplace where Derek could reach him, and he'd blown that by not going to the Hay-Adams. Where could he be?

As he paced, Derek stripped his clothes. He was sweating even though the room wasn't that warm. Down to briefs, he dropped to the floor, hooked his feet under the edge of the bed and began doing rapid sit-ups.

"Why?" he mumbled to himself at the top of each sit-up. "Why? Why? Why? Why? . . ."

There was no way into the Watergate garage. It was strictly valet, security was tight. Karen tried to think of a solution and finally opted for a story. She burst into the lobby of the Watergate Hotel and charged at a sleepy desk clerk.

"Where did he go?" she demanded, grabbing the counter as if she wanted to rip it in half.

The clerk backed up.

"Where did who go?"

"I saw him come in here. He was driving a dark blue Chrysler. He hit my car two blocks down the street and kept going, the son-of-a-bitch. And I saw him turn in here."

The clerk stepped back.

"I'm sorry, Ma'am, but you must be mistaken. No one has come through the lobby in the last forty minutes. I've been here the entire time, and I can assure you—"

"But I saw him turn the car over to one of the parking attendants. Please check, or I'll have to call the police."

The clerk made a decision. "I believe maybe I'd better call the police," he decided.

Karen panicked. The police she didn't need.

"Are you sure he didn't come in here?"

The clerk paused in his dialing.

"I'm absolutely sure," he said with grim determination.

"Well, he must be around here somewhere." She shook her head, and walked as quickly as possible toward the front door.

It was almost too easy for Michael to get into the private garage under the Howard Johnson's Motel. All he had to do was use the side door to the lobby, bypassing the front desk, then duck into the elevator. He could have gone straight down to the garage, but instead he decided to play it safe. He went to the fourth floor, walked down a flight, then called the elevator and pushed the button for the first level of the garage. He'd seen it in an old "Rockford Files."

It took him ten minutes to wander through the parking grids. And there it was. The blue Chrysler, its engine still popping with heat, was parked on the second level. The doors were locked, but at least they knew where Derek was.

Michael left the same way he'd come in, and all he got from the front desk was a nod from the clerk as he passed to the side door. He saw Karen running across Virginia Avenue as soon as he hit the sidewalk.

"We've got to get out of here," she said, grabbing Michael by the shoulder. "I believe the clerk in there is calling the cops."

"What? Why?" Michael began to walk faster.

"I couldn't get into the garage. I tried to get the clerk to help, and he became suspicious."

They kept walking back in the direction of their car.

"I found him," Michael said. "He's at the Howard Johnson's. His car's there."

Karen stopped in her tracks, then pulled Michael around the corner. "Are you sure?" she asked.

"It's there."

"Now, we've got to stay, no matter what."

Derek stopped at 150 sit-ups, and still he hadn't answered the question "Why?"

He jumped to his feet, feeling alive again, small beads of sweat rolling down his face and chest. There was only one thing he could do. He'd have to call Manning Hall again and get to Quince. He'd have to demand some answers.

When he had showered and changed into fresh clothes, it was 9:30. Michael would have been dead by now if he'd gone to the Hay-Adams as instructed. Derek decided to make the call from one of the museums on the Mall. He picked the Hirshhorn.

Twenty minutes later, Derek stepped onto the sidewalk in front of the Howard Johnson's and hailed a taxi on the other side of the street. Until he knew what was happening, he decided it was best not to take extra chances. The rental car was best left out of sight in the basement parking deck.

"Where to?" the driver asked without enthusiasm.

"The Hirshhorn Museum."

The driver grunted. It was a short fare. Then he pulled into traffic.

Derek glanced down the hill at the Kennedy Center as they started off. If he'd looked the other way, up 25th Street, he might have seen Michael running to jump into the beige Chevrolet that had already pulled into the street.

The taxi driver headed down Virginia Avenue, made the quick right and left required to get onto Constitution, then jockeyed for position, moving into the right-hand lane as he approached 14th Street. Things wouldn't be open for another five minutes, but already there was a line of tourists around the Washington Monument.

The driver had glanced in his rearview mirror several times as he maneuvered through the Washington traffic. There was a car back there—a beige Chevrolet—and it was following them.

He checked out his passenger in the same mirror, noting the nice suit, the clean shave, and the combed hair. He decided there might be a tip in it.

"Listen, mister." He coughed. "I don't know if it means anything, but there's a car back there following us."

Derek's face turned a deathly pale. Now he knew why. Michael wasn't at the Hay-Adams because somehow he'd picked up Derek's trail. He'd been on him all night.

"Thanks." He tried to laugh it off. "I think it's a competitor."

The driver eyed Derek suspiciously in the mirror.

"Any change in where we're going?" he asked.

"No," said Derek. "Keep heading for the Mall. I'll let you know if I change my mind when we get there. And keep an eye on that car."

Garrett had been driving around in circles for three hours. He had close to two hundred men in a thirty-square-mile area looking for a beige Chevrolet or any sign of Michael, Karen, or Derek, and now he was on the street trying to do what all of those men were failing to do.

He thought he saw the car at every corner, at every alley, but it always turned out to be a white Ford, a cream-colored Dodge, a pale pink Nissan.

Then there was static on his radio.

"This is Blue-Boy-One," he said into the transmitter.

"This is Unit 716. I think we've found your boy."

"Where?"

"A beige Chevy, Virginia license RXY-888, just moved into the right-hand lane on Constitution Avenue. Looks like he's going to make a right at 14th Street. That'll take him past the Mall."

"Roger."

"Shall we intercept?"

"Negative!" Garrett shot back. "I'm on my way, but that's a negative. Keep him in sight. Do not intercept."

Garrett was less than a half mile away. He reached out the window and popped a red light on the roof of his car.

Karen Daniels didn't like it. There was something about the way the taxi was moving. It wasn't normal, not with the quick jumps and starts that all D.C. taxi drivers use as they maneuver through traffic. This one was being too cautious.

Then she figured it out.

"He knows we're back here." She looked at Michael. It was up to him to make a decision now.

"Move," Michael shouted. "Let's get him."

Karen grabbed the wheel tight in her hands, and hit the gas. The car jerked to the right, almost sideswiping a panel truck.

The taxi driver saw them coming just as he made the right-turn onto 14th Street. Before he could turn left onto the Mall, a dozen high school students dashed in front of the car.

"Mister, that car is speeding up." The driver was beginning to worry about just who he might have in the car. "Looks like they want to catch us."

Derek dropped a hundred-dollar bill on the front seat of the taxi.

"Get me out of here!"

The driver hit the gas just before the light turned green, swerving to keep the car under control as he entered the parade of traffic around the Mall. This was a mistake. He knew it as soon as he made the move, and so did Derek.

Now the taxi was trapped. There was nowhere to go. No parking was allowed on the Mall before ten o'clock, and at two minutes to ten cars were slowly searching for the last available spaces.

Derek glanced out the rear window for the first time, but he couldn't tell which car it was.

"It's tan-colored," the driver noted.

It was four cars behind them. Derek could see Karen Daniels behind the wheel, Michael Manning at her side. Their eyes met just as the taxi driver hit the brake, coming to a complete stop.

Directly in front of them, a school bus had just flashed its no-passing signals in front of the Smithsonian and begun unloading a herd of young children.

Derek dropped another twenty-dollar bill over the seat and stepped from the taxi. His crisp suit was soaked with sweat. For the first time in seventeen years Derek faced the absurdity of his own failure.

He ran through the crowd of children, his mind clicking at top speed. Maybe the Hirshhorn was still his best choice. It had three circular floors of galleries. He would lose Michael in the confusion.

When Michael and Karen saw Derek take off, Michael opened the door with his right hand and jumped from the car. His left hand automatically reached inside his jacket to find the revolver.

Michael and Karen looked at each other, but now it was too late for words. He slammed the door and ran in pursuit of the phantom.

TWENTY-EIGHT

One of the Hirshhorn guards was just opening the front door as Derek joined the group gathered at the entrance. There were perhaps fifteen people, but by moving through the crowd Derek was second through the revolving door.

By the time Michael got there, most of the others had already entered the museum. He scanned the faces, deciding that maybe this was a trick. It would be just like Derek to fake entering the building, then circle it and head back toward the Mall.

Michael stepped into the central court, the pounding water of a large fountain making it difficult to hear anything else. The cylindrical inner glass walls of the museum stretched above him. He kept his eyes on the windows as tourists began to appear in the galleries that surrounded the inner perimeter of the building.

Most of the people were young—too young to be Derek. There was a woman with a stroller. The glass was dark, but he could see two young girls giggling at a series of nude sculptures as they passed through one of the galleries. Two young boys were not far behind, trailing the girls.

And then there was Derek. He was moving through the galleries like a cat, staying close to the wall but making it seem natural, as if he were just getting a better look at the small sculpture in the cabinets.

Michael watched, not knowing what to do. His mind wouldn't work, but his hands moved on their own. He pulled the revolver from his belt, and somewhere off in the distance he heard a woman scream.

Michael lifted the gun and fired. He closed his eyes. Glass shattered on the second floor of the museum, sending a shower of large pieces crashing down into the fountain.

When Michael opened his eyes, Derek was staring down at him from the ragged opening, and he had a large revolver in his hands. Derek fired, the bullet dug up a piece of granite six inches in front of Michael's right foot, and Michael ran toward the front door of the museum, right into the path of waiting museum guards.

"Freeze!"

He heard the word like an echo before he even noticed the four men who surrounded him just inside the door. The up escalator was less then five feet away, but it might as well have been a mile. All four guards had their guns drawn, and Michael had no choice but to stop in his tracks, the revolver hanging loosely in his right hand.

"Drop the gun!"

Michael wasn't sure which of the guards spoke the command. He tried to figure which was the boss, and then he spotted one with stripes on his sleeves.

The boss.

At the same instant, out the corner of his eye, Michael saw Derek coming down the escalator on the other side of the lobby. The big revolver was in his hand, and it was aimed right at Michael's head.

Lowering his shoulder, Michael charged into the guard with the stripes on his shirt. A shot echoed through the lobby and one of the guards took a bullet in his chest. The shot had been meant for Michael. This was it.

The showdown. Derek and him.

Michael rolled away just as another shot sounded. A second guard moaned in pain, grabbing his shoulder as he fell to the floor. There were screams from all directions as tourists ran for cover.

Michael fell against the wall, out of Derek's range, and looked at his hand, surprised to see that he still had the gun. He stood, took a breath and stepped back into the open, ready to shoot at anything that moved.

Derek was gone, creating a wave of screaming, panicked tourists as he raced back through the central court toward the Mall. Michael got a glimpse of him as he passed a window, but Derek moved too quickly for a shot. Michael ran in pursuit.

Quince Garrett was six blocks away when he heard gunfire. Michael and Derek had found each other. Almost at the instant he heard the shots, his radio popped to life.

"Shots fired. On the Mall. The Hirshhorn. We're moving in. All units. Respond."

Garrett couldn't wait for the traffic. He bounced his car over the curb and raced to the lawn in the center of the Mall.

Michael came through the central courtyard of the Hirshhorn just in time to see Derek cross the street and disappear down into the museum's sculpture garden. Several startled tourists came running up the steps, their frightened screams marking Derek's trail.

Michael darted across the street, his gun drawn. Just as he got to the wall he heard another shot. He fell to the ground, but the shot wasn't for him. He glanced over the low wall. The glass in a small cubicle on the opposite wall was shattered, and the guard had collapsed through the opening.

Michael ran for the steps, down into the garden. He had no time to think. He had to keep moving, always forward. If he stopped, or hesitated, it would be too late. He'd be dead, and Derek would be gone.

He stumbled down the steps, twisting and turning, looking in every direction at once. He saw nothing. He was all alone. Derek was not in sight.

Then there was a voice.

"Mikey." It didn't really sound like Derek. It was out of breath. Frightened. "You can turn around, Mikey. It's all over."

Michael slowly turned, and still he didn't see him. Then he looked up. Derek was sitting on the edge of the wall, the large revolver resting in his lap, the barrel pointing in Michael's general direction. Derek looked exhausted. Defeated.

"It's all over, Mikey. You did it. You've caught your phantom, and now there's nothing left but for you to die."

Michael wanted to go for it. There was a chance. He wanted to drop to the ground, and try for a shot, but he knew it was hopeless.

Derek could read his mind.

"I promised you a chance, Mikey. I said it might not be a fair one, but you've got your chance. Go for it. Draw on me."

Derek tightened his grip on the revolver but kept it in his lap. Michael was perhaps twenty feet away. They were close enough to see every twitch, to feel every thought behind the uncertainty of the eyes.

Michael was ready to go. He felt his heart pumping. Just as he hit the ground, swinging his gun to fire, something came running up behind the wall—it was Karen!—and she tackled Derek with the full force of her momentum. A shot went off, but it was wild as the two figures tumbled off the wall, falling ten feet to the hard ground between two smooth bronze sculptures.

Derek climbed shakily to his feet, pushing Karen's limp body away from him. He turned quickly and stared into the barrel of Michael's revolver. Derek was unarmed. He'd lost his gun in the fall.

Michael fired, but in that instant Derek ran for the steps. Michael fired again. The bullet hit the wall three feet behind Derek's sprint. It was too late. Derek had made it to the steps, and he was gone. Up and out. Back to the street level, running with all his speed down the center of the lawn toward 14th Street.

Michael ran toward Karen, but she was screaming and crying at the same time.

"Get him! Get him!"

Michael took off in pursuit.

Quince Garrett couldn't believe it. He'd just bounced his car onto the lawn when he saw the distant figure heading straight in his direction. Everybody else was running for the sides, but not this figure. He was still a long four blocks away, but even at that distance Garrett knew who it had to be.

He floored the gas, the car catching hold in the damp grass and picking up speed.

Derek saw the car off in the distance, but he didn't care anymore. It was all over. He was unarmed. Sirens were sounding all around him, and Michael had won.

Tears of failure streamed down his face, but suddenly there was a glimmer of hope. A police car bounced over the curb and pulled to a stop in front of him. A fat policeman was stepping from the car on Derek's side, while his partner scrambled from the other door.

If he could just get there fast enough . . .

Derek made a dive for the fat cop. They wrestled, falling to the ground, and the policeman's revolver was loose. Derek pulled it free and fired point blank into the cop's stomach, rolling away just in time to fire again, catching the cop's partner as he circled the car.

Now. Now, he had a weapon. Now he could face anything. He glanced behind him. Michael was a good fifty yards away. There was still time.

Panting, Derek climbed to his feet, ripping off his sportcoat as he began running down the lawn again. The police cars now stayed on the street, pacing him down the mall, but ahead the single car still raced straight at him.

When man and car were a hundred yards apart, Derek took a firm stance and lifted the revolver. He took his time, trying to control his breathing. He fired once, and the glass shattered. He fired again, and he hit something.

The car swerved, tried to straighten up, but then it twisted hard to the right and flipped, rolling over and over, tearing up huge clods of grass and earth as it came to a stop on its roof.

Quince Garrett was out of it. He was unconscious, but he was still alive. His shoulder had been shattered by the bullet. His right leg was broken in two places.

And Derek was running again. A hundred yards in front of him was 14th Street, but the traffic had stopped. Police cars blocked the whole end of the Mall, ten of them parked end to end, policemen leaning over fenders and trunks, guns drawn, all aiming at him.

And fifty yards to the rear was Michael. Alone. Gun drawn.

Derek slowed his step. There was nowhere to go. He lowered the dead policeman's revolver to his side and bowed his head, crying like a baby.

Then he turned. If there had to be an end, it would be with Michael. They had shared too much. It had to be this way.

Michael saw Derek come to a stop, but his own legs kept moving. Something in his stomach tightened. He was exhausted, but it was more than that. He knew how it would have to end.

Michael slowed to a stop. He and Derek were ten yards apart. Both were breathing heavily, guns down at their sides. The sirens still sounded, tourists still screamed, and the police bullhorns echoed a demand that both men drop their weapons.

"Michael, that's close enough," Derek panted.

Michael swallowed deep, his head pounding. He had to get his breath.

"Let's do it right, Michael." Derek showed Michael the revolver in his hand, then lowered his hand to his side.

Michael could see what was happening, but he couldn't believe it. Derek was still challenging him. Derek wanted to draw, and something inside him said it was the only thing that would be right.

Michael showed Derek his gun, and lowered his arm until it came to rest at his side.

"Michael." Derek's voice was weak and sad. "You know that I never meant you any harm. It was all a game. That's all any of it was. A game."

"I know, Derek. And you were the best."

Derek smiled across the few feet of grass, then he made his move. He was quick, but Michael was quicker. The two shots seemed to be fired at the same instant, but it was Derek who fell backwards with a pain greater than anything he had ever felt in his life.

There were tears in his eyes, but then he laughed, a subdued laugh, a victorious laugh. It wasn't over yet. As long as he breathed, Michael wasn't the winner. He still had the gun in his hand, and there was still a single bullet left. Michael would not win. Lying flat on his back, gasping for air, he raised the revolver to his own head and pulled the trigger. He would not allow Michael to kill the phantom.